Marten Claridge lives in Edinburgh. His first novel, *Nobody's Fool*, was shortlisted for the 1990 Fulbright Raymond Chandler Award and his second novel, *Midnight Chill*, is also available from Headline.

Slow Burn

Marten Claridge

For the Claridges,
Pim & Tony, Mike, Salli & Rob

Day spins undreamed of dreams
mirrors mirror
snarling double-talk
telling you dirty
your own best nightmares.
Turning frost to black ice
you skid throught the night
wake howling
to the cool suck of the moon.

From Hilary Lazare's *Melt Down*

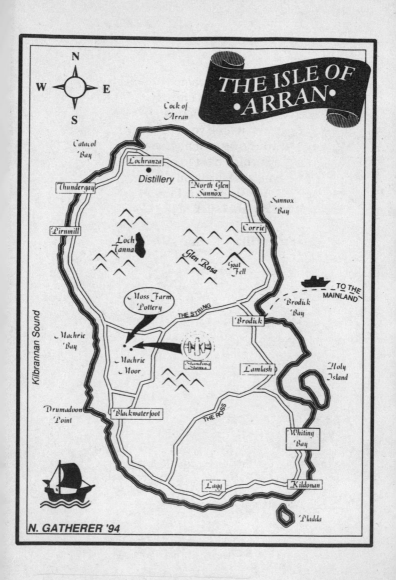

Book One

The Arousing Thunder

*'The woman holds the basket, but there are no fruits in it.
The man stabs the sheep, but no blood flows.
Nothing that acts to further.'*

Stab, stab, stab.

In the light of the new moon, the glint of the Machrie Water as it glides between the trees is the same cold hue as the blade of steel he wields in his wildly plunging fist.

Spurt, spurt, spurt.

Blood in his eyes, his hair, his mouth. On his hands, his clothes, his boots. Warm blood, sticky blood. All over the stone, the killing stone, the cropping stone.

Gideon: he who crops, hews, cuts down.

Gideon Byrne has his own adage: he who crops gets drenched in blood. Even when he shouldn't. Even when it says so explicitly in the reading.

So why the blood?

Why hadn't it read, *The man stabs the sheep, and geysers of blood spurt all over the place*? Why hadn't it said that?

Maybe the Book of Changes, the *I Ching*, wasn't all it was cracked up to be. Maybe it *was* fallible. There was certainly nothing wrong with his interpretation of the reading. There it is on the cropping stone, the sheep, and there he is standing over it, the man with the knife in his hand, and there, if you rewind the scene a few hundred frames or so, is the man, him, stabbing the sheep. *The man stabs the sheep . . .*

How could any sane man misinterpret that? It was down there in black and white.

Until the bit . . . *but no blood flows.*

Like hell it didn't. More blood in that sheep than any life-deserving creature had a right to. In fact, it was still pumping it out, though its life's momentum was slowing now, the flow sluggish, the blood thick and black as oil, glinting too in the crescent light of the softly sucking moon. The sound coming from its torn throat like a wide pan of water, gently boiling.

Eyes.

He doesn't need to hold it down any longer, its struggles are but those of its nerves. The shadow of the nearest standing stone paints him black as he moves in closer. To peer. To watch its eyes as he pushes the blade of his knife slowly up its nostril.

Does he see anything he hasn't seen before?

Not this time.

The shriek of an owl. The distant hum of a car on The String. Machrie Water hustling down through the trees, dropping from Goat's Leap Pool to the Deep Pool, hurriedly on towards Laidlaw's Bend. The sky black overhead, fringed in chrome, Venus watching over you, admiring your style.

The stars.

Pulling you this way and that and you don't even realise it. Puppet on cosmic strings. All that energy. The same energy you are made of. What a delicate balance. How does the sheep weigh in the balance? Anything at all? How will its passing affect the scales? Create a little more energy somewhere else in the world, cause an earthquake? Hurl a tidal wave at some unprotected shore? Or bring a new life to being? A new sheep, perhaps? One that doesn't bleed when it shouldn't?

You hope.

On a new moon.

Shackle your dreams to a new moon, watch them grow. *Isn't*

4

that what your mother always said? No. Fat chance. She never said anything to offer you hope. Which is why she's secured away in the lockdown ward of the country's first privatised psychiatric hospital for the criminally insane. If she'd offered you hope back then she might not be there today. Simple as that.

Still, Elderburn House is better than Carstairs up the road, where she'd spent the last twenty-seven years. Carstairs is serious moon-howler preserve. People eating themselves alive in there. Getting their brainwaves recharged. Walking around with that goodbye look in their eyes, ready for the off at any given second. Pure mental. Not to mention the high-security aspect. The kind of place they'll only let you out of if you've got an axe in your hand. That's Carstairs for you. Elderburn House is like a holiday camp in comparison. The staff there all wear these name badges – Hi, I'm Betty, have a nice day; Hi, I'm Geoff, enjoy your ECT – it's that kind of place, pioneering. You can get in to visit your mother almost any time you want. Just give them a couple of days' notice and it's 'No problem, Mr Byrne, just pick up your pass at the gate, it'll be waiting for you there as usual.' Easy come, easy go.

Silence.

Venus up there on the sea of the night, you down here on the sea of the Moor, both sailing courses predestined by forces unimaginable, charting the unknown. She launching the new moon across the sky, you launching a sheep into the big forgetness.

It is still now, its blood no longer seeping on to the stone, sliding towards the grass. Back in the days when these standing stones were erected, they believed the blood from their sacrifices fertilised the soil, helped their crops grow. Back then the whole island would have been covered in trees, not a fucking sheep in sight. So they probably sacrificed each other, divorce not exactly being an option in Neolithic times. Let the blood sink into this very same grass here, fertilise their next crop of chips. All the women rubbing themselves against the stones, trying to get pregnant, like shafted by the spirits of their ancestors.

Talk about crazy.

The coast road deserted, waves lapping lethargically on the rocky shore. Moon ploughing a silver furrow across Machrie Bay. Across Kilbrannan Sound, the black hills of Kintyre. Another world. Days long gone and the Revenue cutters would lie off shore there, hope to catch the smugglers plying the Sound by night, the whisky coming down from the stills in the hills above Imacher. Alive then, Gideon would have been celebrated in song, his exploits renowned across the land. Black Byrne. A kind of West Coast Rob Roy. He can picture it, there he is, night like tonight, standing one foot on the prow, his long kilt and sandy hair blowing in the offshore breeze, claymore strapped to his back, the oars gliding silently through the swell, the Revenue cutter half a league off, bearing down, the prospect of battle firing through his veins, a contemptuous smile of anticipation on his lips – yeah, that's the way he sees it, the way it would have been.

The possibilities for adventure back then far greater than the predictable present.

Gideon pulls in, leaves the engine running, climbs out. Sits on the sea wall awhile, breathing in the scent of the Sound, letting the sound of the waves and the lick of the moon wash over him, bring him back down.

Nowadays a superior man has to struggle to find uncharted waters, a cause worth dying for. Like you can't just buckle on your swash and ride into the jaws of death, expect to go down in history with *Legend* after your name. It's just not that easy any more. You have to think things through now, plan a campaign carefully, weigh the pros against the cons, get yourself a public relations officer, airtime on all the major channels, write a book. Like these days inferior people just buy their way into the history books, sell their lies on primetime TV. The senseless ones buying every fucking word. The state of a nation down on bended knees.

Gideon sighs. To hell with them all. Soon their eyes will open and then they'll recognise him for what he is. He can wait. He's good at that, waiting.

The sheep is wrapped in a black tarpaulin. As Gideon lifts it from the back of his car, the sheep almost slips out. He has to stagger to the sea-wall, drop it immediately over the edge. A hollow thunk as its head splits on a rock. Come high tide, it'll drift away, feed the fishes, feed the gulls. And good riddance. He turns back to the car.

Hey, wait a minute.

Someone down there on the beach. Watching him. Sitting on a rock, watching. Man or woman, he can't tell, they're all wrapped up. Does it matter? No, he decides. It's too late now, anyway. Nothing that acts to further. Just climb in the car, head on home – it's been a long tiring night. And tomorrow night will be just as long if he's going to get it right. Go down the south of the island, plenty more damn sheep down there. Fields of them. Mutton on the hoof. No more shitting in his own back yard, getting all excited, going off all half-cocked like he did tonight.

The idea being to think it through, take his time, make sure no blood flows with the next one. Not blame the *I Ching* but seek the error within himself.

The action of a superior man.

2

Sheep.

The wind squalled, snapping suddenly at my uniform jacket. I cursed again and, pressing my cap more firmly to my head, raked my gaze down the hill and south across the restless sea to the lighthouse on Pladda, now standing white against the silvery spray. In the murky distance beyond, the black rock of Ailsa Craig seemed little more than an inky thumbprint smeared against the foaming waters of the Sound. Deep in the heavens thunder rolled.

Below, the village of Kildonan – the ruin of an Iron Age fort, a straggle of houses, a hotel, a farm or two – sheltered in the meagre crutch of hill, cowering, it seemed, from the ragged shoreline where surging whitecaps hurled themselves upon the glossy granite rocks in explosions of flying spume, the dull flat crumps reaching me here on the hill only through rare windows in the ripping wind. I turned the sheep over carefully with my boot, just as the first drops of rain, warm and heavy, spattered on my face.

It had obviously lain there for several days. Maggots squirmed through eyeless sockets, moving deep within the cloven skull. Maggots or brain, it was hard to tell. Around the wound, dried blood, crusted black, still matted the tangle of dirty fleece. Insects crawled and swollen bluebottles buzzed and gorged, buzzed and gorged. The taste of my breakfast returned to my throat as rain thudded into grass, bounced off stone.

The Inuits, I recalled, have more than fifty words for snow. Arranites, on the other hand, have just as many expletives for rain – the most potent of which now formed silently on my lips as I glanced again at the purpling bruise of sky, sighed and shook my head. For the hundredth time that morning I wondered why – why me, why here, why today?

Francis McMorran, Constable of Police, Protector of Sheep.

It lay squarely on a flat rectangular stone embedded in the earth in the centre of the field. I wondered if it was an altar stone, Neolithic, like the chambered cairn I had visited once, there above the sea-lashed cliffs, a mile to the west on Bennan Head? Or even the lid of a Bronze Age burial cist? It was the right size: about a metre by a metre and a half. Or perhaps it was more recent; a *cromlech*, an altar stone, used by the Celts for sacrifices during the Iron Age. I could imagine it: days of old and the Druids and vestal virgins would climb up here on warm summer nights to perform their fertility rites beneath the silvery moon. Knives would gleam and hot blood flow as the soft white flesh danced to rhythms as deep as the earth.

Or then again maybe not, I thought, breathing through my nose now as I donned soft black leather gloves and, squatting, probed the exposed ivory skull with a tentative fingertip. Bone moved perceptibly beneath my touch.

Satanic ritual?

Where the skull had split the edges were ragged, splintered, what appeared to be the result of a single blow from a bluntish instrument, the killing blow. Delivered to the top right-hand side of the cranium with not a little force. Devil-worship, I wondered, or just your average wellie-booted sheep-shagger with a PhD in psychopathy?

At the top of the sloping field, a huddle of bedraggled sheep stood mournfully in the rain, heads turned forlornly in my direction like worried relatives waiting for the surgeon's prognosis. The foremost of them, a ewe, continued to bleat half-heartedly, sounding like the tortured strains of some sorrowful

10

lament. Pitiful. I returned my concentration to the grass around the stone.

It was the second Sunday in June and, until a few moments ago, it hadn't rained in days: the ground dry and hard with no convenient footprints around the immediate locus. Evidence of someone's presence, yes, there in the grass closest to the shallow slab of stone: scuffed back in some places, flattened in others. More than one person? I shook my head, doubting it, as I rose slowly to my feet.

A voice called from down by the road and I turned to watch Tom Tully close the wooden gate and trudge up the slope towards me. The wind suddenly changed direction, slanting the rain into my face. As I turned away, my attention snagged on something dark beneath the dampening fleece of the sheep's carcass. I squatted again and pushed back the stiff, matted hair.

I'd seen them before, many times before. On bodies on cold, wet cobbles, and on bodies on stretchers and cold-room drawers. I pushed back more of the fleece, fingers searching. Found another five similar wounds before I heard the farmer's footsteps approach, and rose to greet him.

Greetings were not Tully's strength.

'Well?' he said.

'Thank you, yes.'

'I meant the sheep.' Tully's flinty eyes bored into me from deep within the shadow of his parka. 'I was right, eh?'

I shrugged. Tully had phoned the Lamlash station early this morning, claiming one of his sheep had been murdered. 'Murder, eh?' Sergeant Yuill had said. 'Then we'd better send McMorran.'

Tully said, 'Head caved in, lying on the stone like that, not much doubt, eh?' He studied me suspiciously as I slowly shook my head.

'No doubt at all,' I told him.

'That's what I told the sergeant. He laughed.'

'He would.'

'He said, "How did it die?" I told him someone had bashed its brain in, and he laughed again. All a big joke.'

'Bashed its brain in first,' I told him, 'then used it for bayonet practice.'

'Say again?'

I said nothing; instead, squatting again, I peeled back the fleece in several places as Tully bent for a closer look.

'Mother of God!'

I said, 'Little or no blood from the wounds, see? Which means they were inflicted *post mortem*, after the sheep had been killed by the blow to the head.'

'You mean someone just walked up and smashed in its skull, then . . .'

I shook my head. 'Whoever did it, did it from behind. Probably sitting or standing astride the sheep's back, like a shearer would, pinning it down, left hand pressing its neck to the stone, right hand delivering the killing blow.'

'You can be so sure?'

I pointed to the patches of flattened grass on each side of the stone. 'That's where he planted his feet. See?'

Tully snorted. 'The hell d'you know he wasn't left-handed?'

I looked up at the sky again, darkening overhead, clearing to the south. 'It came to me in a dream,' I sighed, indifferent to the farmer's suddenly narrowed eyes. I *had* had a dream this morning, that much was true. One of those turgid swamp-like dreams, deep yet rich in colour, emotions playing heavy on the organs, and peopled by strangers somehow intimate. It must be the island air, I thought; in the city, it had always seemed that my formless dreams dissipated as readily as the morning haar over my native High Street.

Tully studied the sky, the way all farmers do, warily, with mistrust. He said, 'Is that how you solve all your cases? By dreaming?'

I rose and, peeling off my gloves, jerked my head towards the nearest house, the roof of which was just visible above the line of trees at the top of the field. 'Who lives up there?'

'Woman name of Hastie.'

'Alone?'

'If you call twenty-plus dogs "alone".'

I almost barked. '*Dogs?*'

'Mostly strays. She takes them in.' Tully scratched his stubbled chin. 'Why? What's the matter?'

'Nothing,' I lied, as a sudden shiver convulsed my body. 'Nothing at all.'

Tully frowned. 'You think she might have seen something?'

'You tell me.'

'In the stars, maybe. She's into all that stuff, you know – astrology, charts, psychic phenomena, UFOs, what have you.' Tully obviously was not, feet firmly on the ground, standing there as though planted. 'Off her tree, if you ask me.'

'Living with so many dogs,' I said, 'I'd have to agree.'

'I've nothing against them personally – have three of my own, in fact. But Ros, well, every now and then one of hers gets on to my land, chases the sheep. Scares the living shit out of them. Couple of years ago one of her Alsatians killed a ewe and its lambs and the whole thing ended up in court.'

'What happened?'

'Dog was put down and we haven't spoken since.'

'You think this is her revenge?'

Tully watched as a busful of tourists wound slowly down the hill, turning down towards the village of Kildonan. 'It crossed my mind,' he said eventually.

'And yet?'

'And yet I find it hard to imagine.' Tully chewed his lip for a moment, then shook his head. 'No, not hard,' he decided, 'but impossible.'

I made a scribbled note in my notebook, then changed the subject. 'When did you last count the flock?' I asked. 'I mean, last see this sheep alive?' Feeling suddenly as though I were the principal actor in some ludicrous farce, as though any second now Tully would throw back his parka-hood to reveal Jeremy Beadle, microphone, leer and all.

'Thursday?' Tully massaged his chin, looking to the sky for confirmation. Then studied his shoes to stretch the moment, before losing his gaze in the distance. 'Yes,' he said, 'Thursday. Must've been later on in the afternoon – back of five, maybe six. Any help?'

'That stone,' I said, nodding towards the slab on which the dead sheep lay, 'how long has it been there?'

'You want the exact date?'

'It might be relevant.'

'Give or take a few thousand years, for ever.'

I managed a smile. 'I saw a burial cist in the Heritage Museum, the one discovered in the Brodick Castle grounds. The lid must've been about the same size as this, same kind of stone.'

'If this were a cist or a fallen standing stone – or, for that matter, anything else of arguable historical value – you wouldn't be able to get near it for all the geologists. No, Constable, you can take my word for it, it has no ancient or religious significance. It's just a stone.' He glanced at me askance. 'You're getting wet.'

'It's the rain,' I said, turning up the collar of my uniform jacket. Water dribbled down the back of my neck. Not even midday and I was all out of curses.

'You finished here?'

'I'm finished.'

Tully indicated the sheep. 'What should I do with . . . that?'

'Roast it delicately in its own juices?'

As we trudged down the slope to the cars, Tully said, 'You mentioned a bayonet . . .'

'A reasoned guess. The almond shape of some of the wounds suggests a double-edged knife.'

'A bloody thin one, whatever,' Tully observed.

14

'Not,' I shrugged, 'if you allow for the skin's elasticity.'

'Aye?' Thunder crackled overhead and a heavy warm rain fell now like molten glass from the cracking sky. 'I s'pose you'll be looking for witnesses then?'

'Aye,' I said. 'There's a few of your sheep I still want to interview.'

Tully opened the door of his Land Rover, climbed in. 'You don't like me, do you, McMorran?'

'Nothing personal. It's Sunday.'

'Ah,' Tully said. 'That explains everything.' He slammed the door and drove off.

3

Lamlash police station could never be called a teeming hive of activity. There might be a smaller station, a quieter one, on some remote part of the Western, Outer or Northern Isles but I had yet to hear of it. Here there was no hustle and bustle, no incessant ringing of phones, no constant stream of irate offenders being dragged noisily through the system, no endless hubbub of raised voices against a background of hammered typewriter keys, personal radio static, squealing tyres and wailing sirens. No. Here there was little more than the wailing wind and hammering rain.

'That you, Sarge?' The voice belonged to PC Jim Tennant and came from the small kitchen behind the holding cells. As did the smell of coffee and bacon, the pop and sizzle of frying eggs. I felt a sudden sharp pang, realised I hadn't eaten since I'd come on shift at seven this morning, hadn't even thought about food after examining the maggot-ridden carcass of the sheep.

I said, 'No, it's me,' and peeling off my fluorescent jacket, hung it to drip on the floor behind the door.

'Oh.' Jim Tennant stood in the doorway, still in his civvies, spatula in hand. Twenty-four years old, tall and lean with dark boyish looks, in early for the back shift. 'You hungry?'

'As a wolf.'

Tennant said, 'Coming right up,' and returned to the kitchen. I plugged my personal radio into the recharger on the public counter, flipped open the Duty Officer's Journal. There were no new entries. Good. I flopped into a chair behind one of the back-to-back desks, stretched out my legs. The rain had eased off a little now but still spattered intermittently against the steamed-up window. I was thinking of the warm coal fire in the hotel bar when Tennant returned, bearing plates and cutlery.

'That do?'

I said, 'No complaints about the service so far.'

'That' comprised several slices of bacon and black sausage, two fried eggs, grilled tomato, mushrooms, and a couple of potato scones. I grabbed my knife and fork, and spoke through a mouthful of mush.

'You're in early, aren't you?'

'Argument with the wife.'

'She ever dumps you, Jim, you've got yourself a lodger.'

Tennant said, 'Might be sooner than you think,' and sat down opposite. We ate in silence, rain rattling the window, thunder still a throaty growl in the darkening sky.

'The Sarge around?' Tennant asked eventually, wiping his plate with his last bite of potato scone.

'Out working on the Ryder kid,' I told him.

'Again? Christ, why doesn't he just throw the little fucker in front of a jury?'

'Or better still, a train.'

'They'd find him guilty the moment he walked in the courtroom.'

'Maybe so. But when Sergeant Yuill wants a confession, nothing less will do.'

My tone of voice did not escape the young PC. 'What is it between you and Yuill?' he asked. 'I mean, from the moment you met, you've been like a pair of pit bulls tearing each other to shreds.'

'Call it a healthy professional rivalry.'

'Call it a steaming pile of shit.' Tennant collected together the plates and took them back through to the kitchen. 'You want coffee?' he called.

'Sure, spoil me.'

'Did you see Monica this morning?' Tennant asked over the sound of the boiling kettle.

'Sort of.' Monica Kemp was the only female police officer on the island, a WPC, currently working the night shift. 'She didn't hang around.'

'Busy night, did she say?'

'Quiet—' I broke off as lightning flashed across a sombre sky, counted the seconds, seven, until thunder crackled, then resumed: '—for a Saturday. A couple of Breaches, one Assault, one DUI. All visitors.'

Most offences on the island, I had already learnt – especially during the summer months and the Easter and Glasgow Trade holidays – were committed by 'visitors'. Most common among these were petty thefts, vandalism, careless driving, tax discs, licences, breach of peace, driving under the influence, weekend assaults, that kind of thing. Less common were crimes such as robbery with violence, rape, assault with the intent to ravish, and Contravention of the Protection of Animals Act. It was all, I thought ruefully, a long, long way from my days as an Edinburgh detective with the Scottish Special Crimes Squad.

Tennant returned with two mugs of steaming coffee. 'She call Bob out?' Bob Gillies, the most senior PC on the island, with fourteen years' service under his belt, the last four on the island.

I shook my head. 'No need, she said.'

'And you? Anything exciting happen this morning?'

'It's all in the Journal,' I said, nodding towards the public counter next door.

'Something about a sheep . . .'

'Yuill's sense of humour. Just mention the word "murder" and he says, "Send for McMorran." Try it sometime.'

'Someone *murdered* a sheep?'

As the rising wind soughed and moaned, I told him briefly of the morning's events. Tennant was still smiling when I finished.

'What's so funny?'

'Looks like we have ourselves a Ripper.'

'A *sheep*-ripper.'

'Aye, the headline, I can see it already.' Tennant slurped at his coffee, elbows planted on the desk, both hands cupped around the mug. 'Splashed across the front page of the *Arran Banner – Jock the Sheep-Ripper Strikes Again*.'

'You ever hear of anything like this happening before on the island?'

'There *was* this guy once,' Tennant said after a moment's thought, 'which must've been not long after I came over 'cause I remember thinking, Holy Moly, maybe the stories you hear about what goes on on the islands *are* true – you know, the sheep-shagging jokes, what d'you call a guy from Skye with more than one girlfriend, that kind of thing – or at least maybe a little truth behind them, no smoke without fire, if you know what I mean?'

'What *do* you call a guy from Skye with more than one girlfriend?'

'A shepherd.' Tennant's smile was a dazzle of perfect teeth. 'But this guy I'm talking about, Gibson I think his name was, had to move across to the mainland. I mean, can you blame him, Frank, he walks in a bar here and everyone points him out and says, "See him, he's the one got caught slipping it to some poor nannie." Because that's what happened. Ask Bob Gillies. He was the man spotted the car pulled off the side of The String, looks up and sees this guy and a goat silhouetted against the skyline, the guy giving it laldie, moaning so loud he never even hears Bob approach until he taps him on the shoulder and says, "I think you better come quietly, sir."'

I was still laughing when one of the phones began to ring, the black one.

Tennant reached across and picked it up. 'Lamlash Police.' I watched with a wry smile as the young PC's expression passed from exasperation to resignation. 'Yes, ma'am . . . An emergency, you say? . . . And what time was this? . . . I see. And it answers to the name of . . . Tiddles, yes, I've got that . . . Un-hunh, of course . . . As soon as I can, ma'am.'

The dangers of rural policing.

Rain fell like iron bars outside the window, stotting off the roof in a wild tattoo as thunder clapped, then boomed directly overhead. The school across the road now little more than a vague shadow, the road awash and gutters running. Jim Tennant had left the stuffy warmth of the office twenty minutes ago, climbing reluctantly into Mike 30, the squad car, with a scowl on his face as dark as the skies above. I was still sitting at the desk writing up my case report when Sergeant Yuill returned.

Yuill shrugged out of his overcoat, hung it up behind the door, threw himself down behind the opposite desk and, smoothing back his greying rain-slicked hair with both hands, said, 'The Greatest Living Detective has returned, I see.'

I glanced up with a snappy retort already half-formed on my lips but decided no, not now, and, shaking my head, returned my attention to the report in front of me. Back in the city, I brooded morosely, the Administration Department had a whole bloody floor in the Force HQ, with banks of computers manned by legions of clerical civvies whose express purpose in life was to free cops like me from the paperwork chains that had previously bound us to a desk for sometimes days on end. Out here on the island, though, with a limited budget and plenty of time on our hands, we have to do all the paperwork ourselves.

'Didn't take you very long,' he now added, his tone implying I should have spent the rest of the afternoon standing in a field with my neck running rain.

This time I looked up from my report and, unable to keep the edge from my voice, said, 'No problem. Back in the city I'd usually clear up at least a couple of murders before breakfast, leaving the rest of the day to concentrate on something *really* important – you know, like hunting down sheep-shaggers and bringing them to justice.'

At forty-eight years old, Adam Yuill's most remarkable feature was his nose, a legacy, the story went, from youthful bouts in one too many a welterweight ring. It had been broken twice and reset askew, and now dominated an otherwise plain and sallow face, overshadowing the shallow sockets in which moist eyes drifted like glossy black pebbles caught in the tide. He said, 'But you're not in the city now, are you, McMorran. You're just a plain country bumpkin cop.'

'As you always take pleasure in reminding me.' Six months now I'd been stationed here on Arran, one of four PCs in a combined force of five officers and six Specials. Everyone else on first-name terms and it had taken until only last week for Yuill to drop the 'Constable' in favour of 'McMorran'. Still, little progress was better than none at all. I called a mental truce and, pushing my case report aside, leant back in my chair. 'You have any luck today?'

'With the Ryder kid?' Yuill shook his head. 'Still claims alibi.'

'The so-called girlfriend?'

'Aye. And lying through her lovely little teeth, I'm sure of it.'

'So work on her,' I suggested. 'Tell her Ryder's been two-timing her. Usually does the trick.'

'You think I haven't tried?' Yuill shook his head again. 'No, he's got something on her, maybe dope, I don't know. Anyway, she's more frightened of him than she is of us.'

Sad indeed, I thought, the day a seventeen-year-old ned could evoke more fear in a fifteen-year-old schoolgirl than the combined force and wrath of the law and justice systems. Something vital, I felt, had been lost to our profession somewhere along the way.

'So what next?' I asked.

'What I'd like?'

'If you want.'

'Get the little shit on my own through the back and see how smart he is then. That's what I'd like.'

Through the back where the two small holding cells were situated.

'He could be telling the truth.'

Yuill curled his lip. 'Did you see the surgeon's report? The photos?' Twenty-two years a sergeant and just two years short of his service, he was a man whose metronomic moods could swing from one humour to another in the space of a single conversation. I told him no, not yet.

'Bruises the size of saucers on her thighs, on her back. Scratch-marks on her shoulders, her buttocks. Rectal tears, vaginal tears – I need to paint you the picture? The guy who did this is a fucking animal.'

'And in your mind Ryder fits that bill?'

Yuill stared out through the blinds, the window still running with rain. 'No remorse,' he said, voice as distant as his eyes. 'He shows no remorse.'

'What is this, a hunch? You? Sergeant Sceptic?'

'Fuck, she IDed Ryder, McMorran, mask or no mask.'

'But she never saw his face. Nor any distinguishing marks, nothing you could use in a court of law.' The Devil's Advocate was sitting at my shoulder taking notes.

'I *know* he did it.' Yuill almost sighed himself unconscious. 'Look,' he said, 'Ryder, he doesn't act concerned he's a suspect in a crime that could put him away for five-ten years, he says sure he knows her, the slag's got a rep. He says she likes it rough, he says ask anyone, any of the lads she hangs about with, how she likes it twos-up, threes-up, any way she can, this is what he's saying about a lassie fourteen years old, same age as my daughter. And you expect me to swallow that? Not a chance, McMorran, not a bloody chance.'

'But no previous, Sarge, not even a whiff, you say, that he's done this kind of thing before. Violence, sure, intimidation, sure, the typical schoolground tyrant, okay. From what I've

23

heard about him, I can believe that. But rape, especially this vicious kind of attack, usually you have a few pointers early on, you know, Intelligence: peeper reports, flash reports, indecent assault reports. Failing that, at least rumours. But from all accounts, as far as sexual deviancy is concerned, Ryder is clean.'

'The violence is there, McMorran, you can't deny that. Rape's not about sex, it's about power. You know that. It's assault, and nothing less.'

'Sure, I know that. But I also know you need proof.'

Sergeant Yuill muttered something about printing the little shit's genetics over a hundred-mile radius, then lapsed into silence, elbows on desk, head in hands, broad, blunt fingers massaging his heavily furrowed brow. Another flash of lightning, another growl of thunder. I waited until the sky was quiet before I spoke.

'What about all that devil-worship stuff Ryder keeps going on about? The sacrifices up on the Moor, at the Stones. You believe it?'

'Fantasy, pure fantasy. Sure, there's a bit of it about, but it's harmless, man, harmless. The days of human sacrifice are over.'

'Maybe they are. But animal sacrifice? And what he was saying about the goings-on in that hall? I wouldn't exactly call that harmless.'

'Look, McMorran, an island community this size, to a certain degree you have to learn to live with one another, accept that some people do things differently, have differing tastes and beliefs, make their own kind of entertainment. A lassie wants to join one of these pagan cults and lie naked on a table in the centre of a stage while all the men in the hall take it in turn to fuck her stupid, well, as far as I'm concerned, and as long as no crime is committed or reported, that's her choice. Whatever turns you on.'

'And Ryder claims what? That the girl, Julia, is into all that?'

'That's what he says.'

'And you believe him?'

Yuill thrust his chin aggressively forward. 'McMorran, it's been a long day and you winding me up is the last thing I need. I believe only what I know for a fact and what I know for a fact is that I've found no one I've interviewed so far who can corroborate one single claim that Ryder has made. You want my opinion, he's a pathological liar who wouldn't know the truth if it fucked him up the nose. And as far as all this pagan shit is concerned, this so-called devil-worship, I doubt a ned like Ryder would even get a look-in. Take my word.'

'You doubt?'

Yuill sighed again, weary comment, it seemed, on the ways of a world not of his making, nor to his liking. 'Up yours, McMorran.'

'No harm in checking it out.'

Yuill glanced shrewdly in my direction. 'Why the sudden interest? You pick up something on Tully's sheep you think might be connected?'

'It's possible. When Tully called it murder, he described it right.'

'Shit, McMorran, a sheep's a sheep.'

'Sure, but when you find one stabbed fifteen, maybe twenty times, you have at least to consider the motive. It's not slaughter for profit, it's not accident or suicide, and it certainly isn't a *crime passionnel*—'

'You can never be too sure,' Yuill smiled.

'—which leaves us with one very distinct possibility.'

'I don't want to hear it, McMorran. Not today.'

'Ritual sacrifice,' I said. 'In other words, murder.'

Yuill sighed. 'I should've given this to Bob Gillies.'

'The day before his holiday?'

'So I should've gone myself then.'

'You'd've reached the same conclusion.'

'Okay, okay.' Yuill held up the palms of his hands in a gesture of defeat. 'So you think the sheep was killed, what, as some kind of sacrifice?'

'It's possible.'

'Now you don't think so.'

'I don't know what to think yet. When I arrived I found the sheep on a slab of stone in the centre of the field. Dead a couple of days, though possibly less. Tully says he can last be sure he saw the sheep alive on Thursday evening, five or six. The last few days have been pretty warm, which would account for the state of decomposition and the maggots.'

'Bad?'

'You want to go on a diet, go take a look.'

'So,' Yuill said, flicking back through his desk diary, 'Thursday night, and no later than—'

'Friday morning.'

Yuill looked up from the diary. 'You want to know what Thursday night was?'

'Don't tell me. A full moon.'

'A new moon.' He slammed the diary shut. 'Maybe you have something after all.'

'And maybe it's just a coincidence.'

'You're a cop, McMorran, you don't believe in chance.'

'A cop, yes, but paranoid, no. Like you, I prefer to rely on facts.'

'So give me some facts.'

'Cause of death, then. What appeared to be a couple of heavy blows to the head, skull crushed in on both sides of the cranium.'

'Weapon?'

'I'd say a hammer, possibly a ball-peen. Both wounds about as wide and deep as a golf ball.'

'What like, the ground?'

'Dry when I arrived.' As I spoke, another peal of thunder ripped the ever-darkening sky apart and I turned towards the steamed-up window just as the cloudburst slanted in, heavy balls of rain exploding on the pane like translucent insects on a pebble-starred windscreen. 'But probably a quagmire by now,' I added as lightning lit up the sky again, forking towards the earth.

Yuill sighed. 'No footprints then.' He picked up a pen and began doodling absently on his blotter.

'As such, no. But on each side of the stone the grass was pressed flat, most likely where he planted his feet—'

'*He?*' Black pebble eyes snapping to my face.

'Sarge – give me a chance, will you?'

'Sure.' Another humourless smile. 'Carry on.'

'Nice of you.' I returned the smile with interest. 'As I was saying, the way it looked – in my *expert* opinion – he sat astride or stood over the sheep, pinning it down with one hand while he delivered the blows with the other.'

'Right-handed?'

'Or left, take your pick.'

'How about access?'

'Gate at the bottom of the field. I found a couple of tyre tracks down there in the mud, but Tully says that's where he usually parks his Land Rover and they were both deep enough for that, the treads similar.'

'But washed away by now.' The rain against the window still relentless, both of us having to raise our voices.

'Well I didn't think you wanted me to secure the locus.'

'Bloody right.' Yuill glanced at his watch. It was big and solid, a replica Seiko Oyster he'd bought last year on holiday in Greece, about as subtle as the Crown Jewels and maybe only twice as heavy. 'Okay,' he said, 'tell me about the stab wounds.'

'Five definites, at least a dozen possibles.'

'Possibles?'

'Like I said, decomposition was fairly advanced.'

'Blood?'

'On the stone beneath its head, plenty. From the stab wounds, nothing.'

27

'Inflicted *post mortem*, then.'

'Exactly.' I had his full attention now.

'Kind of knife?'

'Double-edged, I think, possibly a bayonet. As for length, I couldn't say. That would need an autopsy.'

'You're not seriously suggesting—'

'I told Tully he could roast it.'

'And knowing him, he probably will.' As suddenly as it had struck, the storm abated, passing swiftly out into the Firth of Clyde, the rain gradually easing off as the sky brightened to the west, a patch of blue clearly visible amidst the shifting strata of cloud beyond the school. Yuill glanced back down at the doodles on his blotter. 'You come across him before?'

I nodded. 'February, in the Mountain Rescue Team. Mind the young German couple got trapped on Cir Mhor? Guy who broke his leg coming down off the Saddle, took us all bloody night to bring them down? Tully was part of the team.'

'An awkward bastard, Tully. Thinks we've nothing better to do than settle his bloody right-of-access disputes. You ask me, I'd say that's what this is, this business with the sheep. One of his neighbours, maybe had it up to here, goes out in the dead of night and takes it out on one of Tully's sheep. Can't say I'd blame him.'

'*Him?*'

'*Touché.*' Yuill began doodling again, cubes within cubes. 'You pick up anything else?'

I flicked through my notebook. 'The name Hastie ring a bell? Rosalind Hastie?'

'Cottage up the hill, woman who takes in all the strays?'

'Aye, her. Tully says she's some kind of mystic. Anyway, you can see the roof of her cottage from the field.'

'Tully thinks *she* was responsible?'

'On the contrary,' I said. 'He thought the idea impossible.'

'And you? Did you speak to her?'

'All those dogs around?' I shuddered. 'No chance.'

Yuill made a sound which could have been mistaken for a laugh. 'You should've become a handler instead of transferring out here. Learnt to overcome your fear.'

'I don't want to overcome it, just avoid it.'

'Reminds me of a story my predecessor told me,' Sergeant Yuill said, his mood suddenly expansive. Perhaps the release of atmospheric pressure, now the thunderstorm had passed, of had also lifted a weight from his mind. 'Doyle, Sergeant Doyle. Working Strathclyde now, I think, part of the Robbery Squad. Told me about the time he pulled up this middle-aged couple, they'd been staying in Whiting Bay, you know, the caravan park, and he pulls them up on the Lamlash–Brodick road, they're late, you see, rushing to catch the ferry, and so he asks the guy behind the wheel if he owns a dog, and the guy says, "Sure, it's in the caravan." So Doyle says, "Are you sure, sir, did you put it in there yourself?" and the guy says, "No, my wife did," and the wife turns round and says *she* didn't put it in the caravan, she thought her husband had. So Doyle asks the guy where the dog was the last time he saw it, and the guy looks at his wife and they both say in unison, "Tied to the back of the caravan – why?"' Yuill burst into a fit of laughter that subsided eventually into a racking cough. 'Still . . .' he added, smearing the tears from his eyes, 'this sheep business, McMorran – don't get carried away. This isn't any bizarre kind of ritual or pagan sacrifice, you can strike that idea right out of your mind. Nevertheless, you'd better go speak to the Hastie woman – you never know, she might have seen or heard something. For the rest of it, find out what you can, sure, even give it a couple of days if you like. But like I said, it'll most likely be some kind of farming dispute, something petty like that. Chances are you'll not be able to prove anything, so just tie it up to your own satisfaction. Final report on my desk, say, Wednesday morning.'

'You know what worries me?' I said, pushing back my chair, climbing to my feet. 'The possibility that the kind of person who can do that to a sheep will soon get bored and move on.'

'To what? Dogs?'

'Either dogs,' I said, 'or policemen's daughters.'

'McMorran?' Yuill glowered. 'Get the fuck out of here.'

With a warm fire waiting in the hotel bar, a hundred wild and willing women couldn't have persuaded me to stay. I changed swiftly into my leathers, donned helmet and gloves, then stepped out into the drizzly remains of my day.

4

'...*Spying above with sharp eyes*
Like a tiger with insatiable craving. No blame.'

Watching.

He stands motionless beneath the ancient beech, the balmy night enclosing him, secure in this pocket of power. He has been there minutes or hours – he no longer knows nor cares. Time is not the issue here. Restoring a sense of balance is.

Especially after all that business with the sheep. After the mess he made of the first, having to go out the following night, find a fresh one. All the way down to Kildonan before he found what he was looking for. But worth it in the end, this time the man stabbing the sheep and no blood flowing at all – the *I Ching* spot on.

All it takes, a little perseverance.

Gideon can smell him in there, the old man Thomas. Smell rotting bowels. Body sweat so strong Gideon can almost lick it off his lips. And booze. Stale booze, beer and whisky. The man unable to breathe unless he has a drink in his hand. Lording it down at the hotel bar like every word he speaks is a pearly drop of wisdom. All those boring old stories about his life in the yards, all the great ships he welded. Listen to him long enough and you'd end up believing he built the whole fucking fleet single-handed. Royalty dropping by to shake his hand, ask his advice about where best to break the champers on the bow. Sure. 'Course they did. Stands to reason. Guy was a welder, worked with a blowtorch and one of them metal masks on his face. Talks like the world's leading marine architect.

Gideon can hear the old man's wheezy breath now. Can imagine his fat bulbous nose with the ugly bushes of hair sprouting from the nostrils, waving like reeds in his breath. The way they did that afternoon he swaggered into the pottery like some stompy wee dictator and finally lost his petty little temper. The day he joined the cropping list.

Gideon looking down into the cottage now, through the living-room window, watching him sitting there, another comatose TV supplicant. Why don't they just invent some kind of cap you put on your head and it scrambles your brains in privacy? Like you don't have to inflict it on the rest of the sentient human race. Man invented that would make a fucking fortune.

'Course it was all that Baird's fault, guy was a typical scientist, had to try and invent something because it hadn't been invented before. As though it was a challenge. Like Mount Everest, people climb it 'cause it's there, the world's highest midden. Put the Oprah Winfrey Show in every house in Britain – the challenge there is obvious. Worth wasting a lifetime for.

Only good thing on TV is the news. Gideon contemplating the last few months buying one of those satellite dishes with the twenty-four-hour news channel. Rig it up so he can watch it while he works, keep an eye on the Home News, see how the hunt for him is progressing. Maybe find some new inspiration there.

Arthur Thomas pushing himself out of his armchair now, through to the kitchen to make another cup of tea. The commercials must be on, Thomas obviously not in a buying mood, happy with his washing powder. Gideon also looking at his watch now, thinking why waste any more time, it was clear Thomas was in for the night, not going anywhere. He would just have to wait, maybe come back tomorrow night. Get a good look around the cottage then, get a feel for the man, the private man, see what makes him tick.

And what will make him come unwound.

The Oriental woman in the Philadelphia Eagles starter jacket at the end of the bar met my eyes again, the merest of smiles ghosting across her lips before she turned away. So brief and fleeting the smile that I wondered if I'd imagined it, had conjured it up from the wishing-well of my ego to fill the emptiness and alleviate the boredom, both of which ached within me this evening like some grievous, inexplicable loss. Or maybe she was smiling at someone else, I thought, the man standing next to me, perhaps, now collecting his change from Freddie the barman, asking when the bar closed.

'November.'

'I mean tonight.'

'When you've had enough, mate,' Freddie replied, 'that's what time we close.' Watching me as he said it, the look in his eyes provocative, as if to say, *You're a cop, what you going to do about it?* My answer, of course, *Why shit in my own back yard?*

She was in her mid to late twenties, with a small round face framed by shiny black shoulder-length hair. Her small snub nose sat delicately above rosy lips which she glossed frequently with her small pointy tongue. Korean? I wondered. Japanese? Or a Filipino? Her teeth were even but for two sexy little eyeteeth which she used every now and then to chew at her full lower lip. Her clear black eyes swept the room with confidence, her gaze alert, curious and alive as she sat side-on to the bar, drinking pints of Real Ale and rolling her own, a pouch of tobacco and a pile of notes weighted by coins next to her elbow.

She had been sitting unmolested since I had entered three and a half pints ago, and I was brave and getting braver. Her time was up.

'Pint,' I ordered, draining and then pushing my empty glass towards the barman, then turning on my stool to survey the room. Back of eleven and it was already busy, mostly hotel guests crammed around the half-dozen Arran-shaped tables by the fire while the regulars either sat or stood at the bar. At the no-armed bandit near the steps up to the dance hall – a long, low wooden extension tacked on to the side of the hotel, where they held ceilidhs on Saturday nights and folk-gigs during the Folk Festival – a couple of black-leathered bikers punched away their money, watched warily by a short-haired mongrel stretched out beneath a nearby table where a middle-aged woman sat on her own, sipping whisky and writing postcards. I turned back to the bar and caught the Oriental woman's eyes on mine, so I raised my eyebrows in question and made a drinking gesture with my hand, then watched her smile politely, shake her head and look away. So I counted out the exact change, making a meal of it as I felt my neck redden, thinking *Shit, what a fool*, as I slid the coins purposefully through a puddle of beer to the barman, *who d'you think you are, Mickey Rourke or what*, sank a third of the pint to cool the creeping flush, *when will you ever learn*, glanced around with a little too much unconcern, *just because she's on her own doesn't mean she craves your company*, then studied with the intensity of concentration I normally reserved for crime scenes the label on the bottle of Edradour just to the left of the till. Established 1825, eh? And a ten-year-old Single Highland Malt to boot. Now that *was* interesting. Very interesting. Perhaps if I drank enough of it, I'd forget what a bloody fool I'd made of myself, imagining a ghost of a smile as an explicit invitation to—

'Thanks for the offer,' she said, hand resting for a second on my forearm, 'but I think I've already had enough.'

Her English as flawless as her skin. Oxford? I wondered, or Cambridge? Taller than I'd thought, and perhaps a little older. A faint nicotine stain between first and second fingers of her right hand, a plain gold band on the second finger of her left. Sweatshirt beneath the starter jacket, UCLA. Pale-blue jeans, neither baggy nor tight. Plenty of curves in all my favourite places. Her scent subtle, the kind of subtle that costs a lot of money. Money and American fashion ... she had to be Japanese.

'But I'll join you, if you don't object?' Without waiting for a reply, she hitched herself up on to the neighbouring stool.

Object, me?

'Do,' I said, 'please.' Then rubbed a finger around the inside of my collar where the sweat still prickled. 'My name's Francis. Francis or Frank, take your pick.'

'Nice to meet you,' she said, holding out her hand. Her grip was neither limp nor strong, just confidently feminine. 'My friends call me Kyoko.'

'May I be your friend?'

Her laugh was genuine, if a little wary. 'You can call me Kyoko.'

It was a start. 'You're from Japan?'

'Wakayama. You know it?'

I shook my head. The only places I'd heard of were Tokyo, Hiroshima and Nagasaki – and the latter two were not exactly great conversational gambits.

'It's a fishing port. Agricultural kind of city. Not very big, population around four hundred thousand.' Kyoko exhaled at the ceiling, stubbed out her cigarette. 'Now four hundred thousand minus one.'

'You're living over here?'

She shook her head. 'Business. I'm here with my uncle.'

'Your English is very good.'

'It should be, I was at university here.'

'Cambridge?'

Her eyes opened out like sun-kissed flowers. Black orchids. 'How'd you guess?'

I shrugged modestly, took a swallow of beer and said nothing.

'Do you live here? In Brodick, I mean.' She pronounced it Bloh-dick. It wasn't the first time I'd detected a subtle mid-Pacific twang to some of her vowels. I told her aye, a wee cottage behind the hotel that I shared with an empty fridge and a family of mice.

'It's a lovely island.'

'"Scotland in Miniature" is how the travel brochures describe it. Highlands in the north, lowlands in the south, sheep bloody everywhere. You're in business, you say?'

'My uncle's in business. I'm, well . . .' She shrugged, thought about it for a second, then sighed heavily. 'Let's just say I don't know what the hell I'm doing.'

'I know the feeling.'

'You do?'

'The sign of troubled times,' I said, taking another hefty swallow of beer – my own sign of troubled times. 'So what were you doing before you decided you didn't know what the hell you were doing?'

'You'll laugh.'

'Probably.'

'I was a prison officer.'

I didn't laugh. I reassessed her. She looked just as good. Maturer, in fact. Which was even better. I took another sign of troubled times and asked her how the hell.

'I'm not too sure really. One of the reasons, I suppose, because there's a prison in Wakayama. After I came back from university I was under a lot of pressure from my father to join his company. But I could see myself, you know, thirty years from now still sitting behind the same old desk, looking out the same old window at the same factory wall and wondering where the hell my life went.'

'So you became a *prison* officer?'

'I know it sounds strange – but yeah, that's what I did. I thought I'd be able to make use of my languages – there are a lot of foreigners in Wakayama prison – and maybe change the way prisoners are treated, like in a more humane way. Idealistic stuff, I know, but why not? I was young. My father, though, was furious. Hasn't spoken to me since.' She smiled ruefully, took skins and tobacco from the pouch on the bartop and rolled up a smoke, matchstick thin, then lit it off a book of hotel matches. Claridges, London. She was a veritable cache of clues.

'How long are you staying?' I asked.

Before she could reply, a man approached the bar and pushed between us. He was in his early fifties, grey-haired and lanky, and stooped like a crane. A heavy tweed overcoat smelling of woodsmoke and rain hung from wide sloping shoulders. His nose was a hooked beak, his dark eyes beady beneath an overhanging brow, his mouth a pinch of puckered flesh around large, uneven tobacco-stained teeth. He ordered a pint of Eighty Shilling and began searching his pockets for change. Kyoko had to speak around him.

'I haven't really decided yet. My uncle has another round of meetings in London in a couple of weeks, I may go with him, I may not.'

'What kind of business is he in?'

Kyoko shrugged. 'This and that. Nothing very exciting.' Said with an air of total boredom. 'And you?' Kyoko said. 'What do *you* do for a living?'

Here we go, I thought.

'Nothing very interesting,' I shrugged, inwardly cursing the necessity of such social obligations as small talk. At the end of a hard day's shift all you want to do is throw off your uniform, relax, and be treated as any other normal human being. The last thing you want is someone asking that dreaded, loaded question. Ruin a relationship before it's even begun.

'That's an answer?'

'This and that. Clean the streets, you could say.' And anyway,

39

what did it matter the hell I did for a living? Does the job make the man, or the man make the job? It's what you put *into* life that you get out of it.

Or so I keep telling myself.

'You're a street-cleaner?'

'Don't believe a word of it,' said the man at the bar without looking up as he counted out change for his drink. His hands were bloodless, bony-knuckled claws with long, nicotined nails. 'He's a cop.'

'Thanks, Alec,' I sighed, 'I appreciate that.'

Kyoko said, 'You're a cop? A real-life detective?'

'Don't mention it,' Alec Brodie said to me. And to Kyoko, 'A beat-cop, hell, a glorified shepherd. Ask him.'

'Is that true, Francis?'

Resignedly, I told her aye, it was true. Anyway, the danger had passed: she hadn't slapped me or moved away, nor let that look – the one every city cop sees a hundred times a day – cloud her clear black eyes. And she was calling me Francis.

'Francis? *Francis?*' the old man mimicked. 'Christ Awmighty!' He paid off the barman and then turned to lean his back against the bar. 'I mean, what kind of man's name is that? Frank – that's what his name is, dear. Frank.'

You can walk into any bar, I thought, any bar in any dark, forgotten, godforsaken corner of the world and find an Alec Brodie there, propped against the bar with a drink in his hand, holding forth like a king over his court. A friendless man who knows so much about everything that nobody wants to know because no one in their right mind wants to be wrong all the time, nor constantly preached to, corrected and patronised by someone whose only talent in life is an unfailing ability to clear a bar several hours before closing time. Unfortunately it was clearly my predetermined lot in life – or perhaps some obvious weakness in my face evident only to the world's greatest bores – to become a human receiver to the endlessly broadcasting Brodies of this world.

Kyoko shot me a glance. 'Aren't you going to introduce me to your friend?'

'No.'

The old man sipped from his pint. 'Alec's ma name,' he said, wiping the foam from his lip with the back of his hand. 'Alec Brodie.'

'And poaching's his game,' I added, taking a sip of revenge, a mosquito sip of blood. 'Alec, do me a favour?'

'I hear you found a sheep this morning, one of Tully's.'

'So?'

'Just saying.'

'Well why don't you say it—'

'Murdered, I heard.'

'Okay, you've made your point. Nothing happens on this island you don't get to hear about. Now would you please—'

'Stabbed, the word is, at least a hundred times.'

'A slight exaggeration.'

'Maybe I *will* have another drink,' Kyoko said, intrigued now by the twist the conversation had taken.

'Eighty Shilling?' I asked, then called over the barman, ordered up a couple more.

Brodie: 'So how many times then?'

Kyoko: 'Someone *murdered* a sheep?'

McMorran: 'Five, maybe more.' Wishing now I'd stayed home in my empty little cottage, spent the evening watching the mice eat my socks and fornicate on the kitchen sideboard.

Alec Brodie, though, was enjoying himself. 'A sacrifice, I heard. One of they cults that like to go out in the full moon's light, drink a chalice of blood and dance nekked in the early-morning dew.' With a throaty chuckle and a wink at Kyoko.

'You mean,' she asked, 'that goes on over here?'

'You wouldn't believe the things go on over here,' Brodie told her, ignoring my obvious discomfort. 'In fact it minds me of something happened across the Sound,' he added, 'must be, aye, seventeen, eighteen year ago now.'

41

'Kilbrannan Sound?'

'Aye. Carradale Point on the Kintyre shore.' Brodie flapped a hand in the direction of the bar, vaguely west. 'Used to be a herd of maybe thirty feral goats over there until they were slaughtered. March, I think it was, nineteen seventy-six. Two-thirds of the herd, including the old billy, shot and decapitated, their carcasses left piled in cairns to rot.'

'Gruesome,' Kyoko said with a shiver and grimace as I continued to look out over the bar, feigning disinterest. In truth, I was listening very hard.

'They find out who did it?'

Brodie told her no, not exactly, but theories there were plenty. 'You see,' he said, 'whoever was responsible arrived and left by boat.' Pronounced with an air of divine revelation, as though it explained the secret of the universe, everything. Both Kyoko and I looked at him with puzzled frowns. He sighed wearily, shook his head and sighed again. Alec Brodie was top of the Premier League of Sighs, runaway leader.

'Look,' he explained, as though to a backward child, 'there's a road there, and tracks that give much better access. Why go to all the trouble of using a boat? Unless . . .'

'They sailed across from Arran,' I said.

'Exactly,' Brodie said triumphantly. 'If they'd come from the Kintyre mainland, they'd've used a car. Stands to reason.'

'And no one knows who did it?'

'Did I say that?'

'You said there were theories,' I reminded him.

'Theories and proof – you want me to teach you your job, man? No wonder they transferred you out here.'

Kyoko asked. 'You're not from Arran, then?'

I paused a second before replying, but in the presence of Alec Brodie even that was half a second too long.

'Look at him,' Brodie sighed, 'his face, the colour of his skin. That's a city face. People step out of a prison after fifteen years, they have the same pallor. Or better. I've seen healthier-looking corpses cut out of car wrecks, ghosts, even, with a more colourful complexion. That haunted look – you know where that comes from, doll? From living in the city, always looking over your shoulder, always being chased in your head by demons who look just like your neighbour or boss or milkman or travelling shoe-salesman. Believe me. A thousand years from now and city-dwellers will've evolved into long-necked swivel-heids, fearful mutants with bulletproof skin, rushing here and there in a paranoid frenzy, afraid they'll waste a few seconds somewhere along the way and miss something worth killing or dying for.' Brodie ran out of breath, had to stop and refuel. Sank the rest of his pint in two hefty swallows.

'No,' I told Kyoko, taking advantage of Brodie's vocal incapacity, 'Edinburgh.'

'Yeah?' she said, giving me her wide-open eyes.

'Yeah,' Brodie replied on my behalf as he beckoned the barman and ordered the same again. 'One of our cool east-coast cousins, my dear. Wait'll you hear this.'

Some people can only talk with a drink in their hand. Unfortunately they're often the same people who can't *stop* talking while there's a drink in their hand. So while we waited with bated breath for Brodie to reload his hand, I turned my thoughts to goats. Goats and the Devil and the Deep Blue Sea.

If goats are symbolic of the Devil, I mused, then of what are sheep symbolic? In religious terms, the answer was obvious: in the scriptures, Jesus was referred to as the Lamb of God, and his followers as his flock. Perhaps . . .

My attention returned as Brodie cocked his voice on a gulp of frothy beer and cleared his throat.

'You're looking at a disgraced man,' Brodie continued as though after but a second's respite. 'Frank here used to be a high-flying detective on the mainland – an inspector, no less – in one of those fancy crime squads they took straight from TV, all screaming tyres and gunshots, you know the kind, chasing international gangsters across the country, picture in the papers every time he so much as farted – if you'll pardon my French, hen.'

'I don't believe it,' Kyoko said, shaking her head as she looked from Brodie to me, back to Brodie again. But forgive me, I'm a man and my gaze is male, and I was watching her breasts and the way they swayed beneath her sweatshirt with just a little delay as she shook her head. Anyway, this was a story I'd heard before.

'Nor does he,' the old man muttered. 'The last pictures he had in the papers weren't so flattering at all. Were they, Frank?'

Here we go again, I thought.

'No,' Brodie answered for me, 'they most definitely were not.'

'Why don't I go sit in the corner, let you finish your story in peace?' I suggested. 'I'm obviously not needed here.'

'See?' Brodie said to Kyoko. 'The man's a celebrity and he feels left out. I know – he wants to tell you the story himself, his own way.' Brodie put down his pint for a second to patronise her hand; patted it, the way you would a child you don't want to know. 'Forgive me, dear, I'm just an old fool who talks too much.' He picked up his pint again. 'Okay, Frank? I'll leave you alone now, let you tell it the way you know best, the way it was. And don't miss out the bit about the headlines. I know you don't like to talk about it, what they called you and that, but—'

'What headlines? What did they call you, Francis?'

'Killer,' Brodie said. 'They called him a killer cop. That was the headline: *Killer Cop Disciplined For Excess Force*. What d'you think, dear? Good, eh?'

Good, I thought, was not the word.

6

'**M**cMorran?'

'What?'

'Yuill. You busy?'

'Is that why you rang? Middle of the night and you want to know if I'm busy?'

'Middle of the day, McMorran, and some of us have work to do.'

'And some of us have days off we like to sleep in on.'

'Then you chose the wrong profession.'

'You're telling me?'

'I just received a call from the distillery up in Lochranza, the Glen Chalmadale.'

'What about it?'

'They found a dead sheep in their water-tank.'

'Is this a joke or something? Is this what I have to look forward to every time someone discovers a dead sheep, you're going to call me out? Have a laugh with the rest of the boys?'

'It's not just an *ordinary* dead sheep, McMorran.'

'Not another one, please don't tell me that.'

'There do appear to be certain similarities.'

'Such as?'

'The manner of its death, for a start. We're not exactly talking natural causes here.'

'That's all I bloody need.'

'So why don't you take a wander round there later on,

see what the score is? Maybe have a word with Findlay Farquharson, calm the man down before he has a bloody heart attack. He thinks someone's trying to put him out of business.'

'I wish they'd hurry up and succeed, give us all a bit of peace and quiet.'

'Kid gloves, McMorran, and I mean that. I don't want Farquharson calling up his bum-chums in office, kicking up a stink. Not yet, anyway.'

'Just let me know when.'

'We'll see.'

'You want me in uniform?'

'Nah, no need, I told him you were coming.'

'Thoughtful of you.'

'Oh, and McMorran? How about taking a tour of the island, get some sun?'

'What the hell for?'

'I thought maybe you'd appreciate a shot at the Ryder kid. Rattle his cage a bit, let him know we haven't forgotten what a little shit he is.'

'Do your dirty work, you mean.'

'Dirty work? Man, I'm offering you a bonus here, something to make your day. You don't want it, I'll go myself, no problem.'

'Rattle his cage? Or his bones?'

'You're a big boy now, McMorran, you decide.'

Something I've noticed. People come here from the mainland, holiday, whatever, they spend the first couple of days bombing round the island as though auditioning for Bullit with the wife screaming in the back seat and on the verge of delivering quads. I know I did. Overtaking cars for no other reason than they're in front of you. It's crazy. Force of habit. And while you're stressing out your heart trying to beat some time-bomb clock, they're making their own time, dancing to a gentler beat. Think about it. You're on an island a little over twenty miles long, with only fifty-six miles of coastline and three main roads: one which follows most of that coastline, and two – The String and The Ross – that traverse the island. So where are you going to go in such a godawful hurry that you need to risk your precious life to save but a few worthless minutes?

Anyway.

West out of Brodick The String climbs steeply between the heather-mottled flanks of An Tunna and Cnoc Dubh, before dropping into Glean An-t-Suidhe, the Glen of Rest, where it follows for a while the course of Machrie Water, now a molten flow of silver caught in the sun, glinting sporadically through a sparse screen of saplings below to the right. The glen glorious this morning, a lustrous patchwork of pink and green, purple and gold beneath a crystal blue sky fringed by fleeting wisps of cloud. Days like this, balanced between a warm machine and a simmering sky, I can almost believe in gods and their benevolence.

Now as the glen opened out and The String dropped south towards Blackwaterfoot, I found my thoughts dwelling on danger. Women and danger. What is it, I wondered, about cops that some women find irresistible? Their sense of power? Their potential for violence? Their moustaches? I'm never too sure. In a way some of these groupies remind me of the kind of people who stand and stare at accident scenes, or the pavement banquets of jumper remains. Ghouls. I mean, I've had pillow talks in the past that make some of my interrogations – sorry, interviews – seem like romances in comparison. *What's your worsest memory? You ever seen a guy with his head ripped off? Is it true that a body that's been lying for a week in an airless room at the height of summer is gonna burst like an over-ripe melon the moment you try to turn it over? You ever seen that happen? You ever have to kill a man?*

Morbid or what?

Cruising now, Kilbrannan Sound a shimmering sheet of metallic blue to the right, sandwiched, it seemed, between

47

Machrie Moor and the hills of Kintyre. And posing. Sitting erect, right hand on throttle, left on thigh, cool behind shades – who says vanity is not a bachelor's greatest ally? With a long night behind me and a slow day ahead, I was man at his most confident self. Life, take your best shot.

Danger, I thought, and its element – both powerful aphrodisiacs. Some people are attracted to danger almost as much as prime ministers are to scenes of disaster. As though Risk Factor was the latest and most potent perfume by Max Factor. Ask an adulterer twenty seconds before the front door slams. Ask any cop. Ask any psychopath. Ask yourself. Take two normal people and add some attraction, stir in a touch of danger here, an element of risk there, and what do you get? Most probably the greatest sex you ever damn had.

Danger, fear, sex, release.

Kyoko. It had seemed last night that the moment Brodie mentioned the newspaper headline the lights came on in her eyes. Or was I just being cynical? Me – a hard-bitten city cop, risen from the streets, a lifter of a thousand gruesome stones, a man who's seen all he wants to see of the darker side of life and can no longer return to the light – cynical? Well, possibly, just a little. Nevertheless, I'd seen the light spark in Kyoko's eyes. So naturally I wondered, as I had wondered before, if it were not perhaps some kind of romantic endeavour to get as close as possible to that dark and dangerous world denied the general public, that shadowy world of forbidden sin beyond the thin blue line, at once repellent yet somehow strangely attractive. Was that the attraction? Or are we all just fantastic lovers?

Indeed.

Ryder. This is what I knew about Julian Ryder. Seventeen years old. A history of Supervision Orders (44/1B), List G Homes, Secure Units and Young Offender Institutes. Lately farmed out to Community Carers. Known joyrider and small-time dealer in speed, downers, and dope. Proven bully. Convicted perjurer and car thief. Suspected fire raiser, burglar and now, it seemed, rapist. The boy was obviously headed for the big time.

Seventeen years old, I thought, and seventeen years stupid. Anyone who tried to make a living as a car thief on an island, especially an island this size, had to be not just a little bereft of the brights.

I did a slow tour of the village, then back down the street where he lived, found him eventually in the hotel car park, kicking a beer can with a couple of younger boys and watched by a gum-chewing, bored-looking girl. He knew the bike, watched me approach with a twist of his lips, making the sound of a siren.

'Hee-haw, hee-haw.'

What was it Sergeant Yuill had said? *Get the little shit on my own through the back and see how smart he is then. That's what I'd like.* I suddenly knew how he felt.

'Ryder?' I growled. 'A few words. Over here.'

'How about *piss off and die*?'

'I'm asking nicely.'

'Piss off.' Ryder glanced around his audience of friends to see how impressed they were. One of the boys laughed nervously, the girl merely yawned.

'The big man, eh, playing it hard in front of the lassies?'

Belligerently, 'I don't have to talk to you.'

'Either here or back at the station. Like last week, when you told us about your pals, what they get up to.'

'I never told you nothing!'

'Sure you didn't.'

'Don't believe a word,' he exclaimed indignantly to his pals. 'He's just trying to stir the shit.' They glanced at Ryder, at me, at Ryder again.

'If they've got any more sense than you,' I said, 'they'll be heading off any second now.'

And sure enough, they had and they did.

'Just the two of us,' I said, now we were alone. I manoeuvred Ryder back against the sea-wall as he struggled to keep his hard

49

face on. Five-eight, maybe eight or nine stone, fine blond hair hanging lank in a pudding-bowl cut over shallow slit eyes, widening now in my shadow. Gold stud earring halfway up his right ear. 'You like sheep, Ryder?'

'You what?'

I brought my face down to within a breathshot of his. 'Where were you Thursday night?' I snapped, watching his eyes buckle and slide as his lower lip began to tremble. All mouth and no heart, I realised. The kind of ned who'd *need* a mask to hide behind. Maybe Yuill was right, after all.

'Th . . . Thursday night?'

'Anyone vouch for where you were?' Keep the little shit jumping.

'I was—'

'Last night, Ryder, I want to know every move you made. Minute by minute. You can't account for one and you're going in, clear?'

'But—'

'I said *clear?*'

'C-c-clear.'

A pair of gulls wheeled and screeched over the tiny harbour at the foot of the Black Water. An outboard motor sputtered to life a hundred yards out in Drumadoon Bay. An old couple came out of the hotel and crossed to their car, watching us warily as we waited for them to climb in and drive off.

'So,' I said, 'tell me about the sheep.'

'What bloody sheep?'

'The one found stabbed to death down above Kildonan.'

'I don't know what you're talking about!'

He looked genuinely confused. He had every right to be. I wasn't too sure what I was talking about either.

'She identified you.'

'Who did?'

'You tell me.'

'I don't know—'

'Say her name, Ryder.'

'Whose—'

'I said say her fucking name!'

'Julia,' he said, his voice a throaty whisper, 'Wallace.'

'That's right, the girl you raped. She's put you there on the night in question.'

'No way! Ask Carol, she was with me the whole—'

'Enough!' I yelled, the word physical in its effect, Ryder flinching back into the wall, trying to hunch his head somewhere down behind his breastbone. I backed off then and turned away, took a few slow paces and a few deep breaths as though to calm myself down, exert a little self-control. Then whirled on him again, but this time keeping my voice low, almost concerned. 'Look, Ryder, I'm giving you some advice for free here, so I suggest you listen carefully. I've been through this same bloody scene so many times I could do it in my sleep. You're guilty – you know it, and I know it. There is no way on this earth you can convince me otherwise. Not all the girlfriends' alibis in the world are going to convince me otherwise. Not even the Pope's personal testimony would make me change my mind. You did this deed and you'll go down for it. Hard. So think about it, Ryder. Think about your girlfriend, Carol. How long do you think you can exert your control over her? How long before she decides she doesn't want to ruin her life for the likes of a jailbound ned like you? A week? A month? A year? Who knows, maybe even longer. But no matter. However long it takes – and we'll be riding her back as hard as we're going to ride yours – we'll be there at your door with a warrant the moment she comes to her senses and tells us the truth. And that'll be you, Ryder, in among the big boys, cheerio. No more Secure Units or YOIs, no more Community Carers, this'll be you on remand, five, six, maybe ten months, crammed four to a cell twenty-three hours a day, and the moment the word comes in that you're the kiddie-raper, you're the whipping post, son, the bendover boy – *you*,' I said, now emphasising each word with a prod of my index finger, '*are . . . gone.*'

I gave him one extra prod then turned on my heel. Stopped a few yards off, glanced over my shoulder.

'Oh, and by the way,' I said, as though an afterthought, 'we found your earring yesterday. At the crime scene.'

Instinctively, he reached towards his ear. Then realised his mistake.

'You bastard!' he spat.

I laughed. He was right.

I headed for my bike.

I took the coast road north out of Blackwaterfoot, taking my time, the sun hot on my back, leather jacket in the pannier, sweatshirt flapping. The breeze was warm coming off the stippled Sound. The forested hills of Kintyre beyond, clad in emerald, in gold. Warm front coming in from Southern Europe, the forecast had predicted this morning, originally from the Sahara. Record temperatures in France and Spain.

I'd believe it when I peeled.

The Glen Chalmadale distillery in Lochranza has a unique status as the smallest distillery in Scotland, the whole contained within a cluster of low, whitewashed stone buildings with red doors in a verdant tree-speckled hollow at the foot of Glen Chalmadale. Approaching up the single lane, you come first to the Warehouse, like a row of squat white cottages on your right, then the Stillhouse where the actual distilling takes place. Opposite that, the small Manager's Office, and a white wooden footbridge leading across a gently coursing burn to Heather Bank Cottage, the distillery shop. Further up the lane, and still on your left, the Old Kiln Buildings adjoin the Malt Barn Reception Centre. Facing that, behind a steep grassy bank, a small reservoir behind a sign that states DANGER WATER. So that you don't mistake it for a pair of fornicating rhinoceroses, I suppose.

52

Anyway, you can learn all this from the brochures on sale in the shop as you wait for someone to come and lead you to the allegedly mutilated carcass of a sheep.

His name, when he came, was Archie McDonald.

'And you,' he said, appraising me with cocked head after I'd introduced myself, 'are the mainland man, am I right? The one in all the papers.'

'Who found it?' I asked as he led me across the bridge. I'd had enough of newspaper talk last night.

'I did.'

We stopped to allow a gaggle of tourists waddle up the hill after their guide, then made our way round behind the Stillhouse. 'When?' I asked.

'First thing.' We stopped in the shade between a bricked-in water-tank on the left and, on the right, what appeared to be some kind of cooling-tank attached to the rear wall of the Stillhouse. 'The Worm,' he explained, noting my puzzled look. 'That pipe coming out the wall there? That's where the alcohol vapour from the still rises. The coiled pipe in the water there? That's the Worm, where the vapour's condensed back into alcohol.'

Whisky and I, I couldn't deny, had staggered many a happy mile together. And although genuinely interested in the process of distillation, at this moment what interested me more was why he had checked the tank. So I asked.

He was a short man, Archie, blocky and solid in his worn blue overalls, his speech and manner as slow and sure as a lava flow. 'Habit,' he said, running calloused fingers through his sandy hair. 'Do it first thing every morning, without fail. See that?' He pointed at a small white cottage further up the path. 'That's where I live. Come down this way to work, check the tank, make sure there's nae wee beasties gone fur a dip. Habit.'

'And sometimes you find beasties?'

'Sometimes,' he shrugged. Like, what did it matter?

'And this morning . . .'

'Yon muckle deid sheep.'

It lay on a bed of bracken on the bank beside the water-tank, beneath a moving blanket of feasting flies. The air hummed. I could already see more than I wanted to see from where I stood.

'Local sheep?'

'How would I know?'

'The markings.'

'What bloody markings?'

'Yeah,' I agreed. Decomposition was more advanced in this case, the sheep here killed at least a day before the other, maybe two. Though there was no apparent damage to the skull, its neck gaped like a surprised black mouth, and there were several stab wounds visible that were not dissimilar from the ones I had seen yesterday. This one had bled, though, had been stabbed rather than bludgeoned to death; somewhere on the island, I reckoned, a lot of blood had seeped to soil. I asked him if sheep ever wandered down here from the hills or up from the village.

'Only the flying kind,' he said. 'We've got fences all round the property here, and if they wander up the road from the village the grid at the gate stops them.'

'*Where* then?' I muttered, I thought, to myself.

'Where what?'

'Where was it killed. The locus, Archie, the crime scene.' As though it really mattered – wherever it was, after yesterday's storm the chances of picking up any significant clues were millions to one, the odds on actually finding the locus even greater. I looked up to find Archie regarding me, his head to one side, the glimmer of suspicion deep in his shadowed eyes. Had I really lost my mind? I wondered.

'Who,' I asked him, 'locks up at night?'

'I do.'

'Who else has keys?'

'Farquharson. The son.'

'You mean Findlay?'

'The one and lonely.'

I forced a smile. 'Anyone else?'

'There's another set in the safe.'

'And who has keys to the safe?'

'Mrs Farquharson.' Whether fair comment or not, and intentionally or not, he pronounced the name *Fuckerson*. With a good deal of spit.

'So the son, Findlay, is first on and last off the premises?'

'Last on, first off. He's consistent, I'll give him that.'

'And he thinks someone's trying to put him out of business?'

'His opinion, not mine.'

'Why would he think that?' I asked. 'Has anything else happened I should know about?'

'Not that I've been told. I only run the place.' Archie glanced at his watch. 'When I've got time, that is,' he added.

'Just a few more questions. I take it the water in this tank is used for the distillation?'

Archie nodded. 'Spring water,' he said. 'Tap it up there on the moor, pipe it down into this tank here. Use it for the mash.'

Mash, I knew, was the mixture of malted barley and spring water.

'And the burn?' I asked. I'd parked my bike down by the footbridge over the stream; had imagined that to be the source of water for the distilling process.

'Like I said, tap it up on the moor. No chemicals that way, see, comes down pure as can.'

'Chemicals?'

'The ones farmers use,' he sighed, 'to make their land more profitable.' As though it was obvious, and me a fool to ask.

'How many work here?'

'There's three of us in the distillery itself, Maggie in the shop, Sue up at the Malt Barn Reception Centre, and the Farquharsons, mother and son.' The latter, said with an air of regret. 'That's the permanent staff, seven in all. Summertime, we usually bring in an extra couple of guides. They're both on today, nice girls, Fiona and Moragh.'

'Where is he now, the son?'

'Who knows?' Another glance at his watch. 'Drove off in a mood about an hour ago, saying he couldn't afford to wait all day on some brain-dead PC who couldn't tell the time.'

'Your words?'

'His.'

'Mm.' I filed it away. 'And his mother?' I asked.

'She'll be in tomorrow. You'll get more sense out of her anyway.'

I couldn't wait.

I thanked Archie for his time. He nodded tersely, turned and disappeared through the back door of the Stillhouse and, for the second time in as many days, I found myself alone in the presence of murdered mutton, staring absently at a teeth-bared and grinning rictus, with the word *sacrifice* still a chorus in my mind.

There was something odd, I felt, about the sheep's death-mask expression. It seemed almost human with its teeth bared in such a vicious snarl. To my mind, sheep don't snarl. Snarling's for predators, carnivores. A defence mechanism to signal attack.

What the hell was I doing here? I wondered again. Why wasn't I sitting out front of the hotel with my feet up on a table, a glass near my hand and the sun on my face, doing what most normal people do on a summer's day off, sit back, relax, and watch the world stumble by? Good question. Maybe Archie's sidelong glance had said it all – why waste my time? It was just a sheep after all.

Except no. It was more than that, more than just a sheep: it was evidence of a very sick mind. Behind these crimes something evil squirmed, some cold malevolence in quasi-human form. I could feel it the way a shiver chills your spine and hackles rise in the presence of something feared but unseen. Sense it in a way I could never explain.

And as I'd told the sergeant yesterday, I *was* worried:

someone who enjoys killing sheep *will* eventually tire of sheep and turn to more challenging and more rewarding victims. To me it seemed logical, a natural progression. In every violent act, there is a history of escalating violence in the perpetrator leading up to that act. Rapists, for instance, do not just wake up one morning and say, 'Right, tonight's the night I'm gonna commit my first rape.' No. They are social inadequates who have a history of sexual offences that increase gradually in severity over the years. They start off as fantasies, instilled, say, by some experience in early puberty – walking home after school, for example, the pubert sees a woman undressing through a bedroom window. So that night he fantasises about her, and next day he makes damn sure he's there at her window same time as the previous day. He becomes a peeper; maybe peeps on other neighbours, begins stealing panties off washing lines. Does this for a year or so, gathering courage. Devours pornography, fuel for his fantasies – which become more adventurous, more ambitious. A couple more years go by and he progresses to flashing, minor acts of indecency. Now he's brave and getting braver, he's on the prowl, looking for someone to act out his fantasy. Maybe he has a record, but so what? All this time, he's been learning from his mistakes, getting better at what he does. He knows what he's doing is wrong, is against the law, but it's a compulsion now, the brakes don't work. It's no longer about sex, either – it's the exercise of power and control, driven by frustration and anger. And when finally the act of violence does take place – when he tries to force reality into his fantasy and finds that it doesn't work out the way it does in his mind, in other words, that he has failed – it is not the end of a fantasy, no, only the beginning of a new and infinitely more dangerous one.

And so it is with killers. They, too, have a history of progressive violence spawned in fantasy. They have practised on little animals since they were kids, staking down frogs, insects, birds, piercing them with needles, burning them with cigarette ends, stabbing matches through their eyes. Dropping kittens out of tower-block windows, or trussed-up puppies into fires. I have heard them talk of such things. Dominic Bain, for instance, the serial killer who terrorised the Morningside area of Edinburgh last year, was now talking to psychiatrists and behavioural scientists out at Carstairs, the long-term hospital for the criminally insane. Revealing for the first time the twisted fantasies that had driven him to murder four pre-pubescent children in half as many months. I have watched a few of the taped interviews and it is not pleasant viewing. There are no rules in fantasy, believe me, none at all.

So yes, this was more than just the slaughter of a sheep, and no, I wasn't just wasting my time on a sunny afternoon when I could've been doing a hundred other things I wanted to do . . . like, well, for example . . .

Forget it. I had nothing else to do. And I was, I admit, intrigued now, my professional curiosity piqued. With yesterday's sheep, I'd been left no clues. Today's, however, had given me direction. It had been placed in this water-tank for a purpose. If I couldn't find a witness, I'd concentrate on motive and opportunity. Somewhere there were answers to who had brought the sheep to this place, how, and why.

Answers I was convinced I would find.

'*. . . clarity within, quiet without. This is the tranquillity of pure contemplation. When desire is silenced and the will comes to rest, the world-as-idea becomes manifest. In this aspect the world is beautiful and removed from the struggle for existence. This is the world of art.*'

The eyes of the dead are mirrors. Mirrors of mortality. They reflect the one great, unavoidable truth. That to live is to die.

As the man at your feet has died.

You turn your eyes from the lifeless body to the window where you bury your gaze in the distant shoreline, somewhere beneath the sun-glazed sky, yet above the slab of slate-blue sea. You see . . .

The old man's neck, like wedged and kneaded clay, blue-lipped mouth a soundless snarl in his red, bloated face. And his eyes, comical almost, the way they bulge, trying to express a million things all at the same time, all the good reasons why he shouldn't die yet. And there behind those pathetically pleading eyes, as though death was supposed to have meaning or be understood, the universal question:

Why?

A question you cannot answer yet.

So you continue to stare through the window. You see high clouds drifting across the plains of the sky. You see the ferry from Ardrossan, *Caledonian Isles*. You watch it carve through the straggle of yachts towards the island, your thoughts no longer chaotic explosions in the dark, blinding you to reason. No, the waters of your life are still now, calm and reflective. Half a mile out, you reckon: half an hour before it spills its belly on the Brodick Pier.

How time intrudes.

Again your gaze is drawn like a magnet to the dead man's eyes. You notice that when you concentrate hard enough you can see your own reflection, twinned and distorted in those glazed and misted orbs, your broad face twisted, yes, grimacing, as you stare down with fascinated horror at your hands ... which you clench now, clench, clench, clench.

Yes, *your* hands. The hands of a potter, the hands of a killer.

You look at them, these fine, creative hands of yours that bring to life such subtle form from senseless clay. You study them intensely, as though enthralled by some fantastic new discovery. Concentrating on every line and curve as you would a freshly turned pot, noting texture and shape, pattern and colour, every whorl and pore and wormlike vein. *Destructive hands are the hands of creation,* you think, *the hands of change.*

And you *have* changed. You are the hand of creation now, the hand of change. You are alone, rogue, your destiny locked like a runaway train to its tracks, your every act propelled by forces unleashed the moment you dared, yes, dared become God.

This is what you believe:

That only Gods are truly lawless and only the lawless can truly become God. Why? Because laws exist only for fools. They are made by fools, worshipped by fools and kept by fools: those threatened by the thought of freedom, those ashamed of their innate animal urges: life's agoraphobes, who need limitation lest they suffocate, who can shine only in conformity and fear utterly the absolute, the unknown. The Senseless Ones, you call them: born into this life an explosion of senses, of miraculous awareness and infinite power, yet content to exist shackled and blind in prisons of their own making. Living life as though a life sentence. Invertebrates. Modern humankind.

An aeon of wasted evolution.

For instance. Arthur Thomas, the man at your feet. You knew him well. You made it your point. You are like a farmer, you see, you cultivate and then you crop. Like you have cropped Old Thomas, former welder, now retired. Old Thomas who worked a lifetime on the Clyde building luxury cruise liners he never got to sail in, look at him now, all wrinkled and worn by a lifetime of mental inertia and pointless existence, forty years wasted on a deafening shopfloor amidst the shrieking steel and leaping sparks, day in, day out, the same grinding monotony of asinine repetition, performing the programmed cycles of a senseless automaton, no more than a machine but less than a man for selling his life cheap to a prick in a suit just to slowly grow old and die in a stultifying cocoon of graceful consumerised comfort. Hah. And where had it got him, this old man Thomas, now totally retired from all manner and matter of life? Exactly nowhere.

But you digress.

Because you have other beliefs . . .

You believe that to destroy is to create. That nothing comes from nothing. That we are clay – from the earth we came, and to the earth we shall return. That as children we are kneaded and pounded, prepared to the right consistency then centred on the wheel and moulded, shaped and formed to standards long extinct. Once hardened, we are then dipped in the glaze of passive acceptance and fired. We become receptacles, mere vessels from which others may drink the essence of life, yet—

How time intrudes.

Not *time*, you suddenly realise, but *sound*. Not the high-frequency pitch in your head, the coursing energy that drives your thoughts, not that, no, nor the voice, *her* voice, but something else, something alien, incursive, unwelcome, *impure*.

The sound of *them*.

Coming from outside, beyond the window through which you absently stare. Somewhere down there, yes, along the potholed

61

track that passes the croft, descending into the trees on its winding way down to what the Senseless Ones call humanity.

So you freeze. You let panic ice your veins. As your scalp bristles, you allow your senses to overload.

For instance.

Smell.

You smell faeces. The acrid smell of putrefying bowels. That of Old Thomas at your feet. You recall now those moments stretching to oblivion and back when your hands met around his neck, thumbs pressing deep on the carotids, closing off the blood to his brain, crushing the voice-box, the explosion, yes, it was like an explosion as his sphincter muscles gave way and he stopped kicking then, relinquished the struggle as his trousers filled, life fading from his eyes like the dying picture on a TV screen.

Other smells too. The smell of age, and the old man's deodorant mingled with sweat. Of a meal recently cooked: mince and tatties. Coffee. The scents all there, residue in the cleansed air. And from outside, still clinging to your nostrils, a fragrance of wet pine.

Trees, another thread through your life's rich tapestry.

The forest behind the croft descending almost to the back door, the way you had approached, *ingress*, coming down through the forest, silently, a stalking beast, every footfall placed to perfection as you follow the burn sluicing down the hill, urgent over polished stones, propelled, like you, with a sense of direction, driven forward, downward, by forces unreasoned, you, seeing every now and then through the dark alleys of pine carpeted in soft needles and brittle twigs the curl of smoke from the chimney rising through the rain-freshed air towards a sky released from cloud, warmed by sun, blue now, the soft, gentle blue of summer. You recall no thought of murder in your mind as you crept through the forest's womb, a sense of freedom, yes, of godlike potency, to do whatever came to mind, but murder, no, just a little exercise, stretch the psychic muscles, a taste perhaps, but no more, from the brimming chalice of your power.

But something had gone wrong.

Old Thomas who should not have been at home, who should have been blowing his pension down in The Clauchan Arms as he bored all the tourists with riveting tales of his dockyard days, was not there at all. No. He had come home early.

And you never heard him.

Until it was far too late.

We are but colliding atoms, you believe, our actions and reactions but cause and effect, our struggle to control our lives but a blind arrogance, a vain attempt to invest meaning on the meaningless. We are mere pinballs – nothing more, nothing less.

Again the sound – louder now, demanding attention.

A car, no, the engine's growl deeper than that, a Land Rover, yes, coming up the track, the pitted road that follows the course of the burn down into Brodick, that insidious nest of vipers, a Land Rover, climbing towards the croft, the ferry in the distance, docked at the pier, Christ, how long have you been standing here in this timeless zone, this limbo, struck motionless by the force of your thoughts, the weight of your actions, while all the while the ferry spills its reeking belly on to the Brodick Pier and you're standing there slackjawed, savouring death's sweet delights, the Land Rover crunching up the track, heading for the croft. You try to think, try to remember if there's another croft further up the glen. Yes. No. A ruined bothy. But inaccessible, even to a Land Rover. Must be Forestry, then. Okay. A visitor for the old man or someone on his way to chop even more trees down. But either way you know you have to move because the spell is shattered now and consciousness intrudes like daylight on a dream, reluctance dragging at your heels until the Land Rover rounds the corner and the glint of sunlight off its windscreen ignites a flash of anger within you, a fission that fires you into motion as you realise the hunter has suddenly become the hunted.

You move. Away from the window, avoiding the overturned TV and coffee table, the debris of shattered crockery ground into the carpet. Towards the kitchen, the back door. You don't look at *him*, no, you grant him nothing, not even in death. *His* fault he lies there twisted and cooling on the floor amidst all the broken pottery, some of it yours. You didn't want to kill him, how many times must you repeat that, it was *never* your intention, not for a second, to launch him into the great forgetness. But in he strides, arrogance in his what-the-fuck-are-*you*-doing-here voice, standing at the door, arms akimbo, filling the small room, this shrine to porcelain and chintz and fusty days gone by, with his macho presence and puffed-out peacock chest, secure in the sense of his own supremacy; oh such a flaw, such a fatal mistake, how easily manipulated is such a man, how *vulnerable*.

So you don't spare him a glance as you back towards the door, no, you tune your senses, concentrate on the Land Rover and the pitch of its engine as it continues to climb towards the croft, its roof in sight now, a hundred yards, maybe more, as your fingers close on the handle, leaving it, as always, until the last moment, the moment of almost certainty . . .

The Land Rover drives on by, the sound of its engine receding behind that of your pounding heart.

You have another belief.

Life is only worth living walking hand-in-hand with death.

You return to the body. You kneel by its side. You tear open the front of the old man's shirt. Touch his neck, pulling the slack skin taut. Mm. Work still to be done.

You lick your lips.

8

You have to be flexible.

That's what the Sergeant told me six months ago, my first day on the job, his second sentence. 'You have to be flexible,' he said. 'And that means you expect to be called in on your rest days and, come summer – when you've got maybe five times the island's population to cope with – you have to be prepared to work two or three weeks without a single day off and, if you're lucky, with only one or two double-shifts back-to-back just to keep you sleeping on your feet.'

And here we were in June, and it was happening already. Jim Tennant phoned in sick this morning, Monica Kemp was on court duty on the mainland, and Bob Gillies was on holiday in Ibiza. Which left the Sergeant on call, and me, on my second official rest day, lumbered. And back in uniform. The thin blue line now little more than a dotted blue line.

So I was being flexible. *Feeling* flexible: like a soggy leaf of lettuce I sat in a sweltering wee office in the Glen Chalmadale Distillery, trying hard to summon up even a single shred of yesterday's enthusiasm to the job in hand: sheep. To make matters even more difficult, in the early hours of this morning I had broken from the clutches of terror, suddenly awake in a sheet-clinging sweat, with my heart a panicking pump. Who else do you know has nightmares about vampire sheep?

Exactly.

Flora Farquharson was a tall woman in her early fifties, dressed in a navy-blue suit, white silk blouse, red chiffon scarf.

Around her neck, half a dozen chains of varying widths and sizes; on both her wrists, bracelets and bangles jangled; on each of her fingers, rings and bands. All gold. Her grip a few minutes ago had been firm, her perfume, Chanel No. 5, almost a memory. Her posture was erect, her gaze direct, and she wore her long ash-blonde hair loosely tied back. She sat forward now over her desk, hawkish blue eyes locking on to mine over the golden steeple of her fingers. 'Please explain,' she said.

From the window of her office I could look across the burn and the white wooden footbridge to the wide double doors of the Stillhouse open to the afternoon sun, and watch Archie's young assistant shovel steaming draff from the mash-tun into a waiting farmer's wagon, the sweat on his face and bare back like a glossy pink varnish. I was happy merely to watch – and explain.

'Whoever put the sheep in the tank,' I said, facing her again, 'had to know that that particular water is used in the distillation process.'

'And how, young man, do you arrive at such a conclusion?'

Young man? I liked this woman already. But I was not blind to the fact that she was already there ahead of me, merely wanted me to spell it out, perhaps add flesh to some skeleton she had formed in her mind.

'Why put it in the tank then?' I said. 'Why not just dump it on your doorstep or a dozen far more obvious places? Why go to all the trouble of hefting a dead-weight up that embankment and through that screen of trees to the top of the tank? It couldn't have been easy. No, what we're looking at here is someone who wanted to cause you damage, cost you money, contaminate your run.'

She fingered the heaviest gold-link chain on her breast. 'And you believe this "someone" was once in my employ?'

'That is my theory, yes.' Christ, I was beginning to talk like her – obviously too many Agatha Christies before lunch. 'I mean, who else would know which water to contaminate?'

'I imagine any one of the seventy thousand visitors who pass through these gates each season.'

'*And* has access, motive and opportunity?' I watched her pale eyes cloud.

'What exactly are you trying to say, young man?'

I changed tack. 'Your son, I understand, is of the opinion that someone is trying to put you out of business.'

'My son has many opinions, Constable, many of which I do not share.'

Which was not exactly an answer to my question. 'And *this* opinion of his?' I pressed.

'Perhaps you should ask him about his opinions, and me about mine.'

'What is your opinion,' I sighed, 'concerning his opinion?' This was proving harder than pulling teeth. In the last minute or so, the atmosphere in the room had cooled, her opinion of me, I imagine, now doing a swift one-eighty.

'I have no evidence to suggest that anyone is trying to put us out of business, Constable. Does that make you happy now?'

No, it did not. But it would do until I had more to go on. I made a scrawled note in my book. 'Since no sheep can get on to the property,' I said, without looking up, 'it must've been transported here. Which suggests either someone with access to the gate keys, or someone who has had access in the past. Tell me, how long since the lock was last changed?'

Her gaze strayed to the window, her tense profile in sharp relief. 'That would be . . . just after the break-in. End of March.'

'Break-in? What break-in?'

'Your good Sergeant Yuill would know about that – he handled all the details.'

I made a note. 'And you?'

'I was in Edinburgh,' she said airily. 'On business.' As though that explained everything.

'Your son, then?'

'He was here.'

'Is he here now?'

She sighed. 'I don't know where he is. He was supposed to be here an hour ago but . . . I do wish he would ring, just to let me know.'

A man one could rely on, it seemed. 'Back to my original question,' I said. 'Do any of your ex-employees spring immediately to mind? One dismissed since March, and probably with a sense of grievance?'

Flora Farquharson leant back in her squeaky wooden swivel chair, again regarded me down the curve of her nose and over the spire of her steepled fingers. I sensed waters running deep behind her still blue eyes.

'John . . .' she said eventually. 'French. Worked here for three years as a general handyman. Left under rather a dark cloud in March.'

I looked up from my notebook. '*You* fired him?'

She shook her head. 'My son,' she said, her voice a confessional whisper, almost apologetic.

A point here needed clarification. 'Your son, Findlay, manages the distillery,' I said, 'while you manage . . . ?'

'The administration, mostly. Findlay's useless when it comes to figures. Mathematical figures, that is,' she added, in a vain attempt at levity.

I ignored the comment. 'And I take it there was a difference of opinion concerning the dismissal of John French?'

'In business, Constable, these things happen.'

Well, I'd never have thought. I recovered from my surprise and asked why French had been fired.

'From what I understand, things were going missing. Small amounts of petty cash, a bottle of malt here and there.'

'And French was charged?'

'No. We decided not to press. That kind of thing always creates adverse publicity.'

'Or perhaps the charges would never have stuck?' I suggested.

Her smile was brief, cool and dismissive. 'I wouldn't know, Constable,' she said, glancing pointedly at her watch. 'I would imagine that was more your department than mine. Now, if you'll excuse me?'

'This is where we cool the wort.'

We were in the Stillhouse, Archie and I, both in shirtsleeves, up on the iron gallery, watching the straw-coloured wort flow over the brass vanes of the red trough refrigerator. About the size of four squash courts side by side, the Stillhouse is a colourful network of vats and pipes and dented copper stills. Red, blue, black, white – everything in the Stillhouse has a colour, Archie had explained, and every colour signifies a step in the process. Black for spirit, red for wash, blue for faints and low wines, white for water. In between questions I was getting the condensed guided tour.

'The what?'

'Wort,' Archie said. 'It's the sugary liquid we get after the malted barley and spring water have been mixed and heated in the mash-tun below. We drain it off slowly, then pass it up here to the refrigerator for cooling.'

'So you never heard a sound?' I asked.

'Not a thing.'

'Not a thing?'

'I work hard and sleep hard.'

'And your wife?'

'Is no longer my wife.' He wiped the sweat from his brow with a sleeve, and said, as though by rote, 'The cooled wort is then passed into one of these washbacks over here.'

I followed him down a few steps to stand at the railing overlooking two large pine vats. 'Okay,' I said, 'so tell me about John French.'

'Why should I?'

'Because you liked him? Because you don't believe he was behind the petty thefts?'

As a shot in the dark, it hit its mark. 'Damn right,' Archie said. 'John was a good man, honest as the day is long, a damn fine worker. Forgotten more about this job than Farquharson will ever know.'

'So why was he really fired?'

Archie shrugged. 'Clash of egos, who knows? Man like Farquharson, all you have to do is look at him the wrong way and you can find yourself out on your ear.'

'Didn't his mother intervene?'

'It must be hard for any mother to admit her only son is a total arse. But as long as his decisions don't affect the profits of the business, she seems happy to go along with whatever he says.'

That's the trouble with people like the Farquharsons, I thought: other people's lives and livelihoods are nothing to them but playthings. I have met so many of these rotten pillars of society that I often wonder why the roof hasn't yet fallen in on our heads.

'So what do you think of Mrs Farquharson?' I asked.

'She knows her stuff, I'll give her that. Since she took over running the distillery after her husband died, profits have almost doubled. It was she who had the Old Malt Barn converted into a Reception Centre.'

'Seventy thousand visitors a year?'

Archie nodded. 'Before that, lucky if it was one thousand. Aye, she knows what she's doing.'

'John French,' I said. 'Is he local, married?'

'Incomer from Ayr, wife and two kids. Live in Lamlash.'

'You know his address?'

Archie scratched the top of his head. 'Wrong tree, son, John's not your man. What you're looking for here is a psycho; a nutter, not a family man like John.'

'Unfortunately,' I told him, 'nutters come in all shapes and forms. Of course our lives would be a lot easier if they were all hideously deformed and limped around the streets with hate-crazed eyes and slavering mouths and bloodstained axes in their hirsute hands. But they don't, Archie, they look like the man next door, that nice quiet man who keeps himself to himself and is always polite and goes to church twice a week and takes in damaged birds and tenderly mends their broken wings. He can be a loving husband, father, lover; a lorry-driver, a security guard, a civil servant – whatever he publicly wants to be. Privately though, behind closed doors, he sees a different man in his mirror, a man caught in the web of his fantasies, trapped by the force of his desires, tortured by the devils he's spawned in his mind, and accused by the voices of his victims. He's a man picking at the wounds of his past, resentment simmering, anger on the boil, alert to the slightest slight, always waiting for that opportune moment when victim and lust collide, and the power of life and death is his and his alone.'

Head cocked, Archie's expression now was one of shrewd reassessment. 'You speak like you know them well.'

'I've known a few,' I said, 'and that's a few too many.'

I thought of Dominic Bain, hospital cook by profession, child-killer by desire. 'Such a nice boy,' his neighbour had said after Bain's arrest, 'so kind and thoughtful. I just can't believe it.' Whoever can? Try it sometime: take a neighbour or someone you think you know well, see if you can judge the tenor of their innermost thoughts. Ask yourself do you *really* know them well, do you *really* know what goes on in their lives the moment their doors are locked and curtains drawn? What form do their fantasies take, what outlet their desires? The same as yours? Not so kinky, or even kinkier? Scary thoughts indeed, and ones we'd rather not acknowledge, if you please. Which is why we're always so surprised to learn that that awfully nice young man next door has been boiling the heads of his lovers and frying their hearts in garlic and onion before burying their remains underneath his floorboards to dig up again every once in a while for a little necrophiliac relief.

'Archie,' I said, 'I'm sure John French is exactly what you say

71

he is – a conscientious worker and a good family man. But a complaint's been made and I have to check, you know that.'

Reluctantly, he relinquished the address, a council house in Lamlash. I noted it down. 'So,' I said, nodding towards the two large pine vats, 'is this where you add the yeast?'

Archie seemed mollified by my continued interest. He brushed his fingers through his silver hair, and said, 'Aye. We have to keep the temperature fairly constant – between twenty and thirty-two degrees centigrade and the yeast can sometimes take up to fifty-six hours to convert the sugar into the low-strength alcohol we call "wash".'

'Smells strong enough,' I said. 'Has anyone ever been overcome by the fumes?'

'Not by the fumes, no,' Archie said, dropping his voice and leaning close. 'But one of our workers did drown in this vat a few years ago. Took him three hours to die.'

'Three *hours*?'

'Aye, well he had to climb out twice for a piss.'

That's me for you – the kind of guy who'll play straight-man to anyone who happens to think they have a sense of humour. So I didn't laugh, I didn't even smile. Instead I tossed him a deadpan 'Yeah?' then thanked him for the tour, and said I'd be back in a couple of days for the second half. He shrugged and asked if I'd finished with the sheep; I told him yes – and oh, maybe he could give me a ring if he thought of something else, like someone else with a grudge against the Farquharsons. Or whatever. He said he would. I climbed into Mike 30 and left him there frowning, wondering if I'd really taken him seriously, unsure, but definitely not putting it past me. It's a hazard of a cop's life.

It's one of life's undeniable facts: that if you're a cop you're devoid of a sense of humour. It's what the public fervently believe. They come up against you, say, once a year – you've pulled them over for speeding, or careless driving, or their car

72

insurance; or maybe they're a witness to some accident, or are merely 'helping you in your enquiries' – and what you do in that first encounter is commit probably the biggest mistake you can ever make in your life as an officer of the law: you fail to smile at some pathetic crack you've heard a million times before, or you fail to laugh at some nervous little joke that's about as funny as the holocaust. Which is usually the precise moment they jump to the conclusion that one of the essential prerequisites for a career in the police is a complete and documented absence of anything that might be considered a sense of humour.

What they fail to realise, however, is that because of the nature of your job, you cannot afford to smile. To smile is to be human. If you are human, if you *appear* human, then you are fallible, vulnerable, and insecure; you can be reasoned with, persuaded and dissuaded. And as an officer of the law, an instrument and extension of that law, you cannot be seen to be either fallible or flexible. To smile is to give away your power, your omnipotence, your control over a person or situation. A smile dilutes your authority, can ruin your career and, in some extreme cases, prove fatal. So this cold, indifferent public façade is nothing less than body-armour, protection. You change for your shift, last thing you do is put on your humourproof vest, then it's out into the world with your straight face on.

And another factor the public refuse to recognise is that without a sense of humour a cop would probably end up cold polisalami on the end of a rope, a pavement banquet for two, or in the lock-down ward of the nearest crackpot college. Okay, so sometimes the humour is a little on the black side of sick, but that's only a reflection of the world we live in, and life as we see it. In such a tragicomic life, we become inured to the tragedy and reliant on the comic. It is how we survive: either laugh or crack up.

It was just someone's bad luck that I don't find mutilated sheep funny.

9

The ferry cut through the sea of glass, flanked by shrieking gulls. The early-afternoon sun hung shimmering over the port bow, wispy threads of cloud combed high across the blue dome sky like the few last strands of an old man's vanity. It had turned into another blistering day, temperatures hitting the high twenties and, unlike this morning, the air was now hot and lethargic before a sluggish and sultry wind. Me feeling likewise.

So far, a day wasted.

I'd been cited for this morning at the Kilmarnock Sheriff Court, the case down for 9.30 a.m. The first boat off the island departs at 8.20 a.m., and usually takes about fifty-five minutes to cross to Ardrossan. Last time I did the same trip to court, I'd arrived at 9.45 a.m. The staff there know that witnesses from Arran aren't going to arrive before then, and any Fiscal who starts proceedings any earlier is swiftly going to have his head examined for woodworm.

However, when I awoke this morning, it was to a churning dark sky, squalling rain and snapping wind. I knew the score even before we set sail. We got to about half a mile out from Ardrossan when the captain obviously decided it was too risky – the wind-whipped currents too strong at the mouth of the harbour – and left-turned us up to Gourock. Arrived there 11.45, by which time I'd been on the purser's phone, and there was a squad car waiting to take me to Wemyss Bay. From there another mobile drove me down to Irvine where yet another car was waiting to drive me to Kilmarnock. I arrived in court at 12.20 only to be informed there was a deal on the cards, that the guy had changed his mind and was going to plead guilty, would I mind hanging around another ten minutes just to make sure. Ten minutes later, sure enough, he pled, and that was it, a morning's busted arse for nothing.

I watched a pair of gulls gliding alongside, the apparently effortless ease with which they rode the thermals suddenly evoking within me a sense of envy that surprised me in its absurdity. Envy, I thought, envy what? This is Frank McMorran here – Man at his supposedly Most Confident Self – not some flying grease-bomb with a brain the size of a wart. What the hell could I envy a gull – apart from its freedom, I thought, and the fact that every year it wintered somewhere distant, somewhere hot? Nothing, you see, nothing; it was just one of those days when my moods seem to swing with every shift of the breeze, every minor fluctuation in tide and temperature, every four doubles of single Highland malt. So I took another sip, savouring its strong and heavy smokiness, watched now as the screeching gulls wheeled and dive-bombed a shoal of flotsam.

What did I know? I knew that two sheep had been stabbed and bludgeoned to death within the last week, both within two, perhaps three, days of each other. They had been left at different ends of the island – one where it had died, the other not – in places where they would obviously soon be discovered. I knew, as well as I could ascertain in the circumstances, that both sheep had been stabbed with the same instrument, most likely a long-bladed bayonet, though only one had died from its stab wounds. I knew the name of my first and only suspect to date, and where he lived; and I knew that by the end of my shift I would be able to say whether he was guilty or not. I knew that thunder clears the air and whisky clouds the mind, and that the force we call evil always destroys itself in time. I also knew that one too many whiskies too early in the afternoon makes a total mush of my mind. So I returned the empty glass to the bar and, as we slowed towards the Brodick Pier, made my way down to the disembarkation hatch.

Yuill went off shift at four, leaving me alone with my hangover on the back shift, Monica on call should I need assistance. Week-night like tonight, I wouldn't have much to do anyway, maybe a few D&Is after closing time, noise complaints, a drunk driver, what the hell, nothing serious, nothing I couldn't handle standing on my head in a flushing toilet bowl. Figuratively speaking, of course. And if I had time later on, I would check out the Ormidale Hotel bar again – strictly in the line of duty, of course – and see if Kyoko was there, what kind of mood she was in. Like fun mood, cute mood, or on-your-bike mood. Decision made, I then settled down to the chore of paperwork, catching up on my last two days' reports, answering the phone only twice in the next hour, one from Yuill telling me where to look for the distillery break-in record, the other a cold-feet, last-minute hang-up. I searched the filing cabinet, found the record, but little in the way of results. The case was still open, the culprit unknown, motive, clues and suspects adding up to a nice round nothing. No prints, no discernible MO, nothing seen or heard, nothing stolen, vandalised or destroyed, nothing, nothing, nothing. After a tenth cup of coffee, I pushed back my chair, grabbed my cap and PR, locked up the office and headed for air I hoped would clear my fusty mind.

'John French?'

'Who wants to know?' A slight, wiry man in his early forties, with ruffled dark hair and the bemused air of an academic. Tone, though, belligerent.

Sometimes you just have to come at them hard right from the word go. Fuck etiquette, fuck rights, just make them understand who's boss around here, in total control. Save yourself a lot of trouble and wasted time.

I said, 'You know why I'm here.' With the sneeriest sneer I could fit on my lips.

He stepped back, jaw dropping, working on words that would not come. One hand on the door, other picking at one of the large leather buttons on his plain grey cardigan. To the left, a small book-lined study, a pair of half-moon reading glasses lying on the desk where a small grey computer hummed. To the right of the study, stairs, carpeted blue, and climbing. From a room down the hall a radio blared, the six o'clock news just coming on, with Mr Average here in his slippers and the smell of something garlicky-good coming from a kitchen I could hear but could not see. A woman asking who was that at the door, dear.

I said, 'Why don't you tell her, French? And tell her why.'

'B-b-but...' He shook his head, a confusion of expressions struggling for dominance on his face. Confusion won. 'I don't... I mean, what...'

'Tell her about your urges, French, how you like to satisfy them.'

'L-l-look,' he stammered, 'there must be—'

'What? Some mistake? I doubt it. I mean, consider the evidence. One month you get fired from the Distillery in circumstances described as more than acrimonious, and then what? Next thing you know they're fishing mutilated sheep out of their spring-water tank, and you think there must be some mistake?'

'Darling, who is it?'

It was then that French surprised me, his face suddenly crumpling into a gushing spring of tears, hands falling limp to his sides, head shaking from side to side as his lost and haunted eyes searched for any kind of shelter from the violent storm of his emotions. I offered him that shelter.

'Come on, John,' I said, 'let's go talk. Sort this whole silly mess out.' Hand on his shoulder, I led him without resistance back into his study, sat him down at his desk. A framed photo sat on the VDU: John here, wife and two kids, boy and a girl, all holding hands, skipping along some sun-splashed street, laughing, happier days then.

'John?' his wife called again, this time with more insistence. In the photo, she was taller than her husband, younger and darker, very much in love with her life.

'Tell her I'm a friend or something,' I suggested. Bonding. Masculine conspiracy. It all helps.

'Only a colleague, dear,' he called, 'from the Society.' Voice stumbling for a moment before picking itself up again, gaining strength. Not too much strength, I hoped. Saying now, 'I won't be long.'

'Better not be. Dinner's in twenty, colleague or not.'

John French knuckled his eyes, found a hanky in his pocket, blew his nose. 'It's not what you think,' he said eventually.

'What isn't?' I stopped prowling the room, sat down on the edge of his desk.

'These stupid bloody tears.' He blew his nose again, just as angrily. 'It's not guilt, you know. I haven't done any of those crazy things you accused me of. It's just, I don't know, bad timing, all coming at the same time, the way it always does.' Beginning to ramble. I nodded agreement, slipping his leash. 'You know, demands here, demands there, always attacking in packs. Fucking coyotes, that's what they are, coyotes with suits on, smirking behind masks of superiority, rubbing it in, one thing on top of another, the final straw, you know, the one that breaks the camel's back, doesn't have to be anything to do with anything else, Christ, any excuse will do, so long as you don't keep it in and bottle it up, mm, best get it out in the open, the light of day and all that, don't you agree?'

'Always.' Sympathetic sounds. 'Nail on the head, John.' That kind of thing. Anyway, I did agree. It would make my life a hell of a lot easier, Saturday nights, stand outside the emptying discos and watch all the macho wee neds sobbing in each other's

79

arms instead of kicking each other to pieces. I said, 'Kick a man when he's down, eh?'

'You don't know what it's like. How it feels, how they make you feel, walking out the door with all your stuff, kids screaming as they watch the TV and video go, they don't understand, to them it's like watching a robbery in progress and they're looking at you to stop it, to protect them, to save their TV, and you can't, you can't, a couple of payments down and these bastards want to make you feel *that* high—' a millimetre between finger and thumb '—in front of your family, your neighbours, what do they give a shit, waltzing in from the city the way they do, you know, all in a day's fun, make a fucking show of it as they load up the van, wave the car keys in my face and say, *Good enough to borrow, mate, good enough to pay back*. Bastards.'

'They took your car?'

'And bloody welcome to it,' he spat. 'More trouble than it was worth.' A lie. I knew it and he knew it. Angrily, he tapped a couple of keys on the keyboard in front of him. The screen went black.

'Tell me, John, when did all this happen?'

'Month, six weeks, something like that. Ask the neighbours.' Fish began to swim slowly across the computer screen, accompanied by the sound of popping bubbles. Tropical fish, coral fish, angel fish. Seahorses. Underwater flying toasters. Mm. I wondered how many hours a day he spent watching these fish as he wallowed in the energy-sapping swamp of his own self-pity. I wondered also why they hadn't repossessed his computer.

I said, 'Night before last, Sunday, where were you?'

'Here. Not watching the telly, me, the wife, the kids, the dog. Why?'

I made a note. 'And last Thursday?'

'Same. In fact, every damn night last week.'

I'd ask Monica to check later with French's wife – and their kids and neighbours. Investigation is by necessity the compassionless process of gathering facts and corroborating facts.

'The Distillery,' I said. 'Does it open on Sundays?' A question I should have asked Archie McDonald yesterday.

'Every day. The process is a continuous one, you can't stop it halfway through. Unless your name's Farquharson, of course.'

'Mm,' I said, 'Farquharson . . .' Letting the name hang there for a moment to concentrate his thoughts in the direction I wanted to go.

'Man's not got a bloody clue.'

'But at least *he's* not a thief.'

His head snapped round, eyes blazing so fiercely I felt a sudden flash of apprehension: the man behind *those* eyes I could easily imagine inflicting the frenzy of wounds I'd seen on the carcasses of the two slain sheep. I had to remind myself that the beast that lies within us does not always sleep, and that the forms of its desires are seldom conscious ones. John French's voice was a barely restrained shriek.

'He's worse than that, he's a . . .' he spluttered, searching for the right word, '. . . liar.'

An anti-climax perhaps, but I always prefer at least two sides to any story.

'He said you were on the pockle.' Me talking about a man I hadn't even met yet, probably the only guy on the island who I hadn't.

'Pockle?' His voice still shrill.

'A bottle here, a bottle there, fingers in the petty cash. Pockle.'

John French clutched his seat and, breathing hard, stared at the floor, shaking his head, sitting there like John McEnroe two sets down and just not believing it, holding himself in as every cell in his body screamed for release, but fighting it, I could see, deep breaths now, counting to ten, marshalling his thoughts, regaining control, retaining what last vestiges of dignity I and the world had left him. His voice, although still a little tremulous, was serene.

'When I was seven years old,' he said, still staring at the floor, 'I was caught shoplifting from the local Woolworth's. I can still remember bits of it vividly, and once in a while I even revisit the store in my nightmares. I remember the moment the store detective's hand fell on my shoulder as one of absolute terror. If he had dragged me out the back and stood me in the yard in front of a firing squad, I would not, I tell you, have been any less terrified. I was rooted. I had wet my pants. I was crying, I think, even before the full weight of his accusatory eyes fell on mine. After that, I can't recall much of the detail, only the sense of being led along dark corridors deep into the bowels of the building towards rank dungeons against whose dripping stone walls I felt sure I would be strung, alongside all the other naughty little boys, for all eternity. The whole journey, without a word from the store detective, seemed to take hours. When it ended, it was not in a dungeon but a small white windowless room with a table and two chairs at which the store detective sat me down, placing in front of me that pathetic originator of my sin, the object of my temptation.' French raised his eyes from the floor now, meeting my gaze unflinchingly as he continued. 'You know those kits they used to have, maybe you're too young, but they had these kits, like bus-conductor kits, with a wee plastic machine that churned out the tickets, and you'd have clips for the coins and a conductor's cap and I forget what else. Anyway, that was for other kids. I didn't want to be a bus conductor, no, what lay on the table between us was a Z Cars kit. Plastic whistle and handcuffs, warrant card, peaked cap, notebook and pencil, hell, maybe even a truncheon. Aye, that's right, I wanted to be a cop. You find that funny? Yeah, well, maybe it is. But it's true, ever since I can remember. I applied when I was nineteen, but I knew the answer even then, I'm too small, but I had to, you see, I had to try. Anyway, I don't know

82

why I'm telling you all this – you're a good listener, I'll give you that – but from that day on, after the police came and drove me home in shame, I have never stolen again.' He turned to watch the fish on the screen, his voice now a weary sigh. 'And personally, I don't care a damn whether you believe it or not.'

'So who was dipping their fingers, if not you?'

'No one was. That's the thing, you see, nothing was going missing. Why do you think no charges were brought against me?'

'The scandal would've been bad for business?'

French dismissed the suggestion with a contemptuous flick of his hand. 'Because there was no proof, that's why. The only person in the whole distillery who knew anything about any thefts was Farquharson. It was as much a mystery to his mother and everyone else as it was to me.'

'Archie McDonald suggested it might have been a clash of egos.'

'Look at me, man. You call what you see an ego?' He shook his head in answer to his own question. 'Though Archie could be right in a way. You work at the Distillery, you have two choices: agree with everything Farquharson says, or leave. Anyone who offers the slightest competition in any department, anyone who might dare suggest he could have made the minutest of errors or slightest misjudgement, is immediate history. Sam, the guy whose job I filled? He'd worked there almost thirty year, since he was a kid, knew the place inside out, could take the heart of the run blindfold, not miss a drop, and what happens? Second day on the job, in walks Mr Know-it-all, fresh out of college with a certificate in Business Management in his pocket and about as wet behind the gills as a newly spawned monkfish. Spies Sam leaning on a broom as Archie's shovelling draff, orders him to pick up a shovel and help. Sam laughs and tells him to go take a runner – probably the first time anyone ever said that to him. So what does Farquharson do? He tells Sam if he can't pull his weight in every department, then he's

83

surplus to requirements. *Surplus to requirements.* Week's notice and Sam was out the door. And that's Farquharson for you.'

'Did you and he cross swords, then, at any time?'

'I needed the job, Christ, look around you. Family to support, mortgage to pay, all that stuff on the never-never, I wasn't going to risk all that for a moment's false pride, or ever say anything but *Yes, Mr Farquharson, whatever you say, Mr Farquharson.* Anyway, it wasn't that hard. He arrives late and leaves early, all you have to do is keep out of his way, laugh at his silly jokes and stare at him in amazement when he offers you the benefit of one of his numerous philosophies.' French shrugged. 'I could handle it.'

'Obviously not, though. Something went wrong.'

'Hormones, that's what went wrong. Man can neither keep his hands to himself, nor his trousers round his waist. Take a look at the books sometime, see how many seasonal guides have lasted more than a couple of weeks since Farquharson arrived on the scene.'

'You caught him at it?'

'Several times, in fact,' French said, reaching for his half-moon glasses, settling them upon his nose. 'It's as though he wants you to catch him, all part of the kicks. And partly, you know, showing off, rubbing your face in his power in order to confirm his own sense of superiority.'

Enter Dr John French, Psychoanalyst.

I said, 'The same woman or different ones?'

'Always different. I'm sure his only successes were initial ones, the girls soon getting wise and knocking him back.'

'And then getting sacked?'

'Like I said, go check the books.' In fact, the John French in front of me now was barely recognisable as the man I had bullied in the hall not twenty minutes ago. He seemed to be growing in front of me, in both stature and strength, adding now, 'And what does he care, anyway? As hirer and firer, he has them in and out on a conveyor belt. A permanent ad in the *Glasgow*

Evening Times keeps them rolling in, the prettiest one gets the job and never has to wait more than a couple of weeks.'

'And his mother knows about this?'

'She's not blind.'

Love is blind, even the maternal kind. 'You said you caught them several times...'

'First two times were during the afternoon, up at the Reception Centre. He always took them there, would "somehow" forget to lock the door. I'd walk in and he wouldn't be at all surprised or angry or anything, would just say something like, *Come to see how it's really done, John?*'

'A right charmer.' I glanced at my watch; French's dinner would be ready soon. 'And the last time you caught him?'

'A Monday night, I'd been on late, getting things ready for Archie in the morning. Had locked up and was on my way home, was just this side of Brodick when I remembered I'd left Mary's birthday present back at the work. You know what it's like, there are some things in life even worse than death, so I drove all the way back, and when I arrived, the front gate was open and there were lights on up at the Reception Centre. If I'd seen his car there, I wouldn't have bothered investigating, but I didn't, so I approached cautiously, decided to go round the back where there's a small window, see what the score was. And there he was, Findlay Farquharson, writhing naked on the floor as one of the guides pissed on him.'

'You what?'

'My thoughts exactly. In my surprise I must have made a noise, banged my head on the window or something, because she looked up and saw me and said something. All I wanted to do was get the hell away from there, which is exactly what I did. Without Mary's present, I might add.'

'So how long did it take him to sack you?'

'A week. Apart from Mary, I never told anyone what I'd seen. You're the first. I wasn't sure she'd recognised me, you see, and even if she had, that she would tell him. But she must've done because a week later, out of the blue, Farquharson summoned me to his office, accused me of theft and asked me to open up the boot of my car. So I humoured him, and said, *Fine, go open it yourself, it's not locked*. And he did. And what did he find? Why, surprise surprise, a case of Glen Chalmadale. So in a big theatrical scene, he sacked me there and then, no notice, nothing, leave the premises forthwith.'

'You never locked the boot of your car?'

'How could I?' French exclaimed. 'The lock was burst, bloody thing kept springing open. It was no secret, either. Anyone could have put the case in there, anyone.'

'He have any other evidence against you? Witnesses?'

'Nothing but his own word.'

I said, 'A case of whisky in the boot of your car is evidence enough to prefer charges. So why didn't he?'

'He knew that if he did, I'd tell everyone what I'd seen that night.'

'Why didn't you do that anyway?'

'It would have seemed like sour grapes.'

'Is the guide still working there?'

'Never saw her again. I reckon he must have paid her off immediately with a large bonus to keep her face shut.'

The interview was drawing to a close. 'So what's next, John, get another job?'

French laughed bitterly. 'What, now that Farquharson's put the word about that I'm a thief and can't be trusted? Not a chance. I've applied for more than half a dozen jobs since then, never even got as far as an interview. One I applied for recently, Farquharson heard about it and made a point of calling on the employer to let him know how untrustworthy I was. The guy told me when I went for interview, said he was sorry but . . . And that was me, the most qualified applicant for a job I'd really enjoy doing.' French removed his glasses, began polishing them with his hanky. 'And you want to know something? I wish it *had* been me who put the sheep in that tank. I wish I had that kind of courage.'

'Maybe you have,' I said, 'but you just haven't looked in the right place.' I asked him which recent job he'd applied for.

'Assistant,' he said, 'at the Field Studies Centre in Lochranza. I'm fully qualified, though.'

'To what?'

'Teach geology.'

Which explained all the books that lined the walls. I put away my notebook and rose to my feet. 'Enjoy your meal,' I said. 'We'll talk again.'

'We will?' Asked apprehensively as he walked me to the door.

'You know what it's like – questions beget questions beget questions.'

I walked back down the road, climbed into Mike 30 and sat there for a while looking out across the calm blue of Lamlash Bay to the heathered green and purple hump of Holy Island. True, questions beget questions beget questions. They also beget answers. And this evening several questions had been answered. Most importantly, that of John French's guilt. Although I'd witnessed momentarily a flash of intense anger, it was no more, I thought, than that of which we're all sometimes capable. I was certain that if French *had* been a thief he would not have reacted in such a manner. As for the slaughter of the sheep, French had had his car repossessed almost six weeks earlier, and the sheep in the water-tank had been transported there Sunday night; he also had an alibi for the nights in question. Of course, all these facts would have to be checked – I'd ask Monica to confirm the family alibi, and Jim Tennant to find out from friends and neighbours if anyone had either lent French a car, or seen one parked outside his house in the last couple of weeks – but, with the instinct that all experienced cops gain after years on the job, I knew that French was innocent of the sheep's slaughter, and its subsequent deposit in the Distillery's water-tank. I had lost my prime suspect.

My *only* suspect.

But I *had* discovered something in the process: an increasing desire – no, *determination* – to meet this much-maligned Findlay Farquharson. The man with a taste for urine facials. The man who'd once referred to me as a 'brain-dead PC'.

The car radio crackled to life. Divisional Control at Kilmarnock.

'Mike 30,' I rogered, making a mental note of the time. 'McMorran.'

Control's voice was one I hadn't heard before. 'We've had a call from a worried relative. Seems her brother was due across here this afternoon but never arrived. Not answering the phone either. Name of Thomas, Arthur Thomas. Mean anything? Over.'

A Drunk and Incapable on a once-a-week pension-day basis, nothing more. 'Ravensbank Cottage?' I said.

'The same. Can you stand down?'

Stand down? If I stood down any further I'd fall asleep. I said, 'Er, roger, Control, five minutes.'

'Run a quick check, would you, make sure everything's all right?'

There were only two places Thomas would be at this time of the evening. It would take me ten minutes to reach and check out his cottage, another ten to check out the pub. After that, I would check out the Ormidale, try and find Kyoko. 'Call you back in half an hour,' I said. 'Over.'

'Roger, Mike 30, half an hour.'

10

'When three people journey together, Their number decreases by one.
When one man journeys alone, He finds a companion.'

Chamber.

Gideon sits in his armchair in front of the glowing peat fire, watching the dancing flames. Might be summer up there in the other world but down here in the chamber below his workshop – what with the cold stone walls and bare stone floor – it gets kind of cold at night. Only times he doesn't need the fire is when he's got the kiln firing – but that's been quite a while now since the last time. Perhaps too long.

He rattles the bones in his fist.

In the old days – the days of Confucius, say – they'd throw yarrow stalks when consulting the *I Ching*, because vegetables are related to the sources of life. Nowadays most people use coins, three of them. Gideon, though, prefers bones.

He rattles them in his fist now, concentrating on his question. That's what you have to do, see, keep your question in mind as you throw the bones, keep it concise and to the point. No generalisations. Then you throw them – bones or coins – six times. Each time you throw, there are four possible configurations: three heads; three tails; two heads and a tail; and two tails and a head. Each throw giving you one line of a hexagram. There are sixty-four hexagrams. Once you have your hexagram, you look it up in the back of the book, then consult the reading.

Gideon's hexagram tonight is *Sun/Decrease*.

As he searches through the book for the reading, he hopes it will mean – at the least – a sudden decrease in his tax bill.

Bitch would lock you up, toss you in the wardrobe like she did her dirty knickers, sometimes for days on end while the legions of men marched in and out of her house, her room, her bed, her body.

'What about the kid?' some of them would ask. 'Shouldn't you give him some food?'

'Nah,' she'd say, 'he'll just want more. Anyway, d'you want to fuck him or me, lover-boy?'

'We-ell . . .'

And those were the lucky days. Some days she'd take the mood, tie you to the bed, force you to watch her at work, laughing all the while at your discomfort. Other days, she'd force you to join in, take the switch to you if you struggled, even if you didn't, lie there playing with herself and making lewd jokes as some brutish ape forced himself upon you, into you, tearing you, splitting you, before tossing you away like some disposable fuck by the side of the road.

Leave the bitch gagging in the ditch, move on.

No wonder you are what you are.

Why did you never tell anyone? How many times have you asked yourself that question? And always the same answer. Tell who? And if you had found someone, someone you could trust with your life? No chance. You were feared to. Feared no one would believe you; feared more that they would, that they'd no longer look at you as a person if they knew the kind of things those men did to you, those unnatural acts that made you what you are, not a man, not a woman, not a live human being any more but something else, inhuman, cold, a machine, not your fault, no, theirs, they made you what you are, they created you, forged you in pain, made it so simple for you, so easy, to take a life in your hands, any life, and break it into little pieces, tear it into shreds, rip its tender throat apart

what a sweet neck, eh, Harry, hasn't he got the most gorgeous neck? There's something about necks really gets me going, I just want to, you know, I get this sort of urge to sink my teeth in deep, feel the warm blood flow like cum between my lips, I think I must've been a vampire, eh, in my last life

the way some of the men would bite into your neck as they thrust at you, yes, you've seen it on TV too, lions, tigers, wild dogs biting the necks of their mates as they mate, only a natural progression, evolution in a way, the process of natural selection that you should now take pleasure yourself in a little shredding of throats

don't worry, Jack, he always cries. It means nothing, he just wants a little attention himself, he gets jealous, you know, of his Mammie, doesn't like it when she gets all the fun, has to spoil it for her, eh, which is when he gets the switch, doesn't he, when he gets put in the roasting tin

after a while you got used to it, the dark place, the dark warm place that smelled of iron and grease and coal and carbon and a hundred years of cooking spills. After a couple of hours, yes, all feeling had gone from your limbs and you got kind of used to it, would find yourself sinking into the warmth of a womb, not hers, no, never hers, but the big one, the womb of forgetness, a subterranean labyrinth along whose endless winding corridors your imagination could safely roam, where there was no good and bad, love and hate, happy and sad, joy and pain, no guilt or loneliness, nothing but a comforting warm nothingness that, for hours becoming days, you filled with the dark, rampaging force of your fantasies.

Fantasies where someone always paid the ultimate price, and the only limits were those of your imagination and your will to go beyond them.

But someone always paid.

Gideon has to give it some thought. The thing about the *I Ching*, right, is that it doesn't always make sense. Like you have to bear in mind it's older than the Bible. Older than Confucius, older than the stone circles out on the Moor there. They didn't know how to write proper English in those days. They talked a different kind of sense then, one to do with imagery. So he has to give this some thought. He looks again at the reading.

When three people journey together, Their number decreases by one. When one man journeys alone, He finds a companion.

So what? Big deal. The only number decreased by one is the local population. Decreased by one Arthur Thomas. Who should've stayed down in the pub a little longer and not come home early.

Gideon sitting there now, not sure about things, needing a sense of direction. Like if he'd thrown the *I Ching* on Monday night before heading up Glen Rosa to check out Thomas's cottage, the old fart might still be alive today, boring the pants off another busload of tourists down in the hotel bar. Gideon might've got a reading which said, *For fuck's sake don't go up to Ravensbank tonight, the bastard's going to come home early*. Or, *Stay at home and play with yourself, Perseverance furthers*. That kind of thing. Which just goes to show it doesn't pay to take the Book of Changes for granted.

When one man journeys alone, He finds a companion.

Okay. So Gideon could be the one man journeying alone. Fairly straightforward, that. Gideon has always journeyed alone. It's the way he prefers it. He's a loner, a solitary man. Master of his own destiny, all that shit. Has the strength of his own convictions, no companion required.

Until now, it would seem.

Schooldays. On the perimeter of the school grounds, out beyond the playing fields, there was a copse. Afternoons when you were plunking off class, you'd head out there with your satchel of goodies and crawl through the tangled undergrowth into the cool, dark heart of the copse where no one else ever went. It was good there, your own tiny domain in which to play God. And you had a host of unruly subjects there who needed to be shown the error of their ways. Field mice. Beetles. Sparrows. Caterpillars. Spiders. Starlings. Once or twice, a grass snake.

So you had to devise a variety of punishments to fit their assortment of devious crimes. The most common crime, of course, and one guaranteed to make you mad, was when they tried to escape. That's when you had to resort to your box of goodies, in which you kept matches, string, needles, cotton, lighter fuel, three or four knives, a scalpel, and cigarettes.

Sparrows you liked best because you could stake their open wings to the ground with sharpened twigs and then go to work with the needles and cigarettes, taking your time. Mice were always so difficult to hold still.

Your favourite schoolday memories.

Companions. Thing about companions is they always have minds of their own. Like they're always wanting Gideon to compromise, meet them halfway. Which is kind of hard for a superior man to swallow. Because there are certain things in life over which you should never compromise. Cropping, for instance. It just wouldn't work. The bitch is there in your hands, say, heading for the strangle, and she like suddenly demands a compromise, wants you to leave her half her life. Or wants you to strangle her with only one hand. Or insists she half-strangle you as well. It just wouldn't work.

And another thing. Companions like to get in your mind, poke around in there, see if they can fuck up what you haven't already fucked up for yourself. They ask you things like, *What are you thinking?* Allow them in your mind and they think they have a right to control it, censor it, rearrange the furniture.

They like sharing things, too. Have all these silly sayings to justify their nosiness, like a problem shared is a problem halved. Is it fuck. A problem shared is a problem discussed behind your back by half the island's inhabitants. A problem shared means articles in all the national rags.

Of course, the other thing about companions is that none of Gideon's has ever survived.

* * *

93

Your worst memory, though, is of the first day of term when your mother dragged you, screaming and kicking, to your new school. She'd made you wear the pink cotton dress she liked so much, and had tied your long sandy hair in bunches with pink ribbon bows.

'Look at you,' she'd said as you struggled to break free, 'you're so much prettier than the other girls.'

True or not, when the time came for roll-call in Assembly and the teacher asked you your name and you said Gideon, it did nothing to still the uproarious laughter that followed. You still feel it now, in reliving the memory, the sense of utter shame and absolute humiliation you felt as you sat crying on the floor amidst the wild, shrieking laughter.

From that moment on life became a nightmare. The teacher took you to the headmaster, who sent you home with a letter for your mother. Your mother tore it up and delivered you to school the next day in the frilly red polka-dot dress, with your hair perfectly plaited. You had three fights before Assembly and the headmaster called and told your mother to come and fetch you from school. By the time she arrived, you'd ripped your clothes to shreds and were cowering naked in the headmaster's toilet. Eventually he broke the door down, and when you got home your mother whipped you with the red leather belt. On the third morning, two events occurred that would drastically change your life.

First, the headmaster met you – in your pastel yellow ra-ra skirt and tights – and your mother at the school gate. With him was a woman from the Social Work Department, who accompanied both you and your mother home. There was a lot of shouting and slamming of doors, and the sound of glass breaking. That afternoon, when the Social Worker saw the ugly weals on your back, bottom and legs, you were taken into care.

The second incident had a far more profound effect on your life. Someone leaked the story to the local press and two days later it was taken up by several of the national tabloids, and suddenly you were the laughing stock of the nation.

You became then what you have been ever since – outcast.

11

Sod's law.

Back in the city you never knew when you were going to walk in on a bloater, so you always carried a couple of cigars in your shirt pocket to help disguise the stench a little. As a street cop it doesn't matter that much, you get the call, *Mr or Mrs Housebound Neighbour isn't answering the door*, and you're already prepared for what you might find. You kick down the door and the heat knocks you back and what little you breathe you breathe through your hanky as you storm through the rooms as fast as you can, spot the swollen body with its discoloured skin, then get the hell out of there as fast as you can. Stand gasping in the hall as you call the fatal in, then wait for the plainclothes to arrive on the scene. Back in the city, the likes of me. The poor bastard who has to stay in that room, checking this, checking that, until long after the pathologist and body have gone, was it accident, suicide or murder? So yeah, cigars became a habit. Until I transferred out here.

Like I said, Sod's law.

Because Arthur Thomas was well past living. How many days I couldn't be sure, not from where I stood at his living-room window, peering in. But days, yes, definitely a matter of days. I could tell by the flies; the flies and his skin. While in life he'd been a small wiry man with sallow skin hanging slack between sharp bones, in death he had ballooned right out so that now it seemed as though all his clothes were several sizes too small, pinching, like those of the Incredible Hulk about to rip under pressure. His skin now the colour of an overripe banana. A bloater, Mark 3.

I took mental note of the time.

Ravensbank Cottage was what Kyoko would call *charming* – a typical wee croft of rough-hewn, white-painted sandstone set beneath a grey-slated roof with a chimney at each end, and black-framed windows each side of the front door, which was also painted black. A rose bush on one side of the door, a clump of ferns on the other. A gravel path led from the front door around the side of the building. The lawn over which I'd crossed, not much more than a week's growth since its last trim.

Flies, I thought.

Flies signified access, a door or window open somewhere. And that meant an airflow and a body that would most likely be cool, and therefore not liable to burst at the first tentative touch or stink enough to make me meet my lunch again.

I hoped.

Stroke? Heart attack? I could see no external signs of cause from where I stood. Yet something, I felt, was not quite right. I tested the window and it too was locked. I went round the back.

The back door was ajar. It opened on a small dark kitchen. I pulled on my gloves, pressed my hanky to my face and pushed open the living-room door. Immediately began to retch. Forced it back down and, through streaming eyes, surveyed the scene.

I've always felt there's a unique kind of silence that surrounds the dead, the sound of timelessness, of eternity. If you listen, you can hear it. Even in the city, where so many noises demand your immediate attention. It's what they call a 'deathly silence'. It was comparatively easy out here – tucked against Glen Rosa's rising forested flanks and embedded in a twilight calm a mile from any road – because all I had to do was isolate it from the sporadic twitter of finches, the plaintive bleat of a sheep, and the distant strains of a car as it struggled up The String.

And, of course, the monotonous drone of the flies that filled the room.

His head lay at my feet, eyes already turned, only the creamy haemorrhaged whites now staring up at me. Around his throat a seething scarf of metallic black and blue. *Buzz, buzz, buzz.* Bluebottles crawling over thin, bloodless lips drawn tight over glistening dentures, darting in and out, nesting in the cool caverns of his mouth. A circle of crusted blood beneath both head and neck. His arms straight along his sides, and a broken vase at his feet, soles facing the window through which I had first peered. The overturned table to my left, an armchair to my right, on its side, the top of its back resting in the ashes in the stone hearth. Broken crockery all around, no bull in sight.

Okay, I thought, a spot of deductive reasoning. Arthur Thomas is sitting in his armchair watching TV, the evening news or something. Maybe a report comes on, someone he knows has died; or worse, Celtic have just bought back Roy Aitken. Whatever. Suddenly he has a heart attack. Shoots to his feet, *arrgh*, clasping his chest. The armchair falls into the fireplace. Whatever it is hits him again. Eyesight clouds. Blood roars in his ears. He clutches at the mantelpiece for support. Staggers, sending all the crockery crashing to the floor. Somehow smashes the TV as he stumbles backwards now, four or five paces, maybe trying to get to the phone. Collides with the coffee table, knocks it all flying, then collapses to the floor, rolls over on to his back, lays his arms down by his sides, and dies.

Like hell.

It was the arms by his sides that was all wrong. Too precise. They looked as though they had been carefully arranged, positioned in such a manner by an undertaker. For effect.

Like all the broken crockery. There was far too much of it to be accidental. And the shattered vase at the victim's feet – the larger shards fanned out from its base, placed, it seemed, like the petals of a sunflower. I thought of Van Gogh. Of paintings. Of props.

Of murder.

Experience being the mother of intuition, there was no doubt in my mind. I have seen far too many to be fooled. It looked fairly straightforward: Arthur Thomas had walked in on a burglary in progress, there'd been a struggle, and the old man had been viciously attacked. Probably hit about the back of the head – where all the blood had pooled – as he tried to get away.

Except...

Except there was more to it than that. And more, even, than the artistic arrangement of the body and the positioning of the broken vase. Something that felt dreadfully familiar, that I'd recently seen or read or heard. Again, intuition. Current cases and reports, rumours and impressions filtered through my mind, but they were too many, too vague, and all they did was log-jam. So I let my eyes slowly sweep the room again, hoping some other detail might trigger my memory, give shape to this stalking conviction.

Nothing. They returned to the body. Always to the body.

In a murder, it's not only your best piece of evidence, the epicentre of your investigation, but also perhaps your only link to the killer. And it will often tell you more about the perpetrator than any amount of further forensic evidence collected at the locus. So it was inevitable that my gaze should eventually return to the body and settle again on the swarming flies around the old man's head and throat. And it was the throat that did it, triggered recognition.

Realisation rose within me like a heavy gob of bile.

A folded newspaper lay on the table against the wall. It was two days old, I noticed, Monday's. I used it as a swat, to disperse the horde of feasting flies.

Arthur Thomas's throat had been ripped apart. Not cut, but ripped.

By teeth.

I was looking at what appeared to be the Fangman's seventh victim.

* * *

'Roger, Mike 30, go ahead, over.' The same Control.

I said, 'Re Arthur Thomas. Control, I'm up at Ravensbank Cottage. Suggest you wake the Duty Officer, tell him it's a Priority One, I've got a suspect Code Four Four – repeat, suspect Four Four – and it looks like a job for the Dentist, over.'

'Dentist' being the codename for the murder squad set up eight months ago to track down the killer the press had already dubbed the Fangman. In these days of multiple multiple-murderers, it seems the use of such epithets is increasingly necessary in order to keep track of who the hell's killing who.

Control did not reply immediately. Probably summoning the Duty Officer while typing the relevant details into his computer terminal. Eventually: 'Roger, Mike 30, please repeat.'

I repeated.

He said. 'You have a phone there?'

I gave him the number; I'd been expecting him to ask. We didn't like broadcasting detailed information on the VHF, there were too many hungry freelance journos listening in. And all the ghouls, of course.

'Okay, McMorran, secure the locus and stand by. The DO will be in touch shortly. Over.'

A half-dozen blackface sheep stood beyond the fence, giving me the dead-eye glare as I replaced the handset and climbed from the car. I smiled. At least I wouldn't be chasing sheep-molesters for the next few weeks, I thought.

Foresight never was my strong point.

So I returned to the cottage with, I must admit, a growing sense of excitement. Ever since I'd set foot on the island six months ago, I'd felt as though I'd been buried alive, in a state of suspended animation, confined to a kind of semi-conscious coma in which I spent every day just waiting for it to end, to suddenly come to life again, for something exciting to happen, Christ's sake, *anyfuckingthing*, so long as it got the adrenaline flowing, lifted me from this stultifying sense of lifelessness.

And now something had.

Some people suggest that victims and killers are somehow attracted to each other; sometimes that is as true as it is inevitable. But there are also officers I've known and worked with who have said – whether only half in jest, I'm not too sure – that killers and McMorran are just as similarly attracted. Maybe so – I've had my fair share, perhaps more. Hence Sergeant Yuill's *Murder? Better send McMorran* jibes; something he probably picked up on the grapevine when he'd heard about my transfer. But it's easy to get fanciful. You know, romantic talk about Good and Evil, Yin and Yang. Opposites attracting, Karma, natural justice, all that stuff.

All that shit.

Because in the real world, that's all it is. You find a young girl lying on a white shag carpet with her hands pantie-tied and brains dribbling out, it's not exactly the time or place to contemplate the metaphysical forces at play here or the philosophical ramifications of the circumstances confronting you. No. Yin and Yang don't come into it. What you're trying to do is catch up with the brainsick who did it before he does it again.

You have a murder locus in a house, your first question is how did the killer get in – was it a forced entry, or did the victim invite the killer in? In most cases you immediately learn something you might not learn if the locus were anywhere else: that either killer and victim were acquainted, or killer and victim were not acquainted. So I studied the locks on the front and back doors carefully, then checked all the windows, both inside and out, but found no evidence that entry had been forced. Which didn't tell me anything, not on an island where the old folk still leave their doors open like they always did in the old days before times changed for the material worse. The killer could have walked in or been invited in. Square one. I began making notes. Time of first and second radio contact, arrival at the locus, discovery of the corpse. Actions. Then a description of the locus, noting position of body, furniture, windows, doors. A small diagram. First impressions. Arrows showing probable ingress, probable egress. Time on the carriage clock, stopped at 5.15. Details like that. Little things. The date on the newspaper, and where I had found it.

I still didn't approach the body. Arthur Thomas could wait, he wasn't going anywhere. Original crime scenes, on the other hand, tend to disappear fast. The moment people start arriving, things get moved, touched, stepped in, contaminated, trampled. Fingerprints can be added or smudged. Fresh traces are brought to the locus, each one a potential red herring. My old boss Jim Aitken, former Commander of the Scottish Special Crimes Squad, had his own way of putting it: *You can murder the victim only once*, he would say, *but you can murder the locus a million times*.

The phone rang. I picked it up carefully by the earpiece, between two fingers and thumb. I hoped the ID Branch wouldn't be taking earprints.

'McMorran.'

'Sergeant Dowie,' the voice said, 'Divisional Duty Officer. Any developments?' Educated accent, Edinburgh or the Borders. Mid twenties, a little arrogant, a little unsure. Seven words is all I need.

'He's still dead,' I said.

'And you, Constable, are on a charge. Any other hilarious comments you'd like to share with us?'

Just my luck, a college graduate still in love with himself. Reading straight out of the manual, I wouldn't bet.

'I'll save them for when we meet, Sergeant, I'm sure you can take a joke.'

A few moments' silence as he thought that one through. Then, 'Well? Get on with it, man!'

'Sir?'

'Your report, for God's sake!'

'What report?'

'What report, *sir*.'

'That's what I said, sir, what report?'

Theatrical sigh, four out of ten. 'Fucking hell, Constable, are you a total moron or what?' I placed the accent as straight out of Fettes – the Edinburgh college, that is, not the Force HQ just down the road from it.

I said, 'No, sir, it's *Frank* McMorran. With an F.'

'Lord help us.'

Indeed. I wondered what a ham-shanker like Dowie was doing out in Kilmarnock, so far removed from the politically orientated arseholes that need such a damn good tonguing if youthful ambitions are ever to be achieved. I hoped he wasn't part of the murder squad.

'Sir?'

'Tell me, Constable,' as though to a child, 'has anyone else arrived yet?'

I had to think about that. 'No, sir,' I said eventually.

'You're alone, then?'

'With the deceased, sir, yes.'

'Of course, with the deceased. Thank you, Constable, for reminding me.' Voice definitely strained now. Muffled, as he covered the mouthpiece. Then, 'Don't touch a thing, Constable, not a thing. In fact, go back outside and wait for your sergeant to arrive, ETA thirty minutes.'

'And Dentist?'

'Don't you worry your overheated little brain, Constable, we'll call Dentist out the moment Sergeant Yuill confirms.'

I said, 'By which time, *sir*, they'll have missed the last ferry.'

'Let me be the judge of that, McMorron.'

'Sir,' I pleaded in a wounded voice, 'there's no need to call me a moron.'

'God save us,' he sighed, and hung up.

I replaced the receiver and approached the body.

Maggots, I recalled, don't like light. Which is why they feast away on the inside. Leaving the skin intact to act as a kind of sunshade. One more good reason why one should never move a bloater or a partial decomp.

Still, nothing ventured . . .

12

Chopper.

They'd had to commandeer one of the Sea Kings from HMS *Gannet* at Prestwick because the Force helicopter had been grounded due to financial cutbacks incurred by new fiscal policies politicians liked to call 'streamlining'. Most of the coppers I knew called it 'cheapskating'.

'There it is.' WPC Monica Kemp pointed into the twilight at a flashing light in the south-eastern sky. Still four or five miles out. She nodded towards the wooden shack where there was a switch for the floodlights, and said. 'Might as well turn them on now.'

I went and flicked the switch, then returned to her side to watch the chopper's approach. The pad was pitted tarmac, small and seldom used, squeezed between a sand plant and the shore just south of the Brodick Pier. Seldom used, Monica had told me, because of the sand from the plant: the pilots didn't care for the amount sucked into the vents.

Monica said, 'First body I ever saw, Christ, I can still see it now, made everything I've seen since seem tame by comparison. Guy'd knelt on the floor, this happily married family man, wrapped his lips around the barrel of the shotgun he'd just used to kill his wife and kids, pulled the trigger, bang, brains all over the wall ten feet away, bits of skull, I tell you, actually *embedded* in the wall, blood dripping off the ceiling and he's kind of sitting back on his heels with the top of his head completely blown off, grinning it looked like, with what little was left of his mouth.

Sergeant I'd attended with didn't move fast enough, I threw up all over his nice clean boots.' Monica chuckled. 'Rice pudding with strawberry jam . . . I used to love it. Now all I see is brains sliding down a bloodstained wall.'

'That was the farmer, wasn't it? Bad harvest or something, over in Fife.'

'Fife nothing,' she scoffed, 'farmer no way. We're talking middle-class suburbia here, Frank, nice detached three-bed-roomed villa on the outskirts of Inverness, the kind of place estate agents buy and don't expect to lose their job, or their wife to another man.'

'That's what happened?'

'In a nutshell, aye.' We stood shoulder to shoulder, WPC Monica Kemp and I, she the tallest woman I'd ever stood next to who wasn't wearing handcuffs. Rangy was the best word to describe her build: tall, wiry, strong. With ash-blonde hair cut short back and sides and ice-blue eyes straddling a long and broken nose, lips fleshy, mouth wide, dimple on her chin. Daryl Hannah she was not – but who the hell had Daryl Hannah? Certainly not me. And I didn't have Monica either; she liked her men small, successful and at a distance, her husband currently partner in an up-and-coming young firm of Glasgow-based lawyers, and someone she only saw four days every couple of weeks. I admired her style.

The chopper only a mile out now, a shadow more than just a flashing light in the darkening sky. Lights from the pier, the village and the houses on the far side of Brodick Bay flickered across the water, silver on black, the peak of Goatfell beyond rising into deep indigo.

'How long were you in Inverness?' I asked.

She stared for a moment at her shoes, the reflective quality of her stance reminding me instantly of Harry Todd, my former partner at the SSCS – now retired from the force and dying of boredom (he says) working security for some city-centre shopping precinct in Edinburgh – who also tends to scuff and stare at his feet when dipping in the well of recollection. I wondered where Monica was at that exact moment, and what telescoped emotion encapsulated that particular memory now fading behind her eyes as she raised and shook her head, focused on the chopper's approach.

'Too bloody long,' she said, the tone of her voice silencing before they were born any thoughts I might have had of pursuing that specific line of conversation. Fair enough: she had her Inverness, I had my Lockerbie. Subject closed. 'C'mon, we better get in the car,' she added, nodding towards the sand plant. 'Unless of course you like sand jammed in every pore of your body?'

Our doors slammed in unison. I flicked my handset over to UHF, skipped through the channels to see what was happening on the mainland. There seemed to be a lot of movement and ETAs – this no doubt the murder squad swinging into action – but nothing except the density of communication to alert anyone using a scanner. Not that it really mattered: the news would leak before the hour was out. If the police force were a ship, Harry used to say, it would sink without trace.

Monica rummaged in her bag, pulled out a pack of cigarettes, fired one up. Said, 'I know you and Sergeant Yuill don't exactly see eye to eye and have agreed to disagree on every subject under the sun, but I think this time, Frank, he may be right.'

'D'you have to smoke?' I said with irritation.

'Did you have to fart?'

I wound the window down an inch. 'So you also think this is a copycat?'

'It stands to reason. None of the others were male or found murdered in their own homes.'

'Maybe not. But Thomas has one thing in common with all the other victims – his throat chewed out.'

'As has been widely reported in the press,' Monica said, winding down her window an inch, blowing her smoke out the

107

gap. 'And why such a sudden change in MO? Why change from murdering women on the mainland to men on an island? It doesn't make sense.'

'Every such killer has his own kind of logic,' I said, able now to make out the silhouette of the chopper half a mile out, descending. 'It doesn't have to make sense.'

'I still think the Sarge is right.'

'Okay, so explain all the broken crockery.'

'Simple. There was a struggle, a fight, you saw it, Frank, the table overturned. Anyway, hasn't broken crockery also been mentioned in the press?'

'Once.' Briefly, in passing, no significance attached. And how was I so sure? Because like serial killers, their hunters also read everything they can about their opposition, their enemy. It's no coincidence that the majority of serial killers have been found to possess extensive collections of books on murder, pathology and, in particular, mass and serial murderers. It is one more thing hunter and hunted, cop and serial killer, have in common: a shared obsession with serial murder. So yeah, for me, it was only natural that I followed the investigation in the papers, cut out the stories and filed them away, tried to make what sense of them I could and phoned every once in a while an ex-colleague of mine now assigned to Operation Dentist to pick his brain, see what, if anything, the investigation had come up with. Last time I'd phoned, John Fullerton had seemed distant, cool; I don't know if it was something to do with me or the investigation – perhaps he just didn't want to add credence to the rumour currently circulating in both force and press that the hunt for the killer was no further forward than the day the second victim was found lying in a ditch just outside the mainland village of Moscow. Eight months ago – and only a few weeks after I'd caught up with the Edinburgh Hangman, Dominic Bain, in the forested hills of Ballaig. You bang one away, it seems, and another leaps to take his place.

Monica said, 'There you are then, it was in the papers.' She exhaled noisily, flicked her cigarette end out the window. 'Did you ever meet him?'

'Who? Thomas?'

'Mm.' We wound up our windows in unison.

'Same as you, I imagine, a D&I once in a while, nothing serious. Couple of times I thought to hell with this, you know, all the paperwork, and just ferried him home, poured him into bed.'

'You too?' Monica flashed the high beams a couple of times, and we both watched in silence now as the Sea King angled in out of the eastern sky, whipping the sand around us into a frenzied storm, the car rocking gently on its suspension. A minute later it was down, the rotors slowing as the rear door slid open. We climbed out and, clamping our hats to our heads, went forward to meet the men who, spilling from the helicopter, now struggled under the weight of all their professional equipment and overnight bags towards the Land Rover I'd left parked just inside the gate. Six men in all, all plainclothes, and all wearing that heady air of excitement that only a murder can invest. One of them, laden with bags, saw me, nodded, broke away.

'Frank McMorran,' he said. 'In the flesh. How's it going? I hear you were the lucky man.'

He looked older than I recalled, the hair at his temples grey now, and a lot sparser on top. The eager sparkle, though, still there in his deeply hooded eyes. We shook hands.

Monica stepped forward. 'Okay, now you've bonded . . .'

'Monica,' I said, 'this is John Fullerton, Detective Inspector. John, meet Monica Kemp, WPC.' Their greeting was a formal nod in each other's direction. I asked Fullerton who'd been assigned the locus.

'You're looking at him.'

I was looking at a medium-built man wearing a raincoat and hat on a warm summer's night. A man in his mid to late forties with deep-set eyes planted like raisins in a plain doughy face. A

109

curt, abrasive man, highly proficient at his job, a widower whose wife had been caught in the crossfire of warring Marielitos, gunned down in front of his eyes in a Miami shopping mall four years ago, and who now devoted all his energies to the fight against violent crime. Even to ex-colleagues like myself, he was not a man to cross.

I said, 'Ready?'

'You drive. Throw all the bags in the back. And you, luv,' he said, nodding to Monica, 'can follow with the rest of the lads. Okay, let's go.'

I winked at Monica who was standing there seething, tossed her the keys and watched her turn on her heel, march stiffly across to the Land Rover. There is something that excites me about an angry woman's walk, something to do with danger. Perhaps I am the only one; Fullerton had also followed my gaze, but wore a puzzled frown.

'What's wrong with her?' he grunted. 'Her bad week or what?'

When you sit your inspector's exam, the papers are hermetically sealed and come complete with a Government Warning: *Sensitivity Can Seriously Hinder Your Chances of Promotion*. As I climbed in and started the car I marvelled again how whole decades of social progress can just pass some people by like they never even happened. And though personally not a very good example of A Desperately Right-On New Age Man, I am at least aware of certain socio-sexual issues. And once in a while am even sensitive. I also happen to *like* the women I like.

So I smiled now as Monica did a perfect high-speed handbraked skid that cut me off and sprayed the car with gravel, then had to turn the smile inward as Fullerton's open mouth snapped shut and his face set in harsh lines as he glowered after the Land Rover's rear lights now leaving us for dead. I stalled. Felt him glow in the passenger seat. Stalled again.

'Jesus Christ, McMorran!'

'Sorry, sir.'

I quaked silently behind the wheel.

I can't deny it, the absolute envy and sense of exclusion I felt once we arrived back at the locus. I was rural, I was uniform, I was totally ignored. Yuill and Tennant had been despatched to the neighbouring farm and cottages, and now that Fullerton had pumped me for all the relevant detail on the journey up, I felt like the uninvited guest at a party, the one who wishes he'd dyed his hair green and not worn a suit. I made for the night air.

'Hey, McMorran,' Fullerton called, 'stick around. You want to make yourself useful, see if you can rustle up some coffee.'

I think it was at that precise moment as I faltered at the back door that I realised finally – and for the first time felt the full force of – the effect that demotion had really had on my life. And also for the first time since my arrival on the island I seriously considered walking out that door with a *fuck you* on my lips and two fingers in the air, just load up my bike and head. Head off, head anywhere, head fast.

Monica caught my eye and winked. Her revenge may have tasted sweet but my smile was not. 'Who's for coffee, then?' I asked through clenched teeth.

Everyone, it seemed.

'Oh, and McMorran?' Fullerton said as I turned for the door. 'Let's leave the kitchen as it is, eh – like wait until the lads here've finished with it?'

Lucky he reminded me.

I didn't have any success in the first bar I visited but the second – a small hotel fronting the golf course – had exactly what I wanted in its public bar.

'Monday afternoon,' the barman said. 'Must've come in straight after opening, because he was already halfway down his pint when I arrived. Left like I said, Monday afternoon.' Pint glass in hand, he gestured at the four fonts. 'You want anything?'

I thought about Popes and bears, Catholics and woods. And the consequences.

The bar was small, low-ceilinged and smoky, sparse yet bright and warm, with its half-dozen punters scattered evenly about the room, the music from the jukebox just loud enough to keep the two bikers playing pool tapping their feet, and just quiet enough for me not to have to repeat myself.

'Ten coffees,' I said, 'to carry.'

'You serious?'

'And a cup of sugar.'

'All milk?'

I nodded. 'You remember the exact time Thomas left?'

The barman wrote down the order, scratched his head of long snarled hair with the tip of his pencil, then looked off over my shoulder. 'Back of four, I'd say, maybe half past. Him and wee Fergie McGrath got in an argument and started shouting so I had to ask them to leave; wasn't all that long before I went off at five. What's it all about, anyway?'

'Nothing serious,' I said, then asked him what the argument was about. He tore off the order sheet, nodded towards a wizened old man in the corner. 'Why don't you ask the wee man yourself?'

I did.

'Why? Whit's up wi' the ol' bastard?' Fergie McGrath snapped, squinting at me suspiciously through thick, wire-framed spectacles. There were ash-marks on his suit trousers, and what looked like an egg-yolk stain on the front of his burgundy jersey.

'He's in a little trouble, sir, and there're one or two matters we need to clear up.'

'Like whit?'

'Like why you argued?'

McGrath exhaled in a long whistling sigh. 'Jest one o' they things,' he said with a shrug. He perched nervously on the edge of the seat, hunched forward over crossed legs, hugging his side

112

with one hand as he smoked with the other, the cigarette moving barely an inch from his lips, gathering ash. 'The man lived and breathed for the sake o' a good argument. And Monday's was nothin' special – fitba', if you must know.'

'And yet you almost came to blows, I hear . . .'

'Aye, ken.' McGrath shook his bony head. 'Arthur wizne hissel'. Not at a'. In fact, Ah've no' seen him like that since Mo Johnston signed fae the 'Gers.'

'Like what?'

'Broodin'. Like he had somethin' heavy, ken, on his mind. I mean, he wiz already half-cut when Ah come in – an' that wiz back o' two.'

'Any idea what he had on his mind?'

He cocked his head, glanced at me shrewdly. His build and posture, like his mannerisms, birdlike. 'Whit kin' o' trouble did you say, son?' Sparrow-like.

Maybe when you reach his age you can smell death, and the scent of it still clung to my clothes. Or you get used to seeing it, reading the signs in the unemotional tones and eyes of officialdom.

'The terminal kind.'

He stared at me for a long minute. 'The terminal kind, eh?' He cleared his throat, stared some more. 'Monday afternoon?'

'You may be the last person who saw him alive,' I said.

'Last Ah seen, he wiz headed up yon road.'

'In which direction?'

'Hame.'

'Alone?'

'Aye.' Fergie McGrath took a long, slow draught of Guinness, replacing the glass on the table with almost exaggerated care.

'What time was that?'

'Five.'

'You sure?'

'Ah can tell the time, if tha's whit you mean.'

113

'And you've no idea what he had on his mind?'

'Did Ah say that?' He looked at me for a long moment. 'How?' he said, his voice a rasp.

'Murdered.'

He nodded slowly, as though it all made sense now, his eyes drifting from mine to the window, out across the moonlit golf course to the silver-flecked bay beyond.

'Artie wiz no' the kin' o' man to imagine things,' Fergie McGrath said, his voice a distant murmur on a laboured, whistling breath. 'He wiz a practical man, son, liked to use his hauns. So when he said someone was watchin' his hoose, Ah believed him.'

'He said that?'

The old man nodded. 'From the woods, ken, at the back o' his hoose. Always the same place, he said. So Ah went up wi' him last week – he was feared tae hissel', case the boy wiz there – took me tae the spot. *Ah* never seen naebody, son, but Ah seen the grund there flattened, ken, like footprints. *Somebody'd* been there, ken, waitin', Ahm sure o' that.'

I took out my notebook, drew a quick plan of the area around the cottage as I remembered it: the lane leading up past Glen Rosa Farm and Cottage, curling round the lip of the hill to Ravensbank Cottage, the field with the Standing Stones below, Glen Rosa and its Water to the left. And finally, the treeline.

'Show me,' I said.

He took my pencil and after studying the crude sketch for a moment, marked a cross just inside the treeline up the hill behind the house. 'There,' he said.

I thanked him, took his address, thanked him again, then told him someone else would probably come and ask him the same questions all over again and maybe take a statement, but not to worry, it didn't mean he was a suspect, it was only normal routine in any murder investigation, you know, check each fact once, twice, then a hundred times again in the mostly vain hope that some new and possibly vital piece of evidence might

114

emerge, and make the hours of tedious repetition door to door almost seem worthwhile.

His expression as I left seemed almost sympathetic. A trick of the light, no doubt.

'Fined two and a half grand and bumped back down to uniform all because you were unlucky?' Fullerton clucked twice and shook his head, blew on his coffee and clucked again. 'I'm not calling you a liar, but that kind of ruling is usually evidence of some pretty serious misdemeanour, correct me if I'm wrong.'

I didn't correct him.

He'd beckoned me outside 'for a quick word' a few minutes ago and we now stood by the open front door of the cottage, bathed in the wash of headlights. David Hunter, one of the duty doctors from Lamlash Hospital, had arrived only moments before my own return and was now working on the body on the living-room floor; I could just see the top of his sandy hair through the window to my left.

'Rumour has it you killed a man,' Fullerton continued, pushing back his hat and regarding me with empty grey eyes. 'Supposedly in the process of arresting him.'

'So why ask?'

'I prefer facts.' Grey hat over grey hair, grey mac over a grey suit and black shoes. DI Fullerton.

I shrugged. Sometime in the last few weeks, or maybe hours, his manner towards me had changed. Apart from our initial greeting, Frank had become either McMorran or Constable. Unsure of the reason, I was naturally wary. 'There'll be an official record of the Fatal Accident Inquiry,' I said. 'And another somewhere of the disciplinary hearing, no doubt. All the facts you could ever want.'

'I'm trying to do you a favour here, McMorran.'

'Yeah?' I said, studying the line of trees that curved round behind the cottage. 'I ask myself what. Then I ask myself why.'

Fullerton pulled on his thin cigar, dragging it back to life.

'You have respect in the . . . right quarters, shall we say? A lot of people reckon it was you who finally brought the Hangman to justice.'

'You've been listening to too much gossip,' I said.

'But is it true?'

I hesitated a moment, contemplating denial, then told him yeah, it was true, almost.

'And that you made a deal?' He must have glimpsed the fleeting surprise on my face. 'So it is, eh? Well, well.' He seemed genuinely pleased.

I turned away, cursing my lack of control. Follow the lane round the cottage another twenty yards or so, I thought, and the treeline retreats up the hill away from the roadside. Up there somewhere. And perhaps a couple of cigarette ends ground into the earth or a piece of torn fabric clinging to a branch – or even, if today was a day worthy of miracles, a perfect impressionable footprint.

'You did a deal,' Fullerton said, 'and let your boss take the credit.'

But by now my face was set, I was the inscrutable Charlie Chan. 'Arthur Thomas believed someone was watching him,' I said. 'From the trees round the back.'

Fullerton was not to be put off; he dogged me across the lawn to Mike 30. 'Bumped down for two years,' he persisted, 'then what, a review? Pass the exam again and they bump you back up? Is that it?'

The torch was in the glove compartment. I flicked open my notebook, found the map I'd drawn. Glanced at it briefly before directing the powerful beam into the trees. 'X marks the spot,' I said.

X appeared to be a tall beech, one of its lower branches leaning into the undergrowth, torn half from the trunk, I supposed, by lightning.

'Okay,' Fullerton sighed. 'Tell me.'

I repeated my conversation with Fergie McGrath. Fullerton

scratched his long chin and examined my map as he listened. When I finished, he placed his polystyrene cup carefully on the bonnet, said, 'Okay, McMorran, show me.'

'Maybe we should wait until morning,' I suggested. 'In case we . . .' I broke off. Did something move out there as I played the beam over the trees near the beech? An animal? A man? Or merely shadows dancing?

'In case we what?'

'Destroy vital evidence?' But my voice held little conviction; we both understood the importance of evidence discovered during the first few hours and days of a murder investigation: time has always been our greatest enemy.

'Gimme the torch,' Fullerton growled.

I didn't. Instead we left the headlights behind, crossed the ditch and climbed through damp moss and long grass into darkness pierced only by the torch beam that I continued to play across the trees ahead with only one thought in mind:

Killers often return to the scene of their crimes.

Fullerton wasn't stupid.

'Think someone's up there?' he whispered, hard on my shoulder as I stopped.

My answer was ambiguous silence.

They get kind of worried and frustrated, this kind of killer, desperate even, when their victims remain too long undiscovered,

Arthur Thomas – two days, maybe three.

keep returning to them, the way Dennis Nilsen did, digging them up, playing with them, doing the gruesome things they like to do to them – gloating, it would seem, over their victims' brutalised predicament, milking every last drop of satisfaction from their deed because this kind of man is more at ease among the dead, it is only in their morbid company that his power is complete, dominance assured.

'Could be a bird . . .' Fullerton breathed.

But they also want *the bodies found, because they feed voraciously on the public shock, absolutely lap up the violent waves of public outrage and indignation that follow each discovery. As though . . .*

In the blackness there, between the trees. Movement heard, not seen. Furtive rustlings in the undergrowth. Of flight? Stealth? Or purely imagination? Fullerton bent down and

the victim is only ever truly dead in their eyes when he is beyond their reach – that is, discovered, carried off, lying in a cold-room drawer somewhere, mission accomplished.

picking up a stone, hurled it in the direction of the sound. There was a high-pitched squeal followed by something small panicking through the undergrowth; a cereal killer of the fieldmouse variety perhaps, but that was all.

'A fucking rodent,' Fullerton said, releasing his breath with as much relief as mine. 'Come on, let's see if we can find the spot, have something solid to show Kettle in the morning. You know what he's like.'

I stopped dead. 'Kettle?' It was almost a yell.

'Aye, the Commander. Flying in, first chopper in the morning.' Fullerton's teeth glinted in the torchlight. 'I hear you've met,' he grinned.

Yeah, I thought, bad dream suddenly becoming a nightmare, we'd met.

Book Two

The Abysmal Water

13

'Deliver yourself from your great foe.
Then the companion comes. And him you can trust.'

'**S**corpio,' he tells her, squinting through his heavy thick lenses at the curve of her neck. Nice lines, he thinks, almost Grecian.

'I knew it,' she twitters, hand like a sparrow fluttering at her throat. 'As soon as I walked in and saw you working there at the wheel, I knew it. I said to myself, Ros, this man is a man of the Earth. At first I thought Taurus, I don't know why – well I do actually, I always feel one should go by first impressions, the sub-conscious *is* a powerful ally if only we choose to recognise it, don't you think? – but then I noticed those *be-eautiful* pots over there and the word that sprang immediately to mind was "perseverance" because really they must have taken you absolutely *ages* to perfect and that's one of their most positive aspects, Scorpios, their indomitable perseverance. But,' hand to mouth, as though to stem the flow, 'I'm gushing. You must excuse me.'

She reminds Gideon of someone, past, distant past.

Her looks? A head of long red curls framing a fleshy red face brought alive by piercing green eyes that crinkle at you, seem to pin you down, seeking agreement. Or her voice, her manner of talking? Full of breathless enthusiasm and a tendency towards overemphasis. Or the way she dresses? Kind of arty, with jacket, blouse and canvas jeans in various shades of woodland green, the baggy look. Or her age? Mid forties, but still there, her lines tight, not saggy yet, figure well moulded beneath her clothes, has the look of someone who looks after her bod, takes a lot of vitamin pills – probably has nothing else for breakfast but.

And diet pills. Or else a dozen lines of speed to account for how she can't keep her mouth shut any longer than it takes to grab enough breath to stay alive until the end of another monologue. How had she introduced herself last week, the first time she came in? '*Hastie. Rosalind Hastie – but call me Ros, everyone else does.*'

Not that Byrne had been paying too much attention that morning: the slaughter of the sheep the night before, instead of appeasing his appetite, had only served to accentuate it, leaving him hungry. That was the trouble with snacks.

So, Moon sucking at his bones that morning and he had to stand there and listen to her nervous prattle, how she'd moved to the island almost a year ago now, had bought a cottage down above Kildonan, had always been interested in pottery, and did he do lessons? And, as always, he was polite. He nodded and clucked and sighed and agreed in all the right places, said he'd let her know if he ever decided to start up a class, but at the moment, what with it being middle of the season and hardly having the time to breathe between firings, and then serving in the shop all at the same time, there was scarce enough time to even slip out in the cool of the night and slit a sheep's throat for the fun of it.

Or words to that effect.

A little off-centre perhaps that morning, but he'd noticed her lines. Maybe didn't quite connect that she reminded him of someone in his past, but he did recognise the strong curve of her neck to shoulder and note the smooth low ridges of her clavicles, hidden today beneath her buttoned green blouse.

'You'd be *surprised* how many potters are Scorpios,' she was

122

saying now, checking both her silver earrings to make sure they were both still there, watching you from aslant. 'Or maybe you wouldn't, meeting as you probably do so many more potters than I . . .'

He doesn't interrupt to tell her he goes out of his way to avoid all other potters. That he abhors their middle-class liberalism, their false values, their overwhelming need for conformity.

' . . . but I'm sure someone's done a study *somewhere*, the influence of natal elements over one's profession, it would be *awfully* interesting, don't you think? I mean it really *is* about the elements, isn't it – earth, water, wind and fire – because after all, what is pottery but a product of the elements?'

What are human bodies, he wants to tell her, *but earth and water, blood and bone.*

Which starts him thinking.

About *her* bones.

Then he remembers who she reminds him of.

Simone.

The ding-dong of the pottery door bringing him back. It's Ros Hastie coming in. Byrne, sitting at the spinning wheel with a wedge of clay nicely centred, frowns: he can't remember her leaving. One minute she's standing there talking this and that about his stars, next she's backing in through the door telling her frisky collie bitch, 'Stay, Jess, stay! We don't want you smashing all the nice Mr Byrne's pots, now do we?'

Which is damn bloody right. First time she came in, she let the bitch loose with its nosy nose nudging and happy tail swiping what must've been at least half a dozen of his small delicate vases on to the stone floor. Which had made him think of Hector, that silly old Hector whose fate long ago could so easily become the collie's if it entered the workshop again, began smashing up his pots.

' . . . I mean, what with all the police flying in, it must be pretty serious.'

Byrne comes back again.

'Police?'

'Coming in by the 'copter load, I hear. All last night and this morning, I reckon they must be drafting the whole force in.'

'Why?' he croaks, throat suddenly dry. 'What's happened?'

Ros Hastie covers her shocked mouth with the tips of her fingers, takes a sharp intake of breath. 'Murder,' she whispers, eyes wide in mock disbelief. 'An old man, I heard, living on his own near Brodick. Glen Something-or-other.'

'Rosa?'

'That's it, Glen Rosa. Apparently a policeman found him last night lying in a pool of blood.'

'Policeman?'

'The youngish one, you know, fair hair, McSomething-or-other, the one used to be an inspector, was it, in the city? He found the body. Lying there, I heard, for several days at least.'

Sixty-four hours, to be exact.

'My God,' Byrne exclaims, 'is nobody safe?' And her description of the cop who found the body coincides with that of the cop with the torch last night, the one with the sensitive ears who seemed to be staring right through the screen of trees, penetrating the sheer wall of darkness, looking right into Byrne's eyes as he crouched there in the undergrowth thirty yards back, trying hard to still the rampant pounding in his chest.

'There's talk that it might be that one from the mainland, the Whatsit, who's been killing all those women with his teeth.'

'The Fangman?'

'Mm,' she says, voice laden with foreboding, 'him.'

Nicknames, Gideon Byrne has found, take time getting used to. You have to grow into them. The Fangman, he felt initially, was too tabloidy. Diminished his status and belittled his mission, trivialising the importance of what he is trying to *say*.

Say it with bodies.

But even in murder one must learn to adapt. And, well, he must admit, the name *is* growing on him. He can see it now has more potential than he previously thought. *Fangman*. Like Batman. Maybe he should get himself a cape and a mask, wear his Y-fronts over his tights.

'All the chief constables, too.'

He must've missed something. He keeps doing this lately, drifting in and out of reality, losing whole chunks of conversations, hours, sometimes days. Like he's there but he's not there. Weird.

'Sorry?'

'Flying over for the photo opportunity,' she continues, ignoring Byrne's blank stare. 'They're setting up a local command centre, I think he called it, across in Lamlash. And the TV . . . I've seen two of their trucks already, you know the ones with BBC on the side, they're parked down at the foot of The String, which is probably as close as the police will let them get to the actual scene . . .'

Why is she here?

'Pardon?' She seems shocked, taken aback.

Pardon what? Byrne stares at her, puzzled.

'Why am I here?' she says. 'Is that what you asked?'

Shit. Now he's speaking his thoughts aloud.

'I just wondered,' he says lamely, looking down at the mug he's been turning. It's a misshapen blob on the wheel. He glances along the bench, sees half a dozen mugs he can't recall turning, but all of them fine, flawless. What's going on?

'*Wondered?*' As though wondering was against the law, something distasteful.

'I mean, it *is* a bit off the beaten track here.' Miles from fucking anywhere, to be more precise.

The friendliness has gone from her eyes. 'I like it out here,' she says, her posture wary, manner defensive, tone hurt. 'It's quiet, peaceful, there's a sense of tranquillity I like that surrounds the stones.' Pause for breath. 'And I hope you don't take this the wrong way but I felt the other day that it might get a little lonely, that perhaps you'd appreciate a visitor once in a while.'

Why today, though, and talking about the strangle and the police? Maybe she was psychic or something. People into all that horoscope stuff often were. Like on a different wavelength.

'What's *your* star sign?' Byrne asks, his mind jumping all over the place, like not quite under control.

'Guess.' She's smiling now, probably celebrating some small victory in her mind, the clouds blown instantly from her eyes.

'Taurus.'

She looks at him agog. 'How did you know?'

'Luck,' Byrne says modestly, knowing she won't believe it. He watches her reassessing him, head cocked, hand stroking her chin. He wonders how she would look at him if he was wearing a mask. Say a mask made from leather, leather patches of different shades, one that fitted the contours of his head perfectly, with a zipper for its mouth and some kind of gauzy material to veil the eyes. Something like the mask he's been designing in his mind for a while now since he read that book. The whole idea, he has found, excites him, and now he's already getting a hard-on just wondering about how the woman here might react.

'Well, well, well,' Ros Hastie says, 'we have an expert here.' Something sly – or is it shrewd? – in her eyes. Careful, he tells himself, don't underestimate this woman. She might come in useful later on.

'And you're right,' he says, looking coyly away. 'Sometimes it does get a wee bit lonely out here.'

Better make out a shopping list.

'What about at night?' she asks. 'Doesn't it get a bit creepy?'

Where to buy leather, though, that was the question.

'Sorry?'

'You know, with all these stones here, all the history of this moor. I mean there must've been, what, hundreds, maybe

126

thousands of sacrifices performed out here, by the Druids, what have you. Think of all that bloodshed, what gory scenes these stones have witnessed down the years. If it was me, I'd not be able to sleep at night, I'd be too damn scared.'

It would have to be soft leather, too, perhaps offcuts.

'You get used to it,' Byrne shrugs. 'After all, it's only your own imagination. The sounds are just ordinary night sounds.'

Where do you get offcuts without arousing curiosity? Somewhere on the mainland, obviously. And you'd need a special needle for the leather, a thimble, and a zipper, a short one. Black gauze for the eyeholes.

'What about the cultists, the ones who come out here on certain nights of the year and perform rites of sacrifice?'

'Games,' Byrne tells her. 'Nothing but games.'

'Mm.' Like she disagrees. He lets the silence hang there until she can't take it any further. 'I'd still find it spooky,' she adds, her voice trailing off as she picks up a shallow blue bowl from the display, turns it in her hands.

Spooky, yeah.

Last night he'd dreamt about bones. He seems to be dreaming more now than ever before, his sleep a riot of confused emotions, with strange, formless forces, sensed rather than seen, battling for supremacy across the wasteland of his subconsciousness. Difficult at times to tell the difference between his daydreams and nightdreams, his fantasy and reality. Because what starts out fantasy soon becomes reality. No wonder he awakes slippery as an eel, vacuum-packed in sweat-drenched sheets, his whole body aching from exertion, exhausted even as he turns to face the onslaught of another day. Onslaught, yes, because this is the onslaught season when tourists in their summertime hordes climb the Moss Farm road, following the signs for the Standing Stones, the stone circles, the chambered cairns, up across the Machrie Moor, coming as they could not help to Moss Farm, ruins all those years ago when he'd first come to the island and set eyes on the place, ruins since who knows when, hundred-odd years or more, but Byrne's bungalow and workshop now, Moss Farm Pottery, set in a hollow in the shadow of the stones, three low buildings, cottage, workshop, storeroom, invisible when the blanket mists come down and settle over the moor as they do autumn, winter, spring, earth, water, air, like living in the clouds, his own little world enclosed by the mists of time. Walk up out of the hollow through the layer of mist and he's in another world, a world not of his making, where life has no meaning, no value. Walk back down, it's like descending the steps into some nether world, not just some world but his world, one definitely of his making, where different rules and logic apply, uncompromised fantasies.

'I mean, those stones and circles,' Ros Hastie continues, 'they're ancient. We're talking Neolithic. Bronze Age. The sign over there behind your storeroom, I was reading it the other day, says we're talking about 3500 BC to 1600 BC. That's a lot of years in anyone's language. And it says the Moor was a centre for ceremonial and burial activity all that time. If that's not spooky, tell me what is.'

So Byrne tells her about the two burial cists some guy whose name he forgets excavated over by the nearest circle to the pottery. Where that single red sandstone stone still stands. And how one of the cists contained some pottery which disintegrated on handling, how the other one contained some flint flakes and a skeleton all doubled up like it was caught by a lava flow while squatting over a hole having a shit.

'I know, I know.' The woman getting all worked up, her eyes wide, hand at her throat again, playing with that weird-looking pendant. 'That's what I mean, spooky. Especially the pot they found in the other circle. Some kind of food vessel, wasn't it?'

Yeah, a tripartite, divided into three parts by its two horizontal mouldings. Or Byrne's own theory, that it was in fact a burial urn where they placed the ashes of the recently cremated. Bone-ash. Or look at it another way, bone-earth.

'Bone-earth,' he says. 'Know what that is?' Show the woman if you want to be a potter you have to know a fucklot more than just how to turn mugs for tourists. You have to know the manner and matter of the materials you're working with, and as a craftsman you have to be totally at one, you, your pot, the elements, the earth you come from and return to, yin and yang right down the line, no half-measures, no compromise, no half-hearted notions – this is what Simone taught him – that pottery is some kind of therapeutic hobby and all it takes is learning to control the clay as it spins on the wheel. No. Life, death, bone, blood, earth, water, air and fire, all play an essential part in the cosmic pottery of the now.

Tasty Hastie is shaking her head of red curls. She doesn't know what bone-earth is. She doesn't know what life is.

'There are more than two hundred bones in the human skeleton,' he tells her, 'made up of fibrous tissue and bone-earth. Bone-earth in turn is made up of phosphate and carbonate of lime. I use both in my straightforward glazes.' Sounding now like that fucking professor patronising the kid in his class who couldn't read but everyone thought was subnormal and took the piss out of. Gideon Byrne. Who knew more about life and death then than any of them would ever know.

So he tries to explain this growing philosophy of his, put into words the vague images of elemental progressions he feels in his bones to be true. 'What I'm saying is you make a pot, it's not just a pot, something lifeless, inanimate, it's alive, as much a part and product of the earth as we are. Life comes from the earth, nowhere else. Every day we walk on the bones of our ancestors, we eat food nourished by the bones of our ancestors, what we take out of the earth we put back in – we live and we die. Full circle.' He stops there, aware his voice is raised, that Hastie has taken a step back and is giving him that shrewd look again, of almost apprehensive assessment. And that damn dog scratching at the door outside, yelping.

'Exactly,' she says. 'Full circle. What I was going to say. How they find a pot in the cist from around 2000 BC, so they were making pots here then, and now, almost 4000 years later, here you are making pots yourself. Like it has a certain cosmic symmetry, this place.'

Here she goes again, off into the stars.

'Which is one reason I would like to draw your chart. I can feel it sometimes, there are forces at work here, in this spot. I think you can feel them too, at least subconsciously, it's why you're here, doing what you do.'

Byrne shakes his head. He's too busy, he tells her. What with the tourist season in full flood he's firing the electric kiln once a week at the moment and tomorrow he's going to have to start the woodfire one, lot of hard work there, three days, hardly time to sleep at all, he has to keep the temperature just right or lose a couple of months' work just like that, so with that and tending the shop he won't have a single spare second for any stargazing of the myopic kind. No.

'I could always help out in the shop here, you know,' Hastie persists. 'When I'm not serving customers, I could work on your chart. And you could concentrate on your firing.'

Byrne tells her he can't afford to take on staff. It's the truth. Business is all to hell the last few months ... but that's something he won't let himself think about.

'Hell, I don't want paid. It'll be fun.' Looking all girlish at him now, clasped hands, excited flush. Will probably start skipping round the workshop any second.

But what she's saying makes sense, someone to watch over the shop for the next few days while he fires the kiln would be a great help, give him time to think things out – like what to do now he's brought the whole mainland police force over to the island. And, try as he might, he can't deny the growing excitement, the thrill of improvisation he can sense birthing inside him.

When one man journeys alone, He finds a companion . . .

Realms of possibility opening out before him now. Tasty Hastie, and her uncanny resemblance to Simone. Bringing it all, refreshingly, back. And astrological charts – perhaps a stimulating new twist to an old ceremony, another dance with danger. Dust off some of his youthful fantasies, bring them to life. And masks, definitely masks.

But no dogs, he tells her. Let that be understood.

She beams, crinkling her eyes at him. 'It's a deal. What time do I start?'

'Have you ever seen the dawn?'

As she skips out the door he wonders again if he really knows what he's doing. No, he decides, probably not. But what the hell.

If you can't get what you want, get what you can.

14

Midday Thursday found me on traffic and crowd control, stationed at the foot of the lane to the cottage and using all the subtle skills of communication I'd developed over the years to restrain the growing horde of reporters and TV crews eager to get closer to the action.

'I asked you twice, pal, now fuck off back behind the cordon.' I led the scruffy, potbellied hack back to the road, held up the cordon for him to pass under.

'It's nice to be nice,' he whined. He had the lugubrious face of a dachshund, with a frame of mousy hair hanging lank like droopy ears.

'I know,' I said, 'but it gets so boring.'

A crowd of about twenty men and women stood around in tight knots by the side of The String, some smoking, pumping each other for information and speculating into mobile phones, while others adjusted lenses and checked microphones, smoothed unmanageable hair and rehearsed suitably sombre expressions for the live lunchtime broadcasts. Two of the reporters I recognised as crime correspondents for the *Herald* and the *Scotsman*, the rest, judging by their press passes, were Sunday and daily tabloids. One young woman stood self-consciously by the mouth of the lane, ignored by everyone else, ostracised it seemed for nothing more than a lack of big-city experience. In the cluttered office of the *Arran Banner*, I was sure her employer would now be hastily resetting Saturday's edition.

'When we going to get a statement?' someone asked.

'Soon as the brass arrive.'

'You been saying that all day.'

'I've been meaning it all day.'

Four hours' sleep, eight times disturbed, on a lumpy horsehair mattress on the lockfast floor of the Lamlash station. And now this, a freak sun suddenly alone in a powder-blue sky, and my shirt clinging to my back, my hat to my head, my tongue to the roof of my mouth.

'Hey, McMorran! How's it feel to be back in uniform?'

In my mind's eye, the image of a mutilated sheep.

'Like I've been reborn.' I muttered. 'In hell.'

'There are those on the force who say that you and death walk hand in hand. Are natural companions.'

'You writing a book, Jimmy, or what?' Jimmy as in Slater, as in freelance crime reporter for one of the nationals. He was a runt of a man who hid, behind Jack Russell features and a tangle of fair curls, a mind sharp enough to shave with.

'No, but I could open one on you. Like two-to-one you're off the investigation within the hour.'

'No takers,' I told him, shaking my head. I'd turned down the volume on my personal radio but not before I'd heard confirmation that the chopper was airborne. ETA far too bloody soon.

'You heard the saying, find a murder and you'll find McMorran?'

'One time too many, every day of my life.'

'There's a new one. Find a TV camera and you'll find Kettle.'

Which was about as new as TV itself, I thought, turning to watch the BBC Scotland linkman, hair now perfectly in place, go through a dry run of background commentary in front of a gap in the hedge, through which the cameraman could zoom in on the Glen Rosa Farm and Cottage. Better footage in the wrong cottage, it would appear, than simply filming the line of trees that concealed Ravensbank.

Why sheep? I wondered.

'You remember that name, McMorran?'

Half a dozen cars came over the hill and nosed slowly down The String. I ducked under the cordon and, with a ZZ Top flourish, waved them through the slalom of TV trucks. The cameraman, perhaps overwhelmed by such excitement, almost missed the shot.

'Commander Harlan Kettle.' Slater's mouth was at my shoulder, yapping. Why was it that all the reporters I met resembled dogs? 'The bane of your life, McMorran, come to steal your show again. What d'you make of that?'

Karma, I thought. Maybe I should have shown that little shit Ryder a bit more politeness on Monday. Kissed his tears away. I retreated back behind the cordon, as though it were a soundproof barrier Slater's words could not transgress. No such luck.

Slater flipped open his notepad, extended it to arm's length and squinted. 'PC McMorran, formerly a detective inspector with the Scottish Special Crimes Squad, did not reply.' I hoped he was only pretending to read. 'When pressed to comment on his relationship with the officer commanding the investigation, McMorran replied—'

'We're just good friends.'

Slater popped his biro and, with exaggerated care and concentration, wrote two words on his pad, speaking them aloud as he did so. 'Bum . . . chums.'

Would this day never end? I looked up The String towards the sky, fringed by Stronach Wood on the left and Glen Shurig on the right, hoping to spot a more compassionate bird of prey there, a buzzard perhaps, or, hovering over hill scrub, a knife-winged kestrel. I saw only the purposeful flight of one hooded crow.

A ripple of excitement suddenly stirred the pool of reporters. Slater tucked his notepad in a pocket, held out his arms in a shrugging gesture of what-can-I-do?

'I mean, gimme something better to write, Frank, and I will.

135

Good copy's just kinda short right now.' His dialogue one Lou Grant show too many.

I said, 'Where are you staying?'

'Castleview. Room 104.' His smile not quite wolfish, more that of the terrier that caught the rabbit. 'If I'm not in, leave a message.'

Or tear your fucking room apart.

'No names,' I growled.

'Strictly non-attributable.'

'That's what I said.'

He hurried back to join his colleagues.

I climbed into Mike 30, reversed it off the centre of the lane, parked by a gate. The chopper had landed. The TV crews waiting there for its arrival had phoned to alert the crews waiting here, hence the excitement. Perhaps if I pulled my hat down over my eyes as he passed, I thought. Or, if he drove right on by, and no one up at the cottage mentioned who found the body last night, or the name of the man on duty at the foot of the lane, then I might still survive the day.

No one can say I'm not an optimist.

Perhaps I have my great-aunt to thank for that. She was one of those people so full of life, so vibrant and positive, she made those around her stand out like pale imitations of life, sad ghosts lost in a limbo of self-doubt. She couldn't walk, Aunt Joan, she could only stride. Even in her eighties, when cancer began to eat away her throat, she still strode the globe with the same sense of purpose and determination as she had done half a century before. There was a world out there, and she had to see it.

The radio crackled to life. I heard Monica at the landing pad report to Yuill up at the cottage. ETA five minutes. A moment later, Yuill was through to me, issuing instructions I'd already carried out. He finished with, 'Oh, and McMorran? Not a word to the press, eh. Zip it tight is the order of the day.'

'You know me, sir.'

Yuill signed off on a static wave of doubt.

She had never married, Aunt Joan. The impression she gave was that it was too mundane an existence for someone who truly wanted to live; leave that to the drones, the accepters of their lot. Instead she lived alone in a big rambling house near Thornhill, guardian of a thousand paintings, all her own. She loved to paint the sea; the east coast for its fishing ports, the west coast for its magnificent sunsets. Would send me postcards from all over Europe with little crayoned sketches, a man walking his cat along the banks of the Rhine, trawlers berthed in a small French harbour, colourful barges on an Amsterdam canal. Arran, too, held a special place in her heart. She came every summer for two weeks of hill-walking and playing the numerous golf courses. As I remember her, a slight, diminutive woman yet strong and wiry, with perpetually windswept hair, a steely grey that eventually turned to white. She wore tweed and brogues, ate no meat or salt or butter, survived solely, it had seemed, on fish, vegetables, and yoghurt. And huge afternoon teas, of course, with unbuttered scones and jam.

Why these sudden memories?

There was movement among the crowd of reporters as two cars rounded the bend so, tugging the peak of my hat down over my eyes, I climbed from Mike 30 and approached the cordon, ready to put my years of intensive training into practice and raise the plastic ribbon for the cars to pass.

They didn't pass. The lead car stopped at the entrance to the lane and was immediately engulfed by the pack of reporters, scrapping like jackals for a chunk of the carcass. Cameras flashed, microphones and mini-recorders were thrust like daggers. As was always the case, I heard him before I saw him.

'Gentlemen, please, I have nothing to say at the moment – as you can see I have only just arrived. I will make a full statement as soon as I have talked to my officers and surveyed the locus.'

'When will that be, Commander?'

'The sooner you let me pass. Now . . .'

I moved in. 'Stand back, please, let the cars through.' I pushed and pulled at reluctant bodies. 'C'mon there, out the way.' The pack parted, the white Audi nosed through. 'Move along now.' I was doing my duty, far too engrossed to glance towards the passenger seat of the car as it passed.

Ten yards up the lane, the Audi skidded to a halt, reversed. 'Constable!'

My heart dropped over a cliff, fell screaming into blackness. I turned and saluted. 'Sir!' I couldn't help the smile.

He did a double-take. He squinted. His mouth fell open. He stared. Words formed on his lips. He frowned. The words dissolved. He glared. Moments stretched to a minute. Then his fat, fleshy lips stretched in a cold, malevolent smile. He'd reached a decision. Still holding my eyes, he snapped at Monica behind the wheel.

'Drive, woman, dammit!'

The Audi sped up the lane, followed quickly by the Ford. In the back seat of the latter I recognised the squat, round figure and shiny bald head of Silas Kerr, Strathclyde's chief forensic pathologist. I'd met him once three years ago, lecturing at a detective training course I was on. In a different life, it now seemed.

I climbed back into Mike 30, returned it to the middle of the lane, wound down the window and cut the ignition. Ran a finger round the inside of my collar, longing for a cool liquid lunch in a tall glass. It was turning into one of those balmy summer afternoons when all you want to do is lie back, leave the world behind, wallow in lazy memories. Of carefree childhood days unfettered by the chains of pride, obligation and responsibility, unspooked by demons from the past.

The reporters had now returned to their various huddles by the side of the road, most down to shirtsleeves now, wearing shades, smoking, looking the kind of cool that only a pack of wild dogs can affect.

It happens all the time this, I thought, something we see,

hear, smell, think, triggering off memories from our distant past. Sometimes we're conscious of what's happening, more often we're not. And there are so many of these forgotten memories lying dormant back there, little pieces of ourselves, like frames on a cutting-room floor, discarded, albeit temporarily, just waiting for the right scenario to trigger them off.

I was seven when my mother died, and it was my Aunt Joan who took it upon herself to educate me in the great outdoors. For the next seven years I accompanied her on these annual trips to the island, and struggled to keep up with her as she stormed over heather and scrub, scrambled up mountains and ridges, crept through dark, soundless forests, pointing out this bird, that animal, this tree, that formation of rock, halting only when inspiration demanded she dash off a sketch. I remember she used her rubber a lot. And it was on one of these walks I saw my first golden eagle, high over Glen Catacol to the north-west, on a day not much unlike today, the sky clear, the air warm, the sun dazzling. We stopped and watched it ride the thermals high above the crags and the Nature Reserve, as though effortlessly, for at least twenty minutes before, almost simultaneously, my Great-Aunt Joan's unleashable enthusiasm focused on something else, some rare kind of moss or lichen, I seem to recall, and the great bird dropped out of sight behind the eastern crags.

'Where's it gone?' I cried.

'Spotted lunch, I imagine.' She was kneeling in the heather, backside in the air, examining lichen.

'Lunch?' I wasn't the smartest of kids.

'You like lamb, don't you?'

I'd only had it once. 'I like the mint sauce best,' I said.

'Well, a tender young lamb is the golden eagle's favourite meal at this time of year. When it can't get a lamb, a dead sheep will do.'

'A dead sheep?' The golden eagle must truly be a powerful bird. I imagined one climbing towards its eyrie on the towering crags above, fully grown sheep in glistening bloodied claws. If it could lift a sheep, I was thinking, what about a skinny little boy with suddenly apprehensive skyward eyes?

'They rip it open with their beaks and talons, take what they can back to their eaglets.'

'What about people?' I was busily checking the sky. 'Do they eat them, too?'

'Only wee boys who ask silly questions.'

I smiled now at the memory.

I heard the Land Rover first, turned in my seat to watch it round the bend, draw up alongside. Monica climbed down. I joined her in the sun.

'I see you make friends everywhere you go,' she said, adjusting the set of her hat.

'Who now?'

'Kettle. Mr Politeness Personified.'

'We've shared some bad times,' I admitted.

'Is he part of that past you don't want to talk about?'

'He *is* that past,' I sighed. 'Nemesis should take lessons.'

'I am.'

'And I had you down as the goddess of love.'

She prodded my chest. 'In your dreams. Frank, in your dreams.'

'You've known all along?'

Her laugh was almost infectious; I found myself smiling.

'Since the day you first tried it on.'

'I did?'

'The day you arrived. You didn't waste any time.'

True, I hadn't. I'd thought my prayers had been answered. 'Why die of patience?' I shrugged. 'Life is short.'

'Mm, and getting shorter by the second. You've been summoned.'

'Kettle?'

'Mm.'

'Shit.'

'And he's boiling,' she said.

'What's new?' I was suddenly in not very much of a hurry.

'He's calling you black.'

'Just picking up where he left off.' This warm summer's day now a howling winter's night in my mind. I nodded back up the lane. 'What's happening up there?'

'What you'd maybe call a crime scene, what I'd call a lesson in chaos. But they seem to know what they're doing.'

'They should do, they've had plenty of practice.'

'What's that make it now? Six?'

'Seven they know of.'

'If it is the Fangman . . .'

'My thoughts entirely. Has anyone interviewed the neighbours yet?'

'What d'you think I've been doing all morning, buffing my nails? If only.' She studied them now. Habit. They were chewed to the quick.

'No luck then?' I asked.

'No one saw or heard a thing. Apart from all the hillwalkers, of course.'

'At this time of year . . .'

'Hundreds. And a few of them park their cars up near the cottage. Then there's the campsite.'

'You have been busy.' Nothing fancy, the campsite, a couple of brick toilets and a basin in a field between parking space and the burn. No more than half a dozen tents, mainly couples. Families tended to camp in Lamlash.

'Like I said, some of us have to work.' She glanced at her watch. 'Anyway, I'm to spell you here.'

I nodded towards the pack of reporters beyond the police cordon. 'Tell 'em nothing,' I said.

'What could I possibly tell them that they couldn't make up better for themselves?'

'So much cynicism,' I sighed. 'And in one so young.'

'See that telegraph pole, Frank?' she sighed, pointing up the lane. 'Do me a favour and go sit on it.'

I climbed into Mike 30, the sudden blast of heat evaporating the smile on my face. It was like stepping into a kiln. I turned the ignition, then asked as an afterthought, 'You ever seen a sheep that's been disembowelled by an eagle?'

Monica frowned. 'No, why?'

'Me neither.'

15

'**J**ust the phone,' Kettle asked, 'nothing else?'

The body had been removed in the early hours of the morning, now lay in the Lamlash Hospital morgue, awaiting Silas Kerr's post-mortem examination. Where Arthur Thomas had lain there was now a taped outline, and while two of the forensic team, in white coveralls and on hands and knees, vacuumed the carpet with mini-cleaners, two more processed evidence in clear plastic bags. The air in the living room was warm, stagnant and stale, and despite the open doors and windows, still laden with the stench of death.

'And that window,' I added. I'd tested it for access, had obviously left prints there as well. Through it I could now see the video team at work as the photographer loaded his equipment into the back of a car. Two other officers climbed in and the car drove off.

'But you didn't touch the body?'

'No, sir.' Well, it was only a little touch.

'Had to restrain yourself, eh?' Kettle hurled his gaze around the room in a series of jerks, aggression driving his every mannerism. He hadn't changed much in the eight months since I'd last seen him pacing up and down outside the DCC's office at Fettes, waiting to give evidence at my disciplinary hearing. He was still a huge block of a man, planted now in the centre of the room like a standing stone, his head of red hair cropped close to the skull, less the beacon than it used to be, widow's peak a shallow wedge on the crags of his forehead. 'What about the newspaper by the body?' he demanded. 'You touch that?'

I nodded. 'Found it on the table there, used it to swat away the flies around Thomas's neck. Monday's, you'll notice.'

'I'm not blind.'

'No, sir.' The pathologist Silas Kerr entered from the hall leading to the front door. He wore half-moon spectacles now, and a preoccupied air. He lumbered across to the dining table, sank with a sigh on to one of the chairs, began writing in a loose-leaf notebook.

Kettle ignored him, loaded his voice with sarcasm. 'Is there anything you didn't touch?'

'My toes, sir.'

He hurled me a look of utter contempt. 'In that case, I'll mark you down for a physical refresher course. The intensive one. See if that loosens you up.'

'Thank you, sir.'

'Show me your pocketbook,' he snapped.

I handed it over. He flicked through the pages, came to the most recent entries. 'What the fuck d'you call this?' he demanded, squinting with distaste at my notes.

'Shorthand, sir.'

'A crippled hand, more like it.' He peered at my diagram of the locus. 'So you think Thomas disturbed a burglar, then?'

'It's a possibility.'

'With no sign of forced entry?'

'Old habits die hard out here,' I said. 'Some people still don't feel the need to lock their doors. Like locking your door is an admission that the twentieth-century disease and all its malignant symptoms have finally invaded the island. That times have changed.'

'They have, McMorran. Or hadn't you noticed?'

'They have a saying out here, that an open door is an open mind.'

'And in Thomas's case, an opened throat.'

I couldn't argue with that. I said, 'Check with his sister. She might know if anything's been taken.'

Kettle grunted, flicked through several more pages, frowned. 'What about this Fergus McGrath? Last person we know who saw Thomas alive.'

'He might be able to tell you. He was a friend of Thomas's, probably came up here often.'

'A friend of the deceased,' Kettle sneered, 'who just happened to have an argument with him on the afternoon he died, and was the last person to see him alive? You don't class that kind of coincidence as remarkable, McMorran, worth further investigation?'

I recalled the look on the old man's face when I told him Thomas had been murdered. McGrath was no actor. I said, 'He's your suspect, not mine.'

'Meaning?'

'Meaning I'm just an ordinary PC now. Such decisions are out of my hands.'

Kettle snorted his derision, tossed my notebook back. 'Out of your hands is right. You've got as close to this case as you're ever going to get, McMorran. From now on you don't come near the locus, you concentrate on your outstanding caseload. Sergeant Yuill tells me you already have an ongoing investigation that requires the singular benefit of your vast experience. A case of sheep-shagging, I understand.' The smile was in his voice, almost a purr, the cat with clotted cream on its whiskers.

'Yes, sir. Both shagged to death by a knife with a nine-inch blade. Must've been one hell of a shag.'

'You serious?' His purr a sudden growl.

'Even sheep have a right to life.'

'Save me your questionable ethics, McMorran, just give me the bones.'

It took less than a minute to tell him what I'd learned so far.

'See any similarity to this case?' he asked.

'Apart from both being the product of sick minds, no.' But even as I said it I felt a slight shifting in my mind, as though something dormant there were slowly reawakening.

Kettle must have glimpsed a reflection of that sudden awareness in my eyes. He raised an eyebrow in question. 'Yes?'

I said nothing, and was saved any further inquisition as Silas Kerr lumbered over to join us. 'Right, Harlan,' he said, 'that's me. Any time you're ready.'

Kettle jerked his head in my direction. 'McMorran here'll drive you down to the hospital and ID the body. Sergeant Yuill will meet you there.'

'Relatives?' Kerr asked. In Scotland, four people have to identify murder victims to the attending pathologist: two officers present when the body is found, and two relatives, or people who knew the deceased during life, who have no part in the investigation.

'Coming across by ferry,' Kettle said, glancing at his watch. 'Should be docking now. Sergeant Yuill will bring them to the hospital.'

'Photographer?'

'There already with a couple of POs.'

The two men I'd seen leaving with the photographer. I'd been a Productions' Officer myself many times in my early years with the CID, and it was a job I'd never savoured. POs are the evidential links between locus, post-mortem room and forensic laboratories, and it is their responsibility to ensure that all evidence can be traced back to the locus or victim. And because everything in a Scottish murder case must be corroborated, there are always two officers responsible. Even so, evidence can still go missing between locus and lab, and therefore cases weakened or lost, careers ruined.

'Anything else you need?' Kettle asked.

'A good night's sleep.' The pathologist's laugh was strained and guttural as he mopped his shiny brow with his handkerchief, returned it to his pocket. There were dark bags under his eyes and the top button of his shirt was undone, his tie loosened. 'And food,' he added wearily. 'Bring me food that I may live.'

'McMorran, see Mr Kerr gets something to eat. And once you've IDed the body, I want your report written up and delivered to me personally. Tonight. Omit nothing. Is that understood?'

'Sir.'

Kettle grimaced. What he thought was a smile looked more like a donkey braying. 'And then you can get back to your flock.'

'Thank you, sir.'

'Think he lives on the island?'

'The Fangman?'

'For want of a better name, aye.'

I shook my head. 'He'd have to be totally stupid. You've got his blood group, his DNA fingerprint, his sperm count . . . an island this size, population around four thousand, you're looking for a man in his thirties, you could cut the DNA tests down to a matter of hundreds.'

'And that would still take months.'

'This kind of killer may be a few pebbles short of a beach,' I said, 'but he's not stupid. He's killed seven times already, maybe even more, and with each victim he's becoming more professional. Which is why I don't understand the murder of Arthur Thomas.'

'What's to understand?' Silas Kerr said, shifting uncomfortably in the passenger seat. I'd forgotten to park in the shade at the cottage and we were now two man chops strapped to a speeding grill. All we needed was a damn good basting.

'Why he's suddenly changed his MO.'

'Because Thomas is a man?'

'Exactly. All the other victims were women.'

'It happens,' Kerr sighed. 'Maybe he just fancied a change, or more of a challenge.'

147

'If indeed it was the Fangman.'

'And that, my friend, is what I have yet to determine.'

Brodick's main street was thick with traffic from the ferry, which was now docked with bow raised at the pier. Harsh sunlight glanced off the bay, where a host of small yachts sat stranded beneath colourful limp sails on the sheet of metallic blue. Tourists thronged the pavements, many in shorts and sandals, T-shirts and shades, lugging bags full of shopping or browsing through shops on the hunt for souvenirs. As leather-clad bikers posed on black and chrome wheels, kids dragged parents down to the beach, while hillwalkers with knapsacks headed for the glens. Older generations strolled leisurely along the promenade, basked on benches overlooking the bay, and crammed into the cool oases of oak-beamed tearooms. A lazy summer's afternoon beneath a clear blue sky and here was I, stuck behind a bus unloading German tourists, and on the way to a morgue with a mood overcast by the pall of murder and a sudden, explicable urge for violence. And the name of my pain, as the Joker would say, was Commander Harlan Bloody Kettle.

It was at that moment, though, as I waited to pass through the bottleneck, that, from the corner of my eye and in the shifting current of tourists, I saw movement that caught my attention.

Every street has its natural rhythm. As a cop you subconsciously, and continually, tune into that rhythm. Whether you're aware of it or not, you are constantly assessing the ebb and flow of vehicular and human tides, alert for any break or change in that rhythm, something that doesn't fit, that makes you look twice and twice again. Someone running too fast or walking too slow, or making sudden changes in direction. Furtive glances and mannerisms. Two men sitting in a parked car, perhaps, or a youth carrying a sports bag late at night in a residential area where there's no gymnasium. A man in combat gear carrying a Kalashnikov down the high street, people lying in pools of blood all around. That kind of thing. And like now, a flash of heels in a sprinter's start and a middle-aged woman yelling, 'Stop him, he's got my bag!'

PR in hand, I was out the door and across the road in seconds, the snatcher fifty yards ahead, weaving through straggles of tourists, barging through knots, arms pumping, denim jacket and jeans, mid teens, hair dark and short, white trainers with red soles, me in Docs, gaining all the time now as I found my stride, adrenaline a welcome drug in my veins, the chase on, prey in sight, ever closer, heading along the promenade towards the harbour, sweating hard, feeling good, twenty-five yards and he could hear me now, past the hotels, the mini-golf, the outdoor centre, change of direction, across the road amidst shrieking brakes and blaring horns, his breath ragged, a painful wheeze as he veered left, knocked a cyclist off her mountain bike, lost his stride for a moment, saw me, stumbled on, out on to the pier, the ferry docked at the end, passengers waiting to embark but the gangway withdrawn, dead end, son, end of story, might as well come quietly, no point in adding resisting arrest to a charge of robbery, that's it, face against the wall there, spread your legs, you have the right to remain silent . . .

'Three, four years ago,' Silas Kerr said, twenty minutes later, back in Mike 30, the kid glowering in the back seat behind sullen dark eyes. 'Some kind of detective training course.'

'You have a good memory.'

'For names but not faces. You were a sergeant then, weren't you?'

'Mm,' I said. We climbed into the sun through a forest of pine, heading south towards Lamlash. Best stretch of road on the island for putting the foot down, so I did.

'Of course, I heard what happened . . .'

'Who hasn't?'

'Seemed a little unfair, I must say.'

'Call it the balance of fortune,' I said. 'For one side to go up, the other must go down.'

'Do you miss being a detective?'

'Sometimes. Sometimes often. Depends.'

'On the kind of work?'

'On my mood. Today, for instance. The wee ned there, he commits a crime, I'm right on the spot and give chase, and a couple of minutes later he's captured, there you go, under arrest. That's what uniform work's all about, you're on the front line, the issues are invariably simple, etched in black and white. Somedays I prefer the simplicity of that, instead of like CID work, where quite often you're in the grey area in between, trying to build up cases sitting at a desk, fumbling around in the murk for evidence, perpetrators, proof, corroboration, what have you. Other days, in a different mood, I need the challenge of detection, you know, putting the pieces together, solving the puzzle. Comes down, I suppose, to dominance of left brain, right brain.'

'Or no brain at all,' came the sulky voice from behind.

It was that kind of day. As we dropped down the hill into Lamlash, with the forest giving way to a golf course on the left and Holy Island rising out of the shimmering deep blue of the bay straight ahead, we were all three of us united in laughter in the face of our different adversities.

Murder means overtime. Four days ago I'd thought our Lamlash station could never be described as a teeming hive of activity. This afternoon I was proved wrong. Because of the Thomas murder, Sergeant Yuill, currently leading the door-to-door enquiries with John Tennant, had been forced to call in the island's half a dozen Specials. While two of these remained on standby, two were now out on patrol, leaving two to man the station. Monica was busy on one of the phones, trying to find accommodation for a murder squad whose size was increasing with every incoming ferry, and not having much luck. Meanwhile, DI Fullerton, nominally in charge of the investigation and who'd come across with the first chopper, was now in constant communication with Division at Kilmarnock on the other phone, arranging the setting up of a mobile incident room and computer terminals for HOLMES, the Home Office Large Major Enquiry System.

'Having trouble, luv?' he asked Monica, his hand covering the mouthpiece during a lull in his preparations.

She fired him a look only a sneer short of contempt, and said, 'What you want is a bloody miracle. I mean, with the tourist season well under way and the Arran Festival of Folk starting in the next couple of days, just about all of the island's guest houses and hotels are already fully booked. Have been since last year.'

'How many places have you got then?'

'Ten, doubling up. If you want me to waste another couple of hours phoning round—'

'No need to get your knickers in a twist. If we can't put 'em up on the island, we'll just draft them in on the first ferry and out on the last. Save the taxpayer a small fortune, I imagine.' While Monica glowered, Fullerton turned to me. 'Who's the kid?'

'Bag-snatcher. Caught him in the act.' Danny Calder, the name he'd given me, hung his head at my side.

'Booked him yet?'

I shook my head and asked if the interview room was free.

'Two of my boys in there trying for a little shuteye, been up all night. They'd appreciate another couple of hours. You going to detain him?'

'Depends how helpful he is,' I shrugged. 'I can always hold him on a Section Two if he doesn't cooperate.'

'Sure.' Fullerton nodded absently then tilted his chair so that the back of his head rested against the Early Warning Defence System box. 'I understand you saw Commander Kettle.'

'Yeah. I'm off the enquiry.'

'And out of the firing line. Consider yourself lucky.'

I recalled a notice I'd read recently in the *Arran Banner. Lost –*

black neutered tom, blind in one eye, missing ear and half its tail, answers to the name of Lucky. That's how lucky I felt.

'Find anything up in the woods this morning?' I asked.

'Could be your man McGrath was right,' Fullerton said. 'Three partial prints near the spot you indicated, left heel and right toe deep enough to suggest the watcher might well have squatted there a while. We'll have to wait and see what Forensics come up with. Still, that's no longer your concern, is it.'

'Of course not, sir.' No, I find a murdered body on my beat and just shove it to the back of my mind, never again to let my ingrained curiosity linger for a moment on the consequences. I'm kind of funny that way.

'Good.' He returned his attention to the phone, said, 'Aye, I'm still here. What I suggest you do is . . .'

I turned away and ushered Danny Calder through the back into the lockfast not being used for sleeping accommodation, uncuffed him, told him to sit and be quiet. Then I fetched a folding desk and chair from a cupboard in the hall, told Calder to set them up while I collected from my drawer in the filing cabinet all the forms and papers I would need to keep the bureaucratic wheels of law and order properly lubricated. Finally, I humped through the ancient typewriter, then made two cups of coffee and brought them through to the lockfast.

'What about my rights?' Calder demanded surly.

'You have two. One to a lawyer, the other to call a relative. Unfortunately,' I added, 'there are no lawyers on the island.'

Calder sipped his coffee and grimaced. 'Ugh. How many sugars did you put in that?'

'Two,' I told him. 'Tablespoons. You want to call your father?' We both knew that was the last thing he wanted to do. He shook his head.

'Are you going to charge me?'

'What do you think?' I sorted Detention and Voluntary Booking Forms from Report Forms, then wound one of the latter into the typewriter. Calder could wait, Kettle wouldn't. Fullerton had been right – the sooner free of the bastard, the better I would feel. Cut away those chains of the past.

'You said if I cooperated...'

Danny Calder was fifteen, slight, with curly red hair and freckles, dressed now in denim jacket and jeans. I'd seen him only once before, but for me once is enough.

'How's your pal?' I said. 'Julian Ryder.'

Calder frowned. 'How d'you mean?'

'Think about it,' I told him, and began typing out my report.

16

'Clarity of mind has the same relationship to life that fire has to wood. Fire clings to wood, but also consumes it. Clarity of mind is rooted in life but can also consume it. Everything depends on how the clarity functions.'

Simone.

It's uncanny. The way fate plays its fickle hand. The *I Ching* warning you of this, the Book of Changes, when you threw the bones the other night, all that stuff about finding a companion. So it was no coincidence Hastie walking in your door like she did, right time, right place, right age, right size, right bones, right shape. The only problem is – now that Thomas has forced your hand – Ros Hastie lives on the island. And you don't want lightning striking the same place twice, no sir. The next bone-job would have to be over on the mainland, take the heat away. Taking the old man's throat had been a mistake, you realise that now. It was that sheep business, though, getting you all in the mood so that you had to go trawling, make a strangle out of old man Thomas, take his fucking throat out. One mistake compounding another, and you didn't even get a bone-job out of him. You're slipping, man, slipping. Better beware. This whatsername, Ros, put her on the back burner, let her simmer awhile. No immediate hurry. Take your time, suss her out. Treat her as a long-term investment. The longer you defer your gratification, the sweeter she will taste. As you know from your experience with Simone all those years ago.

Five to be precise.

Five years? Feels like ten. Like almost the same day you walked out of the Aphelion Centre for the last time. All those years in between – what happened to them? Blank, you realise, gone. Like sometimes you can only recall from one kill to the next. Hyperamnesia they call it. Said so in one of those books you just finished about serial killers. *The memory of specific, tiny details disassociated from a larger event always forgotten*. Take life as the 'larger event', a strangle as a 'specific, tiny detail', and yeah, that was you when the fever took you, a hyperamnesiac.

But you still remember Simone the way you first met her.

Long red hair, falling straight as the Angel Falls to her waist as she came round the desk to greet you. One shy peek in her large green eyes and somehow you knew it was going to happen with her, the promise there as bold as sunlight, and she had you from that moment on, you were hers and there was nothing you could do about it.

'You're going to be my star,' she had purred, holding your hand as though to kiss it, her touch electric, voice husky, smile awry. 'In my firmament, you, Gideon, shall shine the brightest.'

And from that moment on how you wanted to shine!

You were fourteen then, nearly fifteen, had been up in front of the Children's Panel for a couple of B&Es and your social worker had made a big thing about you being the product of a broken home – alcoholic mother in Carstairs, father dead – and how sensitive you were, how intelligent and creative, how you ought to be given the opportunity to express yourself in a positive manner, through art, or music, or writing, rather than get banged away in an approved school where your natural talents would be suppressed, perhaps buried for ever by an insensitive disciplinarian regime, blah blah blah. No, what you needed was something like

The Aphelion Centre . . .

the fucking what?

. . . a new approach to certain young offenders, revolutionary

156

one might say. It's run independently as a charity, is a kind of spiritual school, with disciplines that encourage positive expression of self through the arts and meditation in a learning environment that is neither threatening nor punitive.

Yah, super.

But you have to admit it changed your life.

You're not sure what first attracted you to pottery – you were still too young then to appreciate the pull of the subconscious, the suck of the Moon – but when you made your decision you had no idea Simone was to be your tutor. Maybe you just felt the need to occupy your hands – huge nervous hands that you clenched, clenched, clenched even then.

The urge . . . well, that didn't disappear, did it? Carved like an ugly scar into your psyche, it was always too deep to heal or forget. Some days you could feel it pulsing like a heartbeat down there in the forgetness, a dark presence lurking, or perhaps asleep or hibernating. And sometimes it would awake; and then you could sense its awesome power, feel its desperate hunger, its absolute need for bloody expression. You feared its demands, yet at the same time you came to need them: at once afraid of its potency as you were excited by it. The Forbidden Fruit Syndrome. Taste it, yes, but confront the issues, not a chance. At least not yet, you would reason, better let it sleep, this malevolent beast, feed it on snacks every now and then when it stirred, tidbits like Zeus, the Centre's cat, and Hector the senile Labrador

ding-dong

some local kids had found staked out in The Copse, a haunt for teeny gropers back then before the dopers moved in and began leaving their used spikes among the pine needles for anyone to sit on.

Better go serve the tourists.

Simone would talk about *le petit mort* and *le grand mort* as though one could be fully experienced without the other. She never really did understand your ... condition. For you they have always been one and the same, inextricably linked. She would lie there and make fun of you, not quite the same way your mother used to, but it was still there beneath the surface with Simone, this sense of superiority, trying to make you feel ashamed of your impotence, laughing, yes, all in fun, yes, but looking at you like you're not all there – bitches all of them, really, under the skin – and you loved her, that's what made it hurt, you loved Simone like she was the air you breathed and without her you would die, and when she laughed, each laugh would pierce your heavy heart like a white-hot rapier and she must've seen it in your eyes but still she'd do it again and again until inevitably she woke the thing inside you and you could bear it no longer, your brain suddenly ready to explode, like it was trapped inside a skull too small to hold it, and you'd haul on your clothes as she continued to laugh, at your anger now, saying things like *C'mon, Giddy, don't take it so seriously, you're overreacting* and crap like that and all you want to do is knock her sprawling across the bed, burst her fucking mouth with your fists, see how funny she thought that was, but instead, no, you'd bolt from her room on a wave of tears, make a headlong dash down into the cellar where no one ever went, down into the dark among the rats and the packing cases and the smell of oil and wood and paint, crawl into the corner at the back by the old creaking boiler where you'd made yourself a nest, a refuge from the storms above, where you'd curl up in the blankets and close your eyes and sink softly into cunts far more satisfying than Simone's could ever be, fantasies that were warm and inviting where you were the hero with a thousand guises out to save the world from calculating bitches who didn't understand that there were certain things more powerful than the flesh, higher laws and orders to be obeyed. You were a soldier then, and you are a soldier still.

And someone had to pay.

The Centre had a cat. It was a friendly mog, loved by

everyone. Simone had found it one day down on the beach, a kitten then, one of five left to drown in a leaky old sports bag down at the low-tide mark. She'd wanted to save them all but couldn't, had chosen Zeus because of the white spot around its left eye, the rest of its fur being black. Had brought it back to the Centre, to be fussed over and overfed. Everyone adored Zeus.

Until Simone wound you up just a notch too far, and you ended up in front of the Centre's Panel.

There were questions they wanted answered. They wanted to know how Zeus got into the kiln in the first place. And why you hadn't noticed Zeus before closing the door, or heard his shrieks as the temperature climbed slowly through the hundreds. Why you hadn't questioned the acrid stench of burning flesh, or thought the seeping smoke strange, somewhat amiss. Yes, they had a lot of questions.

And you had just as many answers.

They hadn't of course believed you. Not one of your puerile explanations. Had finally accepted them, sure, but believed them, no. Had made you well aware of their suspicions, because that was their way, to confront issues rather than hide from them. And you could live with that, because what they called guilt, you called satisfaction.

But they could've asked Simone why Zeus had to die. She might have been able to tell them because she was beginning to get the picture by then. But she never let on, did she, not to any of the others. Maybe all that guilt she was trying to lay on to you rebounded on herself. Maybe she even felt responsible – what you wanted her to feel. If so, she should have learned her lesson. She should have remembered it last time you saw her.

What happened to Zeus.

17

'**N**o way, McMorran.'

'Why the hell not? I mean, you need someone local who knows what's going on, someone the locals can trust, talk to. It makes sense. It's not like I'm asking to be involved in the house-to-house or even command the enquiry, just to be involved, that's all. Man the phones in there or do something, *any*thing. Christ, even make the bloody tea.'

We were standing by the door of one of the two mobile incident rooms set up in the car park of the Arran Heritage Museum at Rosaburn, at the foot of The String. Follow that burn back up the hill a thousand yards and you'd come within fifty of Arthur Thomas's cottage, Ravensbank. Sun high, wispy clouds high, another warm day, another foul mood.

'No way,' Sergeant Yuill repeated. 'I thought Commander Kettle made that quite clear to you yesterday. He wants you out of the picture completely.'

'If not permanently.'

'Well, that seems to be your special talent, McMorran, winding people up the wrong way. With Kettle you seem to have excelled yourself.'

'Flattery will get you nowhere.' An audience of sparrows watched us from a telephone wire, the mild breeze ruffling shirtsleeves and feathers alike.

'And where are you now?' Yuill said, just managing to restrain a sneer. 'Exactly. On the trail of a sheep-shagger, reduced to apprehending teenage bag-snatchers and handing out traffic tickets. Somewhere City, McMorran, you really know how to hit the big time.'

'So why are *you* here?'

'I don't have the illusions of grandeur you city cops love to wield like claymores. I happen to know my limitations.'

Yeah, and ultimately the success of most police work relies heavily on such men. I was just being unfair, giving Yuill a hard time because I had to give someone a hard time – Kettle wasn't here. He was, I understood, grooming himself for the Commander Kettle Show, a five-minute slot on the lunchtime news, *and here's your host with the most, the delightful, the delicious, the most delectable hunk of law enforcement patrolling the streets and keeping us safe from the powers of evil this side of Mel Gibson, here he is, the one and only, Haaaar-lan Kettle.*

Not.

'Aye, well . . .' I said, coming as close as I could to an apology on a morning like this. I watched for a moment a file of young hillwalkers tramp past the entrance to the car park then, nodding towards the north and the cottage at Glen Rosa, asked what was happening up at the locus.

Yuill removed his cap, ran stubby fingers through his grey hair, and sighed. 'You tell me. Must have had at least a hundred officers across on the first ferry this morning. Fullerton mentioned a search of the woods above the cottage – the way he thinks the killer came down – and this afternoon I'm to help coordinate the first stage of house-to-house enquiries. Personally, I don't see why you're complaining; you and Monica will probably be the most relaxed coppers on the island come last light.'

'Monica too?'

'She's like you, McMorran, too fucking sensitive for her own good. Man just has to look at her funny and she's grinding his balls like grist on a mill.' Yuill sighed again and repositioned his cap. 'Best thing the pair of you can do is lay low, try not to rub anyone up the wrong way. Concentrate on your outstanding enquiries.'

'I found your case file on Ryder in my drawer this morning.'

'Aye, it's all yours. At least until I'm reassigned normal duties.' Yuill started to speak but broke off as two plainclothes detectives emerged from the incident room and, ignoring us completely, stretched and smoked for several minutes before climbing into the second mobile. Only then did Yuill continue. 'Did you have any luck with the Calder kid last night?'

I shook my head. 'He's pally with Ryder all right, but not so pally, he says, that he knows everything Ryder does. I tried to sell him the cooperation line but he wasn't buying, must've been watching too much Taggart.'

'First offence, probable fine, there's not much there you can offer or threaten him with. Does he know Julia Wallace?'

'Says he knows her, sure, but only from school, to look at, has never actually spoken to her. On the night in question, he claims he was out with his folks, a ceilidh night at the Corrie village hall. I'll check that out later.'

'Do that.'

'And the sheep stabbings?' I asked. 'You want I continue with that?'

'Of course. Are you any further forward?'

'I'll maybe head up the Distillery this afternoon, have a word with whatsisface. Farquharson.' I hadn't yet told Yuill of my interview with John French, nor about Farquharson's partiality for urine facials, too much happening in the last couple of days to even spare it a thought. But now...

Yuill sucked in air through clenched teeth. 'Softly softly. McMorran. I'm warning you. That's one vicious wee monkey I don't want to catch anywhere near my back. If you've got a single microbe of diplomacy in your bones, I want you to find it and use it. That's an order.'

'Of course, sir.' How I relish orders.

A car turned in through the gates. 'Speak of the devil . . .' Yuill muttered.

. . . and he's sure to come screeching to a halt almost on your toes in a silver-grey Range Rover.

Yuill grabbed my arm. 'And for God's sake, McMorran, don't mention his height. Last year he sued the Council for building the pavements too close to his arse. He's that sensitive.'

I didn't doubt it. The man who jumped down from the Range Rover was most definitely on the midget side of short, the top of his head coming almost up to my right nipple. Power-dressed in a creamy lightweight suit, moccasin-style slip-ons and shades on a cord, Findlay Farquharson exuded the kind of aggressive energy often mistaken for power. With thinning dark hair slicked back from his forehead and tied in a pony tail that barely touched his collar, fleshy lips, uneven teeth, blob nose and crescent eyes in a round tanned face, Farquharson looked like a sickly cocktail of Bob Hoskins, Danny de Vito and Clive James. Like his mother, he wore jewellery as ballast: heavy gold rings like knuckledusters, a simple gold cross round his neck, and a chunky gold Seiko which was, unlike Yuill's, the real thing. He spoke to it now, as he came round the bonnet.

'Haven't got time to fart about, Sergeant, what's the score?'

'Score, sir?'

'Got half the bloody police force trampling over my land in size tens, and do I get a single by-your-leave? I do not. Score as in score on the door, Sergeant, like what the fuck is going on, why have I not been consulted?'

'I'm sorry, Mr Farquharson, but I'm sure you can understand things have been a little hectic here since we found Thomas's body.'

Farquharson looked genuinely surprised for a second, crescent eyes becoming fleeting full moons. 'Body? You mean the old fool's, what, dead?'

'Don't you watch TV?' I said. 'It's been headline news for the last two days.'

'TV's for morons, I've got better things to do with my time. Anyway, who asked you?'

Little men with big cars and enormous egos who hide behind expensive shades and point stubby bejewelled fingers in my direction tend to find my temper short.

'This is a murder investigation, Mr Farquharson, we don't need to ask your permission for anything. I suggest you climb back in your car and go home, and when we need to talk to you, we'll let you know.'

'McMorran,' Yuill ordered, 'that's enough.'

Farquharson snatched off his shades and glared at me until recognition dawned. Finger stabbing the air, he growled, 'So you're the brain-dead PC's been pestering my mother, wasting my workers' time. McMorran. Right. There's a name I promise I won't forget.'

Yuill, his tone mild and placatory, said. 'There are still a few points we need to clear up, Mr Farquharson, regarding this business with the sheep. Perhaps you could arrange a time with the Constable here . . .'

Farquharson glowered, then glanced at his watch as though swinging a southpaw. 'Too busy. It'll have to wait.'

'Next week?'

'If you really must. Speak to my secretary. Tell her half an hour, McMorran, that's all you're getting.' Farquharson swung round on Yuill, cutting me out. 'Right, Sergeant, about the cottage. Your estimation. How long's this going to take, when can I move a new tenant in?'

I should have guessed.

I nodded to Yuill, then crossed to my bike, pulled on my leather jacket and substituted cap for helmet. Although riding my bike in uniform was normally against regulations, due to the abnormal circumstances and the fact that all our cars had been commandeered by the murder squad, I had been grudgingly granted permission to do so as long as my uniform remained mostly concealed. No problem on a shirtsleeve day like today. I started up, turned left out the gates, and headed north along the coast road, taking my time.

On the north shore of Brodick Bay and below the castle stands the Old Quay, relic of the times when Brodick was situated there – rather than on the south side of the bay as it is today – and livestock, goods and passengers would all come ashore at the quay. The tiny stone harbour, though, probably didn't stink so sulphurously bad then. On past the castle gates, passing families on mountain bikes, families on foot, to Merkland Point where glossy seals basked on shoreline rocks as a pair of herons waded nearby, the creeping forest of rhododendron falling back from the roadside now as the sun burnished the golden hills on distant Bute, came blinding in off the Clyde. How, I wondered, could I ever miss the city?

And yet I did, often. Nights, mostly.

The next few miles I was happy to cruise along behind a wagon-train of caravans, let the breeze aerate my mind. I was taking things too personally, getting wound up over nothing. Did I really want to spend the day on hands and knees combing the forest above Ravensbank Cottage, or tramping round the village knocking on door after door and hearing the same reply, though in different forms, nothing, zilch, I'm sorry, Officer, fuck all? No, I did not. There was nothing I could do or add that would make a sod's worth of difference, so why worry, why let that bastard Kettle get under my skin, restring my nerves to tournament pitch? Why indeed?

Corrie. For me the most beautiful village on the island, for Prime Minister Herbert Henry Asquith no less than Europe. You see High Corrie first, a cluster of cottages situated on the kind of raised beach more common on the south of the island, where waves used to pound the hundred-foot cliffs behind. The village of Corrie itself is spread amidst verdant splendour along the shoreline below, where white cottages and bungalows are set

166

back from the road, and red sandstone houses stand in grounds boasting eucalyptus and palm. The quay – built of the same white sandstone mined in the now disused quarries above the village – today offered anchorage to a few small yachts and dinghies, and on the grass nearby, a group of German bikers were picnicking alongside a young girl camcording a collie chasing its tail near the swings. Turning the corner, the road narrowed to squeeze past a tidy row of cottages with postage-stamp front gardens. I pulled over and parked on a small patch of grass by the Ferry Rock, alongside which half a dozen small boats were moored. The blue Sierra that had been in my mirror since Brodick sped on by.

In the village hall, I arrived just as a Ladies' Aerobics Class was warming down, and after much distraction eventually managed to corner a woman on the Management Committee and persuade her that the future of the hall's activities would not be in dire jeopardy if she allowed me to consult the year's Events Diary. I verified that a ceilidh had indeed taken place on the night Danny Calder had claimed, then asked her if she or anyone else would be able to verify his story. She said she didn't know, not herself, but would ask her colleagues on the committee, what was the date again? I left her with the date, my name and number, then strolled leisurely back down to my bike. Sat on the saddle awhile, looking out across the Clyde, wondering what it was like in the old, old days when it took twelve hours to cross from Ardrossan to Brodick by smack. Not so full of tourists then, for sure.

'Francis!'

I recognised the voice, the way she walked as she came down the road towards me, finally her face beneath mirrored shades and floppy hat – but not the glunk she had in tow. Mid leap, my heart faltered and fell. Both were in T-shirts and shorts, wore hiking boots and carried knapsacks. 'Hi,' I said.

Kyoko unslung her knapsack, dumped it on the grass, sighed

dramatically. 'I'm shattered already and I've only been *looking* at Goatfell.'

She looked so good, my eyeballs ached. 'You making the climb?' I asked, nodding towards the mountain's eastern flank rising behind the village.

'Not today, thank God. I have to meet my uncle later. Just call this training.' Kyoko glanced at her companion. 'This is Dave, by the way. He's from somewhere in Wales I can't pronounce without drowning you in spit.'

'Llangollen,' the Neanderthal said. He was your typical rugby supporter but with eyes that could focus. Our greetings were grunts a million years old and his grip as fierce as a man-eating mason.

'This is Francis,' Kyoko told him, 'the policeman I was telling you about.' Now our dislike was entirely mutual. 'The one we saw on TV last night.' She noticed my look of surprise. 'You didn't know?'

I shook my head. I'd come off shift at the back of ten and spent the rest of the night in the hotel bar responding to Alec Brodie's multiple theories on the Fangman's multiple killings with monosyllabic replies while hoping any moment the door would open and Kyoko walk in. No such luck. I hurled a glance full of dislike at the musclehead.

'You were on traffic duty,' she said, removing her shades.

'I was?'

'Near where that murder was committed. I almost didn't recognise you in your uniform.' She began polishing her shades with the tail of her T-shirt. 'Are you involved in the hunt?'

'Sadly,' I said, 'not. They've brought in all the experts from the mainland.'

'I thought *you* were the expert. All that talk the other day . . .'

'Night,' I corrected, with a smile for Dave.

'. . . about how you tracked down the Hangman and cornered him on some lonely clifftop, then dragged his murdering ass off to jail, what about that? Were you just trying to impress me, or what?'

I'd been drunk, but hadn't realised I'd been playing-to-the-audience drunk: fanning her flames. Still, sober or drunk, you say what it takes. Old schoolyard maxim.

'No lie,' I told her. 'Maybe running off at the mouth a bit, but what the hell, we had a good time.' Another benevolent smile for Dave. Kiss on that. Day was getting better by the minute.

'Well, yeah,' Kyoko said, 'I suppose.' With about a millionth the conviction I was hoping for. Dave grinned. Day was getting worse by the second. Where was my PR when I needed it? 'But another murder, Francis! It's just like you were saying, almost *prophetic*.'

'I only said he was due another kill soon. I never imagined it would be so soon or so close to home.'

'But it is the same guy?'

'Post-mortem was last night,' I said. 'They should have the results by now.' I glanced at my watch; half an hour till the lunchtime news. Time to cut losses and cut loose. 'Anyway . . .'

Her dark eyes opened like lips to a kiss. 'You have to go?'

I could have stayed all day bathing in those deep pools of her eyes. But not with Dave looking on. 'Work,' I said, donning my helmet. The Neanderthal curled his lip. 'Well, enjoy your training,' I added, 'and next time I see you I'll tell you about the Goatfell Murder.'

'There was a murder up there?'

I flashed her a smile. 'Over dinner, perhaps?'

She glanced again at Dave. 'We'll see,' she said noncommittally. Which was enough for me. I released the clutch and accelerated up the road.

Clear of Sannox a few miles further on and with the road climbing west devoid of traffic, I opened the throttle wide and hit the ton cresting the rise, feeling ecstatic, the joyful vibrancy that is the essence of life, like I was flying across the top of the world. Dropped down the winding road into Lochranza at a more sedate forty, only to find the same blue Sierra that had passed me in Corrie looming large in my mirror again. When I turned left through the Distillery gates at the foot of the hill, again the Sierra flashed by, the sun reflecting off its windows making any kind of physical ID impossible beyond the fact that it contained two men in shades. I memorised the reg out of habit, parked my bike by the burn, then crossed the log bridge to the shop.

Flora Farquharson was in Glasgow for the weekend, Maggie told me, Archie was most likely in his office having lunch and Findlay had left maybe an hour ago and probably wouldn't be back till Monday. I told her that was no problem, I'd spoken to the man himself and was to arrange a meeting for next week through his secretary.

'Secretary?' Maggie snorted. 'Chance would be a fine thing.' She was a large bustling woman with a plain round face and long mousy hair centre-parted and held behind her neck with a bulky wooden clasp. Standing behind the shop counter, heavy breasts resting on the ledge of her crossed arms, she shook her head and said, 'A very fine thing. No. Instead Muggins here does all his paperwork while he sits behind his desk doing what he does best – nothing. What is it you want?'

'An hour of his time sometime next week.'

'Hold on.' Maggie disappeared through the door marked Private, returned seconds later with a large desk diary. 'Mm, Let's see what he's doing next week. Well, Monday nothing, Tuesday nothing, a meeting on Wednesday, Thursday nothing, Friday nothing, and then a half-day. So, take your pick, Officer, when do you want to make the big man sweat?'

'Monday,' I said. 'I hate Mondays.'

'Good, so does he. Morning or afternoon?'

'Early morning.'

'Eleven o'clock, then.' She made a note in the diary, slammed it shut. 'Okay, you're down. Anything else?'

'A look at your personnel records, if I may. For the last year.'

'Temps, you mean?'

'Full-time, too.'

'Is this about the sheep?'

I told her yes. The shop doorbell rang and a group of tourists filed in, began circulating the shelves of souvenirs. Maggie told them to feel free to look around, then returned her attention to me.

'They're on the computer. You want to read them off the screen or shall I print them out?'

'Would you, please?'

'Come back in twenty minutes.'

Archie was indeed in his office and had just finished his lunch. 'Ah,' he said, 'the mainland man.' Then told me to pull up a seat while he cleared away the dishes, would I join him in a dram? I told him I shouldn't and he told me I would anyway.

'You say you know your malts,' he said, placing two glasses and a labelless bottle on the desk. 'Let's see if you can wrap your nose round this one, tell me what it is.' He poured the two measures, pushed one of them across to me. 'Slainthé.'

'Slainthé,' I said, holding it to my nose. 'Mm, peaty.' Sun splashed through the window on to the desk, the sound of the burn a contented chuckle on the sluggish breeze. There was a handbasin in one corner, two gunmetal-grey filing cabinets in another, a bank of shelves in between, sagging beneath box folders and stacks of books and files. On top of one of the filing cabinets sat a portable black-and-white TV, on, but sound down low. I took a sip of the malt, let it linger on my palate awhile before swallowing. Its course down my throat was smooth and warm, with no phenolic aftertastes.

'One of the island malts,' I ventured. 'I'd say Islay.'

Archie chuckled, tapped his stubby forefinger on the bottle. 'Aye, but which one?'

I ran the eight through my mind. Ruled out the Ardbeg and Laphraoig for their very distinctive tastes, and the Port Ellen and Bowmore for their dryness, found myself left with the Bunnahabhain, Caol Ila, Lagavulin and Bruichladich. The latter two being among my all-time favourites, which this was not, left me a choice of two.

'Bunnahabhain,' I said.

Archie shook his head. 'Caol Ila.'

'Close.'

'Neighbours, in fact. You like it?'

'Indeed.' I nodded at the TV. 'Mind if I turn this up?'

'Feel free.' Archie reached across and raised the volume. Behind a barrage of microphones, Commander Kettle was under siege.

'While there are some distinct similarities in MO, there still exist one or two areas of uncertainty, and while most indications would suggest that Arthur Thomas is the seventh known victim of the man popularly referred to as the Fangman, we are not ruling out the possibility that this may be a copycat killing.'

'Are you saying then, Commander, that you don't really know whether this is the work of the Fangman or not, that you might now be looking for two different killers?'

'All I'm saying right now is we're keeping all our options open.'

'Can you give us any details contained within the pathologist's report, Commander?'

'We believe Mr Thomas was killed late on Monday afternoon. As far as we can ascertain, he died of manual strangulation.'

'Was there any damage to his throat?'

'If you're referring to the Fangman's trademark, there was some damage, yes.'

'Had he been decapitated?'

'No.'

'Do you have any suspects?'

'We are following several promising lines of enquiry at the moment.'

'Do you think the killer may be living on Arran?'

'As of yet, we have no solid indication of where the killer might be

172

living. *Recent studies in America have shown that serial killers love to drive and that they often clock up hundreds of miles in their constant trawling for potential victims. As evidenced by the fact that the Fangman has now killed as far north as Largs and as far south as Cockermouth, near the Cumbrian coast, we cannot rule out the possibility that this man may well be a travelling salesman or lorry driver or someone whose line of work brings him to these areas but who is perhaps based elsewhere.'*

'You mean he could be living anywhere in Britain?'

'I'd go so far as to say North Britain.'

'Do you have a psychological profile of the Fangman yet, Commander?'

'We do, and we'll be bringing it up to date once we have fully assembled and considered all the new evidence. I'm sure you'll be the first to know. Next.'

'Is there any truth in the rumour that the psychic Mungo Spinks has been asked to help in the enquiry?'

'No truth whatsoever.'

'But he has visited the sites where the bodies were found?'

'I believe that to be the case.'

'And will you consider any conclusions he draws?'

'As seriously, yes, as we consider all information offered by members of the public. Next.'

'Have you received much response to your last Crimewatch appeal, Commander?'

'Not as much as we'd obviously prefer but new information is still coming in and, like I said earlier, there are several promising avenues of enquiry which we are presently pursuing.'

'Is there anything specific you would like to ask the public?'

'Yes. We're still trying to piece together the last two or three weeks in the life of Arthur Thomas, so anyone who has been in contact with him during this period, we'd ask them to please come forward. Naturally, all information we receive will be treated in the strictest of confidence.'

'Commander Kettle, the officer leading the hunt for the man who *has already killed seven times. Meanwhile, in Sussex, fears continue for the safety of three-year-old Jason Fairley, who disappeared three days ago while out shopping with his mother. This report comes from...'*

I lowered the volume, returned to my seat.

Archie said, 'I mind the old days when there used to be news on the news. Now all you get is one murder after another, the next one always more horrific than the last. Like we're spawning a nation of killer babies. Those two kids last year in Liverpool, that lassie in Glasgow, that twelve-year-old in Birmingham, I mean, we're talking mindless murders by schoolyard killers, kids who don't even understand what death is.' Archie sighed and shook his head. 'Anyway, I imagine you'll be on double-time for a while, all this business going on.'

'I'm the lucky one,' I told him. 'I get to continue my life of ease.'

'You still investigating that sheep business?'

'Looks like a dead end,' I said, playing it down. 'I talked to John French the other day, drew a blank there, so I've now got Maggie printing out a list of all your recent personnel. But, between you and me, I don't hold out much hope.'

'Have you spoken to Farquharson yet?'

'Briefly,' I said. 'Nice man.'

'Aye,' Archie replied with heavy sarcasm, 'one of the best. Made me bury that bloody sheep right up the hill there, didn't want it contaminating his land, he said. Took me four hours to drag it up there and plant it, middle of that storm, Wednesday, I think it was. I told him it's not my job to bury sheep. I'm Head bloody Stillman here, that's what it says on my contract, not Official bloody Sheep-Burier. He told me I could either bury that sheep or bury my chances of future employment on the island, take my pick. What could I do?'

'What you did,' I said in commiseration. 'I imagine you got a better look at it, though, having to do all that.'

'You imagine right. Couldn't eat the whole day.'

'I was trying to remember last night – writing up my report – whether its throat had been cut. Did you happen to notice?'

'Couldn't help it. Bloody thing stared at me every time I looked at it.' Archie shuddered, wiped his calloused hands on the legs of his blue overalls. 'Cut, aye, possibly. But with a very blunt knife, I'd say, or one of those ones with a jagged edge. Looked almost ripped, if you know what I mean, like torn apart. Not a pretty sight.'

The image of Arthur Thomas sprang to mind. I asked Archie if he thought an eagle could have inflicted such wounds.

'Don't see why not. There's a pair of them nesting up Glen Catacol I see once in a while from the back of my cottage. You think that's what happened?'

'It's possible. Still,' I shrugged, 'we may never know.'

'It won't have impressed the Japs though.'

'What Japs?'

'The ones looking over the Distillery,' Archie said, as though it were a matter of common knowledge. Perhaps it was. 'They're over here for a couple of weeks, directors or something of some distribution company back in Japan.'

'The Farquharsons are selling out?'

'Expanding, I think is the word. Though don't ask me. I'm just the sheep-burier around here. Ask Farquharson, he'll tell you. Or maybe he won't. It's his pet project, you see, all very hush-hush, matter of national security.'

'You've been sworn to secrecy?'

It was Archie's turn to shrug. 'Threatened with the sack is how I would describe it.' He tilted the bottle of malt at my empty glass. 'Sure I can't persuade you?'

I wasn't sure at all, so I thanked him and left before persuasion sank its deadly claws into the willing flesh of my feeble resistance. I collected the printout from Maggie, stowed it in my pannier, rode down into the village of Lochranza.

Some days the road's like a slalom, the gates white and woolly, staring at you blankly from incurious black faces as you try to manoeuvre around them. They graze alongside the golf course and on the grassy peninsula around the ruined medieval castle but today there were only two of them to avoid in the middle of the road. I parked by a phone box, called Monica at the station and asked her to run a quick PNC check through Division, said I'd phone back in a while. I then performed a superhero's swift identity change, swapping helmet and leather jacket for cap and PR. Searched through the folder of forms and papers I'd removed from my desk, retrieved the copy complaint I was looking for, then locked both panniers and crossed the road. I saw no blue Sierra in sight.

The bungalow was set back from the road behind a busy tearoom, was modern, painted white, with a tiny square of cropped lawn each side of the flagstone path. I rang the bell and waited. A copy complaint is a notice served on someone required to attend court to answer a charge made against them. This complaint was for a twenty-year-old joyrider lucky to be alive. He'd got pickled one Saturday night in a disco down in Whiting Bay, had succeeded in pulling a geology student who was over for Easter and staying in the youth hostel there. Had wanted to impress her, show her a few midnight sights before reclining the seats and working on her midnight sighs. Found himself a Beetle – best he could manage at such short notice, keys hidden in the exhaust – drove her down to Kildonan beach, tried a handbrake skid at forty, misjudged his timing and sent the car tumbling down the bank to settle upside down, wedged between sand and rock. She suffered concussion and a broken arm and nose, he nothing but a squashed ego. He opened the door now, barefoot in jeans with hair tousled and eyes rimmed with sleep. Read the complaint between a series of yawns, folded it, said, 'So what happens now?'

'You go to court, you tell your story, they believe you or they don't.'

176

'Will I lose my licence?'

'Yes,' I said. 'At least I hope so.'

Duty done, I returned to my bike, sat there waiting for a woman in the phone box to run out of breath, money or both. Tourists milled everywhere: amongst the sheep around the castle, up and down the main street of the village and around the pier where already a line of cars had formed awaiting the ferry from Claonaig. I could see it now cutting across the breeze-ruffled Sound, a speck of white against silvered blue, the hills of Kintyre freckled in ochre beyond.

'Afternoon, Officer.'

'Afternoon, sir,' I replied. One of my good days.

'Some castle.' He wore a bright Hawaiian shirt and shorts over an expanse of belly, high-top Nikes, no socks, camcorder in one beefy hand, wife in the other, almost a perfect mirror image. 'Kinda old, ain't it?'

Overenthusiastic, overweight and over here. I smiled.

'No one knows who built it, nor when. Thirteenth century, maybe earlier. There's a similar one across at Skipness,' I added, pointing north of the approaching ferry. I glanced towards the phone box, saw the woman there shovelling more coins into the slot. I was doomed.

Mr and Mrs Falconburger, he told me, extending his now wifeless hand, express outta Houston, Texas, US of A only three days ago and having, hell, the time of their lives. Yes sir. Over here for the first time ever, got ancestors sailed out to Canada on the brig *Caledonia*, you know, from Lamlash way back in 1829, something to do with them 'clearings' was going on at the time. Some of the family settled south of Quebec in Megantic County, y'hear, but his kin, hell no, they was pioneers, had enough of the cold, headed south, ended up in Houston when it was little more than a couple a shacks in a sea of shifting sand. Yes sir, and now here they were, on vacation, see if they could dig up a few roots.

Falconburger, I thought. Not exactly a common surname on the island. Nevertheless, as the woman in the phone box finally

177

hung up, I wished them both happy holidays and squeezed into the booth. Called the Lamlash station again. Monica answered.

'Registered to a James Orwell Slater,' she said. 'Home address—'

'Don't bother,' I told her. 'That's all I need to know.'

'Has his occupation down as journalist.'

'For want of a worse word. Thanks, Monica.'

'Problems?'

'Not any more.'

'It may just be coincidence, Frank, or else my ultra-suspicious mind at work here, but I just received a message for you from a guy called Archie McDonald. He asked me to tell you that he's just had a reporter nosing about the Distillery, asking a lot of questions about you. Could it be the same one, I ask?'

'Almost certainly,' I told her. 'Said I'd give him an angle on the Thomas enquiry yesterday just to get him off my back. Looks like he took my non-appearance personally, is now scratching about for his own angle.'

'Does that not worry you?'

'About a few column-centimetres' worth, no more. How's it going at the station?'

'Exciting as hell. I even get to answer the phone when it rings.'

'Me, I'm giving guided tours.'

'At least you're in the sun. When'll you be back?'

'Couple of hours. Two more routine calls at Blackwaterfoot and that's me.'

'You know we're both down for the night shift?'

I told her aye, Yuill had already informed me.

'Fucking great,' she said. 'I've had to ring Bobby, tell him this weekend's out of the question. He was not very happy, I tell you. Neither am I, come to think of it. That's six, almost seven weeks now.'

'He'll wait.'

'Aye, but can I?'

'Which reminds me,' I said. 'I was wondering if you knew the difference between pizza and sex.'

I could almost hear her frowning. 'I don't, no.'

'In that case, why don't we go for a pizza tonight?'

'Frank?' she said. 'Get a personality.'

18

'That which is bright rises twice: The image of FIRE. Thus the great man, by perpetuating this brightness, Illumines the four quarters of the world.'

It is dawn. The second dawn since Gideon began firing midnight on Friday. He has not slept. Has passed through fatigue into mild hallucination. To the west, smoke from his woodfire kiln twists into a sky that is bright and alive with stars. He can see life's energy flow, iridescent over the Moor and encircling hills. He feels wired, plugged in, every sensory receptor ajangle with the force of his existence. Dawn's chorus already in full song and carried on the cool breeze across the Moor from the tree-shaded pools of Machrie Water.

He sits in the centre of the stones. Three of them, towering over him, the tallest about five and a half metres high. Like giant Stone Age spearheads thrust through the earth's crust and blunted by a millennium's elements, crude now against a skyline crystal cut by the sharp morning light. In about half an hour the tip of the tallest will light like some magical torch as the sun crests Ard Bheinn, crowns it in gold. Then it will be time to return to the kiln, begin the final and most demanding phase of the firing.

They call him *monster*. A vicious beast, a sadistic pervert. They know nothing about him, yet they judge him, have already judged him. Gideon, who has spent a lifetime watching them, these impotent cocks and gaudy hens strutting their self-indulgent stuff, wielding shabby TV values like bludgeons in their soap-operatic lives, their pearls of wisdom nothing but paste as they chomp their senseless existence into three-minute bites, content to paddle for ever in the putrid shallows of their minds. There is no bliss in ignorance, only fatal ignorance.

For example. The day before yesterday the commander of the murder squad had exhibited his absolute ignorance for all to see on national TV. Naturally Gideon recorded it – as he does every news programme after a strangle. See the nature of his opposition, how far they're progressing in their futile investigations. Try to read between the lines, fathom the mentality of those hunting him down. So he replays the news conference in his mind, sifting it again for the unsaid.

'We believe Mr Thomas was killed late on Monday afternoon. As far as we can ascertain, he died of manual strangulation.'

Right, and right again. The old fart was already dead by the time Gideon tasted his throat, but not so long gone that the blood hadn't flowed. Well, oozed.

'Had he been decapitated?'

'No.'

No time, no point. Gideon hadn't come prepared for a cropping, had left his toolbox in the chamber.

'Do you have any suspects?'

'We are following several promising lines of enquiry at the moment.'

In layman's terms, they were stumbling around in the dark with their dicks in their hands. If they had anything at all, an arrest would be 'imminent'.

'Do you think the killer may be living on Arran?'

'As of yet, we have no solid indication of where the killer might be living. Recent studies in America have shown that serial killers love to drive and that they often clock up hundreds of miles in their constant trawling for potential victims.'

Too true. Sometimes Gideon spends days on the road, driving

182

it doesn't matter where, just following his instinct, checking out supermarkets, secluded lanes, houses tucked away in neat residential areas away from the road. Dump sites, ditches. Behind the wheel of his Subaru he can drift from fantasy to fantasy, free to follow his will, the power of such freedom a heady drug in his veins. Nights he sleeps in the car, rising early. Delivers his pots to retailers and craft fairs in the morning – sometimes visiting his mother, if he's in the area – then spends the rest of the day on the trail of frails with the right kind of bones.

'. . . we cannot rule out the possibility that this man may well be a travelling salesman or lorry driver or someone whose line of work brings him to these areas but who is perhaps based elsewhere.'

'You mean he could be living anywhere in Britain?'

'I'd go so far as to say North Britain.'

Which narrowed it down to about twenty million people. They really didn't have a clue.

'Do you have a psychological profile of the Fangman yet, Commander?'

'We do, and we'll be bringing it up to date once we have fully assembled and considered all the new evidence.'

Yeah, they'd tried that one out on Crimesnitch. Called in some criminal psychologist, a professor at some university, had him study all the evidence to date, draw up a profile. According to him, Gideon probably lives alone and picks his nose a lot.

'Is there any truth in the rumour that the psychic Mungo Spinks has been asked to help in the enquiry?'

'No truth whatsoever.'

'But he has visited the sites where the bodies were found?'

'I believe that to be the case.'

'And will you consider any conclusions he draws?'

'As seriously, yes, as we consider all information offered by members of the public.'

Now there was an interesting fact, something new. A psychic

on his trail. Like the guy in the States, Peter Kouros or something, he'd go to a scene of a crime, sniff the killer's panties and then tell the police the man they were looking for lived in a house with his elderly mother and wanked a lot. Police, being police, were always sceptical about any sense other than common sense. Gideon, on the other hand, is not. Maybe he should leave a pair of sweaty Ys around the neck of his next strangle, see what Spinksy makes of them.

'We're still trying to piece together the last two or three weeks in the Life of Arthur Thomas, so anyone who has been in contact with him during this period, we'd ask them to please come forward.'

Gideon tries to recall if anyone ever saw them together. Maybe once or twice down at the old fart's local, but not recently and nothing remarkable, just a couple of drunks elbow to elbow at the bar. Gideon had never been invited back to his house, so no gossip there. The only connection between them was when the cheapskate came out to the pottery, bought a whole load of seconds and insulted Gideon even further by trying to wangle a discount, then lost his temper. The day Gideon first took an interest in the man, put him in his book.

'Commander Kettle, the officer leading the hunt for the man who has already killed seven times.'

Seven? Seven?

Seven they fucking know about. Which leaves another two they're unaware of. One bitch yet to be discovered, and one they will never find, not in any ditch in the world. Simone had been different – no, *special* – in every way.

She'd been a *slow* burner.

Kestrel, Kettle, kestrel. Gideon can't get that cop off his mind. Even as he watches the bird circle over the Ashtree Pool he sees in his mind's eye the man's blocky face set in hard intractable lines beneath his white-braided peaked cap, those piggy little eyes the eyes of a stubborn man limited by his imagination and whose fleshless lips have been twisted by a lifetime's condescension. The kind of man, Gideon decides, who needs the framework of a uniform in order to function and survive – uniforms are not made to fit the man, the man is made to fit the uniform. And is therefore ultimately predictable and of little threat.

Yet still he dares to judge Gideon, Gideon who has chosen the path of a superior man. That's what gets to him, the cop's moral tone, his air of supremacy and the utter contempt he doesn't even try to conceal from his voice when he mentions the Fangman and the nature of his deeds. This man who knows nothing, *nothing*, about the importance of Gideon's mission or the commitment and toll it takes to carry it through. Like with . . .

. . . what was her name again? Jean something. Yeah, the widow one he caught coming out of the hairdresser's in Irvine, must be four weeks ago now, last suck of a full moon. Perfect timing, Gideon felt. He'd just delivered his last consignment of pottery – mostly teapots, mugs and candle-holders, maybe a casserole dish or two – to the stuck-up bitch in the cherry wig and half a ton of make-up who runs the souvenir shop in Troon, and he was just kind of cruising the way he does, keeping an eye out, see what the streets have on offer, when suddenly, fuck, before he knew it, she stepped out from behind a parked car and disappeared under his bonnet. Or so it seemed. Truth was he only clipped her, bruised her thigh, knocked her sideways. Luck was no one saw it happen. Gideon's luck, not hers.

Sutherland, that was her name. Jean Sutherland, aged seventy-three, husband killed in the war. Gideon found that out from her purse and pension book in her handbag. She lived alone but had a sister in Edinburgh who was trying to persuade her to go live over there. He discovered that in her letters.

She was in shock when he walked round the bonnet, like that song, shaking all over – legs, arms, hands, head, lips – as though someone were playing heavy harp with all her tendons. Her glasses were crooked on her nose, her green Barbour half-off her tiny shoulders, one of her shoes lying at Gideon's feet. He'd picked it up, sliding effortlessly into charm and concern, two of his better acts, though only when short-lived. In a moment she had a hand on his shoulder as he helped her into the passenger seat, was apologising and thanking him profusely as he buckled her in. Ten minutes later he'd helped her up her garden path – nice and sheltered he'd been pleased to see – unlocked her door, and followed her in.

'We can call your doctor from here,' is what he told her as she led him down the dark hall towards the back of the house. She never reached the phone. Ended up a tumble of bones on Mistylaw Muir.

'I thought I said no dogs.'

'You did, Mr Byrne, I'm sorry,' she gushes, hands fluttering like bejewelled butterflies at her neck. 'But this is a . . . well, an emergency. I really wouldn't have imposed on you otherwise. It's Puffin, you see, he was run over yesterday by some yobbo on a motorbike who didn't even stop.' Puffin is the long-haired mongrel looking very sorry for itself in the basket under the cash desk. 'The vet says fortunately nothing was broken but Puffin's probably still in a state of shock and should just rest as much as he can for the next few days. I know you're not too keen on dogs, Mr Byrne, but really, he'll be no problem at all, he won't even be moving from his basket so nothing will get broken. I promise.'

In the two days that Tasty Hastie has served in the shop Gideon has been forced to concede she has taken in more money than on any other weekend in the last two years. If he could take in that kind of money every week during the summer season he knows for damn sure he wouldn't be having the financial difficulties he's having at the moment. In fact he'd be able to say fuck you to all the small-minded retailers on the mainland who order minuscule quantities on sale or return while demanding wholesale prices that, once he's accounted for time and transport expenses, squeeze his profit margins from pounds into pennies. The only reason he continues with the mainland outlets

186

is the opportunity each monthly excursion presents to spend a couple of days on the road, scouting.

'Okay,' Gideon says finally. 'See it doesn't.'

Ros Hastie peers up at him. 'You look tired, Mr Byrne. Have you slept yet?'

He shakes his head. Thirty hours now. Mind buzzing.

'I'll make you some coffee then. Have you had any breakfast? No, I thought not. Well, I came prepared, just in case. You get on with whatever you have to do and I'll bring it out to you. How's that sound?'

'I'll be out at the kiln,' he tells her.

'And you, darling,' she croons to the mongrel, 'you just stay there and Mummy'll be back before you even know it. There's a good boy.'

Same stupid look on its face as Hector the Labrador. What a silly old Hector. You remember him well because you remember all your kills in the finest detail. Insects, birds, cats, dogs, sheep, humans, the lot. Because you take an interest in your work, you are a professional. You watch, learn, adapt. Yeah, Hector was a good one as snacks go, satisfying in the way that illicit midnight feasts always are, dogs, so stupid, so trusting, so gullible yet greedy, not unlike a few of the bitches you've left lying in ditches

move on

the same big round puzzled eyes when you finally got to grips with them in the big strangle, sent them on their way to the great forgetness

to slave or not to slave

as the seventies' serial killer, Zodiac, would have you believe. Now there was a guy was totally out of his head, off his fucking trolley. You and he have a lot in common – have, because, like you, Zodiac has never yet been caught. Twenty-plus years of bitches in ditches and the guy's still loose, somewhere in California, most like, working in some five'n'dime store or maybe even Governor by now, it can only happen there. Whatever. He's the man to respect, to emulate, because he had beliefs.

And what he thought, what he believed was this, that all his victims would become his own personal slaves in the forgetness, there for all eternity to do his bidding . . . fetch me another pint of lager, princess, then wrap your lips round this

kind of thing.

All in all, not an altogether bad idea, you have to admit.

Zodiac also wore a mask on some of his croppings. Like the time he did that couple out on the peninsula, tied them up and stabbed them, left them there to die but the guy didn't, he survived, he lived to tell the tale and describe what Zodiac looked like, how he was all dressed up to kill, the mask more an actual hood than a mask, but kind of square, flat on top, with a bib that came down over his neck and shoulders, with his own special emblem there, sewn on, a circle with a cross centred over it, the guy definitely living the part, the media identity he was creating for himself. Which is why you admire him. It's good to see someone take a little pride in their work, a little interest. Add those extra-special touches the media love so much, like sending letters to the press, taunting the San Francisco Police Department, giving them coded clues as to his identity and what he was going to do next. Having fun. *Which seemed like a great idea. Send the bastards running all over the place, chasing down red herrings, wasting time, wasting money . . . yes, Zodiac certainly had something there, keep one step ahead, keep them jumping in different directions, they can't afford not to take anything you say seriously, that's the nature of the police, they're reactive, you see, effect not cause.*

So maybe, you think, it's time to cause a little mayhem. Open up a line of communication, send the police on a wild-goose chase or three.

Time, in other words, to throw the bones.

'Thank you,' Gideon says, 'that was just what I needed.'

'Big man like you needs to eat,' Ros Hastie replies, taking his plate. 'Like your kiln there, we all need fuel to keep us going. How long to go now?'

They're sitting out by the woodfire kiln, side by side on a crude log bench, washed by a lukewarm sun. Logs crackle and pop in the firebox grate, white-hot now as combustion roars, nearing its peak.

'Another six hours, maybe more.'

Just before she brought his breakfast out, he'd checked the pyrometric cones through the spyhole, seen the No. 1 cone bent over, the colour of heat in the chamber a pale orange. Time now for reduction – the process which sucks oxygen from clays and glazes – he'd replaced the damper at the back of the chamber, thus restricting the flow of oxygen.

'Six hours?'

'At this rate, at least another three to reach thirteen hundred degrees, then I'll need to keep it there for at least an hour, maybe two, to get an even firing throughout the chambers.'

'That's a lot of hard work.'

'Mm.' Gideon throws another log in the firebox. It ignites almost instantly in an explosion of sparks.

'I mean, you could do all this in the electric kiln, save all the exertion. Sleep in your bed at nights, you know?'

With her? Is that what she's meaning? Is that the weird look in her eyes he's been catching the last couple of days? Gideon hopes not. And can he be bothered explaining his philosophy about firing to a senseless one, an uninitiated? No. A simplified version then, to keep her happy. Because he must keep her happy a little while longer yet. He has a mask to make, and other ideas he wants to try out.

'Too sanitised,' he tells her, 'the electric kiln. Like when you switch it on it's as though you switch yourself off. From the most important part of the process. This way is a lot more demanding but the results are far more satisfying.'

'Did you build it yourself?'

Gideon nods. Tells her how he helped construct one for the Aphelion Centre when he was young, how he made a copy of the plans.

'Aphelion, eh?' Tasty Hastie says. 'What was it, some kind of religious set-up?'

Rehabilitation. But he's not going to tell her that. 'Spiritual. Art and crafts. Yin and yang, all that hippy shit.'

'You know what Aphelion is?'

'A Greek god? A venereal disease?' Another log into the firebox, another explosion of sparks.

She actually laughs. 'No, silly, it's when the sun, earth and moon are in a direct line and exert their strongest gravitational pull. It's one of the most important astrological events of the year.'

'Had to be.' Gideon can feel the Moon sucking already. Waxing gibbous, almost full.

'Funny kind of name for a spiritual centre though. Is that where you learnt pottery?'

'Simone.'

'Sorry?'

'Sorry what?'

'You said "Simone".'

'I did?'

'Is that who taught you?'

'Yes.'

'Do you still see her?'

In a manner of speaking, yes. In the trophy room below, the chamber. But he can't admit that, so he shakes his head, no.

Tasty Hastie swirls the tea in her mug, pours what little is left to the ground, then studies the pattern of leaves that remain. Gideon wonders what she sees there, if it is something to do with him. He picks up another log, tosses it in the firebox where it is immediately consumed by flames hungrier than the flames of hell.

'Was it Simone who taught you how to make your special glazes?' Hastie asks eventually.

'In a manner of speaking, yes.' But again he doesn't elaborate. In fact it was Simone who nicknamed him The Glaze Bore.

She shouldn't have done that. Still, he'd certainly put a glaze in her eyes the afternoon he decided to take fate into his own hands and become what he is.

The day she became a slow burner.

19

All Monday mornings should begin like this.

Sitting on a deserted beach, looking out across a sparkling blue bay warmed by a golden disc of sun in a bright cloudless sky as listless waves lap at the sighing sand and gulls bob on the gentle swell, wheel raucously overhead. A time and place to look out through optimistic eyes on a world of beauty and hope and, for a few moments at least, forget the misery created in the constant sating of selfish desires. I leaned back against the overturned dinghy, closed my eyes and tried to sink into the cool, dark depths of sleep. My thoughts, though, infuriatingly buoyant, kept dragging me back to the surface.

So I stared out across the bay at the humpback of Holy Island, now a mosaic of greens and browns, purple and gold suspended between sea and sky, and let my thoughts run their erratic course. I thought about Monica, and how much closer we had become over the weekend, forced together by the circumstance of Thomas's murder. In that time we had handled three D&Is, one DUI, four noise complaints, two assaults, one burglary, one car theft, five cautions, one collision, one hit-and-run involving a motorbike and dog, one fatal heart-attack and one case of shoplifting. But no more murdered sheep, men or women. Neither of us had slept for more than three hours at a time, had been reduced to snatching what little sleep we could on the lockfast bunks between call-outs.

Earlier this morning PC Bob Gillies had returned tanned and smiling from his holiday in Ibiza and had taken the whole new course of events in his long, relaxed stride. Having relieved Sergeant Yuill from duty, Gillies was now helping DI Fullerton coordinate further house-to-house enquiries in Brodick. Fullerton, in order to be closer to the epicentre of his investigation, had now transferred the command of his operation from our Lamlash office to the small one at Brodick that we share with the Mountain Rescue Team. Although this now made it possible for Monica and I to work almost comfortably from our own office, we were still playing host to half a dozen officers from the murder squad who would come in off their eighteen-hour shifts and collapse immediately on to the bunks and mattresses in the lockfasts and interview room. What little information we managed to glean from them before they bombed into sleep suggested that, in the absence of any new evidence and the overall lack of progress in the investigation, a deep trough of pessimism had now settled over the squad. Commander Kettle, I was glad to hear, bore the brunt of their abuse.

An outboard motor sputtered to life further down the beach and I turned on my side to watch it angle across the bay, two men on board, heading for the jetty on Holy Island. Monks? I wondered. Possibly. The island had been bought a few years back by Tibetan Buddhists as an interdenominational retreat, attracted by the island's rich religious heritage. Two miles long and half a mile wide, Holy Island played host to the cave-dwelling Saint Molios in the sixth century, and the springs in his cave, so my aunt had told me, are still considered to contain strong healing properties. The island now hosts a small herd of wild and very rare Eriskay ponies, peregrine falcons, feral goats and Soay sheep. I have often wondered what it would be like to retreat from the world for three years, three months and three days – but never for long. Perhaps like most of us I need people around me to confirm my worth and existence, to drown the cries of all my fears and insecurities. I lay back down and stared at the sky. I thought about two murdered sheep and one murdered man, and wondered if they could be connected.

I thought about Cathy, whom I hadn't seen or heard from in months, whose last lingering kiss I still tasted in dreams.

I thought of a man out there who had a taste for blood and defenceless old women, who sometimes took their heads for trophies or as some kind of ritual fetish. I wondered how close he was, if he was looking up at the same blue sky as I, what dark and twisted thoughts were now storming through his mind.

I thought about Harry Todd, now retired from the force and working security in a city-centre shopping precinct; wondered if he ever thought about the time we'd been partners, the scrapes I'd got him into, the fun we had had.

I thought about my Great-Aunt Joan and what she'd make of me now, neither artist nor musician, writer nor academic, just a plain fucked-up cop beached on the shores of his profession, taking each empty day as it came and trying hard not to think of a future that only begged the question 'What future?' I thought of the times I'd spent on this very same beach with her, bucket and spade, building castles in the sand and castles in the air beneath her stern and watchful gaze. A lifetime ago.

I thought about Julian Ryder, a kid with the looks but a taste for power, who could go out there and pull a stunner with a flick of his long blond fringe yet preferred to dress up in combat gear and mask, pull a girl into a bush at knifepoint. A girl he went to school with, who knew him by sight: hence the mask. I thought about that. Then wondered how she'd positively identified him. I decided to read Yuill's report again when I returned to the office.

I thought about Findlay Farquharson and our meeting later this morning. I would try to be pleasant, to respect his position as one of the island's major landowners. I would erase from my mind his liking for urine facials, and try hard to forget that he was an arrogant, shortarsed moneygrabber with all the charm of a mugger on PCP. I would, I told myself, try very, very hard.

I thought about dogs. Lots of dogs. Running all over the

place, unleashed, wild. A shiver crawled up my spine. We'd met her on Saturday, the woman who took in dogs and lived on the hill overlooking Kildonan and the slab of stone where I'd found the first sheep, what, eight days ago? It seemed longer. Rosalind Hastie was her name. She'd been walking four of her dogs along the beach at Whiting Bay, late evening because she'd been working all day in some pottery out on Machrie Moor, and was crossing the main road to return to her car when a motorbike suddenly appeared out of nowhere and ran down her favourite collie, Muffin or something, without even stopping. No, she hadn't recognised the rider – everything had happened so fast, you see – nor had she noticed either make, colour or licence plate of the bike, and was I going to stand there all night interrogating her while some greasy long-haired hooligan was getting away with murder. 'He had long hair, then?' Monica had asked. 'They always have long hair, these yobbos,' the woman replied. I said nothing. After taking down the details, I'd been on the point of asking her about the sheep when a call came in for a Code 10, sudden death up in Blackwaterfoot. I told her I would call on her this evening with any new developments. I just hoped she kept her dogs in kennels.

I thought about Kyoko. Kyoko and Dave, the Neanderthal. I wondered what she saw in him that she couldn't see in me, whether she now spent her nights in the vice of his vast rippling biceps. Was that why I hadn't seen her around the hotel the last few days? It made sense. I then asked myself was I jealous, and the knot in the pit of my stomach told me yes, dammit, I was.

So I turned my thoughts to the murder squad, to Fullerton and the pathologist Silas Kerr. I wondered if I should contact Fullerton, try to get a line on their progress so far, maybe try and get a peek at the autopsy report on Arthur Thomas. See if I could add anything to my own personal file on the Fangman.

And I thought of Thomas, ship-welder retired, harmless, perhaps lonely, brought to a violent end on his living-room floor by someone he knew or someone he didn't. A killer with an artistic interest in his work. Whose crime scenes were like canvases on which he painted his cruel fantasies in broad strokes of blood. I wondered about all the broken crockery, what significance it could have in the deranged killer's mind. It had been broken for a reason, arranged for a reason.

What reason?

Then I tired of all this thinking, this insistent inner voice that seldom lets me relax. Surrendered myself instead to the warmth of sun, the hypnotic lapping of waves, the luxurious scent of sea and sand. Closed my eyes and imagined myself lying naked on a deserted beach. Spain or Greece, the sun bearing down on my bronzed skin, the breeze a soft caress on hard muscle. After a while I hear footsteps; they stop and I open my eyes. 'You'll burn if you're not careful,' she says, flicking her long auburn hair from her deep brown eyes. She is naked. No, almost naked. Wearing two bits of white string. Her breasts are firm with nipples the same colour as her hair, the same size and shape as her eyes. Eyes that lick me slowly from head to foot. She has the longest legs I've ever stared at, her skin the colour of burning sand. Ochred silk, sheathed in white. A snaking silver bracelet on her wrist. Teeth like pearls in a passion-flower mouth. 'I don't have any oil,' I tell her. 'Don't worry,' she says, rummaging in her shoulder bag, coming out with a bottle. 'Would you like me to rub it in?' she asks. 'Yes,' I say, my voice a hoarse croak. She kneels by my side and begins to—

'*McMorran!*'

I opened my eyes with a guilty start and turned to see Robocop's prototype striding across the sand.

'What the fuck're you doing out here?' Kettle demanded, jerking his thumb towards the station. 'You're supposed to be in that office manning the bloody phones, not lounging on the fucking beach like you're on some kind of foreign holiday.' His face was purpling as he stormed towards me, rolled newspaper like a baton in his hand. 'There's a fucking murder investigation going on here, McMorran, in case you hadn't noticed. You know, like the small matter of a maniac on the loose, who's already killed seven times and might kill again at any moment.' Kettle halted mid flow, but only to curl his upper lip. 'And you, McMorran, what do you do? You lie on the fucking beach and fucking dream your fucking life away, that's what you do. Then you go blabbing to the press when the last thing we need is some drunken has-been cop blabbing off at the mouth, trying to stir things up because he feels he's been left out.'

'You what?'

'Don't give me that, McMorran, all eyes of fucking innocence.' Kettle jabbed the newspaper at my face. 'It's down here in black and white. Read it for yourself.'

I took the paper, opened it. The headline sprang at me.

Fangman hunt 'a farce' claims demoted Crime Squad DI

All days in Hell should begin like this.

While the hunt continues on the Isle of Arran for the killer of retired welder Arthur Thomas, whom police now believe to be the seventh victim of the man they call the Fangman, life continues as normal for the small island force of four PCs and one sergeant. One of the officers, though, is not all he might seem.

PC Frank McMorran is no stranger to the pages of this newspaper. Eight months ago he was a successful detective inspector in the Special Crimes Squad based in Edinburgh, and was rumoured to be the man who finally brought to an end the evil reign of Dominic Bain, Scotland's most notorious serial killer, now a lifetime resident in Carstairs. Although credit for Bain's capture officially went to the man now leading the hunt for the Fangman, Commander Harlan Kettle, many officers at the Fettes Force HQ are convinced such credit was misplaced.

While Chief Inspector Kettle was consequently promoted to the rank of Commander and placed in command of the SCS, DI McMorran found himself in front of a disciplinary hearing which concluded with his demotion to rank of PC.

Although the exact nature of McMorran's misconduct has not been made public officially, there are those who believe it marked the culmination of a long-standing feud between the two men, a feud which supposedly began several years ago during the Crime Squad's ill-fated investigation into high-level corruption in the Scottish Office. Even though results of the enquiry have never been published, many now believe that its findings bear direct relation to the Fettesgate affair in 1992.

While sources close to the investigation confirm there is no love lost between the two men, PC McMorran refused to comment yesterday on his exclusion from the enquiry. When asked how the investigation was progressing, however, he was only a little less reticent.

'The whole thing's a farce,' he replied bluntly, before returning to his duties directing traffic away from the scene of the crime. A far cry indeed from his days as a DI with the elite SCS.

Mike 30 parked alongside the Distillery's Stillhouse, Monica and I waiting for Farquharson to show. Eleven thirty, and our patience stretching with every passing minute. I tossed the newspaper on to the dash.

'I get my hands on the little shit, he's dead.'

'You don't need any more trouble, Frank. That's two disciplinary charges against you in less than a week. One more and you know the score, you'll be out on your ear.'

I said, 'If Kettle has his way, I'm out anyway.'

Somehow the prospect didn't worry me; on the contrary, it excited me. I wondered if subconsciously I had turned a blind corner, could now see a straight ahead. Time would tell, as it always does if you listen hard enough.

Here in the Distillery time marched to its own routine step. Five minutes ago a tractor and wagon had pulled up outside the Stillhouse, and now a bare-chested Archie McDonald was busy shovelling draff through a hatch and into the wagon. Steam from the draff dissipated quickly in the warm breeze.

'Exactly,' Monica said. 'So leave Slater alone. If you go breaking his bones, you'll be doing him a favour, giving him even more of a story. No, Frank, best you just forget him, get on with the job.'

'A week ago, I was doing fine.'

'You were bored out of your bloody skull. Then Arthur Thomas gets murdered and suddenly you're a different man. Like you've finally come alive. You know, I used to sit in the office and watch you sometimes, wonder where the hell was this rogue cop I'd heard so much about, how the stories must've been exaggerated out of all proportion. I tell you, I was disappointed. A little life in the office is exactly what it needs.'

'Nothing short of ECT.'

'That may be, Frank, but don't get me wrong. The boys are fine to work with, no problem at all. It's just they're so ... conventional. You know, wife, kids, mortgage, their lives already packed and wrapped, everything in its right place, like they're just going through the motions. You, on the other hand, are the opposite. When I heard you were coming, I thought, great, at last, a bit of life, some excitement.'

'The trouble with reputations is living up to them.'

'My heart bleeds.' Monica lit up a cigarette, inhaled greedily. 'So what else did Kettle have to say?'

'That what I do in the middle of a manhunt is lie on the fucking beach and fucking dream my fucking life away.'

'He caught you sleeping?'

'Resting my eyes,' I said. 'Thinking summery thoughts.'

'Read dirty thoughts. Orgies in the sun with a bevy of blue-eyed beauties feeding on your privates, no doubt. Or buxom blondes in skimpy swimsuits asking you to rub oil on their backs as sloe-eyed virgins on their hands and knees beg you for a night of unbridled passion. Am I right?'

'Closer than you think,' I chuckled.

'Typical.' Monica snorted, exhaling noisily. There was a tenseness about her this morning, her easy banter coating a hard edge reflected in the aggressive manner of her smoking. 'A man has only to close his eyes to subvert the whole female race.'

'Subvert, hell. We all need some gratuitous sex in our lives. And fantasy, they say, is the red hot chilli of life.'

It was Monica's turn to chuckle. 'Your life, maybe . . .'

'You're telling me *you* never fantasise?' A group of tourists emerged from the Malt Barn Reception Centre, began walking down the lane towards us.

'Of course. But—'

'That's different?'

'I get to live them out, that's the difference.'

'You and Farquharson both.' I told her what John French claimed to have witnessed through the Reception Centre window.

'Whatever turns you on,' Monica said.

'Definitely not that kind of thing.'

'It's harmless enough, Frank. No crime there between two consenting adults.'

As the huddle of visitors crossed the wooden footbridge to the shop, Findlay Farquharson came out of the Centre and strode down the hill, face set in a fearsome scowl. Monica stubbed out her cigarette and we climbed from the car and adjusted our caps in unison. Synchronised policing in action. Farquharson was not impressed. He held up both hands, as though to ward us off.

'Nope,' he snapped, 'no bloody chance. Not today.'

'Sir,' I said, 'may I remind you that it was you who called us out last Sunday.'

'That was then, McSporran, this is now. Priorities change.'

'I'm sure they do, sir. Unfortunately, though, I can't just

201

abandon my enquiries because your priorities have changed. A crime has been committed and it's my duty to investigate it.'

Farquharson swept his glare the length of Monica, then settled it on me. 'Look, Constable, I've got two of my guides off sick and four busloads of visitors arriving any second for the guided tour. I haven't got time. It's as simple as that.'

'Off sick,' I said, 'or never to return?'

Blood suffused Farquharson's neck. He took a step forward and prodded my chest. 'I've heard about you, McSporran—'

'McMorran,' I corrected, brushing his hand away. I was trying very hard to be both polite and respectful, even when I knew the struggle wasn't worth the effort. Farquharson ignored me, blustered on.

'. . . so you better watch it, pal. If you think you can come over here and act the same way you do back in the city, you've got another think coming. Make accusations like that here and you better make them stick or find your arse sued right out of court.'

'Accusations?' Monica asked.

Farquharson rounded on her. 'You keep out of this, Constable, it's none of your damn business.'

The look in Monica's eyes suddenly became a reflection of my own. Not very pretty. She turned away, fists clenching, to watch a German tour bus turn in through the gates, park alongside another. I could almost hear her counting to ten.

'I think we ought to keep calm, if you don't mind, sir,' I said in my most patronising tone. 'Like treat each other with a little respect?'

'*Respect?*' Farquharson shrieked. 'You call walking off with my personnel records "respect"? You call making veiled accusations "respect"? I call it "criminal and insulting", McSporran, and that's damn sure how I'm going to describe it to your superior the first chance I get.'

'And you, sir, can be sure that I will be putting it down on record that you have been nothing short of obstructive in our dealings and that you have not only come close to assaulting an officer in front of a witness, but that I also have good reason to suspect that you are consciously concealing a crime for the single purpose of financial benefit. I'm sure your Japanese visitors would be very interested to hear your explanation on that subject.'

Monica looked at me askance while Farquharson looked ready to burst, his stature seeming to balloon in anger.

'Or not, sir?' I added, smiling sweetly, beginning to enjoy myself, back on home territory.

'Who told you that?' Farquharson spluttered. 'That's confidential information, dammit.'

Deadpan, Monica said, 'I'm sure you can rely on the rest of the island to keep it under their hat, sir.'

He glowered at her again but seemed unable to speak. Wormlike veins jumped in his neck, latticed his pulsing temples.

'An hour of your time is all I'm asking,' I reminded him.

Sunlight flashed off gold as Farquharson waved his pudgy hand in the direction of the recently arrived tour bus. His voice rose and continued rising. 'An hour. You want an hour of my time. Okay, no problem. I'll just tell them to climb back on the bus, come back next year. And the other three buses booked, I'll tell them the same. I'll tell them I haven't got time because a bloody sheep has died and the police are treating it as a major fucking enquiry because that's the way it is over here, people care more about sheep than they do about dragging the nation off its knees and out of recession. Is that what you want me to tell them?'

'It's a fair assessment,' I told him, 'but I don't think we need to go quite so far. If you'll just give me a time when I can return tomorrow, then we'll go about our duty and let you get on with your work. Otherwise . . .'

'What? You'll arrest me?'

'It would be my pleasure, sir.'

'And mine,' Monica added.

Farquharson recognised the blue brick wall for what it was. He made a show of adjusting his shades, smoothing down his slicked-back hair with both hands, checking the hang of his stumpy ponytail before sighing heavily and shaking his head. 'Okay, okay, I get the picture, you have your duty to do. I'll give you the time you need but don't think for one moment your behaviour here this morning will go unreported. The Chief Constable is a personal acquaintance of mine and a man who does not take such matters lightly.'

'Yes, sir,' I said.

'No, sir,' Monica added.

Farquharson seemed appeased by our apparent contriteness. 'Right then. I've a very important meeting in the morning, so it'll have to be after that, say . . .' he glanced at his heavy gold Seiko, '. . . one o'clock.'

'One o'clock,' we said.

'What kind of thoughts,' Monica asked, 'can put such a frown on a man's face on a morning like this?'

'Sad ones. Like Frank McMorran, keeper of the sheep's peace.'

'You're thinking about sheep? Sad indeed.'

'Wondering what other dumb animal can evoke such a common hatred yet claim such a prominent place in its country's history . . .'

'Politicians?'

'Apart from politicians.'

'Grouse?'

'Well, I suppose the grouse is also pretty dumb.'

'Almost as dumb as the morons who flock yearly to slaughter it,' Monica said.

'Morons like Farquharson,' I said, changing gear and checking the rearview mirror. 'Greedy entrepreneurs who wield their economic might like bludgeons, destroying lives and communities and always in the name of progress.'

204

'You mean profit.'

'Exactly. The same kind of profiteers who sold us down the London road in 1707.'

'You're in a foul mood today, Frank, what's up?'

'Kettle,' I said. 'And Farquharson. The Duke of Diplomacy and the Prince of Charm. They ought to team up, go on tour, The Total Dickhead and Bastard Show.'

We were heading south on the west coast road, sun blinding in off the Kilbrannan Sound, the hills of Kintyre rising majestic to the west, with the lofty peaks of Beinns Bhreac and Bharrain to our left. Ahead of us crawled an English tour bus, behind us a black Nissan, the flow of traffic intermittent in the opposite direction.

After several minutes' silence in which I endeavoured to pass the tour bus ahead, Monica asked, 'What did Farquharson mean by "accusations"?'

'His guilty conscience talking,' I told her. 'I was insinuating that his two guides were not off sick this morning but had left because of his unsolicited attentions. According to Archie McDonald, they would not be the first.'

'Is that why you took his personnel records?'

'A copy of them. You want to know something? In the last two years the Distillery's been through thirty-one guides. None lasted longer than three weeks.'

'What, you think one of these guides put the sheep in the tank as some kind of revenge?'

'I doubt it,' I said. 'None of them live on the island, all came across from the mainland. Mostly from Glasgow, it seems.'

'Don't shit in your own back yard kind of thing?'

'Exactly. Apparently Farquharson's got a continuous ad in the *Evening Times*, and conducts interviews once a month in some city-centre hotel. Casting couch and all, I wouldn't be surprised.'

'Guy should be locked up,' Monica said. 'Better still, castrated.' She glanced in the rearview mirror, frowned, then took out a cigarette and lit it. 'So what next? Trace all the former guides, check their alibis? Seems like an awful waste of time.'

'I'm sure Yuill will agree. The only reason he wants me to look into it is to keep Farquharson happy. Unfortunately for him, the more I look into it, the unhappier Farquharson becomes.'

'What a shame.'

'Isn't it. Anyway, I give it two days.'

'Until what?'

'Until Yuill pulls me off it.'

'So you believe Farquharson really is pally with the CC?'

'There's always the chance. The Lodge isn't as choosy as it once was.'

'I'm sure.' Monica stubbed out her cigarette, studied her nails for a moment. 'So . . . are you just going to let it drop if Yuill says so?'

'Not a chance,' I told her. 'There's definitely something going on up at the Distillery. I don't know what the connection is with the sheep I found down at Kildonan, but there must be one. And the explanation, I'm sure, lies somewhere up at the Distillery.'

'You mean the motive?'

'Someone put the sheep in the tank for a reason.'

'As yet unknown.'

'Right. So we must look for means and opportunity.'

'Access and transport?'

'Exactly. Who has access to the keys for the gate, and a car to transport the dead sheep?'

'And considerable strength as well, Frank. Sheep aren't just walking balls of wool, you know.'

'The Farquharsons, Archie McDonald, his two part-time assistants, and Maggie.'

'What about John French?'

'And John French. Have you seen his wife yet?'

'Shit,' Monica said, shaking her head. 'I forgot.'

206

'Doesn't matter. If all else fails, we can come back to her.'

'Exclude Maggie and Mrs Farquharson, and that leaves you four good suspects.'

'They're both big women,' I pointed out.

'Six then. So who do you think did it?'

'Farquharson.'

'Me too.' Monica glanced in the rearview mirror again. 'You know that Nissan's been following us since we left the Distillery?'

'Mm,' I said. 'Like we've been following this damn bus.'

'But the bus wasn't in the Distillery car park when we left.'

'Good point.' It was hanging back about fifty yards, sun reflecting off its windshield, happy, it seemed, with our snail's pace behind the bus. I couldn't see the driver, nor whether it had any passengers.

'Press?' Monica asked.

'But not Slater. He drives a Ford.' As we approached the village of Pirnmill, I said, 'Let's see what he does now,' and, without indicating, pulled into the hotel car park. We turned in our seats to watch it pass.

'Male or female?'

'Couldn't tell,' Monica said. 'But alone, whoever it was. Wait a minute . . . he's pulled up. Now his hazard lights are on. He's just sitting there. You want me to run a check?'

'Aye. You do that while I go and introduce myself.' I grabbed my cap and climbed out.

Monica reached across and gripped my arm. 'Frank? Take it easy, okay? No more disciplinary charges.'

'Not even a small one?'

20

Drumadoon, 'hill of the fort'.

Not much of a fort if you're expecting ramparts and flying buttresses, murder-holes and moats. But if it's the Iron Age you're into, then this is your fort for multiple orgasms. Personally, though, straggles of large stones and grass-grown banks don't do much for my libido, so I wasn't quite as excited as the kid. He was going wild, making aeroplane noises with his arms spread, climbing the banks and dive-bombing bemused-looking sheep. His mother, Irene Wallace, and her daughter Julia were strolling along ahead with Monica, getting on well, it seemed. Lucky them. They didn't have a six-year-old explosion of unlimited enthusiasm to control.

'Bobby!' I yelled. 'Leave that sheep alone!'

'But look, it's smiling!'

Well, through the eyes of a child, I suppose a grimace of sheer terror can easily be mistaken for a smile.

'That's what I mean,' I told him, sweeping him off his feet and on to my hip. 'It's dangerous for sheep to get too happy.'

'Why's that?'

'Because basically they're sad creatures.'

'Why?'

'Because they look so stupid.'

'Why do they look stupid?'

'Wouldn't you look stupid if you had all those teeth in your mouth?'

Bobby giggled and pulled my cap down over my eyes. I stumbled and nearly lost my balance. Pulled my cap up again.

Bobby yelled in my ear, '*You* look stupid!'

I put him down. 'That's because my father was a sheep.'

'He wasn't!'

'He had little black button eyes and teeth at least twice the size of his mouth.'

'He didn't!'

'He did. And he had these huge flappy ears that he'd use to swat away the flies. And spindly long legs like matchsticks, like he was walking on stilts.'

'You're lying!'

'Perhaps just a little.' I squatted down next to Bobby, removed my cap. 'What's your Dad like? Has he got big flappy ears too?'

'Yes,' he giggled. 'And a big red nose.'

'Yeah? What does he do, your father?'

'He's a forestry man.' Said with a mixture of pride and awe.

'Chops down trees, eh? That's exciting.'

''Tisn't. It's boring. *I* want to be a policeman when I grow up.'

Hey, kid, slow down, I thought. Don't make any hasty decisions. Be a pop star or a football star and follow your dreams – don't become a slave to your fears and sentence yourself to a lifetime of constant warfare.

Sometime I should listen to my own advice.

I said, 'Maybe one day I'll show you round our office, if you'd like that. Take you for a drive in the Panda.'

Bobby's small round face clouded over. 'My Dad says I mustn't talk to policemen. He says they're ... *nasty* men.'

'Am I a nasty man, Bobby?'

He had to think about that. But not for long. His face lit up again, enthusiasm rekindled. 'I tell you what,' he said, 'I'll be the bad man and you have to find me.'

210

Monica and the Wallaces had stopped by the solitary standing stone, Monica, it appeared, doing most of the talking. She caught my eye briefly. Her expression seemed troubled.

'Close your eyes and count to a hundred,' Bobby ordered.

'Don't go too far,' I told him, 'and keep away from the cliff.'

He sprinted away, scattering sheep in all directions.

The sun blazed high over the Mull of Kintyre, the hills hazy in the distance and, if I squinted hard enough, I could just make out the hills of Antrim, little more than a blur on the horizon. The view from the Doon here is one of the best on the island. Look west across the Kilbrannan Sound to the hills of Kintyre as, a hundred feet below, sloppy waves chew lethargically on the columnar basalt cliffs. Look north across marshes and woodland to the peaks of Beinns Bharrain and Bhreac; north-east across Machrie Moor to the peaks of Beinns Tarsuinn and Nuis; east across farms and summer-green pastureland, the villages of Torbeg, Birchburn, Shiskine, Shedock, to the slopes of Ard Bheinn bronzing in the sun, and the unfinished fort just visible on Cnoc Ballygown; to the south, the disused quarry, the golf course over which we'd walked, and the wide sandy beach leading round to the village of Blackwaterfoot. You want to breathe a bit of history and steep in local legend, follow the path north from the fort, walk along the raised beach below the sandstone cliffs and you'll come to the King's Cave where Robert the Bruce whiled away his waiting days watching spiders try and try again. Maybe I too should follow Bruce and the spider's example, I thought. Try to put the murder out of my mind and rediscover the relaxed state of mind I was just beginning to enjoy before Kettle and his crew invaded our peaceful patch.

'Frank!'

I replaced my cap and made my way down.

Julia Wallace was saying, 'But why? I've already shown the other policeman.'

'We have to be sure, Julia,' Monica told her gently. 'We need to double-check in case we missed something first time round.' She turned to me as I approached. 'Julia's going to show us where it happened.'

'Good girl.' I looked around for Bobby but he was nowhere in sight.

'He went down there,' Julia said, pointing down the path, her tone and expression sullen. She was a small girl for her fourteen years of age, dressed in denim jeans and jacket, maroon sweatshirt and pink trainers, with her straight ash-blonde hair tied back in a ponytail and her fingertips tucked in hip pockets. Her whole manner suggested 'tomboy'.

We followed the steep path down from the fort on to the raised beach, along the foot of the sandstone cliff. I spotted Bobby crouched behind some scrub but pretended not to notice. I wondered what a fourteen-year-old girl was doing out here after dark and all alone. Whether she really had been alone. I then tried to imagine the sheer horror of her experience, the terror she had faced, the excruciating pain . . . But I'm a man, and as a man I'll die, never able to truly understand the mental and physical torture and torment that women who have been raped are forced to undergo.

But I'm human also, and though I show little pity I have as much as anyone else, and what I wanted to do right then was take her in my arms, this scared little girl, and hold her tight, comfort her with words of soothing tenderness, tell her how this would never happen again, that she was safe now, that everything would be all right.

What I did, though, was nothing.

'There,' Julia said. 'That's where he was hiding.'

'There' was a clump of bushes, a tangled copse at the foot of the cliff, surrounded by weeds and nettles, grass a foot and a half high. I asked her in which direction she'd been walking. She pointed back along the way we'd come.

I pushed my way into the bushes, shirt and trousers snagging on thorns. There wasn't much to see, nothing that Yuill hadn't seen for himself. No scraps of clothing caught on a thorn, no fag-ends in the dirt, no convenient books of matches to send me checking out all the sleazy red-light bars for a man with a limp called Moose. Shame. I backed out and brushed myself down.

'Where were you when he attacked?' I asked.

Julia looked around, then at her feet. 'Here.'

Four yards from the bushes.

'And he dragged you into those bushes?'

Nod of head.

'There was no one else about?'

Shake of head.

'Did you see anyone before you were attacked? Pass someone on the path, perhaps, or up at the fort?'

Another shake of head. 'No.'

'So you saw no one at all?'

Her eyes snapped from the ground and zeroed in on mine, both barrels blazing. 'I told you, didn't I?' she cried. '*I – didn't – see – anyone!*'

Monica stepped between us, pushed me away. 'That's enough, Frank, can't you see she's had enough?'

'Call it a day?'

Monica nodded. 'You go find Bobby. We'll catch up.'

'There's a lot of tension in that girl,' Monica said after we'd been driving in silence for several minutes. We were heading up The String on our way back to the station. 'She's like a booby trap, Frank, one wrong move and you feel she's going to blow up in your face. The mother, too. It's like they're reacting . . . almost feeding off each other's anxiety. Did you notice anything strange about Mrs Wallace?'

213

'Her cardigan?'

'Exactly. A day like this, sun beating down, and she wears a thick woolly cardigan. It wasn't as though she was cold either, the sweat was pouring off her. I mean, you could see her obvious discomfort. So why didn't she take it off?'

'Good question.'

'And every time I asked Julia a question, it was like she'd glance at her mother for permission to speak.'

'What are you saying?'

Monica shifted gear and thought for a moment before replying. 'Something's not right, Frank. I can't quite put my finger on it. It's lots of little things, not exactly inconsistencies, but . . .'

'Was her story the same?'

'Almost word for word. She'd taken some sandwiches along to her father who was working late that night—'

'Forestry Commission?'

'Right. They've a plot on the Tor Righ Beag, wouldn't have taken her more than half an hour to walk. This was early evening, about seven o'clock. Then, on her way back, she decided to sit and watch the sunset over Kintyre, and fell asleep. Woke up and it was already getting dark, so she headed home. That's when she was attacked.'

'She describe the mask?'

'Now she's sure it was a black balaclava.'

'With Ryder inside it.'

'You want to know something she didn't tell Sergeant Yuill? She and Ryder were sweethearts last year.'

'Julia and Julian,' I said. 'That's interesting.'

'Only lasted a couple of months, though, then Ryder chucked her for his current girlfriend, Carol.'

'Fury of a teen-love scorned?'

'Frank, she didn't make this up. You saw the medical report, the poor child was viciously assaulted.'

'Yet no witnesses,' I argued. 'She says she saw no one along the way, but think about it. A beautiful summer's evening, sun setting over the Kintyre hills, it's a popular walk up to the fort and down along the raised beach. You saw how many people were out there this afternoon. I find it strange that she saw absolutely no one.'

'These things happen, Frank.'

'And the bush where she said her assailant hid. Apart from all the thorns and nettles, there's hardly enough room there for a rabbit to hide, let alone the likes of Ryder.'

'You think she's lying then?'

'If not lying, then not telling the whole truth.'

We reached the top of the glen, began coasting down the other side, Brodick Bay opening out below, a fringe of cloud hanging over the horizon.

'What I don't quite understand,' Monica said, 'is why Mrs Wallace burned her daughter's clothes.'

'Like she was purposely destroying evidence?'

'I wouldn't go so far as that. I mean, I can understand her actions to a point. I'm sure if I was raped I would want to get rid of everything that might remind me of the experience. You know, like a sort of cleansing.'

'But she must have known we would want to examine the clothing for fibres and traces.'

'She says it never entered her mind.'

'Which is why we have no evidential corroboration of her daughter's story.'

The radio crackled, came to life. I rogered. It was Yuill wanting to know when we were coming in. I told him ten minutes, then signed off.

'No corroboration of any kind,' Monica said.

Adam Yuill was not a happy man. 'That's all I bloody need,' he snorted. 'The Divisional Super climbing down my throat because it's taken us three weeks to find a suspect, and now you're saying you don't think Ryder did it.'

'Not that he didn't do it,' Monica corrected, 'only that there seems to be more to this than meets the eye.'

We were all there, the whole island force gathered together for the first time in months, Yuill, Tennant, Gillies, Monica and me, drinking tea, catching up on news, the kind of session that goes on in every police canteen in the country, bar none.

'Certainly looks like it,' Bob Gillies agreed.

'Worth looking into,' Jim Tennant added.

'Okay, okay,' Yuill said, holding up his palms in a placatory gesture. 'You're probably right. So what do I tell Division?'

'A week,' Monica said. 'Two at the most.'

'You've got a week.' Yuill made a note on his pad. 'Have you been in touch with the Social Work Department yet? No? Okay, do that first, see if they've anything on the Wallaces on record. Then try her school. Teachers, friends, classmates, whatever. We need to find out as much as we can if we're going to take this any further.' He turned to me. 'Meanwhile, you concentrate on Ryder, McMorran. I'm sure you know what to do. What about the car you caught following you?'

'One passenger, male or female. It drove off as soon as I started towards it.' I consulted my notebook, read him off the description and licence-plate number. 'PNC has it down as a hire car, rented from a company in Edinburgh. Man I spoke to in their central office said it must've been hired from one of their local branches, that he'd find out and ring me back.'

Yuill glanced at Tennant. 'Did he call?'

Tennant shook his head.

'Okay,' Yuill said. 'Better follow that up, McMorran, we don't want any more adverse publicity. If there is a section of the press assigned specifically to you, then we'll have to ground you. Those, I'm afraid, are Commander Kettle's orders.'

Everywhere I turned, it seemed, Kettle was banging nails in my coffin. How long before he decided to bury me? I wondered. And did I really care any more? I didn't want to think about that, not yet, so I turned my blind mind's eye to the answer and asked Yuill how the murder squad were getting on.

'Their camp, it seems, is split,' he replied. 'Was Thomas killed by the Fangman or was he killed by someone closer to home. They've interviewed just about everyone over the age of six in Brodick and are still none the wiser. Thomas apparently led a quiet and simple life, had few friends and no enemies, and his only vice was the horses, a couple of quid a day on forecasts that never won him more than enough for a two-night binge. His friend, Fergie McGrath, the one Thomas had an argument with on the afternoon he died, has an alibi as tight as a homophobe's arsehole. So he's been ruled out as a suspect.'

'What about prints?' I asked.

'None so far that fit the Fangman's. Either he wore gloves, or . . .'

'. . . he wasn't there.'

Yuill shot me a look of exasperation. 'Or he wiped down all the surfaces he touched. The evidence tends to support the latter. There were no prints at all found on any of the door handles.'

Bob Gillies said, 'Seems their only hope is HOLMES now. They're ploughing everything they come up with into the computer, are just sitting there hoping for bells to ring and flags to fly.'

'Bet you wish you were still lying on the beach in Ibiza,' Tennant said.

'Too right.' Gillies was in his middle thirties with an average copper's build set beneath a long, lugubrious face scarred by years of professional scepticism. 'Little ray of sunshine' was not his middle name. He'd served four years on the island and swore he'd retire from the force rather than return to mainland duty. 'These cops,' he continued, 'they come across from the mainland and think they're fucking *it*. Kids hardly out of school telling me to do this, do that, make the bloody tea, treating me like I'm some kind of inferior scum that has to be humoured.'

217

'Scum?' Tennant said. 'Lucky you.'

'The worst is that sergeant, came over yesterday. Pimply wee Yah named Dowie, must've come straight out of Oxford.'

'He's the one put Frank on a charge,' Monica said.

'Then you'll know what I mean,' Gillies told me. 'Thinks he's God's bloody gift to detection. Thinks Inspector Morse is true to life. Fancies himself as the "thinking man's detective". Sits on his arse all day long trying to find his little grey cells.'

'You don't like him, Bob?' Yuill's smile was the first in days.

'Like is not the word.' Gillies glanced at his watch. 'Shit, is that the time? I better get back before his Lordship solves the whole case in a flash of accidental inspiration.'

Bob Gillies grabbed his PR and left. Monica followed suit soon after, finished for the day but on call tonight. Jim Tennant went through to one of the lockfasts, found an unoccupied mattress and promptly started snoring. Yuill sat at the typewriter and banged out reports while I sat at the desk and stared out the window, seeing nothing but the chaos caused by wild and wicked thoughts on the rampage. Eventually I sighed and reached for the phone.

'Ormidale Hotel.'

'Hi, Tommy. Frank McMorran here. You know if Kyoko's around, the Japanese woman?'

'She's been out all day, Frank, not a sign. Is anything wrong?'

'No. Doesn't matter.'

'You coming in tonight?'

'Are cops great lovers?'

'See you tomorrow then.'

Smiling, I cut the connection. Then dialled the number for Rosalind Hastie.

Dogs. I hate dogs. Whatever shape or size. However big and soppy their eyes. All I see are bared teeth and slobbering jaws. Childhood phobia. I glanced nervously around the garden.

'It's all right, Officer, I put them all in the kennels as soon as you phoned. Care to see them, now they're safely behind bars?'

It was all I lived for.

She led me round the side of the cottage, the cacophony of barks, growls and yelps increasing in volume and intensity as we approached the enclosed wire-mesh compound. My bowels churned.

There were ten kennels on each side of the central walkway and as we passed each one, Rosalind Hastie made the introductions.

'This is Lindy, and here's Loppy, and say hello to Bundle, isn't she just sweet? That one there is Oliver, and over here, Misty . . .'

I recognised a dachshund, Alsatian, Labrador, Scottie, spaniel, Old English sheepdog, Jack Russell, setter, Chihuahua, greyhound, boxer, St Bernard, and spotted a couple of hybrids I couldn't even begin to recognise. I was glad, though, to see no pit bulls, Rottweilers or Dobermanns. Nor any poodles or similarly permed rodents.

'. . . and this poor darling is Puffin.' Puffin was a collie, curled up in his basket, sucking on a blanket and looking very sorry for himself. Rosalind Hastie turned to face me. 'Did you get him, then?' she asked, tucking a loose strand of red hair back inside her scarf, wiping her hands on the legs of her blue overalls. 'The hooligan on the motorbike?'

Ruefully, I shook my head. 'Not yet, ma'am.' With no description of bike or rider to go on, our chances of catching the culprit had been limited from the outset. Earlier this morning Monica and I had watched the boarding of the second ferry to Ardrossan, before going on to our fruitless interview with Farquharson, and on the off-chance had stopped two BMW touring bikes before they embarked. After questioning both German couples for several minutes, we took their passport numbers and let them go. Which was about as close as we were going to get, I felt.

'I suppose with this murder hunt going on you have far more important things to worry about than who tried to kill Puffin.'

'There might be an element of truth in what you say, ma'am,' I told her. 'Nevertheless, we will continue to do the best we can.'

'Call me Ros, please, I'm not the Queen Mum.' She led me back out of the compound and closed the gate. I began breathing regularly again. 'So why are you here, then, Officer? Or should I call you Inspector? I read the papers this morning, you see, never realised we had a celebrity on the island.'

Celebrity? No, please. Last thing I wanted right now was to be buried in a television graveyard of has-beens and never-weres. I still had a heartbeat.

'It's about your neighbour's sheep,' I said, as we walked slowly across the unmowed lawn.

'Tully's? The one that was stabbed?'

I pointed down the hill in the general direction of the killing stone. 'Just down there.' From where we stood, I couldn't see the stone because of the trees and hedge surrounding her property. 'Could be as long as ten days ago,' I added.

Ros Hastie sunk her hands in her overall pockets, stared off to the south where, thirteen miles out, Ailsa Craig rose shimmering from the mirrored Clyde like a pyramid through a heat haze. 'There's evil on this island,' she said eventually. 'I've sensed it for a while.'

I asked her what she meant.

'The signs are there. These are times of great change, Officer, as we move from the Neptune-governed Piscean age into the Uranus-governed age of Aquarius. Little wonder then that the confused and spiritually underdeveloped are drawing from the shadow sides of Neptune and Uranus.'

You what? Again I asked her what she meant.

'You deal in facts,' she said, turning to face me now. 'I deal in energy and its sources and areas of expression in the three worlds of mental, emotional and physical.'

'You're an astrologist.'

'Some people think so,' Ros Hastie chuckled. 'Others call me witch. You know the score, a middle-aged spinster living alone in a cottage on a hill, into mysticism and all these dogs . . . I'm sure they imagine me cackling over a bubbling cauldron, chanting "*Eye of newt, and toe of frog, wool of bat, and tongue of dog*." Probably think I turn myself into a hound of hell at night and go out slaughtering sheep. Is that what you heard?'

'Not quite, no.'

'Then Tully thinks I stabbed his sheep.'

'Not at all. Your cottage overlooks the stone where it was killed. I thought you might possibly have seen something. Did you?'

'Ten days ago?'

'Between a week and ten days.'

'Nothing out of the ordinary, certainly no sheep being slaughtered by the light of the moon. I think I'd remember that.'

'What about cars parked down by the gate?'

'Tully's Land Rover sometimes. No other car that I've noticed. Tell me, Officer, what's your sign?'

'Capricorn,' I told her.

She regarded me askance for several moments. 'Mm,' she said, 'could be. Capricorns definitely have what it takes to make a good detective. By the same token, because of the duality in the nature of this planet – what the Chinese call "the pairs of opposites", like yin and yang, the basis of the *I Ching* hexagrams – Capricorns also have what it takes to make a good criminal.'

'So I could be either saint or sinner,' I said.

'Exactly. It all depends on the factors involved, what sign's ascendant at your time of birth, what energies therefore influence your personality. For instance, if you had Mercury square Pluto in your chart, I'd say your speech would tend to be incisive, yet tactful when it suited the purpose, and that your moods can swing from zeal to pessimism.'

'You've been following me,' I said.

Ros Hastie laughed. 'I'd also say you probably take unwise risks to achieve your desired ends.'

'Story of my life.' We were standing between a couple of ageing spruce by the hedge now, looking down over the field with the stone, the road into Kildonan, the hotel, and the lighthouse on Pladda beyond. Only a few wisps of cloud hung between us and the rest of the universe. 'You mentioned hexagrams,' I said, 'and ... eaching?'

'The *I Ching*,' Hastie explained. 'It's an ancient form of Chinese oracle, also called the Book of Changes. Like I said, it's based on the principle of yin and yang, and the duality of life. Very interesting, if you're into that kind of thing.'

'Unfortunately,' I told her, 'an oracle's testimony can't be used as evidence.' I turned my back on the view to study her cottage. Like Arthur Thomas's, it was white and squat with black-painted woodwork, but larger overall, the attic converted, with two dormer windows now reflecting the brilliant southern sky. 'Can you see the stone from your upstairs window?' I asked.

Hastie frowned. 'I told you I saw nothing.'

'And I believed you. Force of habit, I suppose, ask a question once, ask it a thousand times. You ever hear of a guy called Spinks? I understand he's some kind of mystic.'

'You mean Mungo Spinks? The medium?'

I nodded. 'Apparently he can visit the scene of a crime, pick up the killer's residue vibes and aura, then paint you a psychic portrait of the guy. Goes into a trance or something.'

'You sound sceptical ...'

'I'm a cop. Everything in black and white, please.'

'I don't believe that for a moment,' Hastie retorted with a dismissive wave of her hand. 'Not after reading all that stuff about you in the paper this morning. Sounds like you took one unwise risk too many.'

'Unwise in hindsight. You were saying about Mungo Spinks?'

'I don't know much, I'm afraid. We work in totally different fields, you see. But I hear he's respected by his peers, and has had several notable successes recently.'

'The Dartmoor murders?'

'Why ask if you already know?'

'I thought you'd be able to tell me more than was printed in the papers.'

'All I know,' Hastie sighed, 'is he was given a scrap of the killer's clothing and taken to the scene of the crime where he immediately fell into a trance. And that he later told police that the killer lived alone with his elderly mother in a small cottage on the moor, that the cottage was near a small stone bridge, and that the killer was mentally still a child and had a bad stammer. The police had apparently already interviewed such a suspect, and when they brought him back in, he confessed. That's all I know.'

I changed tack. 'You mentioned there was evil on the island, that you could sense it. What exactly did you mean?'

'You don't give up, do you, Officer?'

'Not if I want to sleep at night.'

'You take your work home?'

'Only when I take my head home.' I flashed her a smile. 'Evil, you said.'

Ros Hastie hugged herself and shivered. 'Let's go inside,' she said. She saw my apprehensive look, laughed and added, 'It's all right, they're all in the kennels. You're quite safe.'

I followed her inside, moving from warm light to cool gloom, from the wide airy space of her garden to the claustrophobic obscurity of her living room. The scents of dog, of many dogs, clogged the musty air; perfume to my nose they were not. Hastie swept a pile of magazines from one of the armchairs to the floor, bade me sit. I remained standing. Did I want anything to drink, she asked: I told her coffee would do fine. As she disappeared into the kitchen, I took in my cramped surroundings.

Books.

Books everywhere. Crammed on to shelves ceiling-high, stacked in piles against the walls and the side of her desk, some packed in cardboard boxes, others lying higgledy-piggledy on the varnished oak floor amidst a carpet of journals, magazines and newspapers – dating back, I wouldn't have been surprised, to the middle of the last century. What little light squeezed through the small windows now spilled across the desk, the computer, and the scatter of what I presumed were astrological charts.

'Sorry about the mess,' Ros Hastie said, returning with two mugs of coffee. 'I just never seem to find the time to clean up. You know what they say about "tidy desk, tidy mind"? I suppose this kind of sums me up.'

'In my book,' I told her, 'a tidy desk means an idle mind.' I took the proffered mug and indicated the charts on her desk. 'Do you get much demand for this kind of work on the island?'

'Now and again, though not enough to survive on. I advertise on the mainland, earn most of my living there.'

'Does it pay well?'

'You're wondering how I can afford to keep all my dogs?'

However offworldly her manner, Ros Hastie had a mind that was both sharp and intuitive. I wondered if she too was a Capricorn. 'It can't be cheap,' I said.

'It isn't. Which is why I have to take a part-time job.'

'In a pottery, I think you said.'

'Yes. In fact that's his chart I'm doing there,' she said, picking up a sheaf of papers, letting them fall to the desk again. 'Mr Byrne, the man I work for. You'd probably get on well, he's a Scorpio.'

I crossed to the window where several small framed photographs in black and white stood on the dusty ledge. Family poses, serious faces, posterity no laughing matter. I looked out across the unkempt lawn and, without turning, said, '*There's evil on this island, I've sensed it for a while.* Those were your exact words, Ros.'

Ros sighed, put down her coffee, sank on to the chair by her desk. 'I also said these are changing times, and change often instils in us confusion, insecurity, fear of the unknown. Like the planets in our universe we all have our dark sides, Officer, the shadowlands of ourselves that the warmth and light of our lives seldom penetrate. In times of insecurity people who are spiritually weak will often resort to stalking their shadowlands in search of their lost security. Hence evil will out.' Ros Hastie rose from her chair, joined me by the window. 'A little fanciful, perhaps, for someone like you who deals solely in the material world, but . . .'

'Not,' I said, 'if it can help me find out who's been killing these sheep.'

'I don't really see how I can help you.'

'My sergeant has a theory it has something to do with the full moon. I think the sheep may have been used as some form of sacrifice.'

'Pagan ritual, devil worship, that kind of thing?'

'I've heard there's a bit of it still goes on on the island.'

Hastie snorted. 'Kiddies' stuff,' she said. 'Childish games, nothing more.'

'The attractions of sex and sin?'

'In a nutshell, yes. As far as Satanism is concerned, I doubt they could even summon a waiter, let alone the Lord of Darkness.'

'Would the sacrifice of a sheep be part of their ritual?'

'No chance. A chicken, maybe – and knowing them, it would probably be a frozen one.'

The image conjured up a laugh. 'You actually know them?'

'Not personally,' Ros replied hastily. 'But I did go out and watch them once, out on the Moor, strutting their stuff. I was curious, you see, and wanted to find out more. I suppose I found out. Pathetic, really, what some people will do for a bit on the side.'

'That's how you see it then, as an excuse for an orgy?'

'With a little sinful titillation thrown in.'

Now I was getting curious. 'Out on which moor?'

'Where I work. Machrie. Where all the stone circles are.'

'Can you give me names?'

Ros Hastie picked up the framed photograph of two little girls hugging each other, regarded it fondly for a moment before slowly shaking her head. 'Names, no. But if you want to see them in action for yourself . . .'

'Definitely.'

She crossed to the desk, searched through her organised chaos of papers, eventually digging up a large desk diary. She licked her finger and flicked through the pages. 'Mm,' she said, 'aren't you the lucky man. Just as I thought. Day after tomorrow is the Summer Solstice. They'll be out in full force, I imagine.'

'How many?'

'When I was out there, about twenty.'

'Mostly men?'

'More women, I'd say.' Ros slammed the diary shut. 'Are you going to arrest them?'

'Only if they start sacrificing sheep.'

I wondered if it was an offence to slaughter one of your own sheep in such a ritual manner. No, I decided. Only if it was somebody else's sheep, or was on someone else's property, or caused someone offence. Breach of the peace, at most. The issues were moral rather than criminal. Then I suddenly realised that somewhere on the island a farmer was missing a sheep and I still had to find him. Hadn't even thought about it. Christ. Pressure of work was affecting my brain. Now, with more than a hundred and sixty farms on the island, I had a day's worth of phoning to do. Which was all I bloody needed.

I asked Ros where the best vantage point was.

'I hid in a small ditch behind a clump of stones. It wasn't very comfortable, though, and I didn't dare leave until they'd all left, in case they saw me.'

226

'What would they have done if they'd seen you?'

'I don't know. But I didn't want to find out.'

'Could you draw me a map of the area?'

'I tell you what,' Ros Hastie said, cocking her head and placing a finger to her chin. 'Why don't you come out to the pottery tomorrow afternoon and I'll show you?'

I flicked through my mental diary. I had a meeting with Farquharson at one. A lot of phoning to do and reports to type up. No problem. I could do the phoning in the morning and the reports *mañana* . . . which left me the whole afternoon.

'Yes,' I said, 'why don't I?'

The hotel bar was mobbed. I had to push through the crush at the bar and then wait ten minutes before I got served. I ordered two pints and downed one while Freddie poured the second. Kyoko was nowhere to be seen. The sound of fiddle music drew me up the steps into the dance hall at the back. A five-piece folk band were playing on a makeshift stage at the far end of the room. Irish and Scottish reels. A few young couples danced between the tables but otherwise it was standing room only. If Kyoko was there, her disguise was perfect. I retreated to the bar. Ended up talking to a group of bikers from Edinburgh. We talked bikes and pubs, bikes and football, football and pubs. The more beer I drank, the more homesick I felt. The more whisky I drank, the more I thought about Kyoko. By the time I staggered out the door, I was peering at the world through a one-eyed focus.

I stumbled between the cars that crammed the drive. The fresh air hit me and my head started spinning. I leant against a flash black car to regain my balance. My head on my arms, my arms on its boot. I wasn't going to puke, I wasn't going to puke. My senses reeled. I tried concentrating on something. It was silver. I brought it into focus. It said Nissan. I jumped back as though stung. Fell on my arse. Stared at the number plate. It was familiar. Sat there waiting for coherence of thought. Gave up. Climbed unsteadily to my feet. Lurched around the side of the hotel, up the path to my cottage. Took several minutes to open the door. Fell into the kitchen, lay there on the floor awhile. It felt good. For a moment. Then the world started turning again. I could hear the mice under the sideboard. They were laughing at me. Tomorrow I'd get a cat. Someone in the hotel drove a Nissan. Big deal. Had they come here by chance or had they followed me? Who fucking cared? There was a potato-peeler under the cooker. So it hadn't been stolen. I rolled on to my back. There were more than a hundred people in the bar. One of them would drive the Nissan home. Then I could do them for drunk-driving. On second thoughts, not. There was a beer in the fridge. Maybe even two. If only I could raise my head from the floor. I could. I did. If only I could stand up. I could. I did. For a second. I fell into a chair. I was going to puke, no I wasn't. Coffee, that's what I needed. Coffee and another drink. No. Just coffee. Tomorrow was an early start. I docked with the sideboard. Easy. NASA take note. And where the hell was Kyoko, I wanted to know? Avoiding me? The kettle refused to boil. I switched it on. Woman like her'd have boyfriends on tap. Like the Neanderthal. She was probably with him now. I slammed my fist on the sideboard. It didn't hurt as much as the hurt inside. The kettle boiled. I would not give up. Coffee was in the left-hand jar. Now it was all over the sideboard. I would see her again and this time ask her out. Pour the water into the cup. *Into* the cup, I said. I would move on her gently, then seduce her with my natural charm. Be sugar-sweet. Sugar in the right-hand jar. Two spoons, and stir it in. Then drink.

It tasted like petrol. Sweet petrol. Petrol with sugar in it.

I smiled.

Grabbed my keys and the jar of sugar, then stumbled back out into the night.

21

*'Before completion, attack brings misfortune.
It furthers one to cross the great water.'*

It's cool but you don't care. The night seems to wrap itself around you like a warm fleecy coat, the stars above pressing down, a pincushion of flickering lights, the shadows shallow around you, hiding no threat, no unrecognised inner fears, the soft breeze off the sea a portent, yes, carrying scents you cannot immediately identify, and seaweed, oil, pine and salt. The sound of the waves crawling up the pebbled beach like the slithering of a snake, crests wreathing white in the light of the three-quarter moon, sighing in retreat. A night-hawk shrieks. Somewhere in the distance a car growls to life.

Wei Chi.

Moonlight. Some nights it seems to bathe you in its luminescence, wash you clean, picking at your bones the way a vulture might, licking you clean, young bones glistening, blood-glossed in the silvery glow. Other nights, nights like tonight, it sits there, smug and gloating, a pulsing heart in the heavenly body, sucking at your blood the way a baby feeds at its mother's breast. A regeneration, of old blood into new.

Before completion.

Again the intuition of the *I Ching* has surprised you. Its accuracy and understanding of your mission you find at once frightening, exciting, and awe-inspiring. Its advice, the reading, perfect in its simplicity.

The hexagram indicates a time when the transition from disorder to order is not yet completed...

An hour ago when you threw the bones – coins, you feel, are too impersonal – you were lost, floundering, your mission stagnant, without direction, in total disorder. Now the weight of indecision has been hoisted from your shoulders, you know the way forward. Your mission is still on course.

... and presents a parallel to spring, which leads out of winter's stagnation into the fruitful time of summer.

Behind you, dune grass whispers in the wind breezing in off Kilbrannan Sound, the water an oily black flecked with chrome, the pebbles on the beach smooth as muscle, hard as destiny, grey as a winter's day. Inside you, laughter simmers, ready to boil.

Before completion, attack brings misfortune. It furthers one to cross the great water.

Lying at your feet, spread-winged on the flotsam, the maggot-ridden carcass of a rotting crow, life discarded. Such is the nature of existence: one creature's death is another creature's life. So why hadn't the solution come to you earlier, you wonder? It was so simple, so clear, so perfect. Out of disorder, order comes.

A new situation must be created; one must engage the energies of able helpers...

The 'able helper' is already in place. Tasty Hastie had squirmed into your life as though ordained. Why, otherwise, had you offered so little resistance? Not just because she reminded you of Simone, but because of her mysticism: as though both of you are being drawn together by planetary forces beyond your ken and control, both becoming integral parts in the same divine mission. For the moment, the prospect is thrilling.

... and in this fellowship take the decisive step – cross the great water.

In other words, board the ferry and cross the great water to the mainland. Leave a bitch lying in a ditch someplace over there and ... problem solved. Couple of hours after they find her – of course, you'll have to make sure they do find her – and the whole island will be clear of the murder squad. Simple as that. One fell strangle and you'll have cleared up the mess that was Arthur Bloody Thomas, and sent the police off in a totally false direction. Perfect.

Then completion will become possible.

You step out of your overalls, hobble naked across the greasy pebbles and wade out into the mercurial Sound until the water covers your hips. You incline your face to the Moon overhead, feel it suck the surging laughter from your throat: a contented chuckle that in no time at all becomes a triumphant roar directed at the source of all your power. *You are God! You are God!* You shake your fist and bellow at the stars, belittling their impotency. You thrash and splash and scream and cry, you laugh and curse, then dive beneath the midnight swell. There, in the primordial darkness of the universal womb, you baptise yourself in the blood of the Earth. Emerge purified and rejuvenated. Then, laughing still, you make your way back to the shore. As you climb into your overalls, headlights from the Machrie road arc across the sky, the sound of a car retreating to the north.

If only they knew!

You sink to your haunches, lean back against a boulder and project your gathering thoughts across the Sound, burying them deep amidst the shadowy hills of Kintyre.

Completion.

You can sense it approaching, even though the finer details of your mission are not always clear. As though you are but a common foot soldier whose understanding of the complete battle plan is in no way essential to its ultimate success. There are also moments of almost blinding insight when for a split second you can see the whole scenario spread out before you, the paths along which your destiny lies, crystal clear in your mind.

The final outcome, though, remains ever obscure, just off the edge of the map, attracting you like some magnetic force or the gravitational suck of the Moon, drawing you ever closer. And the closer you get, the more compelling it becomes, the more irresistible.

We are but colliding atoms, our actions and reactions but cause and effect, our struggle to control our lives but a blind arrogance, a vain attempt to invest meaning on the meaningless. We are mere pinballs, you believe, propelled into life at the speed of sperm. And from that moment on, our blind eyes instinctively seek, then cling to, the light of existence like moths to a flame. The superior man is but urge and instinct, the inferior man but a robot of his own making.

Like your father.

It was autumn, you recall, the night sky then, as tonight, a silver-speckled dome of royal Dali blue. You were what, nine years old, ten? It doesn't matter. There were waves then, too, though not licking the beach like an ingratiating poodle but pounding in like punches, pummelling the cringing sand: the beach in question far to the north, north of Lochinver on the west coast of Sutherland, up amidst the black granite rocks, the flying spray, the howling winds, the swooping, shrieking gulls.

It was a special treat, staying up late to watch the sun go down, slip into the bleeding sea as you stood silhouetted on the headland amidst the grazing sheep, your tiny hand clasped in his. He said if you watched closely enough you could actually see the world turning. But you couldn't. He said maybe if you were lucky you'd even see the Northern Lights. But you didn't. He asked if your mother was having problems while he was away at sea. He said you could tell him, but you couldn't. You couldn't tell anyone.

'You see, women,' he said, dropping to one knee and smoothing down your hair, 'are not as strong as us men. They're fragile creatures, son, and they crack very easily. You probably know your mother's not been very well of late, and the doctor's

232

said that what she needs is a little time on her own. Which is why he's sending her to this special clinic in the country for a while, so she can get better.'

You remember the relief you felt.

'And you, you lucky wee mite, will be going to stay with your Nan.'

You remember how your relief crumbled, how a cloying sense of gloom arose from its ruins even as your father gave you a gentle chuck, and added, 'I'll be back before you know it.'

That's how you remember him best: that night as he towered over you, almost blotting out the pale crescent moon ascendant over the headland, his farewell eyes focused on the bloodstained horizon over your heaving shoulders, his thoughts already buoyant on seas to be sailed and oceans to be crossed, Mediterranean, Red, Arabian, Indian, South China . . .

Otherwise, your father remains unfocused in your memory, a series of blurred snapshots taken during his infrequent visits home, shining through the haze of recollection like a blinding sun glimpsed sporadically through shifting banks of cloud.

You see him in his uniform, a tall slimline version of yourself, as he turns at the top of the gangway to wave goodbye, the expression on his face, clear in hindsight, one of sadness yet relief.

You see him Sunday afternoons covered in grease, every now and then wiping huge oily hands on the legs of his overalls as he strips down the engine of his white TR3, his only pride and joy, on the short garage drive.

You see him Saturday afternoons sprawled in his favourite armchair, wire-framed reading glasses perched on the tip of his nose as he struggles with the *Daily Record* crossword while watching the horse racing on a black-and-white TV.

You see him weekday evenings tending the neglected garden; climbing the ladder to repair loose tiles and rusted gutters; working in the shed, sawing, chiselling, planing, hammering nails into wood.

You see him Friday nights staggering in from the Gunner's, cowering beneath your mother's whiplash tongue before collapsing dead to the world on the living-room couch.

You see a quiet man, a gentle man, counting down the shore-leave days, impatient for a rolling deck and the clamour of an engine room, a simple life dictated by orders and structured by duty, an emotionally secure cocoon of undemanding camaraderie.

But what you see most clearly beneath the unremitting light of hindsight is a weak man, a man who deserted you, who left you alone to the mean devices of your mother and grandmother. You see a cowardly, selfish man who could not, would not, face the truth of his suspicions, who preferred to run away to sea rather than confront the horror of what was going on.

A man who finally paid the ultimate price for his cowardice. *Completion.*

22

'*Some mornings I look up and see the Distillery sitting there in the hollow, and it's just as though time had stood still. Just how I remember it as a youngster.*'

Findlay Farquharson said, 'Look, I'm in the middle of some very delicate negotiations here, and the last thing I need is the place crawling with cops. Why don't you just ask your bloody questions and leave.'

Which were my thoughts entirely.

'These negotiations,' I said. 'Tell me about them.'

'That's not necessary. They have nothing to do with your investigation.' He was in business-meeting mode this afternoon, three-piece charcoal-black suit, white shirt with a gold-studded collar, black woollen tie. His briefcase remained closed but his portable phone lay ready within easy posing reach.

'Until I decide otherwise, they are very much a part of my investigation.'

Farquharson sat there giving me the evil eye as I leant back and, drumming my fingers on the table, surveyed the interior of the Malt Barn Reception Centre. I was, I hoped, the perfect picture of infinite patience.

'*It begins with the barley we use. It's malted locally for us, the old way, with peat smoke from the ovens adding flavour. It's the malting that adds a lot to the flavour of malt whisky – that, and the pure spring water we use. We tap the spring way up on the moor, so there are no impurities, you see.*'

We sat at one of four pine tables in the middle of the tiled floor, with an unopened bottle of Glen Chalmadale and four glasses on a tray between us. The bottle, I felt, would remain unopened in my presence. Twenty feet above us a couple of fans churned the sluggish air below the pine ceiling, while behind me, a small log fire blazed – for effect, I supposed – in a wide stone hearth, with a pile of logs stacked neatly against the natural stone walls on each side of the chimney. Four brass lamps hung on chains from the ceiling and, facing me across the room, a flight of stairs led up to a small museum of distilling artifacts. To the right of the stairs there was a simple bar, and to the left, a large video screen upon which Archie McDonald recounted – on a loop – the traditions of distilling a 'hand-made' malt whisky.

'The grist is then mixed with the spring water in the mash tun and heated up. The idea is to extract the sugar from the grist. Now when we've got everything we can from the barley, we clear out what's left.'

There were only two small windows, both to my right and overlooking the burn. Through which one, I wondered, had John French made his ill-fated observations?

'Okay,' Farquharson sighed, eventually tiring of his evil eye. 'This is getting us nowhere.' He opened the bottle of whisky, poured two large drams and pushed one across to me. 'So we don't like each other, what's the big deal? We don't have to be in love to get on with our particular jobs, do we? I admit I'm not the easiest guy to get along with. It's a fact. But you don't build up a business like mine by being easy to get along with.'

The excuse of every business executive in the land who enjoys being a total bastard.

'Still,' Farquharson continued, 'why don't we put this unpleasantness behind us and start again? Forge a new era of cooperation between us: I tell you what you want to know so you can finish your investigation, then we both live happily ever after.' He clinked his glass against mine. 'How's that sound?'

236

Like so much shit, I wanted to say. I thought about refusing his peace dram, but then decided against it. Firstly, not to accept a whisky from a Scot is as gross an insult as calling him or her English; and secondly, the Glen Chalmadale is a superb single malt and as such, one of the finest hair-of-a-dogs you are ever likely to taste. So I took the proffered glass and raised it to my lips. 'Sounds . . . fair,' I said. 'Slainthé.'

'To peace in the glen.'

And murder on the bens, I thought, as Farquharson gulped down his dram. I savoured my own a little longer.

We pump the hot sugary liquid – the wort – up to the Morton Refrigerator, the only one still in use in Scotland. In modern distilleries everything is sealed up tight. Me, I like to see the process happening, see that the liquid is running nice and clear.

'Tell me,' I said, 'about John French.'

Farquharson's expression darkened. 'The man's a thief and I fired him. Simple as that.'

'He claims you framed him.'

'And you're prepared to believe the likes of him?'

'Just the truth,' I said. 'When I hear it.'

'Things had been going missing for months, McMorran. Small amounts of money from the shop register, a case of whisky once in a while from the storeroom, stuff like that.'

'When did you become aware of it?'

'April?' Farquharson shrugged. 'May?'

'About the time of the break-in?'

'Near enough.'

'You didn't think they were connected?'

'Why should I? Nothing was taken from the break-in.'

'Yet you never mentioned the pilfering to Sergeant Yuill.'

'I like to run a tight ship here, McMorran, the fewer leaks the better.'

He must have been up all night studying The Business Book of Clichés. I asked him how he thought the sheep came to be in the water-tank.

'Someone put it there, obviously.'

'And how did they get it through the gates?'

'I don't know. With a key, I suppose.'

'And after the break-in, did you check if any keys were missing?'

'Of course. They were all still there.'

'In the key cupboard in Maggie's office?'

'Yes,' Farquharson snapped irritably. 'What the hell are you driving at?'

We only fill the washbacks halfway, because when you add the yeast and fermentation gets going, the wash can froth right up to the top, especially on a hot summer's day.

Which was how I felt right then, frothed right up to the top. Outside, it was a hot summer's day.

'Tell me about your negotiations with the Japanese,' I said. 'Are you selling out, merging or what?'

'Expanding is the word you're looking for, McMorran.' Farquharson's tone was his puke-up patronising one. 'A chance to break into the Jap market, if all goes well, make a fucking killing.'

'Your mother, I believe, disagrees.'

'My mother is old and stubborn. She clings to tradition like skidmarks do your pants. She doesn't understand the way business is changing. That if you don't keep up, you go down. Simple as that.'

Nothing, I knew, is ever as 'simple as that'.

After forty-eight hours we pump out the fermented wash for distilling. The distilling's really what this place is all about. Ours are the same traditional copper pot stills you'll see all over Scotland – only a lot smaller. The bigger one only holds about eight hundred gallons. As they say, the smaller the still, the finer the whisky. It's also a reminder of the time when the stills around here had to be small enough to hide from the Excise.

'At what stage are your negotiations?'

Farquharson closed finger and thumb to within a millimetre

238

of contact. 'That close,' he said, 'to the clincher. But you know what the Japs are like, perfectionists to perfection. They have to examine every tiny detail until they understand not only its function, but its spiritual karma in the cosmic scheme of all things living and dead.'

'Like dead sheep in your water-tanks?'

'Like a dead fucking sheep in my water-tank. Exactly. Which is why I want to get the whole thing cleared up as quickly and quietly as possible.'

'You haven't told them about the sheep? That you think someone's trying to put you out of business?'

'What the hell for? Man, that'd be financial hara-kiri.' Farquharson poured another two drams, again drained his in a oner. 'Anyway,' he continued, 'I changed my mind. If someone wanted to put me out of business, there's a hundred better ways than dropping dead sheep in my water supply.'

'Like murdering one of your tenants?'

'I'll pretend I didn't hear that,' Farquharson said, shooting me another evil eye, squinting it hard in my direction. 'No, I reckon this is just a grudge, nothing more sinister than a petty act of revenge.'

'So who do you think did it?'

Farquharson gave it some thought while I eyed the whisky in my glass and fought to keep my fingers locked.

You know the spirit's on its way from the smell. You'd never miss it – it's strong and clean as it comes through the breathers on its way to the spirit safe. When the spirit first starts coming in, it's full of impurities – the foreshorts – and likewise, the end of the run is too weak – the faints. What we use is the heart of the run, the strong, pure liquor – that's what we're after.

'French,' Farquharson said. 'Who else could it be?'

'French reckons you sacked him because of something he witnessed in this room.'

I'd expected him to explode. He didn't let me down. In the first few seconds the colour of his face changed from pink to red to purple. Then his mouth began working soundlessly, the words refusing to form on his lips, choked off deep, I imagined, by the force of his fury. He looked like one of those bulbous deep-sea fish that never see the light of day.

'That's it. This time you've gone too far.' Spittle dribbled from his lips as he stabbed his forefinger at me across the table. 'I warned you before, now you've had it. Say goodbye to your career, McMorran, it's all over.'

'Judging by your reaction, I'd say French had a case.' If my career was over, I'd enjoy what little of it I had left.

'You know what makes me sick about your kind? You think just because you put on a uniform it gives you the right to the moral high ground. You sit up there with your air of superiority, sniping at anything you don't even begin to understand. You regard yourself as judge and jury, pass sentence without even listening to the case. I've seen your kind, McMorran, you're fucking everywhere. You grow up with a chip shop on your shoulder and have an instant down on anyone who's had it easier than you, who has a better education, who drives a better car. If you weren't a cop, you'd probably be a thief, the same kind of thief as French. Which is why you sympathise with him, why you'd prefer to believe his spiteful accusations, because you recognise him for what he is, just another poor persecuted little prick like yourself.'

I felt my own colour rising, had to hold myself in check.

Tuesdays and Wednesdays, we transfer the spirit into casks. They're numbered to show how many we've filled this year. We fill around fifteen a week – now that's a very small amount indeed. The Glen Chalmadale has to be one of the most exclusive whiskies in Scotland, due to the volume involved. We only produce in a year what big distilleries produce in a week.

'Whatsamatter?' Farquharson growled. 'Cat got your tongue? Just seen your job flow down the tube? There, see, it's just like I said. When it comes to the crunch, people like you are nowhere to be seen. Typical.'

I'd be there. When his crunch came, I'd be there all right. To sweep up the pieces. Cops have memories that put elephants in the shade.

I modulated the tone of my voice. 'French says you have such a high turnover of female guides because of your unsolicited sexual advances.'

'That little shit will never get another job on this island. Like you, McMorran, he's finished.'

'Wrong,' I said. 'He's going to get the job he applied for. You want to know why? Because you're going to ring the Field Studies Centre and give him a glowing reference.'

'Sure,' Farquharson sneered, 'and pigs like you will fly.'

'While a pig like you gets roasted on the spit of his perversions.'

'Are you threatening me?'

'It sounds awfully like it.'

Farquharson leapt to his feet, knuckles white on the tabletop. 'I don't have to take this kind of harassment.'

'Unlike the girls in your employ,' I sneered, rising to my feet. We were now almost nose to nose across the table. 'But that's always the way it works, isn't it, Farquharson. Little men like you need egos twice the size of ordinary men just to feel normal. Talk about chips on shoulders. Talk about microchips. Talk about midgets who have to prove themselves and their manhood again and again, abusing their power, throwing their paunchy weight about, bullying young girls into sexual submission. What d'you think, Farquharson? What if I traced all the girls you've employed in the last couple of years and took their statements? How many could be persuaded to bring charges against you? I'm betting quite a few. What's your bet?'

His breathing was ragged, his face apoplectic, our eyes locked in mortal combat. Silence but for the video and the singsong lilt of Archie McDonald's voice.

'*Sometimes people are surprised to see that new spirit is clear.*

241

However, it's the maturing in old sherry casks that gives the whisky its rich colour over the years.'

Eventually Farquharson buckled, lowering his gaze. With exaggerated concentration he picked up his briefcase and pocketed his phone, tugged at the sleeves of his jacket. His smile held all the charm of an executioner's axe.

'Okay,' he said. 'French can have his stupid job. But you, McMorran, haven't heard the last of this.'

Farquharson shot me one final look full of pure distilled hatred, then the door slammed behind him. I sank down on my chair. I was sweating hard.

'Once a cask is filled, it's away to the warehouse. It'll spend ten years there. The whisky breathes in our local air, which adds to the flavour. Only trouble is that some of the spirit gets out. About a quarter of every cask evaporates – that's over the ten years – we call it "The Angel's Share". I suppose you can't really begrudge them their dram.'

Quite right, Archie, I thought. Just call me Angel.

I downed my share in a oner.

Masao Hayashi bowed twice quickly and offered me his hand. I shook it, nodding twice in return.

'My niece has mentioned you,' he said, inclining his head towards Kyoko at his side. He too was in business-meeting mode, black-suited and black-tied, a slight man in his late fifties with fine grey hair brushed back and a pencil-line moustache etched across the top of his upper lip.

'Likewise.' My smile was lukewarm and half-hearted. The echoes of my session with Farquharson still reverberated in my head, crashing off the sensitive walls of my hungover skull. I was not in the mood for the pleasantries of polite conversation.

'You are a policeman,' Hayashi observed.

Sometimes I need reminding. Right now I didn't.

'I love your uniform,' Kyoko said with a mischievous smile. 'It fits you well.'

'Thank you,' I said, bowing my head graciously. 'How are your negotiations going?' I'm no Albert Einstein but sometimes I can add two and two and come up with four. It just takes a little time, that's all.

Kyoko nevertheless looked surprised. 'Negotiations?'

Masao Hayashi said, 'They are ... progressing, I believe is the correct expression?' His accent was mid-Pacific and not as flawless as Kyoko's. If she'd studied at Cambridge, I reckoned he'd probably studied at Yale. 'Are you here in a professional capacity, Mr McMorran?' He pronounced my name 'Macmorlan'.

'A minor matter,' I said. 'Such is a policeman's lot in a small community like this. Are you enjoying your stay?'

'It is very interesting, yes. The people here are very friendly. We are made to feel welcome. If such hospitality could be exported ... aah, your country would be rich.'

'If we could export our *rain*,' I said, 'our country would be rich.'

Masao Hayashi chortled on cue. 'But your summer is beautiful.'

'A beautiful freak. We haven't seen this much sun since Arran crossed the Equator three hundred million years ago.'

'Is that a fact?' Hayashi glanced at his watch. 'I was wondering,' he said. 'Would you be so kind as to offer my niece a ride? Unfortunately our car would not start this morning.'

'No?' I said. 'That's a shame.'

Hayashi shrugged. 'Someone filled the gas tank with sugar. I understand there was a party at the hotel last night.'

'Part of the folk festival,' I said, feeling my neck and face redden. I ran a finger around the inside of my collar as I put another two and two together.

'The exuberance of youth, no doubt.'

'No doubt.'

I wondered if I'd been seen in the hotel car park last night, cock-eyed, rubber-legged and sugar-handed. It was possible, very possible. I could see my recollection of the event vaguely through a murky post-alcoholic fog, later events not at all.

Hayashi's expression gave nothing away. 'Mr Farquharson and I have a very important meeting this afternoon—'

'At the golf club,' Kyoko interjected.

Hayashi smiled, acceding the point. 'I find golf ideal for business, Mr McMorran. At the same time one may relax, yet compete. There is exercise for old boardroom bones like mine, and oxygen for the brain. You would be amazed how many deals I have finalised by the eighteenth hole.'

'Then I wish you luck.'

Masao Hayashi winked paternally. 'Kyoko-san, however, regards golf as a good walk wasted. Perhaps . . .'

'I'd be happy to give her a lift,' I said.

'There, that's settled then.' Hayashi bowed and shook my hand, bowed again, then said a few words to Kyoko in his native tongue before bowing to us both. 'I hope we can meet again,' he said. He walked back up the lane, crossed the bridge over the burn and disappeared into the office.

'So,' I said to Kyoko, 'here we are.' One of my better opening gambits.

'You've been drinking.'

'Just the usual half-bottle.' We walked down the lane towards the car park. A straggle of tourists wound up the hill, led by a tartan-suited Maggie looking none too pleased. She rolled her eyes heavenward as she passed. The afternoon was hot and getting hotter.

'I can never tell if you're being serious or not,' Kyoko said.

'Don't worry, I drive better with one eye closed.' I asked her what her uncle had said before he left.

Kyoko giggled. 'He said, "Beware the *gaijin*, he slurps from the cup of your beauty."'

'I do?' She was wearing a pleated knee-length Black Watch skirt, a pine-green cowl-necked lambswool sweater under a sleeveless scarlet cardigan, bottle-green tights and black patent suede pumps. Around her neck, a string of deep red coral beads. Business-meeting mode, Kyoko-style. 'What did he mean by that?'

'A thirsty man will do anything for a drink.'

'I will?'

'Sure. Like take me back to my hotel.'

I'd parked Mike 30 in the shade of a tour bus, but the bus had long gone and the car was now baking. 'You realise it's against regulations for us to offer lifts to members of the public?'

'So treat me as a witness.'

'Witness to what?'

'How about a crime committed in our hotel car park last night?'

I unlocked the passenger door, held it open as she climbed in. 'You mean the sugar in your petrol tank?'

'I saw the whole thing.' The ghost of a smile formed on her lips, haunted her eyes.

'You did, did you?' I rounded the car and climbed in.

'It was very funny. He could hardly walk. He kept falling on his bottom.'

I'd wondered about the bruises this morning. 'What else did he do?'

'He swore a lot. He had a big bunch of keys which he kept dropping on the ground. Then he'd fall over trying to pick them up. Then he'd find the right key and just as he was about to open the lock a crowd of people would leave the bar and he'd jump into the bushes. Must have happened at least three times.'

'I wish I'd been there to see it,' I said. The interior of the car was a cauldron, and we the poison'd entrails boiling. I started the ignition and drove out through the gates. 'Would you recognise this desperate villain again?'

'Probably. If I saw him out of uniform.'

'Mm,' I said. 'Why do you think he did it?'

245

'Maybe he was drunk and didn't like me following him.'

'Maybe he didn't realise it was you following him.'

'Would it have made a difference?'

'As your uncle says, a thirsty man will do anything for a drink.'

I turned down into Lochranza. The road was clear of sheep and the village was awash with an incoming tide of tourists from the docked ferry. A long line of hillwalkers trekked past the golf course in the opposite direction, while outside the Field Studies Centre groups of kids lounged on the grass, congregated in tight multicoloured knots. I wondered if Farquharson would keep his word concerning French.

'I thought Brodick was that way,' Kyoko said, jerking her thumb back along the road we'd come.

'A minor detour,' I told her. 'That is, if you don't mind?'

'What choice do I have?'

'There's a bus in an hour.'

'Charming.'

The ruin of the castle stood resplendent in sunlit finery as a dozen or so yachts bobbed on the silvery bay, masts swaying lazily in the warm breeze. As we passed the pier the first few cars in the queue nosed down the ramp and on to the Claonaig ferry.

I said, 'You know what they have in common, Lochranza and your home town Wakayama?'

'Flooding. Mrs Farquharson told us there was a bad flood here several years ago.'

'Fishing,' I told her. 'Lochranza was one of the main fishing ports on the west coast until the end of the last century when the herring suddenly stopped coming up this way. No one knows why.'

'Perhaps they were fished out . . .'

'Not then. They just stopped coming. And suddenly the four hundred or so villagers had to find something else to do.'

'What did they do?'

'Most became seamen. At one time there were more master mariners from Lochranza than any other west coast village. Then the tourists started coming and saved the day.'

'You should be a tour guide.'

I told her about my summers here as a boy, under the tutelage of my Great-Aunt Joan.

'Sounds idyllic.'

'It was,' I said. 'Then.'

We cruised through Catacol in silence, were almost upon Thundergay when I said, 'This is where we first spotted you yesterday.'

'If it hadn't been for that damned bus . . .' Kyoko sighed as the village retreated behind us. 'Anyway, it wasn't my idea.'

'Your uncle's?'

She nodded. 'He wanted to know what the police were doing up at the Distillery. Farquharson kept saying it had nothing to do with the business, don't worry about it. But my uncle, well, he worries about everything. I suppose it's why he's so good at what he does.'

'And what did you find out?'

'Your . . . colleague? Is very attractive, don't you think?'

'I'll tell her you said so.'

'I didn't realise you were so famous.'

'Only in certain circles,' I said. 'And the word is infamous.'

'Picture in the papers . . . my uncle was very impressed. He wondered what such a famous man was doing here.'

'Call it a penance. A thousand Hail Fleecies.'

'He's worried that your investigation has something to do with the Distillery.'

'He's right to worry.' I told her briefly about the sheep found in the spring water tank. 'Farquharson thinks someone's trying to put him out of business.'

Kyoko frowned. 'By contaminating his water with a dead sheep?'

'I know. It sounds ridiculous, doesn't it?'

'There must be a million better ways.'

'And ones which would not be so easily discovered. It's as though whoever put the sheep there wanted it found.'

Kyoko lapsed into thoughtful silence. Not for the first time I found my thoughts straying to Farquharson's mother, Flora, a strong-minded woman who publicly opposed her son's wishes to expand the Distillery's market. I wondered how much say she had in the negotiations. And I wondered again if she could be behind the business with the sheep. She certainly had the means, opportunity and a possible motive. I asked Kyoko what exactly her uncle was negotiating.

'Sole distribution rights,' she said, 'for the Japanese market.'

'Of the single malt?'

'Initially, yes. To make it worthwhile, of course, Farquharson would have to increase production quite substantially. I imagine my uncle's company would then appoint a trading company in Tokyo to sell it as an up-market whisky.'

'Increased production would no doubt mean big changes at Glen Chalmadale?'

'Dramatic changes,' Kyoko agreed. 'Which is why my uncle came. He says for a tree to grow tall and spread its branches wide, it must be rooted in firm soil and receive plenty of nourishment.'

'Your uncle is full of sayings.'

She regarded me suspiciously. 'Or full of shit?'

'You tell me.'

'Well, for a start he thinks the Distillery is in serious financial difficulties. That if this deal falls through, the business might well collapse.'

'That bad?'

'He puts it down to bad management. What he would call weak roots in a barren soil. Mind you, he reckons most Western businesses are mismanaged. Too top-heavy.'

As we passed through Pirnmill, I said, 'Like they say, scum floats. They should have allowed whisky distilling to become a legal cottage industry. Think of all the beautiful whiskies denied us, like the one they used to distil up in the hills there.'

'They had an illicit still up there?'

'Sure. Best place to keep an eye out for the Revenue cutters patrolling the Sound.'

'So they were smuggling as well?'

'Aye,' I said. 'From the caves down on the Imacher shore across the Sound to Carradale, four long miles by the dead of night.'

'Carradale? Isn't that where they found all the slaughtered goats?'

'Mm,' I agreed, inwardly cursing the increasing number of breaches in my memory. However slender the possibility of a connection between the goats and the sheep, I would have to check it out. When had Alec Brodie said it happened? March 1976. Would they still have a record of it in Campbeltown? Possibly. If not the police, then either the local library or in the offices of the *Campbeltown Courier*. I'd have another word with Brodie, if I saw him in the bar.

Kyoko rifled through her bag, found her tobacco and rolled one up. I said nothing. I was by now a resigned passive smoker. With the polluted condition of the earth, sea and air, carcinogens in all I ate, drank and breathed, a few passive smokes a day hardly seemed cause for sanctimonious outrage. Live and let die in breathless agony, that's my motto. Kyoko inhaled hungrily and asked, 'So, is this a mystery tour or what?'

'Call it the wheel of law and order grinding relentlessly on,' I said as we passed Dougarie Lodge. 'I have to see a woman about a sheep.'

I parked beneath the signs that said MOSS FARM POTTERY and NO THROUGH ROAD, and we climbed the pitted track on foot.

'She's a potter?'

'An astrologist,' I told her. 'Works part-time at the pottery.'

'When I was at school that's what I wanted to be, a potter like

249

my grandfather, Toshio. He was famous for his pots, you know. People came from miles around. In Wakayama he was revered, as all great potters are in Japan.'

'So what happened?'

'He died when I was twelve,' Kyoko sighed. 'And my father had other plans.'

'As fathers always do.' We followed the track alongside a crumbled drystone dyke separating fields of lazing and grazing cows, then dog-legged left through a rusted gate and passed our first stone circle which, the Historic Scotland sign told us, is formed of a single row of granite boulders, with the scanty remains of a burial cairn within. There was also a group of three middle-aged couples within and, as we continued up the track, we passed two young couples on mountain bikes, a man walking a Labrador, and two older women taking it slow. The track turned and climbed, looking more like a dried-up riverbed now than anything fashioned by man.

'Just a short walk?' Kyoko said. 'We must've come a mile already.'

Which were my thoughts exactly. I decided then that if I came out here tomorrow night, I'd definitely come by bike. We topped the ridge and the shallow bowl of the undulating moor opened out around us, spread in a patchwork of greens and browns, russet and gold. The telegraph poles that accompanied the track now led down to a cluster of buildings in a small hollow to our left. To our right, a stone circle of two concentric rings, known as Fingal's Cauldron Seat. When Kyoko asked me why, I showed her the cylindrical hole in one of the stones where, tradition has it, the Celtic hero, Fingal, tied his dog, Ban.

'Fingal as in Fingal's Cave?'

'The same,' I told her. I escaped elaboration by trotting down the track to the cluster of buildings.

There were three of them, all of them roughstone with grey-slated roofs, and forming a loose triangle around a grass courtyard dissected by gravel paths. The L-shaped building on the left comprised the pottery, the building on the right the potter's cottage complete with two dormer windows, and the building forming the base of the triangle appeared to be a storeroom. Cord-wood was stacked as high as the gutters against its left-hand wall. A grey Subaru estate was parked, dented, dirty and rusting, alongside. Kyoko caught up with me as I entered the pottery.

'Ah,' Rosalind Hastie said, jumping to her feet behind the counter. 'I was wondering if you'd come.'

'Wonder no more.' I introduced Kyoko and then asked if she'd spoken to her employer. She glanced at the half-paned door to our right, through which I could see a large man in dungarees sitting hunched over a slowly forming pot on a slowly spinning wheel.

Ros lowered her voice and leant close. 'He wasn't too happy at first when I mentioned it, but when I told him you were the policeman in all the papers, he seemed to change his mind. He's one of these news freaks, I think. You know, like reads the paper cover to cover every day, watches all the news programmes on TV, listens to the radio all day long. Anyway, he said he'd talk to you, which is something.' She dropped her voice to a whisper to explain: 'He's not what you'd call the world's greatest conversationalist.'

'No?'

'No. But once you get him started . . . Well, you know how it is. It must get quite lonely out here, the middle of nowhere.'

'Except nights of the full moon,' I said. The potter was still hunched over his wheel, seemingly oblivious to our presence. Kyoko had wandered over to a display of pots in a glass-fronted cabinet, was peering at them intently. The sound of a radio seeped through from the potter's workshop. Radio Four. The man must be really lonely, I thought. I asked Ros Hastie at which of the stone circles she had witnessed the lunar gatherings.

'I'll show you.'

She led me outside and down the path between the potter's cottage and the storeroom, then stopped and pointed west.

'There,' she said.

A hundred yards away I saw a group of three standing stones. Behind it, Ard Bheinn rising into a clear blue sky. To the north-west Machrie Moor stretched towards Gleann an t-Suidhe, the Glen of Rest, overlooked by Beinns Nuis and Tarsuinn and, in the distance, Goatfell. In the foreground a line of low trees cut across the moor, shadowing the journey of Machrie Water as it tumbled towards the bay. Between us and the burn, another standing stone, this one alone, lit by the sun, the same soft gold as the brackened moor.

'And you watched from where?'

She pointed to the right of the three stones. 'There's a ditch that runs round behind the stones. Not very comfortable but you get a good view.'

I turned back towards the pottery and stopped. 'What the hell's that?' I asked. Behind the storeroom and shaded by a crescent of silver birch, it looked like a distorted stone igloo with a tall flue sticking out the back.

'Mr Byrne's wood-burning kiln. He made it himself, you know.' I noted the surge of pride in her voice, wondered if she and Byrne were lovers.

'A man of many talents,' I said, and led the way back inside.

The potter had emerged from his workshop, was now standing next to Kyoko in front of the display cabinet. 'Unfortunately,' he was saying, 'these are not for sale.'

'A pity,' Kyoko replied. 'They are truly . . . original. I have never seen such a beautiful glaze before.'

Ros Hastie stepped in. 'And it's won him many prizes, my dear,' she said. 'Other potters have tried to emulate it but they never succeed – do they, Mr Byrne?' The potter said nothing, and Hastie added, 'The recipe is his most closely guarded secret.'

Byrne meanwhile was measuring me with leisured eye. He

was a large, lumbering kind of man, six-three or four, with a slight stoop, heavily built and in his mid to late thirties. Sandy hair topped his high, rounded forehead, curling over his ears and collar, giving him a certain kind of boyish charm emphasised by large heavy-rimmed glasses with thick lenses that magnified his watery blue eyes and added to his air of innocence. He wiped his huge hands on his dungarees and offered me his right.

'Gideon Byrne,' he said in a voice as soft as crushed velvet. His grip was limp and moist, his skin cold and rough. 'And you must be . . .'

'Frank McMorran,' I said. 'I appreciate the time you're giving me.'

He shrugged away the pleasantry. 'And who's the lovely lady?'

'A friend, Kyoko Tanaka.'

He took her hand, dwarfing it in his, pressed it delicately to his lips. 'The pleasure is all mine,' he purred. A charmer indeed. Kyoko blushed and bowed, retrieved her hand. Byrne spoke to me without taking his eyes from Kyoko. 'You're interested in the occult, I understand.'

'No more than curious.'

'Yet you wish to observe tomorrow night's festivities from my house?'

'As part of an ongoing investigation,' I said. 'Nothing serious, though – a hunch, no more.'

Byrne tore his eyes from Kyoko to regard me unblinkingly. 'This investigation . . . is to do with the murder in Glen Rosa?'

I shook my head and laughed. 'Not quite. A little more downmarket than that. You'll have read about the sheep, perhaps, the one found stabbed down by Kildonan?'

'And there was another one too, wasn't there?'

'Mm. So you see, no big deal, I'm afraid. Just some sick psycho out there who has it in for sheep.'

Byrne lowered his large blue eyes on to mine, regarded me

253

steadily for a moment before saying, 'You better come out before dark, then.'

I told him I would.

'And bring your lady friend, if you like.'

Kyoko smiled but shook her head. 'Sorry, but I'm all booked up tomorrow night. Thanks all the same.'

'Some other time, perhaps?' Gideon Byrne asked. He had a small slack mouth with lips that stretched his face apart when he smiled. 'You can tell me about your grandfather.'

Kyoko was noncommittal. 'We'll see.'

Byrne nodded to me. 'Tomorrow then,' he said, then turned and lumbered back into his workshop, closing the door behind him.

Ros Hastie let out her breath as though she'd been holding it for the whole conversation. 'There,' she said. 'That wasn't so bad now, was it?'

'Was it supposed to be?'

'Well,' she shrugged, 'you know. Sometimes he can be a little . . . well, impolite.'

'I thought he was quite . . .' Kyoko, back at the display cabinet, searched for the right word.

Charming? I thought.

'. . . charming,' she said. 'Not impolite at all.'

Ros Hastie glared first at Kyoko and then at her watch as the three middle-aged couples Kyoko and I had passed back at the first stone circle now filed cautiously through the door. 'Oh, well,' she said. 'No rest for the wicked, I suppose.'

'Nor for the wickedless,' I told her. 'We won't keep you any longer.' I thanked her for her help and left seconds before the pack closed in.

Kyoko had moved on from the cabinet, was now admiring a neighbouring display of teapots and mugs in an assortment of shapes and glazes. A sign above the display warned that breakages must be paid for. Kyoko handled the teapot with care, studying first its base, then its spout and handle. Its glaze was a simple ferrous green, with a blue rim and lid. It seemed strangely familiar. Whether it was the shape or colour, I couldn't be sure.

Kyoko said, 'Mr Byrne is a talented man.'

'And charming.'

Kyoko looked at me askance but I was busy studying a small bowl in the same glaze as the teapot, noting the initials GB etched crudely into its base. Perhaps Ros Hastie had a similar teapot, I thought. Or someone else I had visited recently. *Would you like a cup of tea, son?* is one of the many hazards of the job.

'Why the thoughtful look?' Kyoko asked.

I replaced the bowl and said, 'I was trying to remember where I'd seen this pottery before. No big deal. Just one of those annoying little things that's bound to keep me awake all night.'

'You mean, like putting sugar in petrol tanks?' Kyoko's smile sparked in her eyes, lit up her face. She had the most lovely teeth. 'Are you ready?'

Ready, yes, to crush her to my chest and suck the lips off her face. Ready, yes, to find a quiet place in the sun, strip down and dream the rest of the day away. But ready to return to the boring reality of a seemingly never-ending shift? No, no way.

'Give me ten minutes,' I said.

I circled the group of three standing stones, found the ditch Ros Hastie had referred to and checked it in various places for the best vantage point. I found that the closest I could get for maximum observation and least chance of discovery was about fifty yards from the circle of stones, and thirty yards from a fallen stone that had been cut in half and the halves shaped into millstones. If there was to be any sacrificing done, I felt it would be done there.

I wondered where in the sky the moon would be.

I examined both millstones carefully, looking for traces of

blood I knew I wouldn't find. I found none. Then I sat on one of the stones and looked back towards Byrne's cottage. I could just see its roof and two dormer windows. I wondered how Gideon Byrne felt about the moondancers, whether he watched their antics from his attic window or joined in the moondance himself?

Harmless fun, I wondered, or something more sinister?

Tomorrow I would find out.

As I climbed to my feet and trudged back along the beaten path to the Moss Farm Pottery, it suddenly came to me where I'd seen some of Byrne's pottery before.

In pieces, on Arthur Thomas's living-room floor.

When I rejoined Kyoko her eyes were alive with excitement.

'He's going to make me one,' she said as we walked back down the track towards the car. 'A special one just for me.'

'One what?'

'Pot, stupid! He's going to make me a small bowl using his special glaze. He doesn't do that for just anyone, you know. But in my case he said he'd make an exception.'

'He fancies you, that's why.'

Kyoko laughed, punching me playfully on the arm. 'Frank! Don't be silly. He said he'd do it as a special favour because my grandfather was a famous potter, and also because I'm a friend of yours.' She skipped a couple of steps and laughed again. 'He said he had to keep on the good side of the law.'

'He's probably got a pile of parking tickets he wants overlooked.'

She poked me in the ribs. 'Cynic!' She was walking backwards now, facing me, her smile brighter than the sun. 'He says it should be ready in a week to ten days but he'll ring me at the hotel to let me know when I can come and pick it up. Will you come?'

'I don't know,' I told her with a straight face. 'Three's an awful crowd. You'll maybe want some privacy.'

'Frank!' She grabbed my lapels and pulled herself up on to tiptoes, kissed me softly on the lips. 'I do believe you're jealous.'

I kissed her lightly on the brow. 'I do believe you're right.'

23

'You want my opinion?'

'Naturally,' Gideon Byrne said, with one of his odd little smiles. We were talking murder.

'Well, in my opinion,' I told him, 'the guy's a paranoid schizophrenic with delusions of grandeur. He probably collects complexes the way some people collect butterflies – you know, pins them to his psyche and then examines them in microscopic detail. It's also likely he has a persecution mania and imagines the whole world is against him. And in this case, he's right.'

'Damn right,' Byrne agreed.

It was a nice night for it. The fringe of cloud in the western sky was stained a deep blood red, while to the east the sky was a rich midnight blue, already pierced by stars above the black surrounding hills. The moon had yet to make its grand appearance.

'I'd also say he's an underachiever who feels he deserves better. And judging by his choice of victims, he belongs to either the upper working class or lower middle class.'

Byrne lifted an eyebrow in question. 'How can you tell?'

We were talking about the Fangman. Well, I was talking and Byrne, between yawns, was showing polite interest. He'd obviously not realised when he'd asked me for my personal psychological profile of the killer that he'd opened the door on my latest obsession.

'Because,' I said, 'such a killer usually selects his victims from the section of society that he feels has rejected or ignored him, one that continues to threaten and misunderstand him. Victims who are invariably weaker and more vulnerable than he is, and quite often close at hand. If you look at the Fangman's victims to date, you'll find most of them are well-to-do, upper middle class, and most of them are women most likely older than he is. So what we could have here, in very simplistic terms, is a killer who was brought up by a domineering mother – in the absence, perhaps, of a weak father – and is now killing her again and again in his demonic fantasies. Look at Ed Kemper, the American serial killer. What was almost the last thing he did before he gave himself up? Killed his mother in a manner he'd been fantasising about for years. Cut out her larynx for all the times she'd nagged at him. That's why, when you're dealing with a serial killer, you can't attach too much importance to the identity of the victim because the killer doesn't care who they are, only what they represent in his fantasies. They become mere objects, dehumanised.'

Gideon Byrne yawned. He was slumped in his armchair with his legs stretched out, resting a glass of home-brew on his belly and watching me through half-closed, almost reptilian eyes. In his right hand he held the remote control for the TV, and every once in a while would flick absently through the channels as I talked.

'I'm not boring you, am I?'

'Not at all,' he insisted. 'I find this all quite . . . exciting. Do go on.'

I didn't need much persuasion. I took another draught of beer – Byrne was as talented with his home-brew as he was with his pottery – and continued.

'I think he may well see himself as some kind of soldier, as a swashbuckling hero, perhaps, on a secret mission to save the world. From whom or what, I don't know. But his whole life, as he sees it, is a fierce battle in which he is constantly fighting against impossible odds. The minor obstacles you and I take daily in our stride and regard as merely part of the struggle we call life are no minor obstacles to this man. He sees them all as part of a giant conspiracy to deny him his rightful place in society and the respect he feels he ultimately deserves. So he fights back. And like a soldier, he kills without remorse. His motivation? Like that of "Son of Sam" David Berkowitz, who claimed he was ordered to go out and kill by a visiting demon, "father Sam" – *I voss only follovink orders*. In the Fangman's distorted world of fantasy, his murderous rampage is already fully justified: it is what society deserves for having ignored his full potential. In other words, following orders to do what he wants to do anyway is all the motivation he needs. And such, I'm afraid, is the nature of war.'

'Absolutely,' Byrne said, coming alive. 'Such, indeed, is the nature of war.' He used the remote control to lower the volume of the TV. 'You saw it on the news just now, before the bit on the Fangman. Politicians, diplomats and generals, all outraged by what they call "senseless slaughter". But the bottom line for those in the front line is kill or be killed. Always has been, always will be.'

Which was quite a monologue coming from Byrne.

'Well,' I said, 'that's one way of looking at it.'

'One of many ways.' Inspired by the turn the conversation had taken, Gideon Byrne seemed like a different man: suddenly there was fire in his eyes and emotion in his voice. 'Look at you,' he continued. 'You're out here tonight to investigate ritual sacrifice. Yet there are those who believe war to be the modern equivalent of ritual sacrifice. In the times when the standing stones out here were used for religious ceremonies, the blood of the sacrificed victim was believed to actually fertilise the soil. In the same way, the annihilation of an enemy during war can be seen as guaranteeing the survival – in other words, fertilisation – of one's own clan.'

He must have noticed the surprise on my face because he sank back in his chair and smiled sheepishly.

'Sorry,' he said. 'Sometimes I get carried away.'

'It's certainly an interesting theory.'

'But it's not every day I have a policeman as a guest in my house.' He drank heavily from his glass, wiped his lips. 'In fact, I feel honoured. Your personal insight into the Fangman is fascinating. Tell me, didn't I read somewhere that he always kills on a full moon?'

'Full *and* new moon,' I corrected. 'Which means he's probably influenced by it. You know, like the moon affects the tides. That's why they refer to people like him as "lunatics".'

'You learn something new every day.'

'All that water in our bodies, I'm surprised we're not all ebbing and flowing all over the place.'

Byrne laughed courteously. 'What about the Fangman's sex life?'

'Zilch,' I said. 'Forget it. He's probably homosexual but doesn't even realise it. Most likely he's never had a shag in his life.'

The potter frowned. 'How can you say that?'

'Because these kind of people find normal relationships impossible. The relationships they form are all about power, having the power of life and death over someone. They thrive among the dead. They feel safer with the dead, they're in control. Look at Dennis Nilsen, who supposedly killed for company. Kept his victims under the floorboards in case the urge came over him. Then he'd dig them out and talk to them, play with them for a while before shoving them back under the boards.'

'So why is this Fangman guy murdering defenceless old women? He's not having sex with them . . .'

'He doesn't need to have sex with his victims to be classed a sexual sadist. He probably achieves orgasm by the very act of murder, of strangling his victim to death. Or maybe as he's biting their throats out. Who knows. Or even . . .' I stopped just in time.

'Or even what?' the potter asked.

I shook my head, nothing. 'Talking far too much as it is,' I said.

Byrne shrugged. 'You want another beer?'

I glanced at my watch, told him sure, why not, there was still another hour to kill. But I'd have to watch it. My tongue was already loosening. Another couple of seconds there and I might have told him about the lipstick.

Byrne hauled himself out of his chair, took my empty glass and lumbered through to the kitchen. He was wearing baggy green cords, a plain white T-shirt and worn trainers. I was dressed in black. I glanced around the compact living room. It gave little away about the man who was Gideon Byrne. It said, here is a simple man with simple needs. A man who has no past, or no time for the past. A solitary man. Who devours newspapers and feeds on documentaries and current affairs programmes. Who looks at the world through a TV screen, and is content to watch it pass him by. An armchair philosopher. A tidy, meticulous man, everything in its given place, not a mote of dust to be seen. And from my own experience, a shy man, ill at ease in the presence of others. At once charming, yet abrupt and sometimes rude. He returned with my glass of beer, then excused himself again. I heard the front door close.

A man who drinks alone, sinks alone. I wondered if he sat here nights and drank himself into oblivion. Would I, if our roles were reversed? I decided not. I need people to talk to, to help drown out the voice of my own discontent. I'm a loner, sure, but only when I choose to be. I wondered if Byrne had that choice.

There was ash in the fire-grate, kindling in bundles by the hearth. A pile of old newspapers. A few cheap souvenirs on the mantelpiece, Figueras, Barcelona, Cadaques. A couple of Dali prints on the wall. *Tuna Fishing* and *Narcissus*. Dali's museum was in Figueras, I recalled, and he'd lived in Cadaques. So Byrne was into Dali. Did that tell me anything? Before I could decide, the front door slammed and the potter returned, slumping into his chair.

'Summer,' he explained, after several gulps of beer. 'It's like a never-ending cycle of bisquing and firing.'

I asked him if the recession was affecting his business.

'Recession has nothing to do with it,' he replied, his manner insulted. 'People have been buying pots for thousands of years. It's just that I don't cater for the arty-farty crowd, the kind of people blinded by exterior ornamentation, who can't appreciate the beauty in the simple fitness of form. The pots I make are practical, simple. To be used rather than displayed.'

'Don't you have some of your own pots on display?' I asked, recalling the pots in the cabinet Kyoko had so admired. 'I'm sure Ros Hastie said you'd won prizes with them.'

Byrne glowered. 'That's different,' he snapped. 'Those pots are personal.'

A touchy subject, I realised. Rather than pushing him to elucidate further, I asked him if he'd known the murdered man, Arthur Thomas. He seemed surprised by the question.

'Thomas? Why should I know him?'

'I thought I recognised some of your pottery in his house.'

'A lot of people buy my pots,' Byrne said defensively. 'I don't know them all personally, you know.'

Christ, I thought, here's someone who changes mood even swifter than Sergeant Yuill. Must be the sensitive artist showing through. Not wanting to alienate the man who had offered me the use of his attic window to observe the forthcoming celebrations, I mentally donned kid gloves.

'I'm not saying for a moment that you do, Mr Byrne,' I explained with a placatory smile. 'Only that Arthur Thomas's killer couldn't have liked your pots very much. They were lying all over the place, smashed into pieces.'

'They were?' The potter returned my smile, apparently appeased. 'Well, well. It seems the Fangman has no taste.'

'If it was the Fangman . . .' I said.

'You don't think it was?'

I shook my head. 'There are too many inconsistencies.'

'Because Thomas was a man and the rest were women?'

'That's one reason. Then there's the fact that Thomas was murdered in his own house, during the period when there was no moon at all. It just doesn't feel right.'

'Too much out of character?' Byrne was leaning forward intently again, more secure, it seemed, with subjects other than himself.

'Exactly. The Fangman's like a predator,' I said. 'He stalks his prey. He hangs around places where he knows he'll find his perfect victim – bingo halls, old people's homes, clubs for the elderly, supermarkets. He's like a big cat staking out a watering-hole, waiting for the herd to arrive. Then he'll single out the most vulnerable – in this case old and weak, single and female – and stalk her. Get to know her routine, follow her round for days, maybe weeks, all the while he's playing out these fantasies in his head, anticipating the moment he can isolate her from the pack, get her on her own, someplace he can get to know her a little better, turn fantasy into reality. That is the nature of this beast. And that's why I don't believe he killed Thomas, whose murder had all the trappings of an impulsive, spur-of-the-moment job. The whole thing appeared hurried, unplanned, amateurish. Not like the Fangman, who seems to plan his killings carefully.' I drained my glass and set it down on the table by my chair.

'Another beer?' Without waiting for a reply, Byrne took both glasses through to the kitchen and refilled them. Last one, I told myself, or I'd never get my binoculars to focus.

'So where do you think he is now?' Byrne asked, handing me my glass before sitting down. 'The Fangman, I mean.'

'Hell, I don't know. Probably grinding his teeth away in some grotty little bedsit, waiting for the knock on the door, the one he's been praying for for years, the *coup de grâce*, the final release, the end to all the madness.'

'You could be right.' Byrne yawned again. 'Do you think you'll catch him soon?'

'Soon, I don't know. But eventually, yes. Each time he kills, whether he wants to or not, he gives us something more to go on. It's like he's almost doing it on purpose, you know, deep down wants to get caught.'

'*Wants* to get caught?'

'Sure. It's all to do with guilt and punishment. He knows what he's doing is wrong but he just can't stop. Subconsciously, he feels guilty as hell and, as one of the psychological functions of punishment is the elimination of guilt, he may seek that punishment, again subconsciously, by making mistakes that will eventually result in his arrest. It's why killers like him often return to the scene of the crime. Why they scrawl *Stop me before I kill again* in lipstick on mirrors. They're like runaway trains, the only way to stop them is to either derail them or wait for them to run out of track and crash. Hopefully, we can derail the bastard before he kills again.'

'I wish you luck.'

'Me? No. Wish it on the murder squad,' I said, 'they're the ones who need it. Me, I've got a far more important mission: protect and serve the ovine race. Protect them from the hands of Jock the Sheep-Ripper, and then serve his head in a sweet-and-sour sauce to my superior.'

'And if you don't?'

'Look for my blood on the sacrificial stone out there.'

'Which reminds me,' Byrne said, glancing at his watch. 'They should start arriving soon.' He climbed to his feet. 'I'll show you upstairs.'

They must have gathered down by the main road or perhaps by the Moss Farm Road stone circle, walked it from there. They came into sight in procession, double file, advancing sedately towards the group of stones like a choir down an aisle. All of them wore long white cowled robes and colourful wooden masks, and carried burning torches, flames dancing in the gentle breeze. At the rear, two men carrying a litter between them. The distant murmur of a monotonous chant came to me through the partially opened window.

I was in the attic guest-room, a sparse room with an unlived-in feel, single bed, wardrobe, chest of drawers, and a dressing table I'd had to move out of the way to get to the window. I sat now in darkness, binoculars in hand, the sound of Byrne's TV wafting up the stairs.

I couldn't get Kyoko out of my mind. Not that I wanted to; she felt comfortable there, bringing to life fires too long extinguished. The touch of her lips on mine yesterday afternoon as we returned to the car from the pottery still very much alive in my memory, the happy excitement I'd seen in her eyes seemingly contagious: all I had to do was think of her and my heart would beat faster, my pulse zoom.

I counted eighteen, including the man leading the procession. He was obviously the man with the pointy hat, the one in charge, the Lord High Priest of whatever it was they were worshipping or celebrating. Night of the full moon, Summer Equinox and all, it had to be something to do with fertility. Ros Hastie had suggested as much with her comments on the orgy she herself had witnessed.

The procession arrived at the stones, the two files parting, like water around a midstream boulder, to form a wide circle around the stones. I focused the binoculars on the man now standing in the centre of the circle, arms aloft in apparent supplication. Whether he was speaking or not, I could not tell because of the horned mask he wore, larger and more ornate than those of his acolytes. Apart from its cow-like horns and eagle-like features, its most noticeable characteristic was its nose – or beak – which seemed to hang from the centre of the varnished mask like a thick and flaccid penis, its bulbous tip painted red. He was distinguishable also by the robe he wore, red as opposed to white, with what appeared to be delicate gold embroidery across the shoulders and down the sides of the garment, and a large gold disc centred on his chest – the full moon, I presumed. He was not a tall man, but stocky, and there was something about his gait or the way he stood that triggered within my subconscious mind some faint spark of recognition. Without his robe and mask, I felt sure I had seen this man somewhere before.

I studied the circle of acolytes. As near as I could determine, there were present ten women and seven men. Their robes were plain, unadorned, their masks crude depictions of common animals. Among them, I saw bulls and cats, snakes and dogs, sheep and goats, a fox, a frog, and a bear. Footwear ranged from bare feet to trainers to Doc Martens.

The two men who had carried the litter now broke the circle, depositing it on the grass by the slab of stone I had examined yesterday. They then returned to their places in the circle. The man in red, Penis Nose, began gesticulating again, delivering, I imagined, his sermon, every now and then opening up his arms to the moon now climbing the southern sky.

The Moon. The Mother Goddess. Mistress of the Elements. Queen of Heaven. Keeper of the keys of fertility and the gates of birth, death and resurrection. Bearer of the seasons. In Japan, Kyoko had told me yesterday, the Moon is regarded as a masculine symbol, born of the right eye of some god whose name I'd already forgotten. Something else about a hare living there, with a pestle and mortar. I wondered what ritual they were re-enacting out here, was it death or resurrection?

I also wondered about the Neanderthal called Dave. What kind of symbol did he represent in Kyoko's mind? One of fertility, purely phallic? Or was it more than that, or less? She'd said she had a date tonight, and when I'd slyly brought the question up later, she'd just laughed it away, told me not to worry about her, it was me I ought to worry about out on the midnight moor by the light of the moon. But I still couldn't help thinking about her and Dave, and what they might be doing right this very minute. The habit of suspicion, I find, is also a curse.

There was movement now among the circle of acolytes – the sermon apparently over – it was down-to-business time, a definite sense of purpose to their actions. Produced from the litter, a crude wooden cage. A black-handled knife with an eight- or nine-inch blade. A wide silver chalice. Several bundles of switches about two feet long, half a dozen more torches.

The torches were stacked like the poles of a wigwam, forming a cone. The circle re-formed, closer now, inside the stones. Most of the acolytes had removed their masks. I focused on them all, one by one, saw only three faces I recognised: a middle-aged widower I'd once met in the bar on the ferry: a woman in her early thirties, a waitress in one of Brodick's sea-front hotels; and Julian Ryder – surprise surprise – rape suspect and ned supreme. Perhaps tonight would not be the unproductive waste of time I'd expected.

Ryder, I noticed, seemed to enjoy a position of seniority among the acolytes. It was to him that Penis Nose seemed to issue instructions, and Ryder who now lifted the struggling chicken from the crude wooden cage and held it up above his head as though offering it to the moon. Ryder who then held the chicken – not frozen, as Hastie had jested – to the stone, Ryder who picked up the knife and raised it in the air.

Penis Nose dipped his head once, and the knife came down. Blood spurted from the headless chicken. Ryder held its gushing neck over the chalice as the sound of chanting reached my ears again. When the blood stopped flowing, he presented the chicken to Penis Nose, then knelt and lit the tip of the cone of torches. The chanting became more insistent as the acolytes began circling the fire in a shuffling kind of gait that looked like it had been copied from some bad old B-movie Western. A kind of tranquillised American-Indian war-dance. The word that sprang to mind, amateur.

Unlike the Fangman who – since my discussion with the

potter – was also back in mind. As Ryder now held the chicken in both hands over the leaping flames, Penis Nose plunged the knife into its chest and sliced downwards, opening it up so that its entrails dropped into the fire. I wondered if there was any significance in that – but not for long. In fact I wouldn't have been at all surprised if they'd pulled a barbecue kit from the litter and grilled the chicken on the spot, brought out the buttered rolls. They had me that much in awe. So I wondered instead about sacrifice, a word I knew came from the Latin *sacer facere*, meaning 'to make whole or sacred' – thank you, Great-Aunt Joan.

To restore to life again through death.

Is that what the Fangman was subconsciously trying to do, restore the sense of his own life through the death of others? It wasn't too far-fetched – in the same way that ritual sacrifice is doomed to repetition because of its inability to appease completely, and finally, the appetite of the gods, so too are the sacrifices performed and perpetrated by the serial killer. Once his victims have died, and the role they played in his fantasy are lost for ever, the killer becomes aware that nothing has changed, that he has failed to achieve ascendancy over his past, and that all the wrongs he has attempted to right in the sacrifice of innocents has done nothing but leave him with an even greater sense of unfulfilment.

They'd stopped their shuffle now, were taking it in turns to step forward and drink from the chalice of blood. Blood as the rejuvenating force. So rejuvenating, in fact, that they were peeling off their robes now, all of them completely naked underneath. All but three had removed their masks, Penis Nose one of them. Standing round in just their sandals, Docs and trainers as they waited for all to sip the blood of Chunky the Sacrificed Chicken. Where, I wondered, were the devilled eggs?

And then it was time for the dancing.

What looked like a Gay Gordon, but wasn't. A bastard son of, perhaps. They each took a switch from the bundle and then lined up, forming an aisle that led to the fire. The two furthest from the fire would then run down the aisle as everyone else whipped them – not hard – with the switches, generally about the genitals and breasts. Then they would leap the fire, and form another aisle on the other side. Did this fourteen times – either once for every day of the waning moon or once for every cell in their brains. I couldn't tell.

I heard Byrne climbing the stairs. He popped his head round the door, asked how it was going. I told him they were just getting down to the headline act, the orgy.

'Fucking primitives,' he growled.

'You want to join me,' I said, 'best seat in the house?'

He shook his head, disgust plain on his face. 'You suit yourself, I'm off to bed. You can let yourself out.'

'Appreciate it,' I told him.

'Aye,' he muttered, then closed the door. I heard water running in the bathroom.

Moody was right.

I turned back to the window. Had to wipe the binocular lenses.

24

'The superior man must first remove stagnation by stirring up public opinion, as the wind stirs everything.'

Gideon is already there, waiting, forty yards down the road, engine running. The strangle comes out of the doctor's surgery and stands on the step awhile, rummaging through her wicker basket. She doesn't see him. Beneath her silver-grey perm, her face is set in lines of suffering. Good. Her swollen arthritic calves are sheathed in pale-grey tights, stumps of silver birch rooted in earth-brown brogues. Her heather-hued tweed coat hangs open, revealing large breasts pushing at a pink blouse tucked into a tartan skirt. A gold brooch pinned to her lapel. Gideon can't shake his gaze from those breasts. Already he imagines them, folded and wrinkled, moving like so much unwedged clay beneath the pressure of his fingertips. He rubs the front of his trousers; he is already hard, straining at the zipper as he approaches the border, that no man's land between fantasy and reality, that asensual limbo from which he can launch himself into the sensual, the great adventure. No going back now, he is a pioneer, godlike in his utter potency, the shining light, leading the way that others might follow.

Just a rub away. A strangle.

Mishima wrote that suicide is the ultimate expression of free will – Gideon has his own philosophy: murder is the ultimate expression of free will. Because, ultimately, murder is suicide. It is the cold-blooded and well-reasoned slaughter of everything he once stood for and everybody he once was. With, of course, an added bonus: he gets to take someone else and make them his. Own them in a way they could never own him. Not just for a second or a minute, an hour, day, week, year or lifetime – but for fucking ever. His.

And, unlike Gideon, they will live on.

Their bones will live on.

Her bones.

She's at the foot of the steps now, looking round for a bus stop, a taxi. Anything that will save her the mile-and-a-half walk back to upper-middle-classville, Honeywell, that social shrine to snobbery, with their limestone manses up steep arborous drives, and the kind of net curtains you need radar to see through.

Gideon pulls out and passes her by. Pulls up, though, with a shriek of brakes thirty yards down the road. Reverses back to where she's standing. Climbs out.

Those fucking tits, man.

'Hello again,' he says. 'Can I offer you a lift?'

She recognises him almost immediately. She says, 'Oh, of course – you're the kind man who carried my shopping home from the Co-op last week.'

'I'm going your way if you like . . .'

And of course she accepts. Because her arthritis is killing her and anyway, what does she have to fear at her age? Nothing but running out of cigarettes or gin, or the telly going on the blink. So Gideon helps her into the passenger seat, his forearm brushing against her breasts as he stretches across to do up her seatbelt. She doesn't react – well, a little shudder perhaps – so maybe she liked it, because when was the last time a man who wasn't a doctor touched those breasts? Twenty, hell, could be thirty years. Before the war. So she looks up at Gideon, smiles and says thank you. He climbs back in and drives off. She prattles on about this and that while Gideon tries hard not to listen or look at her. Last thing he wants to do right now is form a relationship; just makes it all the harder come strangle time. *Say as little as you can* is the hard lesson he already learned that one time last year, that social worker strangle, Sue something, the one just wouldn't fucking die, not till he ripped her throat out, was forced, goddammit, to rip her throat out with his bare teeth. Yeah, he'd learned then. He'd also learned that he liked the taste of blood, and especially the way it spurted like cum into the back of his throat, elephant cum, almost drowning him as he sucked her in, her life into his, becoming completely and absolutely his, a lifesize doll to do his bidding, whatever his fancy, whatever his whim. The power of God.

And soon, so soon, he's going to taste that power again, taste this woman in the back of his throat, gorge on her flesh, suck those huge breasts into his mouth, stuff them all in till he chokes, till he can hardly breathe, chew those nipples, chew them right off and swallow them. Probably the same kind of taste and texture as that octopus they served him that one time in Figueras, the little restaurant off the square, the waiter, Gideon can see him now, gangly streak of piss with a pruned goatee acting like Gideon were some helluva sorry kind of scum, looking at him the same way the bitches used to do when they passed him in the street or saw him in the supermarket, the waiter, probably Juan or Carlos or – what was that waiter's name, the one in *Fawlty Towers* always getting the wrong end of John Cleese's temper? Manuel, yeah – Manuel, bringing him that octopus like it was far too good to be eaten by the likes of Gideon when in fact it tasted like shit, the kind of shit you have to sacrifice a mouthful of fillings to before you can even get it textured enough to swallow . . .

Now where was he?

'I mean, what with that awful man still on the streets, one can't be too careful, can one?'

Of course not.

'Which is why I was so glad to accept your kind offer. I mean, that poor housewife, she was taken from Dalry, wasn't she? And before her, there was the boutique owner in Ayr, whose body they found up near Largs. It's disgusting. I shudder to think...'

and she will shudder

'...what those poor women went through, what final agonies they suffered at the hands of this madman. I mean, biting out their throats, taking their skulls, that's...'

inhuman?

'that's ... inhuman.'

Now she's getting there.

The campaign is working. Terror is a turn-on. People are getting the message. They are living their lives with a new sense of keenness now that Gideon has added that heady spice of danger to their petty, humdrum, ineffectual existences. He has reminded them of the bitter taste of evil and now they taste the sweetness of life the better for it. Rather than hunt him down, they should thank him. Make him a national hero. Erect monuments in his honour. Write ballads. Name streets after him. Gideon Street. Byrne Street. Fangman Street.

'Are you sure this is the right way?'

He's already on the outskirts of town, houses retreating in his rearview mirror, making way for fields of grazing sheep and cows. He jerks his thumb towards the back of the car where two cardboard boxes of carefully packed pots remain to be delivered.

'One final delivery and that's me finished,' he tells her. 'All I need to do is drop it off and then I can drive you home.'

'Oh.'

She sounds worried. He sees the first barbs of suspicion tugging the lines of her face.

'I was talking to a friend of mine yesterday,' Gideon says. 'He's a policeman, one of the ones trying to track down the killer. He thinks the Fangman was brought up by a domineering mother and that what he's doing is killing her again and again. Which is why he's picking on older women.'

She sits there, staring straight ahead as her bony arthritic fingers knead the handles of the wicker basket on her lap. She doesn't answer.

'Women your age,' he adds.

Traffic is thin on the B road east as Gideon heads towards the forest. A couple of farm buildings tucked against the hillside north, a tractor turning out on to the road, lumbering towards him . . . then gone, the road empty.

'I think perhaps you ought to let me out here,' she says anxiously, big round eyes pleading. Like a bitch on heat. They all come to that in the end, supplication. 'I really don't want to put you to all this trouble.'

'No trouble at all.'

'If you just pull up here at the bus stop . . .'

The bus stop flashes by.

'What's your name, dear? I bet you have a pretty name, beautiful girl like you.'

She's frightened now, her mouth working but no words coming out. Gideon supposes that's what happens when you grow old, parts of your body just don't function when you absolutely need them to.

'Let me guess . . . Alice? Susan? Mary? How about Rosalind? I like Rosalind, it's got . . . I don't know, character. Like Simone. Hear the name Simone and you just kind of imagine, well, a whore, I suppose, sex in any position, any time. What did you say your name was?'

'Helen,' she says, her small voice breaking under the pressure of not knowing whether to count her future in minutes, hours, or years. 'Helen Falconer.'

'The Helen of my Troy,' he croons. 'Helen. Helen. Helen. Do you mind if I call you Helen?'

She shakes her head. There are tiny globules of perspiration glistening on her fuzzy upper lip.

'Love your tits, Helen.'

'Please let me go . . .'

'Must be all of, what, forty-two? That's some mouthful. I bet you had them queuing up to chew your nipples when you were young. Just queuing up.'

'I want to get out!' No more pleading now, he notices. Of course, it only takes a bitch an eyelash-flutter to turn pleading into anger. He's seen it so many times now it makes him sick.

'My mother was a thirty-six,' he says, pushing the accelerator needle up to the fifty mark. 'Enough, if you know what I mean, but not enough to really get to grips with. She liked to make me watch her while she was doing it, you know. Would tie me to the bed and suck me off as some guy took her up the arse. She liked that. It seemed to turn her on. How about you, Helen? Does that kind of thing turn you on?'

Helen isn't saying. She's too busy crying. Tears streaming down her blotchy cheeks, shoulders heaving but no noise coming out. Pathetic. Kids you expect to blubber; crumblies you don't.

'Never mind, it's not your scintillating conversation I'm after, anyway. In fact, I'd rather you didn't say another word. It makes everything so much easier in the end. Talk is so ... pointless, don't you think? Little more than the bleating of sheep.'

Gideon slows as he approaches the turn-off, the road clear in either direction. Nice warm day, sun shifting between marching ranks of cloud, just the kind of day for a picnic. *If you go down to the woods today . . .*

Which reminds him.

'My mother, yes. Sometimes she'd make me wear a dress, put my hair in pigtails and paint my face. Some of her men liked that, you see. A lot of them didn't even realise I was a boy until they'd ripped my tights and knickers off. Never seemed to put them off, though. They'd ram right in like I was virgin soil. That's what the cop thinks, the one I was telling you about? He thinks I'm a virgin. Or a homo. He thinks I don't know how to relate to people, that I can only relate to the dead. I mean, come

278

on, I'm relating to you, aren't I? I even related to him all last fucking night and what did he suspect? Exactly. Nothing.'

Gideon turns up the track, leaving the main road behind. Fields to left and right, woods straight ahead. He has to drive slower now, keep the wheels in the ruts, avoid the ditches and potholes. He can feel the tenseness in her, a desperate vibrancy in the air as the bitch builds herself up for the big one.

'Please!' she implores.

Gideon hits her in the face, backhanded, with all his force. She chokes, screaming, as she struggles against the seatbelt.

He hits her again. And again. And again. And again. Her struggles cease. Her head sags, dripping blood down the front of her pink blouse. Her dentures hang out of slack, bleeding lips as her moans sough on laboured, wheezy breaths.

Good, he hasn't killed her.

The track bends to the right to follow the line of the trees. Gideon follows it for several hundred yards before he comes to the gate. He climbs out, opens it, drives the car through, closes the gate behind him. She is still moaning softly, her head moving from side to side, eyes half-closed, the nearest one already swelling. He reaches across and slides his hand up and under her skirt. As his fingers work, burrowing between her legs, she offers no resistance. She is hot down there. He removes his hand and sniffs his fingers. Hot and sweaty. He tears at her blouse, sends delicate white buttons flying. Blood from her nose drips on to the back of his hand. Staring at her huge breasts, he licks it off. Her bra is reinforced, fawn-coloured lace, but not reinforced enough – he tears it open and watches her tits fall, like melons in a pair of stockings. Her skin is rough and leathery, her nipples large, flat and round. He takes one between forefinger and thumb and pinches it hard. She screams and tries to wriggle away, so he punches her again.

'There,' he says as she goes limp. 'Didn't I tell you?'

Gideon slips the handbrake and heads for the woods.

* * *

McMorran, that's his name. The cop who fancies himself as an expert on serial killers. Thinks he understands what makes them tick yet can't even detect one sitting right under his nose. Some bloody expert. Sits there drinking your beer and accuses you of entertaining delusions of grandeur. You? Come on. Superior men don't need delusions of grandeur, only inferior men, like him, the cop. Like all cops. Which is why they wear uniforms, to reinforce such delusions. And why he, McMorran, could feel secure in his supercilious, condescending attitude and the overbearing tone of moral superiority in his voice when he talked last night about you, the Fangman.

There were moments, you admit, when you felt like grinding your glass into his face, had to forcibly deflect the impulse by leaving the room on pretexts of fetching more beer and checking the progress of the bisque-firing. Even then for a while you stood by the kiln in the workshop fingering the garrotte-like wire you use for separating freshly thrown pots from the wheel, and considered using it on the cop. Knowing you'd be able to loop it around his neck and take off half his head before he even realised he was dying.

But what makes you special, you see, what distinguishes you above all others, and cops especially, is that you are a superior man. You are in absolute control. Like a farmer tending his fields, you cultivate your destiny. Then you crop.

Gideon: he who crops, hews, cuts down.

So you do not wastefully plant seeds in barren soil, and you do not kill cops in your living room, however pleasant the prospect. No, you wait. First you must cultivate the cop – maybe send him a letter, personalise the relationship – then later you can crop him. Him and the slant-eye bitch. Teach her not to come across so snooty, treating you offhand the way she did when you suggested she come round sometime and talk about her grandfather, the potter. The way all snooty bitches do, looking down on you like you're some insignificant speck of grime dirtying up their pristine world. The way all the stuck-up bitches back on the estate did, all those pretty-pretty officers' wives who thought their shit didn't stink and spent their long vacuous mornings posing in front of their dressing-tables, flicking through

Homes and Gardens *as they pruned this, primped that, painted their pinched faces in the latest garish shades and then spent all afternoon parading around all the fashionable boutiques, visiting the most exclusive clubs, fattening their limp flesh on afternoon teas in all the in places, too good for the likes of you even to spare you a glance, and when they did, say, passing you on the estate or down in the local supermarket, you could see it in their eyes, behind the pitying looks, exactly what they were thinking. The same as the Kimono bitch yesterday evening. Inscrutable, hell.*

But what bones! What a neck! Those lines, the soft curves and supple skin, the tawny complexion. Near perfection! You only saw her for a few minutes yet already she's under your skin, starring in your fantasies. Soon as Hastie was out the way and the pottery locked up for the day, you had to run upstairs, tear off your clothes and masturbate ferociously in front of the mirror. Not once, but twice. And still the bitch dogs your thoughts. Images of her compact body, soft and mellow, crowd your mind, while the memory of her bone structure seems now indelibly imposed upon your mind's eye.

Are they lovers, you wonder, her and the cop? You've tried to imagine them doing it, but images that refuse to form cannot perform. You can get them in position on the set but they just kind of lie there, listless, devoid of life and passion. Put them singly, in turn, on another set, for instance the power play down in the Chamber, and the passion, with you as director, is there in its full screaming intensity. And boy do they perform. Perhaps you should put them both down there together, see if that works. Maybe create a new set, a new play, and have them do each other while you crack the whip. Tie the cop to the bench, have the slant-eye bitch do whatever you say to him. Insert this here, push that in there. Yeah, the idea beginning to take shape now. You must give it some more thought. Develop the set, search out some new inventive props. Bring life to the fantasy, then bring the fantasy to life.

Where there's a will, there's a way.

At one time it must have been a popular picnic area. Gideon can tell by the three pine tables with benches in the centre of the clearing where he's parked the Subaru. But no longer: the overturned litter bins, the long grass and encroaching under-growth tell their own story.

'Please?'

Gideon ignores the strangle's plaintive cry and unloads the toolbox from the back of the estate, dumps it on the table nearest the tree to which she is secured. Already spread on the table are her clothes and the pathetic contents of her wicker basket. And, of course, her teeth.

Gideon opens the toolbox and runs his fingertips lovingly over the assortment of knives in the uppermost tray. The box has been with him almost a lifetime – since Junior High in fact, where he fashioned it to his own design in the woodwork class, the only subject he ever really enjoyed. Some of the knives have been with him so long they have developed their own characters. Shorty. Slash. Pigsticker. Spike. Mr Bones, the Butcher. Slicer. And, more recently, Sheepshagger, the bayonet. Different knives for the cropping of different lives, all razor-sharp, honed weekly, one of Thursday's more satisfying chores.

'*Please* . . .' she moans, 'release me?'

Look at that – life in the old strangle yet.

Humming an old Engelbert number, Gideon strolls over to the tree to examine the goods. Weird. The tune just kind of popped into his head a second ago, one he hasn't heard in years and can't remember the name. It's definitely not the Delilah one, though, that was Tom Jones, the one where he suddenly feels the knife in his hand and she is no more. That's a good one. This one, Gideon feels, somehow lacks the same direct appeal.

Anyway, the goods are looking good. Like grouse, you need to hang them awhile. It kind of loosens them up, makes them a little more manageable, not to mention palatable. Her wrists are lashed together by a thin leather belt and are looped over a stump of branch above her head, so that her feet hang several inches off the ground. The belt is the red one his mother used to whip him with, the one she favoured above all her other instruments of punishment.

Senseless Ones, like the whining strangle here, believe clothing makes them civilised, superior to the undressed races. That the finer they dress, the more superior they are. But the *I Ching* has taught Gideon to believe that quality of life lies not in exterior ornamentation but in content. In other words, that appearances deceive and are meant to deceive. That what you conceal is exactly what you fear. That, naked, we are all animals under the sun.

And what is the strangle trying to conceal? Little more than the degeneration of that once-precious temple where men once knelt in admiring supplication. But look at it, crumbling now, like the painted face of an ageing whore.

Difficult to believe, see her hanging there, all saggy flesh, pockmarks, stretchmarks and wrinkles, that she used to drive the men crazy, treat them offhand, look down her snobby nose at them as she talked all snooty, secure in her power to pick and choose. It's like looking at his mother when he goes to visit her at Elderburn House and sits there and wonders if his memory is playing tricks on him, or is maybe someone else's memory altogether. The woman he sees before him in the visiting room overlooking the vegetable garden is about the same age as the strangle here, and Gideon tries to picture his mother the way she was then, back when she was beginning to unravel, and the men started coming in twos and threes and fours when Gideon's father was away. It's not easy. Like trying to picture the strangle the same way, doing the same disgusting things.

Looking at his mother like looking at two completely different women. What was, and what is.

'Please ... let ... me ... go ...'

She's having difficulty with her breathing, can hardly hold her head up. Giving it the old JC martyr bit, lacking only a crown of thorns. Gideon kneels down so he can look up into her half-closed eyes. The swelling's coming along nicely, he notices,

283

on the right side of her face. The blood's stopped flowing from her nose, is now caking on her chin.

'Hold still, goddammit!'

Like one of those squirming mice back in the copse at school, she just won't keep still. So he grabs her hair and yanks back her head with enough force to choke off the scream in her throat.

Mm, nice throat.

Gideon applies the lipstick carefully. Scarlet for a harlot. It's not easy without her teeth in, but he perseveres. It's a persevering kind of day. Finished, he stands back to admire his handiwork. A little skew-whiff but what the hell, it's the thought that counts.

Sobbing, she implores Gideon with her big sad brown eyes. Not so snooty now, he notices, and her nipples still need a little emphasis. So he paints them too with the lipstick. Yeah, much better; now they look almost alive, garish, the way Simone's used to look after he'd chewed on them awhile.

'*Please!*' she moans.

Bad girl. *Slap.*

Dirty wee bisom. *Slap.*

One for luck. *Slap.*

It's much more fun when they struggle, it like fires him up. Like it takes two to tango. They lie there all limp and listless, it's kind of hard to get motivated, hard to get hard. But no problem now in the trouser department. Gideon may be a day late because of the cop, but the Moon's still out there, full and sucking, weaving its magic spell.

Take the beast out now, he wonders?

No, not yet. Business first.

He returns to the toolbox.

Eeny, meeny, miny, mo . . .

Book Three

The Receptive Earth

25

Rain.

Monica pulled the car off the lane below Ravensbank and parked. We sat there in silence for a while, looking up through the veil of rain towards the cottage. It was the third cloudburst of the day, the air warm and muggy both outside and inside the car. Monica lit a cigarette and blew the smoke at the windscreen where lethargic wipers slapped ineffectually at the downpour, offering only brief glimpses of the murky world beyond. Behind us the south-eastern sky was already clearing over the Firth of Clyde.

'Let me see that letter again.'

I fished it from my pocket and handed it to her. She removed the single sheet of cheap paper from the envelope and read it for the second time – another fifty and she'd catch up with me. There wasn't much to read anyway: two typewritten lines, seventeen words that now resounded in my brain like some taunting refrain from my childhood.

THINK YOU'RE SO SMART MCMORRAN HOW COME YOU
MISSED THE CLUE I LEFT YOU UP AT RAVENSBANK?

Monica returned it to the envelope and studied the postmark. 'Posted yesterday in Kilmarnock,' she observed, stubbing out her cigarette in the ashtray. 'And addressed to the Lamlash office. So why didn't you mention it to Yuill?'

'It was addressed to me, not him.'

Which was not exactly the whole reason I'd kept it to myself. If it turned out to be the hoax I suspected, I didn't want it used by Yuill or Kettle as an excuse to ground me. Nevertheless, suspicion is the standard of our profession and intuition the black sheep – never voiced, and rejoiced only on coming home. I kept my sceptical face on and my feeling about the note to myself. *Que sera, sera.*

'So now what?' Monica asked. 'We forget about the due process of law?'

'That bullshit?' I glanced at the blue-and-white police ribbon cordoning off the entrance to the cottage, and said, 'You want to sit and argue the finer points? Or satisfy your burning curiosity?'

Below the belt, I know – all good cops are driven by curiosity – but for some reason I hadn't yet fathomed I wanted Monica with me when I entered the cottage. She made a face, her expression a struggle between anger and resignation.

'You're a bastard, you know that?'

I said, 'You're looking at the prototype.'

'Aye, the one they traded in for a toaster.' Monica shrugged ruefully. 'Still,' she added, 'I enjoyed my career while it lasted. Shall we go?'

I must admit I like to watch her, the way she seems to unfold when she climbs from a car, the lines of her long, strong legs encased in the taut material of her uniform trousers, her profile set in confident determination.

Makes me feel safe.

The rain was already easing off, the air now refreshed and laden with the scent of grass, rhododendron and pine. A huddle of sheep from the neighbouring farm watched us as we ducked under the cordon and trudged up the short muddy drive to the back door.

I examined the lock for a moment, then, for the second time in a week, dug out the bunch of locksmith's keys I'd 'inherited' several years ago from a grateful housebreaker, since reformed. Last I'd heard he was acting as a home security consultant for a leading retailer of burglar alarms in Glasgow. It takes a thief . . .

'I don't think I want to watch this,' Monica said, shifting uneasily on her feet.

'Relax,' I told her as I fed the first of the thin L-shaped keys into the lock. 'You might learn something useful.'

'Yeah. Like how to break out of jail if we get caught.'

'Caught?' I said. 'By whom?' I removed the first key, selected one the next size up. Tried, as I'd been taught, to picture the internal machinations of the lock by touch. What I saw through my fingertips was an old lock with three simple tumblers.

'*Somebody* should be here to secure the locus.'

'You're so worried, why don't you take a look around?' The cordon, I noticed, surrounded not only cottage and grounds, but extended also across the track behind, and up the grassy incline to the first rank of trees, enclosing the tall beech beneath which someone had patiently observed the comings and goings of the the late Arthur Thomas. Monica caught the direction of my gaze.

She said, 'Fullerton reckons whoever the watcher was probably left his car at the end of one of the forestry tracks on the north side of Glen Rosa, crossed the Water and came down through the forest there on foot.'

'Which would suggest he knows the area well.'

'Or can read a map,' Monica argued.

I fitted another, shorter, key into the lock, searched around for the second tumbler. 'One thing we do know about the Fangman,' I said, 'is he does his homework well. All the murders to date seem to have been meticulously planned – until, of course, we come to that of Arthur Thomas. His is the only one that appears to have been committed on the spur of an impulsive moment.'

'Beware the leopard who changes his spots.'

'Absolutely. The thing about killers like this, they're in a constant process of change. From the moment they first discover they can get away with murder, their personalities are in a perpetual state of mutation. Which makes catching them so much more difficult.'

Monica glanced anxiously around. 'Come on, Frank, get a move on.'

I slid a third, even shorter, key into the lock alongside the other two, found the last tumbler almost immediately. Carefully, I turned the keys. There was a solid click and the door swung open.

'Dear me,' I said. 'Someone forgot to lock the door.'

Monica grinned. 'We better check nothing's been disturbed, then.'

'Lucky we just happened to stop by.'

The kitchen was cool and dark, the air damp and musty. Nothing seemed to have been disturbed so we moved on through to the living room. Here, there was little resemblance to the room I had entered nine days ago to find the bloated corpse of Thomas on the floor. The carpet had since been removed and the stone floor was now partially covered by a grey felt underlay. All the furniture had been stacked in the small dining alcove, and gone were all of Thomas's personal possessions. Patches of grey fingerprint powder still mottled the dark woodwork of doors, windows and stacked furniture, like the baleful symptoms of some fungoid blight. The varnished mantelpiece, I noticed, held not a mote of dust, fingerprint or otherwise.

'He may be a few slates short of a roof,' I said of the anonymous note-writer, 'but subtle he is not.'

Poised like a coiled python in the middle of the underlay, attracting flies, was an enormous turd. And embedded in its centre, a small envelope, about three inches square.

'A calling card in a calling card,' Monica observed, squatting down beside me. 'Must've been really turned on, leaving a monster like that.'

'Reliving the event, I wouldn't be surprised.'

I pulled on gloves and prised the envelope from the turd. Flipped it open and removed the card. Two lines, fourteen words, the same typewritten print as in the letter I'd received earlier this morning.

THE MAN STABS THE SHEEP, BUT NO BLOOD FLOWS.
NOTHING THAT ACTS TO FURTHER.

'What the fuck's that supposed to mean?' Monica asked.

'Trouble,' I said, heart both leaping and plummeting at the same time. Though nothing I could put into words just yet, I could feel it brewing, like a storm gathering on the horizon. A sense of my future suddenly and irrevocably changing course that was almost physical in its force. My shudder was instinctive, uncontrollable.

I slipped the card in my pocket and said, 'That sheep I found down at Kildonan? It'd been stabbed maybe fifteen, twenty times.'

'*The man stabs the sheep* . . .' Monica said.

'After it had been killed by a couple of blows to its head.'

'. . . *but no blood flows*.'

'Exactly. Blood from the head wound, yes, but from the stab wounds – nothing.'

'Which means . . .'

'We have several possible scenarios,' I said. 'One, we have some small-town sicko wanting in on the big time, trying to make out he's Fangman material. Kills a few sheep and then sees a way to build himself up to heights he knows he'll never achieve on his own. Reads all that crap about me in the papers, and decides I'm the perfect kind of sucker to fall for a stunt like this. And—'

'Two,' Monica interjected, 'we have to consider the fact that the Fangman lives on the island and killed the sheep *and* Arthur Thomas.'

'Like I said, trouble.'

291

'Or three, the Fangman killed the sheep and Arthur Thomas, but doesn't live on the island.'

'Or four, the Fangman killed the sheep and the small-town sicko did for Arthur Thomas, and one of them, both of them or neither of them live on the island.'

'Which makes everything so much clearer in my mind,' Monica said.

'Doesn't it.' I stood up and looked around the room for further evidence of the man who'd left the note. Noticed nothing immediately apparent. I crossed to the curtainless window, trailed a fingertip through the layer of undisturbed dust on the ledge.

'How'd he get in, then?' Monica asked.

'Try the bedroom,' I said, studying the catch on the window. No sign that it had been forced. Monica called me through.

'Professional job,' she said. 'Used a glass-cutter on the back window there.'

Here, the carpet was still intact, but the wardrobe, chest of drawers and double bed had been pushed back against the far wall. Windows at the front and back of the room, the latter with a circular hole in the centre of the upper pane, near the catch.

'Must've come prepared. What d'you think?'

'I think your small-town sicko wouldn't have gone to all that trouble, would've just smashed his way in.'

'I think you're right.' There was no trace of fingerprint powder on or around the window, no visible print or scuff-marks on the sill or ledge, and the carpet beneath the window bore no sign of muddied footprints. I asked Monica when the rain had first come on this morning.

'It was already chucking it down when I woke at five,' she said. 'You'll have to ask Bob Gillies, he was on nights last night.'

I made a mental note to do just that.

The sound of a car labouring up the hill shattered the sombre

292

tranquillity of the room in which we stood. Monica rushed to the window.

'Who is it?'

'Trouble,' she said. 'With a capital T.'

Detective Sergeant Dowie has the kind of face that makes me clench my fists, and an expression of condescending contempt that makes me want to use them – relentlessly. His tone of voice is one I now dream of choking off mid sentence with only the most gradual pressure of my thumbs. We are obviously destined to be buddies eternal.

'You have no right to be here,' he snapped. 'This is a secured locus, McMorran, off-limits and nothing to do with either of you.'

We'd met halfway across the sodden lawn. The rain had stopped, and the sky was clear to the south and east but for drifting islands of cumulus in the calm sea of blue.

'Secure?' I said. 'Door wide open and no one on duty – you call that secure?'

Dowie seemed momentarily disconcerted. I hoped he was personally responsible for the security of the crime scene. When he quickly changed the subject, I knew he was.

'What are you doing here anyway?' he demanded. His pale-grey suit was almost as pale as his face, and as sharp as that of Findlay Farquharson, who stood by the open door of his silver-grey Range Rover, in which they'd both arrived. I wondered what *they* were doing here.

'Looking for DI Fullerton,' I said. 'I thought I'd find him here. Instead, we found the window smashed, the door open, no one on duty and a turd in the middle of the floor.'

'What do you mean, turd in the middle of the floor?'

The man obviously didn't know how to move his bowels, I realised. Which would explain his perpetually constipated air, as though he were always on the point of explosion. I suppressed a smile.

'Exactly that,' I said, handing him the card I'd found. 'And this was embedded in it.'

'*The man stabs the sheep, but no blood flows . . .?*' Dowie said dismissively. 'What sort of nonsense is that?'

'No idea,' I shrugged.

'Beats me,' Monica said.

'Which doesn't surprise me at all. That's why I'm a DS and you're still PCs. It's called a modicum of intelligence.'

'Modicum is right.'

Dowie glowered and cupped his ear. 'Sorry, I missed that, Constable.'

'I said you're probably right, sir,' Monica replied.

'I am right.' Dowie slipped the card into his pocket. 'This is obviously a silly hoax. Someone out to waste our time. No doubt about it.'

'Nevertheless, I think DI Fullerton should see it,' I said.

'Oh, you do, do you?' Belligerently, hands on hips, chin thrust out.

'It could be important.'

'I'll decide that, Constable. If I remember correctly, you're not supposed to be involved in this investigation.'

'I am, whether you like it or not.'

'You are? How do you work that one out, Constable?'

'Because whoever left that calling card sent me an anonymous tip-off this morning. Here.'

I handed him the letter. He scanned it cursorily, then scrumpled it up and tossed it to the ground.

'Pathetic, McMorran,' he sneered, 'you really are pathetic. So desperate to get in on the investigation, you'll even stoop to this, writing yourself anonymous notes.'

I felt my voice chill a few thousand degrees. 'If that's an accusation, sir, I'd like it in writing.'

DS Dowie glanced at Monica, then myself, but said nothing.

'Of course, we'll both have to include such a serious accusation in our reports,' I continued. 'And, as officer in charge of the investigation, DI Fullerton will need to be informed.'

'Hah!' Dowie spat. 'Go running to your pet DI, is that the idea? Well, let me tell you something, McMorran, Fullerton's not going to have time for the likes of you or your pathetic attempts to get involved. He's been recalled.'

'Recalled?' My heart threw itself off a cliff. I knew what he was going to say even before he said it.

'Yes, recalled.' Dowie was smiling now, his thin bloodless lips as slack as a fat elastic band. 'You see, the Fangman's struck again, McMorran. A pensioner on the mainland. Female. All his usual trademarks. Which kind of destroys all these fancy theories of yours, doesn't it.'

On the contrary, I thought.

'Where is he now?'

'Fullerton? Packing up, no doubt.' Dowie was grinning now. I turned to Monica. 'C'mon,' I said, 'let's go.'

Dowie blocked my way. 'You'll go when I say so, Constable.'

I could feel my temper straining, like a pit bull at a leash. Monica must have felt it, too. She put a restraining hand on my arm and said, 'Cool it, Frank, it's not worth it.'

Oh, but it was close. I managed to quell, just, the urge to pound his face to pulp, but not the surge of adrenaline causing my biceps to twitch. He must have noticed it, too. His body was braced, his smile taunting. One look in his eyes, and I realised he *wanted* me to hit him.

I backed off.

'Yes,' he said, 'I can see what they mean.'

I curled my lips in response. He didn't like that.

'Stand to attention when I'm talking to you!'

I stiffened, but only to hold myself back.

'That's it exactly, you see,' Dowie continued, small head cocked, arms now folded across his chest, eyeing me up like I was walking meat being led round a pen with a ring in my nose. 'That's what they said in the canteen. Thinks he's above the law, can do what the fuck he likes just because he got lucky a few times and got his picture in the press.' His sneer, in my mind, was already halfway down his throat.

'Yeah,' I said, 'look at me. How lucky I am.'

Dowie sighed, slipped his hands into trouser pockets and looked down at his patent leather shoes for a moment, working on his dramatic effect. When it came, it had all the power and conviction of a damp squib.

'You know what, McMorran?' He was leaning into my face – well, as close as he could get, six inches below, looking up – and prodding my chest. 'You know what? I'm going to show you lucky. I'm going to make you realise how lucky you were before I ever came into your life. Then I'm going to make you sorry I ever did. How d'you feel about that?'

'Honoured, sir.' As I caught Monica's eye, Dowie swivelled to confront her.

'And you, Kemp, better wipe that smirk off your face before you join McMorran here on a charge.'

'Yes, sir.' Well chastened, I could tell.

Farquharson, too, had a smile on his face. He was now leaning against the bonnet of the Range Rover as he avidly watched the scene unfold.

'That's what's wrong with the force today,' Dowie said, returning the weight of his condescension to me. 'Too many people like you who think it's all a game. That rules are there to be broken, and that discipline is just a matter of learning how to march up and down. Well, let me tell you, McMorran, those days are over. There's a new breed of copper now, one that doesn't regard the fight against crime merely as a game, but a war that must be won. Warriors, McMorran, not players.'

I couldn't help the laugh, nor hide the contempt from my voice. 'Kids out of college,' I retorted. 'Snotty wee yoiks who think they can learn the job from a textbook. Who come into the force straight from school, with degrees in this and that and all sorts of letters after their name, and think they know what life's about. Who've never even walked the streets but have all these fancy ideas and ideals they just want to force down everyone's throat to show how fucking clever they are. Warriors? Don't make me laugh, Dowie. Intellectual fascists is more like it. Little men with ideas as big as their overinflated egos. Napoleon. Hitler. Manson. Your friend over there. You.' I laughed again, this time viciously. 'Warriors indeed.'

Dowie's complexion was naturally pale, with high spots of pink on his cheeks, nose, ears and neck. His fine, lank hair was similarly milky, parted at the side, swept back over large, ungainly ears. His wispy moustache was that of a hopeful teenager. If pale can pale, Dowie paled now, as though all the blood from the plains of his face had suddenly been pumped to the plateaux, now flushed and purple. I turned, picked up the crumpled note, and walked away.

'C'mon, Monica. Let's go.'

She, too, was staring at me, mouth open, eyes wide. She hesitated, but only for a second, then fell in beside me.

'McMorran!' His yell was one of helpless fury. 'Kemp! Come back here at once!'

He was still ranting as I turned Mike 30 and drove back down the lane.

Monica let out her breath in a rush, reached for her pack of cigarettes, lit one up with shaking hands. 'Christ,' she said through a cloud of smoke. 'What the hell are you doing to me, Frank? My legs are like rubber.'

'Giving you the ECT you wanted. Remember?'

Monica sighed, took another drag. 'Should've kept my fat mouth shut.'

Suited DCs were loading boxes of files into the back of the Land Rover, a sense of urgency in the air. They all had about them the same heady excitement I'd witnessed on their arrival more than a week ago. All it takes, I thought, is another dead body, and you're one step closer to home.

'Helen Falconer,' Fullerton said, pulling a batch of files from the desk drawer, tossing them into his briefcase. 'A sixty-eight-year-old widow, lives with her daughter in Girvan. Reported missing yesterday afternoon when she failed to return home after a doctor's appointment. Couple of kids on mountain bikes found her a couple of hours ago. Picnic area, seldom used, up in Carrick Forest. No doubt at all it's the Fangman.'

I'd dropped Monica off at the Lamlash office where, she said, she still had a couple of hours' paperwork to catch up on before going off-shift. Maybe so. I had the distinct impression, though, as I drove back up to Brodick, that she'd been unsettled by my mood, felt wary and perhaps not a little fearful for her job. Fair enough. I could live with that. Have had to, in fact, for most of my adult life. It's a hazard of my nature: fools I can suffer – barely – but arrogant fools not at all. It was just DS Dowie's misfortune that he fell flat on his face in the latter category.

Was I going to lose any sleep over the likes of him?

Was I hell.

I said, 'So what about this letter? And the card I found up at Ravensbank?'

'Forget them, Frank,' Fullerton said, emptying the drawers of his temporary desk, his manner preoccupied. 'It's probably just as Dowie said, a hoax.'

'Hoax hell, John. It's a link between the sheep and Arthur Thomas. If the Fangman did Thomas, he most likely did the sheep as well. Which would make him local.'

'You wish.'

'I *know*. Whoever did Thomas was local.'

'Okay, maybe you're right. But that still doesn't mean it was the Fangman.'

'No?' I shook my head in exasperation. 'So now you're saying, what, that we've got two killers out there, both working the same area at the same time? I can't believe you're serious.'

'Look, you're getting too wound up about it, Frank, too involved. I can understand your frustration with all this

298

happening on your doorstep – it must be hell for you. I'm sorry you're not part of the team, and I mean it – we desperately need the inspiration of someone with your knowledge and experience. But you know Kettle. He won't even entertain the thought of pulling you in.'

'All I'm asking you to do is tell him about the note.'

'And when I do, he's going to say exactly what I've told you already: let the new DC of the Thomas enquiry handle it.'

I sighed. 'So who is taking over the investigation?'

'Guess.'

'Not Dowie? Please don't tell me Dowie.'

Fullerton came round the desk, nodding gravely. 'This'll be his first major enquiry. Kettle seems to think he has some potential.'

'Potential?' I said, incredulous. If this was true, I might well have a few sleepless nights ahead. 'Potential to fuck up, maybe; to lead a murder investigation, not a chance. He's just a bloody lapdog, the kind Kettle likes yapping around his heels.'

'Can't argue with that.' The DI crossed to the cork board that ran the length of the far wall, began removing the pinned photographs of the Fangman's victims. He spoke without turning. 'Still, a word of warning, Frank – leave well alone. And I mean both Dowie *and* the investigation.'

'I can't do that, John. It's out of my control. It's become personal. The guy is communicating with me. And it's him, I know it. The Fangman. I can feel it. He either hates me, or he believes I understand him, what he's going through. Either it's a cry for help or I've become a part of his game, a pawn to be lured whichever way he will. Either way, I get to get closest. Be sure to tell Kettle that.'

'Christ, you're putting me in a position here, Frank.'

'Close, John, like something really personal.'

'I mean, you're in enough shit as it stands,' the DI said, swatting angrily at a fly buzzing his head. 'Dowie's probably on the phone to Kettle right this moment, getting the first word in.

You were up there against express orders to stay away from the investigation. You say you were looking for me – okay. I'll believe you. You say Sergeant Dowie accused you of writing and planting the note – okay, the man's that dumb, I'll believe you. You say you got that anonymous letter this morning – fine, no problem with that. But when you try to tell me you didn't show it to any of your superior officers because you thought it was personal – now that I don't believe. Not for a second. It's pure crap, Frank, and don't insult me by denying it.'

I didn't. Instead, I felt a sudden sense of detachment, as though I wasn't really there, never had been. That I was living an out-of-body experience, had somehow slipped unconsciously into a parallel existence of nightmarish quality. That if I reached out to touch John Fullerton, my hand would pass right through him. A whole major murder enquiry going on around me, and no one would listen to me, or even, it seemed, acknowledge my existence. As I struggled with this strange and novel sense of insignificance, I felt a forlorn kind of helplessness begin to well up inside me. Emotion? I thought. Me? I squashed the fucker dead. Then refocused on what Fullerton was now saying.

'And the note. You say it's the Fangman who killed both Thomas and the sheep. I say it now looks even more like a copycat, especially since we've just got another Fangman definite. *And*,' Fullerton pointed a stubby finger to emphasise the point, 'this one's bang on schedule.'

'A day out,' I argued. Full moon had been Wednesday night, the night I'd spent up at the standing stones on Machrie Moor. I realised I still had the night's report to write up for Sergeant Yuill.

'Unlike the Thomas killing, which was at least nine days out. No, Frank. Put that together with the comparatively amateurish attempt on Thomas's throat and all his bones still intact, and what you have is a better case for a copycat than for the Fangman.'

'Thomas's was an impulsive killing,' I said impatiently. 'For all we know a hurried or interrupted one. He didn't have enough time to finish the picture he was painting – that's why it was a botched throat job, why no bones or skull were missing.'

Fullerton ruefully shook his head, then crossed to the cabinet by the window, began pulling files.

'Okay,' I persisted. 'What about forensic comparisons? Hair, fibre, blood, dirt? Traces found at Ravensbank also found at one of the other locuses?'

'Christ, you know the time these things take. We can only roll as fast as the wheels that turn the system. You can be sure of one thing, though: with Kettle huffing and puffing down the lab boys' necks, we'll get any such comparison the second it comes out from under the microscope.'

'Meanwhile—'

'Meanwhile,' Fullerton interrupted, 'you ought to wind down a little, Frank. Have you looked in a mirror recently? Well, you can see it for yourself. You need sleep, lots of it.' He came round the desk, laid a hand on my shoulder. 'Look, you've got a couple of days off now, why not take a trip home, visit a few friends, drink the city dry. Relax. Clear the decks of your mind and forget about all this. Come back next week a regurgitated man.'

I couldn't help but laugh.

'Maybe you're right,' I said.

And possibly he was. Maybe I was getting too involved, taking personally what professionals can't afford to take personally. Maybe I *would* use my weekend off to go through to Edinburgh, look up a few old mates and sink a few jars. And perhaps, over dinner tonight, even persuade Kyoko to accompany me.

'And Kettle?'

Fullerton sighed. 'Okay, I'll see what I can do.'

'Great,' I said, and handed him the evidence bag containing the crumpled letter. 'I can respect a cop who knows when to cover his arse.'

And doing just that were the photocopies in my back pocket.

'And I thought "morbid" was *my* second name.'

'I'm not morbid!'

Japanese women don't laugh, they giggle behind their hands. When I'd asked Kyoko why, she explained that it was an ancient tradition, that in the old days when women married, they painted their teeth with a black paste to ward off evil and protect their mouths from bad luck and disease. Thus, in company, they would cover their mouths when they laughed. 'Nowadays,' she'd added, 'we do it because it's . . . well, kind of charming in front of strangers, and because we saw our mothers and grandmothers do it.'

I said, 'Sitting here in a cosy restaurant, sipping wine and feeling fine, and you want to talk about the Goatfell Murder? If that's not morbid . . .'

'You promised!'

'I did?'

'And anyway, you enjoy talking about murder,' Kyoko said. 'I can tell.'

We were sitting at one of the window tables overlooking the bay, the reflected lights from half a dozen moored yachts flickering across the ermine water like rippled trails of gilded thread. The night was in its late teens, maturing still.

'You can?'

'By the way your eyes change. Someone only has to mention the word and it's like watching neon lights come on.'

'You've been watching my eyes.'

'So?' she giggled, behind her cupped hand. '*You*'ve been watching my teeth.'

'And what lovely teeth they are,' I said. 'No wonder you have to hide them.' We were on our second bottle of Australian red: slowing, yes, but already glowing. 'You know which of your teeth are my favourite? The little eyeteeth, the ones you sometimes chew your lip with.'

302

'You mean I look like a vampire. How flattering.'

I tilted the bottle of wine to her glass. 'More blood, Morticia?'

Another giggle. 'I shouldn't . . .'

'But you will.' I replenished both our glasses, mine needing more than hers. It had been a long time since I'd had a meal to accompany wine – too long, in fact. And longer still since I'd feasted in such pleasurable company. So I was all the more determined to behave especially well tonight, and make a good, favourable impression. I'd just have to ask if I could fuck her stupid another night.

Kyoko sipped, then put down her glass. 'Has anyone ever told you before that your eyes have an attention span of less than three seconds?'

'Not recently.' I glanced at the waiter clearing the table next to ours. Thin, middle-aged and obsequious, he had the furtive manner and features of a weasel. I'd seen him lately, somewhere else.

'Who was she?' Kyoko asked, with a teasing glint in her eyes. 'Your ex-wife?' She'd seemed relaxed from the moment I'd collected her from the hotel almost two hours ago, and was relaxing still. Me, I felt about as relaxed as Indiana Jones in a pitful of snakes.

I told her I'd never been married. Had never hated any of my girlfriends enough.

'And I had you down as the romantic type.'

'Me?' Incredulously.

'Look around you, Francis.' Her voice a soft, contented purr. 'Here we are, in a quiet secluded restaurant, dining on fine food and bottles of wine at a candlelit table overlooking the starlit bay, and you say you're not a romantic? I just wonder what you plan to do next.'

I'd been wondering myself. 'I thought perhaps . . .'

'A walk along the beach, hand in hand, and barefoot in the sand?' Still gently teasing.

'Well,' I said, 'I was thinking more along the lines of . . .'

303

'Yes? A midnight kiss among the dunes?'

'Not exactly . . .'

'What, then?'

Was that a glimmer of disappointment I saw in her eyes? I hoped so. But I was on best behaviour, I reminded myself, and I wasn't going to blow it, not now. I was going to live to love another day.

'A bedtime story,' I said. 'The Goatfell Murder.'

Kyoko sighed. 'I should have guessed.'

'Look down from North Goatfell and you'll see – below the ridge they call The Saddle – Coire nan Fuaran, the Gully of Fire. That's where, in August 1889, a search party uncovered the battered body of one Edwin Rose, a clerk from Brixton, buried beneath a pile of boulders. He'd been reported missing by his brother after he had failed to return to London at the end of his holiday, two weeks before. The body was carried down to Corrie, a journey of about two hours, where police soon established that he'd been murdered.'

'How could they tell?' Kyoko asked. 'I mean, if you fall off a mountain, the injuries are going to be pretty horrific, anyway.'

'Fall off a mountain,' I said, 'and you're not going to have much life left to live to conveniently conceal yourself under a pile of boulders. On top of that, his pockets were empty and his face had been pounded almost beyond recognition – enough evidence to suggest murder in any copper's book. If someone takes a flyer off a mountainside here, that's the first thing I'm going to think.'

Kyoko shuddered. 'You would.'

'Damn right. I'd ask myself, Was he pushed, did he jump, or did he fall? In that order. You want me to go on?'

Kyoko shuddered again, this time spilling a few drops of her wine on to the white tablecloth. She set her glass down, nodding enthusiastically. 'Yes. Please. Go on. I should have brought a jumper, that's all.'

'Here,' I said, passing over my leather flying jacket. 'Put this on.' She slipped it over her shoulders and almost disappeared inside.

'So the age of chivalry is not yet dead,' she said, snuggling in, the warm glow of her eyes becoming a momentary sparkle that threatened to ignite an untimely fire in my loins. I should have worn a sign, I thought, on my zipper: *Danger – Tinderwood*.

'Not by a long way,' I told her. 'You know we still have feudal landlords on the island?'

'So Mrs Farquharson was telling me last night. It seems some of them are not very popular at the moment.'

'Greedy people seldom are.' I took a sip of wine to wash the guile from my voice, and asked, 'I thought you had a date with . . . er, Dave, last night?'

'A date, yes, but with Dave?' She giggled again behind her hand. 'What must you think of me?'

I was saying absolutely nothing. Lest I incriminate myself.

'Dinner with the Farquharsons,' she elaborated with a wistful smile. 'My uncle insisted I go. Even though I told him about Farquharson's wandering hands.'

'You what?'

Kyoko appreciated my reaction; it seemed to settle a question in her mind. 'You know the kind of man he is, touching you whenever he can, wherever he can. Ugh. He makes my flesh creep. But my uncle said I had to accompany him – for the business's sake.'

'And it used to be "for God's sake",' I lamented.

'Business *is* God,' Kyoko retorted. 'Or so the economists who run our country want us to believe.' She took another sip of wine and sighed. 'But let's not talk about that, let's be really romantic and talk about murder. You were saying?'

I had to spend a few moments regathering my scattered thoughts. She really had the most beautiful teeth.

'Edwin Rose,' I said. 'Yeah. After the police had buried his boots down on the beach—'

305

'Buried his boots?'

'It's an old tradition,' I told her. 'Like superstition. You bury a dead man's boots and his ghost won't be able to walk around haunting people. In fact, we still do it to this day. Works very well.'

'You do? It does?'

'Well, how many ghosts've you seen since you arrived?'

She laughed. 'None.'

'There you go then.'

She looked at me askance. 'You're having me on.'

'Perhaps just a little. Anyway, after they'd buried his boots, they soon discovered that, before his death, Edwin Rose had been seen in the company of a man calling himself Annandale. Both men, it transpired, had come across to Arran on the same steamer from Rothesay, on the island of Bute. Police then started looking for Annandale. It didn't take them long. Annandale was in fact a man called John Watson Laurie, a pattern-maker and petty thief from Glasgow. It was Laurie's misfortune, however, that an acquaintance of his had seen both Laurie and Rose together in Rothesay, and had later met Laurie in Glasgow and quizzed him about the mysterious events on Arran. As the body had yet to be discovered, Laurie, alarmed, did a runner, and his acquaintance informed the police. He was subsequently captured in September, and tried in Edinburgh in November. The prosecution alleged that Laurie had pushed Rose over the edge and had then climbed down into the Gully of Fire and robbed the dying man, before completing the job with a rock. Laurie's defence claimed that Rose's injuries were sustained in an accidental fall, and that the defendant had only robbed and tried to bury him. The jury believed otherwise, and found Laurie guilty. He was sentenced to death.'

'And hanged?'

I shook my head. 'Reprieved,' I said. 'On grounds of out-to-lunchedness. Spent the rest of his life in prison.'

'And that's it, the only murder on the island?'

'There was another one more recently,' I said, 'back in the sixties, I think. A police sergeant. Took exception to his wife's extramaritals and took her apart with an axe. No one likes to talk about that one, though. Too close to home.'

'A police sergeant?'

'Yeah,' I told her. 'Like the one they're going to find throttled pretty damn soon if he doesn't get off my back.' I explained about Detective Sergeant Dowie taking over the Thomas enquiry, and our little head-to-head up at the cottage.

'You find her attractive?' Kyoko asked after a moment. 'Your partner, I mean?'

'Monica? Yeah. Terrific pair of legs.'

'Is that all you look for in a woman, a terrific pair of legs?'

'That, and a great set of teeth.' Kyoko dropped her gaze demurely, studied her slender fingers as they twirled the stem of her wine glass. I asked her if she had a boyfriend back home.

She shook her head and smiled ruefully. 'I'm a disgrace to my family,' she said in a tone of self-mockery. 'Here I am, past what we call *tekireiki* – the "suitable age" to marry – without even an offer of marriage. The shame of it.'

'I know the feeling. You're looking at the world's most illegible bachelor.'

'And all those bridal skills I was forced to learn: flower-arranging, how to perform the tea ceremony . . . all gone to waste.'

'Did you learn any of the martial arts?' I asked.

'Not as bridal skills,' Kyoko laughed. 'But I did learn kendo at school, and goshinjutsu when I was a prison officer.'

'That's what, a form of karate?'

'Similar to judo, except we were trained to use sticks and ropes as well – purely for self-defence, of course, to protect both the prisoners and ourselves. Didn't always work, though.'

'I'm not surprised,' I told her. 'Woody Allen said one thing he learnt in judo was that the bigger his opponent, the bigger the beating he was going to get.'

'It wasn't just that,' Kyoko said, chuckling politely. 'If a prisoner lost control, it was, you know, difficult not to lose it yourself.' She was picking her way carefully through a minefield of volatile words with, I realised, the voice of experience. 'In the heat of a dangerous ... situation, it's not always easy to remember the ... disciplines of goshinjutsu. Things can happen too fast.'

'Is that,' I asked gently, 'why your career ended?'

She was twirling the stem of her glass again, intent on the swaying wine as her tone turned introspective. 'Most nights,' she said, 'there were only twelve of us on duty, and we had more than five hundred prisoners to look after. This one night, there was something in the air, a kind of tension so strong you could almost smell it. Maybe it was a full moon. I don't know, but I had a feeling, I just *knew* something bad was going to happen. And, of course, it did.'

She broke off as the weasel-faced waiter approached the table and asked if there was anything else we wanted before he closed up the bar. We told him no, just the bill, and he slunk back through the door marked *Staff Only*. If he'd had a tail, I thought, it would have been between his legs. Apart from a middle-aged couple by the servery and the two waitresses laying out tomorrow's tables, we were alone in the restaurant. I refilled Kyoko's glass, poured the dregs into mine and then, on impulse, reached over and took her hand. She surprised me by not immediately snatching it away. Instead, raising thoughtful eyes to mine, she offered me a rueful smile.

'My uncle will be waiting for me,' she said.

'Let him wait.'

She lowered her thick lashes. 'We have an early start tomorrow. We're visiting some relations of his: a cousin, I think, who married a man from Edinburgh. They manage a small tour guide company there, showing Japanese businessmen around the city. I have to go.'

I tried, and failed, to conceal my disappointment. 'When'll you be back?' I asked.

'Monday.'

My weekend off was suddenly a barren desert stretching as far as my mind could see. I could already envisage the next two days crawling blindly from one sad oasis to the next. 'I could phone you on Monday,' I said, seeking at least for a light at the end of my tunnel.

She regarded me pensively for a moment and I thought, Oh no, here it comes, the knockback. But then she smiled and squeezed my hand, and said, 'Yes, I'd like that. It'll give me something to look forward to.'

This time I managed to conceal at least the extent of my emotions – at that moment, a mixture mostly of relief, spiced through with a heady pinch of excitement – and retrieved my hand in time to accept the bill from Weasel Face. I was counting through my brownies and thinking about a second mortgage on my High Street flat when Kyoko snatched the bill from my hand and gave it to Weasel Face along with her credit card. After he'd departed, and not before he'd granted me a supercilious raising of his eyebrows, Kyoko made what I assumed to be a deprecatory gesture.

'I've got this huge expense account,' she explained, 'and no one lets me use it. Please, let me treat you.'

I had to give it some thought – male pride and all that – but half a nanosecond later I thanked her kindly and slammed my wallet back in my pocket before she could change her mind. Weasel Face returned, Kyoko signed, and Weasel Face departed, ignoring me totally. Did I care? Did I hell. My gaze was fixed on Kyoko's perfect little eyeteeth and the unconscious way they were now chewing at her lower lip. I wished it were my teeth chewing her lip.

She looked up, caught the direction of my gaze, and smiled self-consciously. 'Shall we go?'

'You didn't finish your story,' I told her.

Like water thrown on a campfire, the light in her eyes died. 'I try not to think about it,' she said, a brittle edge to her voice. 'It brings back too many bad memories.'

'I know how you feel.' Thinking about Ruben Maxwell and how memories of that night on the towerblock roof still brought out the worst of my emotions. Some things, I realise now, are better left buried.

'I know you do,' she sighed. 'I suppose I felt you'd understand, having experienced something similar yourself. That's why it just sort of slipped out. That and the wine.' She laid her hand on mine, sent a thrill running down my spine. 'Some other time, Francis, I promise.'

'Sure,' I said, standing. 'Any other time you want. Why spoil a beautiful night like tonight?'

Her smile was thirty-two teeth long. 'Would you walk me back to the hotel?' The clouds were gone and the flying sparks were back in her eyes. She gathered her purse, and stood while I held her chair. 'We could walk along the beach, if you want . . .'

'Barefoot? Hand in hand?'

'We might even stop by the dunes . . .'

I was already at the door, waiting with puckered lips.

26

Her lips traced a soft, slow line from my right nipple to my left, her breath hot on my cool, trembling skin. I felt my nipple harden between her teeth, my breasts swell out as though a woman's, distended with milk.

Kyoko.

Face concealed behind the jet-black curtain of her hair, she sucked like a hungry, feeding pup. Milking me. The feeling not unpleasant as my warm milk spurted. She sat astride my thighs, making small grunting noises as she drank, her whole body moving to the rhythm of her feeding. I was hard and getting harder. My hands moved over her buttocks, spread her cheeks. A moan escaped her lips, deep and throaty, as my fingers sought her heat, probing. She was wet with want. Her tiny nipples hardened like buds in her soft tangle of chest hair.

Chest hair?

She nibbled at my swollen, sensitive nipple. Sharp little teeth, almost feral, biting. Painful. Pleasurable. Hard to tell. Her rough skin rasping against mine. I could wait no more. Found her, split her, filled her. She moaned again. I rammed into her, hard, deep, again and again, forcing my name from her lips.

'McMorran!' Her head banging off the headboard with every powering thrust. *Bang bang bang*. 'McMorran!'

Call me Frank. Call me Francis. Call me anything you like, as long as it's dirty. *Bang bang bang*.

'McMorran!'

She wasn't listening. I looked up into her face. But it wasn't her face, not any more. It was a man's face. DS Dowie's.

I came awake with a scream. Alone in a tangle of sweaty sheets. Empty bed, empty room, empty half-bottle on the floor. Lights on, jeans on, hard-on.

Bang bang bang. 'McMorran!'

Someone at the door.

I staggered towards it, bleary-eyed. Not a dream, I realised, but a nightmare. A wet bloody nightmare! Clock on the mantelpiece said middle of the night. I blundered into the bathroom. Found the rest of my clothes, fresh pukestains in the bath, bloodstains in the sink. Dowie of all people. *Bang bang bang.*

'McMorran!' the voice growled. 'I know you're in there.'

Splashed my face with cold water. There was blood on my lips and my nose was tender. Dowie? I thought. *Screw* him? Sure I wanted to screw the arrogant little bastard. To a fucking crucifix. I washed away the blood with warm water – punch or fall, I couldn't remember.

Bastard, usurping my dream like that. Should be a law against it. Invasion of privacy. Obscenity. Mental torture. Still cursing, I swayed across the hall, unlocked the door with trembling, stiff fingers that weren't my own.

'Took your bloody time.' Detective Sergeant Dowie stood there with a sneer on his lips and another plainclothes detective at his shoulder. Daylight was an even harsher reality, blinding.

Something snapped.

I took a swing at Dowie but somewhere between the intention and the act a whitey came down and I lost balance, coordination and half the contents of my stomach. By the time I'd finished, Dowie was cursing and wiping his shoes angrily on the grass, his colleague restraining him physically.

'Five minutes, McMorran,' Dowie hissed, 'then we're taking you in, ready or not.'

I tried to focus. Found his mean little eyes halfway down his mean little face. 'Go to hell,' I said, and slammed the door.

I was halfway across the room when the door came in. Next thing I knew I was face down on the floor with a heavy knee in the centre of my back and my arms coming out of their sockets as the cuffs clicked on.

Dowie leered down at me.

I smiled back. It was okay, I'd got the idea now. Any second the scene would change and it'd be Kyoko looking down at me, and I'd be cuffed to the headboard and she'd be driving me crazy with her pointy wee tongue, nibbling me to a frenzied death with her sexy little eyeteeth. Then I'd wake up and everything would be just fine and dandy.

Ever the optimist.

The chopper was the same one that had ferried the murder squad out to the island the night I'd found the body of Arthur Thomas. I could tell: it made the same amount of noise.

I was strapped into the jump-seat by the open cabin door as the Firth of Clyde slid by below, looking cool, quiet and infinitely more inviting than this cramped and cacophonous tin can suspended high above its shimmering smoked-glass surface. The pilot's voice crackled in my headset.

'Good morning, ladies, this is your captain speaking. On behalf of the Royal Navy, may I welcome you aboard our special Pigs Will Fly charter service to mainland Britain. We are now flying at an operational speed of a hundred and twenty knots, heading One Three Zero at a height of five hundred feet. Barring the million and one things that might go wrong, our ETA is ten minutes.'

Maybe it wasn't the surface shimmering, I thought, but me. I don't, at the best of times, like hurtling through the air at breakneck speed – too much faith in the fickleness of nature's laws – and this morning was definitely not one of the best of times. My head felt like something slippery on a slaughterhouse floor, my tongue like the insole of a beat copper's boot. My eyes

313

felt like golf balls being wedged from a sandtrap. On top of all that, my body was battered and bruised, and my pride had gone AWOL. I was not a happy man. Nowhere this side of death near a happy man. So maybe the surface down there wasn't shimmering, it was just my mind blowing fuses.

'*For those of our passengers with a nervous disposition who are flying for the first time, let me reassure you that I know exactly how you feel – this is my first time as well. So, in the likely event of a crash landing, let me remind you that you may be lucky enough to find a lifejacket under your seat. If not, then put your head down between your legs and kiss your ass goodbye. I do hope you enjoy your flight, and will fly with us again.*'

I glanced at the two plainclothed detectives to my right; they returned my gaze with equally dispassionate eyes. DCs Matthews and Stone, the Heavy Brigade. Both looking decidedly uncomfortable in their bulging immersion suits as they sat squeezed together on the bench against the cabin wall. Good. They'd been giving me the silent treatment from the moment DS Dowie had placed me in their custody. Was I under arrest? No comment. What the hell was going on? No comment. Where was the stewardess with the drinks trolley? No comment.

Everything seemed so much clearer now.

Except the shimmering Clyde five hundred feet below. Or, I struggled to work it out, a hundred and fifty-two point something metres. Which sounded, sweeter music to my ears, a lot nearer the ground. Heading, what, One Three Zero? Southeast, then – about four o'clock, half-four. Four o'clock from Brodick, I reckoned, was more likely to be Ayr than HMS *Gannet* at Prestwick. Except I could now see a plane lifting off from one of the airport runways and that was to my left through the open cabin door and we were still heading south and a little to the east, more like half-four, which made our destination somewhere to the south of Ayr, maybe Dumfries, but why the hell, I wanted to know, were we heading in the direction of Dumfries?

Gingerly, I rubbed my nose. It was still tender. Punch or fall, I still couldn't recall. After walking Kyoko back to the Ormidale, I'd headed for the bar – I remember that much. Some ceilidh band playing, a lot of stomping going on, the whole place alive, jumping. The Folk Festival peaking. Was I dancing? I hoped to hell not. Though I'd been drunk enough, and just about happy enough – in my book, a lethal mixture. So I probably *was* dancing. And then – what? Vague memories of somewhere else, another pub down in the village, another band playing.

Of getting home, nothing.

We were over the mainland now, losing height as we followed a quiet B road east through open farmland, sunlight keen, glinting off skylights and windscreens alike. A caravan of cumulus trekked across the sky, trailing its shadow over fields of grazing cattle and pockets of woodland set against softly rolling hills. It was the woodland, I think, that finally set the synapses firing and triggered the response my mind had been subconsciously seeking since we'd taken to the air. The last time I'd seen this Sea King was the night I'd walked up into the woods behind Arthur Thomas's cottage and found the spot from which the watcher had watched. John Fullerton had been with me then, and, when we landed in just a few minutes, I felt sure he would be there on the ground as well. We were heading for Carrick Forest.

Locus of the Fangman's latest victim.

Whatever I was in, I was in it deep and it didn't smell nice. DCs Matthews and Stone had maintained their stone-faced silence from chopper to squad car, and maintained it still as we climbed the potholed track away from the lochan and into the forest. I wondered if they were naturally so reticent or whether they'd been given orders not to speak to me. Matthews, suit-and-tied, sweated greasy chips in the back seat next to me, a heavy, lumbering man in his mid twenties, with dark, sluggish eyes and

315

fists the size of boxing gloves. Stone, in the passenger seat, wore a darker suit of grey, and was older, with a sleek, balding head, sallow face and a habit of maybe forty a day. Orders, I thought, or they hated each other's guts.

'So?' Commander Harlan Kettle glared at me expectantly.

'Sir?'

'Cut the crap, McMorran, this is just you and me. No witnesses, no games.' We were alone in the mobile command unit, Kettle slouched on a chair behind the sun-splashed desk, me standing to attention in front of it. It was a command unit much like any other, sparse, without character, door, couple of windows, beige synthetic carpet, plywood desks, folding chairs, *We'll crack crime together* posters on the wall, boxes of files stacked three-high, senior officer slouched on a chair behind a desk. 'So explain,' Kettle said.

'Explain what?' I said, planting my knuckles on his desk, letting my anger show. 'How your pet poodle Dowie broke down my door in the middle of the night and dragged me forcibly out of the house? In *hand*cuffs? I think it's you, pal, who's got the explaining to do.' No witnesses, no games, I was going to make the most of it.

Kettle tapped the pad in front of him with a stubby finger. 'He says you assaulted him.'

'I missed.'

'That you puked on his shoes.'

I shrugged. 'I've had more practice.'

'Somehow that doesn't surprise me.' There was an undercurrent of weariness in his voice, barely discernible, but there.

'No?'

'No,' Kettle sighed. 'I've seen it all before, your problem with the drink.'

'Getting it all in the fridge, that's my problem.'

'Life's just one big joke, eh, McMorran?'

'See me laughing?' I broke away from the desk, crossed to the

316

window where at least the air was in motion, albeit a very sluggish motion. The early-morning sun slipped behind a solitary cloud as I watched DI Fullerton brief a group of young overalled officers on what to look for in the grid-search that would begin shortly. 'You want to know why the drink?' I said, turning to face Kettle. 'Okay, I'll tell you why. I drink when I get lonely, and I get lonely when people stop listening to me. When they start acting like I'm not even there, leave me screaming at the moon. That's what makes me lonely, makes me feel like I ought to go out and seek the company of a damn good drink. Like at least it will listen to me, won't tell me I'm making the whole thing up, writing anonymous bloody notes to myself.'

'Did you?'

I didn't answer. My look was enough.

'I had to ask.' Almost an apology, that was, coming from Kettle. As sunlight angled in through the window again, it caught his face amidst a column of rising motes and I noticed for the first time how drained he looked, his expression at times almost haunted, the bags under his eyes deeper and darker than I'd ever seen them before. I wondered what kind of pressures he was working under now, and how much longer he could withstand them. There were definitely a few hairline cracks in his once unimpressionable façade. Good. He said, 'Dowie is a good cop, McMorran. A bit of an arse, a bit wet behind the ears, but don't underestimate him just because you don't like his educated accent.'

'Arse,' I said, 'is right.'

'Just like you were at his age. No difference. He's as good a cop as you were then, and is certainly no less ambitious. And he also has a problem following orders.'

'You're saying that was off his own bat, then, the unreasonable force, the handcuffs?'

'His orders were to get you aboard the chopper, have you delivered here.'

I thought about the hunger I'd seen in Dowie's eyes, the

317

hunger to succeed, the eagerness to get the job done and let nothing stand in his way. Had I really been like that when I was a newly promoted DS? Had my youthful arrogance also provoked a similar animosity amongst my elder subordinates? It was well possible. Probable, even. Christ, what a little shit I must have been.

Maybe still am.

'So why the sudden urgency?' I said, with not a little rancour. 'Someone found a dead sheep in their coffee? Lost their pet poodle?'

Kettle shot me a baleful look as he climbed to his feet and crossed to the door. 'We'll get to that,' he growled, 'later.' He poked his head out the door and ordered one of the overalled PCs to fetch coffee. 'Make it a flask. Black and sweet. Two mugs. Jump to it, man!'

A 'Derry man, Harlan Kettle came over the Irish Sea in his teens, has returned only twice, once to bury his mother, and once, so the story goes, to spit on his father's grave. His accent's still there, but only when he's angry. Which is often. He strode back to the desk and threw himself down in the seat. Stared at me for a long contemplative minute while his short, blunt fingers played absently with a stub of pencil.

'I should've let Bain take you over the cliff,' he said eventually. 'Saved myself all this trouble.'

'But you didn't.' This was the first time he'd ever mentioned it, saving my life. Since the arrest of the Hangman, our paths had crossed only twice: at the trial of Dominic Bain and at my disciplinary hearing several weeks later. On neither occasion had we exchanged even the slightest recognition of the other's existence; although both on the same ladder, we'd been heading fast in different directions.

'No,' he sighed, 'I didn't.'

'There was a time I wished you had.'

He glanced at me, at first shrewdly, then with growing interest. 'That bad, was it?' The interest in his eyes, I thought, was like that of a cat playing with its dinner. I couldn't forget that all my troubles in the past couple of years were down to this block of a man sitting behind the desk.

Would never forget.

'Bad,' I said, 'is not the word.'

Dark times, those, ones I seldom return to in my thoughts. Certainly not memories I was prepared to share with Kettle.

'So why didn't you resign?' There was almost a note of concern in his voice. 'I don't think I could've handled all that, the demotion, the transfer, the disgrace . . .'

'Resign,' I said, 'and do what?'

Before he could answer, there was a knock on the door and a young PC entered with a flask and two mugs, set them down on the desk and retreated hastily. Kettle filled the mugs, leaving one on the desk for me. I let it stand, remained by the window.

Kettle ran a finger round the inside of his collar, loosened his tie a fraction of a millimetre. 'At the last ACPO conference, one of the chief constables stated that good coppers never resign. I tend to agree with that point of view. What I don't understand is why you go out of your way to cause so much trouble for yourself. You on some kind of professional death wish or what?'

'Maybe it's like you said, good coppers don't resign.'

'They get thrown out, is that it?'

I said, 'Just because I'm down to PC doesn't make me any less the cop I was. People ought to respect that.'

'People do, McMorran, otherwise the disciplinary hearing wouldn't have given you the opportunity for a review next year.'

'If I'm still around . . .'

'Exactly,' Kettle said, sighing in exasperation. 'Don't make waves, they said. So what do you do? You make tidal ones.'

'These aren't even waves, man, they're ripples. I may be trying to rock the boat, but I'm not trying to sink it.'

'Yeah?' Kettle said belligerently. 'So explain last night.'

I rubbed my nose tenderly as I crossed to collect my coffee, using the few moments to assemble what fragments of last night still remained in my memory. There was only one seat in the unit, so I returned to lean against the wall by the window.

'Okay, so maybe I drank a little too much.'

'Not just a little. You were seen by one of my officers. He said you were way over the top.'

'My dancing wasn't *that* bad!'

Was that a quiver of a smile, I wondered, ghosting across Kettle's lips? No, couldn't be, I decided, there was no known precedent. It was just my world continuing to shimmer. Had to be.

'And the fight you picked with the journalist?'

Ah, I thought, and it all came back. The little shit in the brown and rumpled corduroy suit, the one with the notebook and never-ending questions who wouldn't take 'fuck off and die' for an answer.

'Slater had it coming,' I said.

'Perhaps he did. But there are times and places, Chrissakes, times and places. Times when we don't need the press on our side, places like a dark alley in the dead of night, somewhere you don't have a barful of witnesses to contend with. Get the picture?'

Yeah, but he hadn't been there last night. Slater hadn't been exactly sober himself, had given me as much provocation as I had him. I think.

'Okay,' Kettle continued, 'I'm not stupid. I can see now that this is some kind of personal vendetta, especially after the last piece Slater did on you. I don't know what you did or said to the man, but he obviously wants your blood. Fortunately for us, the piece he filed was too late for the early editions and of such a vindictive nature that the editor got me out of bed at some unearthly hour this morning to see if there was any truth in the story.'

'What did you tell him?'

'That I'd find out.' Kettle poured himself another coffee from the flask, blew on it as he watched me through the steam. 'The

320

short of it is,' he said, 'I told the editor that if he wanted to print that story, then his newspaper would be the only one not carrying today's exclusive.'

'Exclusive?' I said. 'Has there been a development?'

'Yes,' he replied. 'You.'

'Me?' My mind was still staggering around my skull looking for a socket to plug into.

'DI Fullerton showed me the letter you received.'

At last. Now it seemed someone was listening. Which was why I'd insisted yesterday that Fullerton show the letter to Kettle: I may hate every breath the man breathes but I can't deny that he's a damn good cop and seldom misses a trick.

'Did you see the card?' I asked.

Kettle nodded, sipped his coffee. 'I had Dowie send it over with your escort. I doubt we'll have much luck but we'll see what Forensics can make of it.'

'All you'll find is Dowie's prints.'

'I know, I know, McMorran, you've made your point. And I've also made sure Dowie understands.' Kettle sighed wearily and rose to his feet, shaking his head. 'As far as you and Dowie are concerned, I've had it up to here. I don't want to hear any more bitching from either of you. This is a murder enquiry I'm trying to run here, not a bloody nursery. I'm prepared to overlook Dowie's reports, but only on the understanding that it doesn't happen again. If it does, well, I need hardly remind you . . .'

Water off a duck's back. 'So you're going to tell the press about the letter?'

Kettle began pacing up and down, hands in pockets, head bowed. The whole unit shuddered with every elephantine step. 'I've already spoken to several of the chief constables on the committee, including the chairman, and the consensus is yes. We feel any kind of communication with the Fangman is better than none. In fact we hope the media attention will encourage him to write again.'

321

'And if it wasn't the Fangman who wrote the note?'

'Then I think when he reads about it, he's going to feel indignant that someone else is getting all the limelight.'

'So he'll rush for pen and paper.'

'Exactly. And if it was the Fangman, then the reservations you express about the note's authenticity should motivate him to contact you again.'

'What d'you mean, *I* express?'

Kettle stopped pacing and looked me in the eye. That look again, Judas in his eyes, the goodbye look.

'What you've always wanted, McMorran, your five minutes of primetime fame. You're going out live on the lunchtime news.'

'I am?' I touched up my bouffant hair. 'You want me to do a Gazza? Burst out crying? Improve the ratings? That kind of thing?'

'Why not just be yourself, McMorran, do a George Best.'

'It takes a worried man,' Detective Inspector John Fullerton said. 'Rumour has it he's taking a lot of stick from the Committee of CCs, and they're being pressured by the Scottish Office, who in turn are being pressured by the Home Office who, as *the* party supposedly representing law and order, are currently under fire in the Commons for their inability to control the rising crime rate. It's just Kettle's bad luck the buck's landed right in his lap.'

'I don't trust the bastard. I think he's setting me up again.'

'Covering his arse, Frank, that's what it looks like.' Fullerton was down to shirtsleeves, his thin face drawn, casting deep shadows around his eyes; long-running murder enquiries have that effect. He carried a thick manila folder which he slapped against his thigh as we walked. 'In case the Fangman and the sheep are connected. At the same time, I imagine, he's using you as bait to draw the Fangman out. Either way, you come out shiny bright.'

'Or dead.'

'Then why worry?'

'I need the overtime.' We followed the dirt track through a short tunnel of trees, broke into warm sunlight again and a grassy clearing with picnic tables and benches and maybe fifty officers on hands and knees picking their way through every blade of grass. A painstaking and often futile task, but then again so is most of the work we do.

'So what else did he say?'

'In so many words,' I said, 'I'm to concentrate on the sheep angle, and assist Sergeant Dowie on the Thomas enquiry.' I then voiced what Kettle hadn't said in any words at all. 'And you're to supply me with copies of all the collated status reports to date.'

'Sure,' Fullerton said. 'No problem.'

I couldn't think of any further advantage to take of my colleague, so I followed him in silence around the perimeter of the clearing to the table nearest the trees, where a forensic team, dressed in white overalls, were hard at work. They were bent over the table, examining it minutely, he with a magnifying glass, she with a pair of tweezers. Half a dozen labelled evidence bags already lay on the bench nearby.

'That's where they found her,' Fullerton said. 'On her back, naked, knees up, legs splayed, hands and feet nailed to the table.'

'Nailed?'

The DI grimaced, nodding his head. 'Four-inch nails, driven right through. You can see the holes,' he pointed, 'there, there, there, and there. Not a pretty sight.'

'So he brought his own nails,' I remarked.

'A right little Boy Scout. Probably has a compass in the heel of his shoe.' He opened the manila folder, pulled out a batch of twelve-by-eight photographs. 'Here, see for yourself.'

Helen Falconer.

You get used to it, sure, hardened against such sights – or so we always tell ourselves. But for each new horror we confront, some freshly twisted mind somewhere else is concocting a new obscenity to shock the world. There are no limits, it seems, to the evil men can do, only the limits of their imagination.

'The attached sheet,' Fullerton said, 'is what we've managed to piece together of her last movements. The bio's a bit sketchy but we're still working on it. There's always a chance . . .'

Chance, yes, that somewhere in the background of one or more of the victims there might still exist a trail that would lead to the Fangman. Perhaps a million-to-one chance, but a chance none the less.

I read the background report, then glanced through the photos, looking up every once in a while to judge distances and angles, trying to visualise the horror of the scene.

The stills had been taken from every conceivable angle, some full-body, some concentrating exclusively on individual wounds, of which there were many. In fact there were few parts of her body to which the Fangman had not turned his sadistic attention. Helen Falconer was a patchwork of bruises, cuts, weals and burns, her skin torn in some places, peeled back in others.

'She must have had a strong heart,' Fullerton observed.

'Unfortunately for her.' The blood caked around her wounds meant she had been alive when they were inflicted. We could only hope she'd not been conscious. 'And this?' The photo puzzled me; I angled it so Fullerton could see.

'Aye,' he said, scratching his head. 'Two bottles, both Portuguese red. Definitely his, though, prints all over. Seems he really did make a picnic out of it.'

'Not a bad wine, either.' Thinking how nice a glass of it would go down right now. Or even . . .

'You know it?'

I nodded. 'Quite popular at the moment. Maybe cost you three, four quid a bottle. You checking out all the local off-licences?'

324

'For what it's worth.' The tone of the DI's voice implying a worth next to nothing. 'I better go check the lack of progress. Back in a sec.' He strode off towards the burly sergeant supervising the inch-by-inch at the far end of the clearing.

Helen Falconer, age sixty-eight, widow. Last seen alive by her doctor's receptionist. Time: 11.15. No sightings between the surgery and the forest but that might change after the lunchtime news broadcast. Son, daughter. Grandchildren . . .

You get used to it, but . . .

. . . but imagine it was *your* mother lying there, naked, degraded, abused and tortured, legs splayed, nailed to the tabletop. This woman who has borne you and devoted her life to you, nursed you through the dark times, asking for nothing, not even your love, who has given and given and given, imagine her, yes, lying there, and the pain she went through as those four-inch nails were driven through the palms of her hands and soles of her feet, imagine that as just the beginning of the pain she would suffer, a foretaste of the torture yet to come, this gentle, trusting mother of yours whose diminishing life is a trail of memories captured for posterity in a chest of fading black-and-white photographs, pictures of you since you were knee-high to a leprechaun, of the men she loved, of happy days, summer days, and she's lying there and she knows she's going to die and she can see from the look in her tormentor's eyes that it's not going to be easy, not going to be soon, the killer standing there swigging from a bottle of wine, somebody's son, toying gleefully with his knife, probably about the same age as her son, perhaps you, and she's thinking of him now as she strains against the nails, *Why isn't he here to help me? Darling George, why aren't you here when I need you?* and the helplessness and hopelessness of her situation overwhelms her, becomes a sudden unbearable weight on her heart, she is alone, alone in the presence of death, and she is so *scared* she can hardly breathe, hardly scream as the knife slices up her right nostril . . .

John Fullerton was back at my shoulder, slowly shaking his

head. 'Could've been my mother,' he said, as though reading my mind.

His mother, yours or mine, I don't think I would have felt any different: the hatred was already welling up inside me, an emotional force that was almost tangible, certainly physical, threatening to rip apart the fabric of my restraint, and firing thoughts of revenge like a rapid burst of dumdums through my mind. I was probably feeling then what the Fangman had felt as he nailed the old woman down: the same intensity of hatred such an act of cold-hearted brutality must surely necessitate. At that moment I could've nailed the bastard down with a smile on my face and joy in my heart.

Social worker, I am not.

'Anything,' I asked, 'on the weals on her wrists?'

Fullerton glanced at his watch. 'Silas Kerr'll have finished the autopsy by now. He wouldn't say much last night except that her wrists had been lashed together, probably by a belt, width about one inch. Impression of the weals was deep enough to suggest she'd been left suspended for some time. That tree over there?' He pointed at a young pine beyond the table where the two forensics were still at work. 'See the stump of branch about six feet up? We found striation marks that may well correspond to those on her wrists.'

'Where's he doing the autopsy?'

'Kilmarnock. There's a case conference up there this afternoon, we'll get his report then.' Fullerton smiled. 'You know what they've started calling him up at the squad? Silas of the Labs. I think he's quite flattered by it. Though no one's taking odds on Kettle becoming known as Harlan Lecter.'

'A loser's bet.' I watched a uniformed PC enter the clearing and walk towards us, circumventing the ongoing grid-search. The sun was melting down, almost directly overhead now, and my fragile mind was beginning to simmer. One word, one thought, clamoured at the forefront.

Lager.

'Sir, that's the TV crews arrived,' the uniform said. 'Commander Kettle asks that you both go down.'

'Thanks, Mason,' Fullerton told him. 'Two minutes.'

As Mason walked away, I wondered if the TV crews would have an ice box in their outside-broadcast van – a natural reaction, I assure you, to the butterflies suddenly rampaging in my stomach.

Call it first-time nerves.

If Commander Kettle wanted bait, I thought, then bait I would give him.

27

'**D**on't you think it strange that the Fangman should contact *you?*'

His moustache looked like something you'd use to sweep a bar-room floor. It seemed to be growing out of his nose, a kind of fibrous ectoplasm that, having now usurped his upper lip, was intent on taking over his whole face. I found my eyes drawn to it as though it was the world's deepest cleavage, something I could easily lose myself in. Had to tear my gaze away.

'The price of fame,' I shrugged, feeling like a condemned man in front of the assembled firing-squad of boom microphones and cameras. I should have asked for a blindfold, I realised, to keep my attention from straying to the reporter's gargantuan moustache. 'Anyway,' I continued, 'we're not absolutely certain the communication was from the Fangman. Perhaps if he gets in touch again, he'll tell us something only he could know. As it stands at the moment, we may well be dealing with nothing more than a copycat, someone seeking notoriety at the Fangman's expense.'

The reporter – 'Call me Bob' – had only one expression, it seemed, one of perpetual startlement. Eyes like a surprised Olive Oyl's.

'Do you think it's possible,' he said, 'that this communication is a sign that the Fangman may want to give himself up, in fact that he sees you in the role of mediator?'

'No. The man we're looking for is too much a coward to face that kind of truth.'

That startled his startled expression. He had to look down at his clipboard to find continuity.

'Er . . . it's possible that the man you're seeking, the . . . er . . . Fangman, is watching this broadcast. Is there anything in particular you would like to say to him?'

Kettle wanted bait, I'd be his maggot.

'Yes,' I said, turning to stare directly into the camera. 'I know you, Fangman, I've met your pathetic kind before. You're what we call a total inadequate. You're not a man, you're just a mean little mother's boy.' I smiled, noticing the astonishment on Call Me Bob's face. I wasn't sticking to the script, his expression said; this wasn't the way to talk to dangerous serial killers, you were supposed to offer them understanding, help. I broadened my smile to the camera and continued. 'Old women, eh? That's really daring of you. What a hero you are. How brave. Of course you have to tie them up or nail them down because otherwise they might frighten you, make you wet your frilly knickers. You cut out their tongues because you're scared of what they'll tell you. Because the truth hurts, doesn't it, Fangman? You dare not look yourself in the eye in a mirror lest you see yourself as you really are. A nobody. An insignificance. Nothing but a social disease I'm going to take great pleasure in wiping off the face of this earth.'

Call Me Bob was looking at me like I'd just stepped out of a flying saucer. 'Surely such an attitude will induce the Fangman to go out and kill again?'

'He's going to kill again anyway. It has nothing to do with my attitude. He's out of control, he can't stop now, not till he's either caught or killed.'

'Is there a possibility he might take his own life?'

'Not a chance. He hasn't got the guts. Killers like him, they're doing it for the fame. For the headlines. Sees his name in the papers, hears it on everyone's lips, suddenly he's *somebody*, the man of the moment. No,' I concluded, 'inadequates like the Fangman can't stand even the thought of pain. He could as much take his own life as he could successfully make love to a woman.'

'Er, yes,' the reporter blustered, trying in vain to regain his former composure. 'The Fangman is obviously a very sick man... But don't you think he needs help rather than condemnation?'

'The only help I'd give him would be up the steps of a scaffold.'

'Or off a towerblock roof?' he suggested, obviously having read up on his research.

I wasn't going to disappoint him. 'It would be my pleasure.' I said.

He turned to face the camera to my right. 'PC Frank McMorran, the officer singled out by the Fangman as a line of communication. Whether or not such a development will lead to the capture of Britain's most wanted man still remains to be seen. Back to you in the studio, Carole.'

'Okay,' Bob said, 'that's a wrap.' Then, turning, he shot me a wink that sent his moustache lurching up his face. 'Any time you want to give another interview, call me and we'll *really* wake the bastards up.' Yeah, sure, I thought, you and me, what a team. His handshake was as limp as a soggy leaf of lettuce. 'Okay, who's next, Gloria? We've got two minutes.'

I broke through the ranks of the TV crews just as a tall, middle-aged man in a black cape was ushered in the opposite direction. A ladder of prominent bones, he was dressed completely in black, his manner and gait haughty, his hooded dark eyes sweeping over the heads of the gathered crews, expression that of a man preoccupied with realities far beyond the mere mortal. Either that, I thought, or he'd dropped a dozen tabs of acid.

Commander Kettle, whom I'd noticed standing behind the soundmen during the interview, was striding towards the command unit. His nod as he passed was one of satisfied approval.

He looked almost content. Christ, I thought, the way things were going we'd soon be fumbling buttons in the back seat of a car, making wild promises of marriage.

Slater had not been present among the assembled ranks of press. I read nothing into it, hoping only that he was in pain wherever he was. I made my way back up the track to the picnic area, relishing for a few minutes the shade afforded by the tree-fashioned tunnel. Back of one and already my T-shirt was caked to my skin.

I passed a group of officers coming down the way and when I arrived at the clearing saw the rest of the grid-search team sitting in groups in the shade, eating their pieces, smoking, drinking from flasks. Fullerton was there too, lying on the grass, head on folded jacket, eyes closed. Snatch it when you can, where you can; something we soon get used to.

The two forensic scientists were sitting under the tree where, they reasoned, Helen Falconer had been left suspended prior to her nailing. I walked past them and found a cool pool of shade where I lay back, hands behind my head, and tried to clear my mind.

But difficult, here, not to think of the horrors experienced by Helen Falconer. As though angry spirits still roamed the clearing, the hate and pain still residue in the warm air.

Why had the Fangman strung her up like game left to hang? I wondered.

There is reason in madness, not necessarily yours or mine, but reason nevertheless. It's the detective's job to search for the patterns and consistency of action, however disparate, which at least give the impression of having been motivated by a reasoning mind. The idea being that you can follow paths of reason from source to resolution and back again.

Trouble was, I didn't have much to go on at the moment – hopefully John Fullerton would come up with the goods tonight – only the generalised details I'd gleaned from newspapers, the photos from this locus, and my own experience at Arthur Thomas's. Not much, but enough to play with.

332

I recalled how, while studying the way in which the broken vase at Arthur Thomas's feet had been arranged – like the petals of a sunflower – I had thought of Vincent Van Gogh. Not just because of his sunflower paintings, but also because he was an artist, a *provocateur* who struggled against great mental odds to get his message across on canvas. And in that respect, though in a less lethal fashion, I felt he was not all that different from the Fangman who, in his own morbid way, was also trying to create a single coherent reality from a multitude of disparate impressions.

The locus is the killer's canvas.

And so you, the detective, have to look at the locus as though it were the killer's latest work of art. What is he trying to say here, you ask yourself, what is his message? What is he trying to tell the world so desperately that he is prepared to sacrifice his life in order to get that message across? Usually it is something quite pathetic and trivial: an anguished scream of protest and anger at a society that has failed to recognise his full potential. The attention-seeker's cry of *Here I am!* and *Look at me!* Murder being the only way to achieve the fame and notoriety he feels he deserves.

And like with all kinds of communication you try to read between the lines. Look a little deeper, for meanings hidden, disguised, obscured. And because what has not been said often tells you more than what has been said, you look for what has been omitted, left out of the picture.

And you ask yourself why he painted this *specific* painting. What was going through his mind at that particular time.

You also look for mistakes. Art is exploration through trial and error, an experimental search for its own perfect individual identity. The serial killer too strives for perfection. As he learns, he adapts and discards. As his fantasies evolve, his rituals become more intricate, his desires more demanding. He experiments, always searching for that sharper edge, that extra kick, trying to sate the insatiable. Experiments, and makes mistakes. So you, the detective, study the canvas from different angles, minutely from every conceivable point of view, looking for that seemingly insignificant incongruity, the wrong thing in the wrong place, the tiny inconsistency that doesn't quite fit, which makes you look and think twice, thrice, raises questions you can't immediately answer.

Like why string her from a tree like so much game left to hang? What had the Fangman been doing while she was there? Sizing her up, whetting his appetite, dehumanising her before he set to work? Or drinking wine, getting a good buzz on, not wanting to rush the moment, knowing the moment he got started he'd be out of control, totally dominated by the power of his lust? How did that compare with his other victims? None but Arthur Thomas had been killed *in situ*; the rest had been taken from the place of their abduction to somewhere like this, a secluded spot where he could take his time, secure in the knowledge that he would not be disturbed. Or perhaps even his own house, I thought, recalling the old barn at the end of Dominic Bain's garden, where the Edinburgh Hangman had brought his prey, played with them awhile before dropping them in the noose and kicking the chair away. Did the Fangman have such a place?

Suddenly, a whistle shrilled, disintegrating the pattern of my thoughts. Lunch break was over. Men and women climbed lethargically to their feet, stretched, then reassembled by the entrance to the clearing to await further instruction. I watched Fullerton make his way wearily across and it was then that I noticed the tall, caped figure of the man in black I had passed shortly after my TV interview. I'd been leaving as he arrived. Which made him news. So I too climbed to my feet and stretched, then ambled over to join him.

He stood there by the picnic table where the forensic team had earlier been working, feet braced apart as though riding a swell, both clawlike hands resting on the silver knob of his cane. A twist and draw, I reckoned, and he'd be on equal terms with any of the Three Musketeers. His mane of thick black hair swept back from a long forehead, curling over the collar of his cape.

Mungo Spinks.

I introduced myself, said, 'We should talk.'

'Why should I talk to you?' he said, his voice and manner terse and uncompromising. 'You're a cop.' Inflexibility also dominated his face, was there in the setting of his eyes, the cut of his nose, the temperance of his mouth, the trim of his moustache and goatee, the jut of his goateed chin . . . even the shadows he cast were sharp and angular. It would be easier, I thought, to change the mind of a pyramid.

'And you're Dr Who, wacko supreme, the Lee Van Cleef of time-travel,' I sneered, watching his face for reaction. All I got was a sleepy reptilian blink. 'So now we've made our prejudices clear, why don't we start again, see if our two worlds can meet on a common plane, get a little cross-fertilisation of ideas going?'

'You mean the Fangman.' No question. He was a few inches taller than me, dark eyes studying me down the length of his nose.

'It's why you're here, isn't it? Or is work so slow you need the publicity?' This time I got more of a reaction, a narrowing of his eyes, a small twitch at the side of his mouth. Good. Perfect composure always makes me want to crack it.

'I watched your interview,' Spinks said, preferring to ignore my comments. 'An interesting approach. Are you hoping the Fangman will come after you?'

'The idea's growing on me,' I told him.

'An eye for an eye?'

'Seems fair, don't you think?'

Spinks shrugged his caped, birdlike shoulders. 'Revenge is but a concept, my friend, not one of Nature's laws. Nature is not fair. It is only human arrogance that demands life be fair, that there be justice, a moral safety net of unnatural laws to tame the hungry, stalking beast within all of us.'

'Arrogance,' I said, 'or fear?'

335

Spinks smiled. It failed to reach his eyes. 'And what is arrogance but a fear of failure? Of being less than human, of tumbling from the lofty heights of perceived moral standards into the bestial insecurity of day-to-day survival? No, my friend, we should be as proud of our mass murderers and serial killers as we are enthralled by their exploits. They are the vanguard of modern society, the yardstick against which we can measure our descent into moral apathy, our plunge into barbarism.'

Not quite the way I saw it, but then I was at the sharp end, mopping up the mess. I said, 'Mungo Spinks? What kind of name is that?'

This time there was humour in his smile. 'The name I was born with, my friend. But I have others.'

Wacko was definitely one of them.

He cocked his head and studied me pensively for a moment. 'Your aura is strong, my friend.'

'I didn't have time for a bath this morning.' I flashed him a smile. 'I understand you were out here at the Mathieson locus . . .'

Mathieson, as in Maureen Mathieson, a fifty-one-year-old housewife from Troon whose mutilated body had been found in a ditch less than five miles from where we stood. The Fangman's second known victim.

'Last November,' Spinks said, using the silver knob of his cane to scratch his goatee. 'Yes. Her daughter asked me to come out. She wanted me to set her mind to rest that her mother hadn't suffered, but I couldn't do that, she *had* suffered, poor woman, suffered quite horrendously. I'm afraid I wasn't much help.'

'So why are you here today?'

He regarded me steadily for a few moments, the way people do when they're considering whether to tell the truth or lie.

'I have *known* this man,' he said eventually, 'the one you are looking for. I have felt his presence. It is not something one can easily forget.' He shuddered, then shook his head irritably, as though to rid himself of some vile, distasteful thought. 'If I can help in any way, I will.'

'I read about your success on Dartmoor.'

Spinks snorted, brushed away the compliment with an airy wave of his hand. 'A mere child compared to this man. Hunt was mentally retarded – challenged, as they like to call it now. The impressions he left behind were clear and simple, his remorse almost overpowering. It was no big deal.'

'And the Fangman?' I asked.

'There is nothing simple about this man, nothing clear. He is a man caught in throes of confused and violent emotions. He lives both in the past and present. Unlike us, for him there is no distinction between the two. His past is as real to him as his present. He is a man living amongst his memories, reliving them again and again and again. He searches in vain for a break in the chain, an escape from the endless vicious circle in which he is trapped. He is like a hamster on a wheel, trying to get somewhere fast but getting nowhere at all. Doomed to a life of constant repetition.'

'You think his sudden desire for communication is an attempt to break the chain, escape, as you say, the vicious circle?'

'A cry for help, you mean? It's possible. But then I haven't been allowed to see the letter, nor informed of its content.' Said with dignified hurt.

I pulled the photocopy from my pocket, handed it to him. He glanced disdainfully at both sides before saying, 'The original would have helped. I can't pick up anything from a photocopy.'

'Nor,' I said, 'can Forensics. You'll just have to wait your turn.'

'By which time all traces will have been erased.' Spinks sighed at such incompetence. 'Still, I suppose it tells us something.'

'It does?'

'*The man stabs the sheep, but no blood flows . . .*' he read as though to himself. '*Nothing that acts to further . . .* Can't say I recognise the quote, but I'm pretty sure I know where it comes from.'

'You do?'

'The Book of Changes,' he said. 'The *I Ching*.'

For several moments my mind lurched from one recent memory to another, searching for the right character in the right scenario. I ended up in Ros Hastie's dark and dusty living room amidst her clutter of books and charts.

I said, 'An ancient form of Chinese oracle, based on the principle of yin and yang, and the duality of life?'

'Something like that,' he said, regarding me speculatively, as though anew.

I answered the question implicit in his eyes. 'Ros Hastie,' I said. 'Maybe you know her. She's into astrology, lives on Arran. Those were her words, not mine.'

'You remember everything anyone tells you? Verbatim?'

I shrugged the question away. 'What do you know about this *I Ching*?' I asked. 'Why would he send me a quote from it?'

Spinks shook his head, stabbing at the grass with his stick as he did so. 'Perhaps you, my friend, know the reason better than I.'

I told him about the two slaughtered sheep.

'Were their killings reported anywhere?' he asked. 'In the local press, on TV?'

'Local press.'

'Which makes him a local man?'

I shrugged again. 'I'm keeping my options open. This guy's not stupid. He could be playing us along, you know, the proverbial wild-goose chase.' I recalled something Spinks had said earlier. 'You said he's "living amongst his memories" ... what exactly did you mean by that?'

Spinks sighed and let his head drop for a second. When he raised it again, I could see the weariness shadowing his eyes. 'Memory, my friend, is the forge upon which we hammer out our sense of identity. Memory roots us firmly in abstracts such

338

as space and time, who and what we are. Imagine then if all your memories were bad ones, painful – a casual stroll down Memory Lane like you were being dragged screaming down the darkest corridors of hell. What would that make you now, my friend? Angry? Sad? Indifferent to suffering? Bad? Would not these merciless memories make you all the more merciless now?'

Yeah, I reasoned, they probably would.

Spinks continued without waiting for a reply. 'And chained to this pitiless past, would you not want to hack those chains away, cut yourself adrift and forge new memories in which you put the world to rights: a new order, for example, which you could control mercilessly with the power of fire and sword? And would not every murder then become just a link in a chain that must be hacked apart, with every stab, punch, squeeze of a strangle, every cut of a saw and slice of a knife, ultimately nothing more than a ritual cleaving from the past, a ritual doomed to repetition if only because of its guaranteed failure to appease absolutely?'

'So he's searching for . . . what? A sense of identity?'

'*I* believe so,' he replied. 'Somewhere amidst all the hurt and pain, the horror of his isolated existence, there is yet, perhaps, buried deep beneath all the anger and hate, a scared and lonely little boy who knows not where he belongs, yet longs with every tortured breath to belong, to be loved, to sink into the warm and comfortable womb of social acceptance, to be *noticed* . . .'

'Stop,' I said, holding up my hand, 'or you'll have me weeping on the collar of your cape. I get the picture. He's a sad wee fuck. But he's also dangerous, rabid. Like needs to be put down. And before he kills again.'

Spinks said nothing. He was there, but not there. He stood with two fingers and thumb pressed lightly to the scarred surface of the picnic table, looking out across the clearing, the distance in his eyes an introspective one, not of this time, I felt, nor of this world. He raised his other hand and pointed.

'That tree,' he said. 'Next to the oak. The one with the

withered branch. He hung her there.' His voice altered in pitch and tone, became a low nasal sneer. '*Always best to let them hang awhile.*' My skin prickled as he continued in a voice definitely not his own. 'Stood here and admired her. He was drinking, feeling good, the power, yes, surging. So much meat. *Those fucking tits, man.* He's got some kind of box on the table, he keeps his tools there. They have pet names and he talks to them. He talks to her also, but she's nothing, just meat. He slaps her the way a cat slaps a mouse. Watching her face. He wants to see her eyes. He's looking for something there, an understanding perhaps, an answer. *The eyes of the dead are mirrors.* There is so much confusion, so much hatred, even now.'

Spinks walked towards the tree, oblivious, it seemed, to all around him. I followed a few paces behind, remaining silent, not wishing to shatter the spell as I felt myself drawn into the scene his words were painting. We could have been alone in the clearing.

'The belt is red,' Spinks said, approaching the tree. 'It's the one his mother used to beat him with. He likes the irony in that. He finds it hilarious. The wine is red and goes well with meat. *Put him in the roasting tin, let him simmer for a while.* It was dark in there, no room for a growing boy to move . . .'

The psychic was in his mid to late forties, his skin babyish in its pale softness. His awkward hands with their large knuckles and nibbled nails looked almost bloodless, as though even the sunlight might bruise them. He frowned now, sniffing the warm air.

'But what smells! A thousand roasted meals. He loves the smell of charred flesh. They'd lock him away for hours on end in an old iron stove at the back of the garage. They lived on a scheme, their house near the end of a cul-de-sac. A sports car at the kerb, white. I don't know where. Netted curtains . . . dark rooms, full of fear. And such confused anger. *Of course, someone always has to pay . . .*'

His voice trailed away. He shook his head, again as though

trying to exorcise some recurrent nightmare. He swayed, then reached out to steady himself against the tree. As his hand came into contact with the bark he let out a loud moan and snatched it away. Sank to his knees. 'No!' he cried. 'No!' Anguish ravaged the contours of his face. 'No-o-o!'

I grabbed him by the shoulders and shook him hard. 'Spinks! Snap out of it!'

We were attracting curious glances from the grid-search teams by now, Fullerton looking over, the question in the angle of his head. I waved him back, returned my attention to Mungo Spinks.

He was still moaning softly, shaking his bowed head from side to side, so I slapped him across the face, not hard, but hard enough to sting. Dazed, he looked up at me quizzically through wide glazed eyes. Took what seemed a long time coming back.

'I'm sorry,' he murmured eventually, still breathing hard. 'I'm all right now.'

I helped him to his feet, led him away from the tree, over to a bench warming in the sun. He sat down heavily, as though he could no longer support the weight of his body. If he was pale before, he was ghostlike now.

'God!' he said. 'I've never . . . never . . .'

'It's okay,' I told him. 'You don't need to say anything.'

'You . . . felt it?' His breath was still ragged.

'I didn't need to. I could see it in your face.'

'That poor woman . . .' His voice trembled. He was more than just shaken; whatever he had seen or felt had pierced him right to the core. I've seen people cut from car wrecks who looked less shocked than Mungo Spinks did at that moment. He noticed my concern. 'Hazard of the job,' he explained weakly, his attempted smile a few thousand watts short of convincing. 'I thought Mary Mathieson had suffered, but . . .' He shook his head and sighed.

'Where's your car?' I asked.

'Down by the road. Why?'

'What you need is a drink.'

'You could be right,' he said, pushing himself slowly to his feet. 'A good stiff brandy, yes.'

What I needed was a long cool hair of the hound.

28

They say that if you look out across the Clyde from Ardrossan the outline of Arran's hills resembles that of a sleeping warrior. Maybe so, but this evening I was imperfectly sober and devoid of any kind of hallucinogen, and all I could see were hills, Goatfell the most prominent among them. It was a glorious evening, the sun over the port bow, the firth as flat as a mirror, the breeze warm, gulls gliding effortlessly alongside. It was the last ferry of the day, though abnormally quiet for a Sunday, and I'd found myself a quiet and sunny corner near the stern where I could browse through the bundle of collator's reports I'd received from John Fullerton earlier in the afternoon. It was not, however, pleasant reading.

I put away Silas Kerr's post-mortem report on Helen Falconer and turned my attention to the summaries of the eight victims.

The Fangman's first known victim had been Susan Hegarty, a fifty-nine-year-old social worker who'd disappeared on Monday 2 August last year. Her naked body was discovered four days later in a ditch at the foot of Whitelee Hill, near the village of Moscow. She'd been partially strangled, but cause of death was through loss of blood induced by heavy lacerations to the throat. There were obvious bitemarks on neck and throat, and both anus and vagina had been savagely mutilated *post mortem* by a sharp object – most likely a broken bottle, as several shards of glass were discovered near the neck of the womb – but there was no pathological or forensic evidence of intercourse.

She had last been seen climbing into what one witness described as a light-coloured hatchback, possibly an Escort, in the car park of her local supermarket. The car was driven by a fair-haired man wearing a green anorak and glasses. Her own car, a navy Metro, was later found in the same car park, with two flat tyres.

A couple of backpackers descended noisily from the upper deck, hurried laughing towards the bow. A woman in her late twenties stood at the rail further along the deck, puffing surreptitiously at a joint. She caught my eye, smiled, turned away. I shrugged – what the hell, it was a beautiful Sunday evening and I was officially off-duty – then returned to the report.

The second victim was Maureen Mathieson, a fifty-one-year-old housewife who lived in a fairly posh residential area of Troon with two of her four children and a husband who was employed as an air-traffic controller at Prestwick. She had last been seen alive on the afternoon of Saturday 30 October in her local supermarket car park, where witnesses had seen her climbing into a light-coloured (blue or grey) hatchback driven by a large man wearing glasses. Her own car was found there later with two flat tyres. Her naked body, again genitally mutilated, was discovered four days later in a ditch on the edge of Carrick Forest, six miles south of the village of Straiton. Again, there were both lacerations and bitemarks on her throat. No bones were missing.

At this point in the enquiry, I recalled, investigating officers believed that the killer deflated the tyres while the women were in the supermarket and then just happened to be around to offer them a lift home. It was thought the killer was a local man and that he and his victims were possibly acquainted.

The Fangman's third known victim was one Eileen Parker, a sixty-six-year-old retired English teacher who lived alone in Largs. Although there were no recorded witnesses to her movements on the day she disappeared – Tuesday 28 December – her car too had later been discovered with two flat tyres in her local supermarket car park. Her partially decomposed body was found ten days later in a ditch on the western perimeter of Prestwick airport. She had been mutilated in the same manner as the previous two victims, and her face and nipples garishly painted with a high-gloss lipstick. And, in another new twist of the killer's MO, he had filleted her left thigh and removed the femur bone.

By the end of the first week in January, Strathclyde police were now certain they were dealing with a serial killer. The three separate murder enquiries were then brought together and Operation Dentist came into being under the command of the newly promoted Commander Kettle. The Home Office Large Major Enquiry System was subsequently installed in the operation's main incident room at Kilmarnock. A week later, TV's *Crimewatch* team devoted a large part of their programme to the three unsolved murders and, apart from the usual appeals for witnesses, also warned women in the area to be especially vigilant in supermarket car parks and, if possible, not to go shopping alone. Dates of the full moon were also broadcast, although no serious weight was attached to this aspect of the killer's MO. Perhaps, in hindsight, that was a mistake. The killer now changed his *modus operandi*.

His fourth victim was thought to be seventy-three-year-old widow, Jean Sutherland, from Irvine. She had disappeared on the afternoon of Thursday 27 January, only minutes after leaving her weekly appointment at the hairdresser's. She had last been seen standing at a bus stop just across the road. One of the hairdressers thought Jean Sutherland might have climbed into a light-coloured hatchback, though she couldn't swear on it. Although the widow's body had yet to be found, everybody concerned regarded her to be the fourth victim of the man known as the Fangman. She too had vanished on a full moon.

The Fangman's fifth victim struck a painful chord close to the hearts of many of the men involved in the hunt for the killer. Sadie McEvoy was the forty-eight-year-old wife of a desk sergeant at the Kilbirnie police station. She'd been abducted from her local supermarket car park in Dalry on Sunday 27 March. Another full moon. She had last been seen talking to an elderly well-built woman in the back of her own car. She was discovered the next day in a ditch by the side of the B road out to Farland Head, west of West Kilbride. Her throat had been bitten out, her genitals mutilated, her face and nipples painted with lipstick, and her femur and humerus bones were missing.

Why did he take their bones? I wondered for the hundredth time. As fetishes? Why not just take a lock of hair or one of the victim's personal belongings? Why bones? Why the humerus and femur bones? Because they were the largest? What special significance could those two bones have for the Fangman? The guy was obviously no surgeon: path reports on Parker, McEvoy, Bryce, Drummond and Falconer all pointed to the killer's definite lack of anatomical knowledge: the flesh hacked from the bones, the bones themselves ripped from their sockets. And then there was the question of the heads.

The sixth victim was a thirty-seven-year-old boutique owner called Margaret Bryce, who lived and worked in Ayr. A divorced mother of two, she lived with her mother who looked after the kids while she was at work. She disappeared after locking up her shop on Monday 5 April. Her Datsun was found in the car park of the superstore where she usually did her shopping on her way home. No witnesses. Two weeks later her body was found, naked and mutilated, in a ditch by the Camphill Reservoir by the side of the A760 Largs–Kilbirnie road. Defensive wounds on her arm suggested she had put up a formidable struggle. Both humerus and femur bones were missing and, in yet another grotesque twist of the killer's MO, she had been decapitated and her head removed. Identification had been by X-ray.

I looked up as a gang of kids chased along the deck towards

me then thundered up the steps. The woman who'd been smoking the joint was still there by the lifeboat, looking out across the water with a smile on her face. Oh for happy thoughts, I thought, and moved reluctantly on.

The seventh victim was a forty-three-year-old nurse from Cumnock. Alice Drummond had disappeared on Wednesday 25 May, reported missing when she failed to turn up for work. She was last seen talking to a well-built woman in her local supermarket car park. Her body was discovered two days later in a ditch by the side of a small B road just outside Cockermouth, south of Carlisle. Hers was the only body to date that had been dumped south of the border. Like the previous two victims, her throat had been bitten out, her face and nipples painted, her genitals mutilated, and her femur and humerus bones removed. She was also found headless.

What did he do with their heads?

The eighth victim was Arthur Thomas. The one that seemed to break all patterns. A man. Found in his own home. Mutilated only in that his throat had been bitten out. No bones missing, no lipstick applied, head still intact. Murdered four days after a full moon, on Monday 27 June. Cause of death, manual strangulation.

I stared at the report for a long time, letting the facts sink in, hoping, I suppose, for a miracle, a flash of inspiration to rise from the pages and slap me round the face. As usual, nothing happened. So I returned the report to its folder, dropped it on to my jacket and let my mind wander. The joint-smoking woman had gone and I was now alone leaning against the rail. We were about halfway across, the sun blinding in across the water, Holy Island crowned in gold six or seven miles ahead.

And, of course, there was Helen Falconer, victim number nine. Very little information in on her yet, house-to-house were still in progress and it would take until tomorrow at least before we had any clear kind of picture as to her movements on the day she died. We knew already that she was a sixty-eight-year-old

347

widow who lived with her daughter in Girvan, and that she had last been reported alive on Thursday afternoon after leaving her doctor's. Beyond that, nothing.

All the women had died from loss of blood. I considered this. All were murdered on a full moon, except the last two victims: Thomas, four days late, and Helen Falconer, one day late. All except Thomas had been dumped in ditches in mostly rural areas. All were women, except Thomas. All with throats bitten out. Victims three to seven inclusive – although this was purely conjecture in the case of Jean Sutherland, whose body was yet to surface – had been painted with lipstick. The last three female victims had been younger than the first four, an indication, Fullerton suggested, that the Fangman was becoming less selective as the form of his fantasies mutated. The killing of Thomas, if indeed the work of the Fangman, only helped, he said, to reinforce that view. I'd then asked him about the well-built women seen talking to Sadie McEvoy and Alice Drummond on the days they died.

'Trust you to pick up on that,' Fullerton had said. 'It's probably our best hope yet of catching the bastard. We think he changed his MO after the *Crimewatch* programme and that what he does now is dress up as a woman, wait until his chosen victim enters the supermarket, then breaks into her car and sits there until she comes out.'

'That's rather a lot of conjecture, is it not?'

'It would be,' Fullerton said, looking pleased with himself, 'if we didn't have a witness.'

The DI had enjoyed the surprise on my face. 'You have a witness? Someone who can describe the Fangman?'

'As far as describing the Fangman goes, not much luck there, I'm afraid. She didn't come forward until several days later and by that time her memory was pretty vague. She said she'd arrived back at her car to find a well-built woman sitting in the back seat. When she asked the woman what she was doing in her car, the woman explained she'd had a dizzy spell and had had to

348

sit down and rest. The witness – whose name I'm not going to give you, Frank – was by this time suspicious: she says she always double-checks her doors and was absolutely convinced that she'd left none of them unlocked. The woman then asked her if she could drive her home, as she had to lie down, and gave her a nearby address. Our witness, though, had noticed that the woman's forearms were not those of a frail old dear, but those of a man, and a hairy man at that. She told the woman to leave her car immediately or she would fetch the police. Then she noticed that the woman had an Adam's apple. She started screaming and the man dressed as a woman dived out of the car, knocked her to the ground and ran away.'

'So why didn't she report it earlier?'

'Shock, she said. She didn't think it was that serious. It was only when, two days later, she found a plastic bag under the back seat of her car that she informed her brother, a retired constable. He, of course, informed us immediately.'

'And in the bag?'

'A claw-hammer and a knife.'

'Prints?'

'None,' Fullerton said. 'And none in the car either. Witness says he wore gloves.'

'What about her description of him?'

'Large. Heavily built, maybe six foot. Blond hair on his arms. He was wearing a scarf and large horn-rimmed glasses and, she thought, possibly a wig. We checked the car for traces, of course, but nothing's turned up yet.'

'Nothing?' I'd asked incredulously. 'When did all this happen?'

'Twenty-fifth of May,' Fullerton said. 'The same afternoon Alice Drummond disappeared.'

'Where?'

'Kilwinning.'

'And Drummond was taken from . . .'

'Cumnock. We're talking twenty-five, thirty miles. So having failed with our witness, he drove south and eventually succeeded with Alice Drummond.'

'So his aborted attempt on your witness could account for the fact that Drummond was younger than most of the other women?'

Fullerton nodded. 'Time was running out for him and he had to have a victim.'

And time was still running out, I thought now, leaning on the guardrail. Running out for us, and running out for his next victim. The next full moon was just over three weeks away, 21 August, and he'd be out there now, I felt sure, already trawling for suitable prey. I sighed at the seeming futility of our investigation, then grabbed my jacket and folder and headed for the bar.

It was quieter than usual and I was served immediately. A few faces that I recognised and only one nod of recognition from them. I took my drink along to the telephone and dialled the Lamlash station. Monica answered. She was just going off duty, she said, was already halfway out the door. I asked her if she would meet me off the ferry.

'How'd it go with Kettle?' she asked.

'You didn't see me on TV?'

''Course I did, it was on every bloody broadcast. You could at least've let us know what was going on.'

'It all happened too fast,' I told her. 'Anyway, I still have a job to come back to.'

'I don't know if I'm relieved or not.' She sounded tired, her voice lacking its usual confidence. 'But yeah, okay, I'll meet you off the ferry. When's it due?'

'Half an hour.'

'I'll wear a red rose so you'll recognise me.'

I laughed and hung up. For the first time since I'd transferred to Arran, I felt like I was going home – and felt good about it. I returned to my sheltered suntrap at the stern and savoured my whisky. It was a Glen Chalmadale. It brought my thoughts briefly back to the Farquharsons, to the mystery of the sheep and then, inevitably, to Kyoko. My weekend off had not been so bad after all – certainly no sad-eyed drift from one empty oasis to another as I had imagined it would be when I'd seen her last. Tomorrow she would return from her trip to the capital and we would meet as arranged. And already, I realised with a certain degree of amused apprehension, I felt as excited as a kid on Christmas Eve. No two ways about it, the island air was definitely affecting my hormones.

And, I would later admit, my highly tuned senses as well.

I never heard a thing. I sensed his presence, yes, a split second before the bottle cracked open my head and I slumped over the guardrail. I saw stars, plenty of them, swirling before my eyes. Beyond them the foaming water below. Stunned, I tried to turn, to gain some kind of foothold, any kind of handhold. Coordination wasn't working. My struggles became desperate as something hit me hard in the middle of my back, driving the breath from my body. I saw more stars. No, not stars but the sun-flecked water flashing by beneath me. I was now doubled over the guardrail, feet no longer on the deck, and I couldn't turn, couldn't move, couldn't breathe. I felt his hands grasp my ankles and I knew what was coming next but there was nothing I could do as he heaved my legs over the rail but watch myself tumble into a whirligig world of sea, ferry, sky, sea, ferry . . .

. . . sea.

29

'If one is not extremely careful,
Somebody may come up from behind and strike him.
Misfortune.'

Mistylaw Muir.

He parks the Subaru off the track, sits there awhile behind the wheel, trying to calm the rampaging thoughts in his head. In vain. Simone is there, as she seems to be almost all the time now, lashing him with her tongue, hardly giving him a moment's peace. His mind is unravelling; he can feel it disengaging, blowing fuses, the whole critical circuit gradually closing down on him. Time breathing like a dragon down his neck – so much to do yet so little time.

Her bones, bonehead, that's why you're here.

Gideon Byrne climbs from the car, starts up the track. He has walked this track five, maybe six times already this year. The ground is dry and hard, pitted in some places, inlaid with rocks in others. The track winds up the hill, squeezed between a drystone dyke on one side and a ditch on the other, overgrown now by a hedge of tangled briars and brambles. The sun is warm on his back, already sliding down the afternoon sky.

Should've killed the nosy cop when you had the chance. Look what he's gone and done now, made you the laughing stock of the nation. You had him there, and then you let him go. Typical.

'So what?' Byrne says aloud. He's got other plans for

McMorran. Plans which involve the Japanese woman whose name he can't exactly remember. Something like *Kimono*. Anyway, eyes that looked at him all snooty like, like all the other bitches who ended up in ditches. So if Kimono wanted a pot with his very special glaze, hell, she would have one. She could have a hundred, so long as she came out to the pottery one last time. Which is why he's out here today on the Mistylaw Muir searching for the necessary ingredients.

On today's menu, the chef's speciality, bone-ash.

Ingredients, yes, because each glaze has its own recipe, its own delicate balance and blend of substances. Aye, he could tell Kimono all about glazes. Keep her enthralled for hours. Simone used to call him 'The Glaze Bore' when he first started out. Then everyone else at the Aphelion Centre followed suit, so he stopped talking about glazes, stopped talking about anything to anyone.

Should've taken the last strangle's bones. Helen Falconer's bones. Then you wouldn't need to be here now on a Sunday afternoon when all good potters should be lying out in the sun getting pissed. But no, you got all carried away, didn't you, you had to take her right to the edge. By which time it was getting far too late for a bone-job.

Not today, though. He has plenty of time, can stroll along up the track just like any other Sunday promenader looking for a decomposed body in a ditch. Every time he'd come up here he'd wondered why he hadn't just dumped her down where he'd left his car. There, she might have been discovered sooner and his power enhanced. But at least now he has an emergency supply of bones.

Jean Sutherland. She was the widow strangle, the one who didn't seem to care very much whether she lived or died. An air of defeatism about her, resignation dulling the embers of her eyes. As though dying beneath your hands was just about the best she could expect out of life. Weird, the way some people just give it up, relinquish the torch of their existence with barely a struggle. To the superior man, the struggle is *life.*

Of course, for most of his pots, Byrne uses fairly straight-forward glazes, making the most of the materials around him. A variety of peat-ash glazes and several kinds of wood-ash glazes are the ones he prefers for the tourist trade. The peat-ash glazes sell best; they tend to look more natural, a kind of velvety grey, the texture oily, the effect varying with each batch of peat. His favoured wood-ash glazes are Scots pine, larch, spruce and fir, all readily available on the island.

The cop, McMorran, you can't shake him from your mind. Not since you seen him yesterday on the news. The things he said about you, degrading you the way he did in front of millions of viewers, making you out to be some kind of . . . what was the word he used . . . inadequate, yes. In that tone of voice he has, of moral superiority, when all he knew was nothing of the man you really are.

On the brow of the hill now, a middle-aged couple, heading away from him. Probably been up to look at the crashed World War Two bomber up there, a Shackleton or something. Soon they will be out of sight and then he can concentrate on the ditch. The marker stone he'd left last time up was still there, balanced atop the drystane dyke. In the ditch opposite, the remains of Jean Sutherland.

So last night you threw the bones to see what you ought to do about the cop. Consulted the I Ching *and came up with the hexagram Hsiao Kuo, Preponderance of the Small. Your 'nine in the third place' gave you the reading: 'If one is not extremely careful, Somebody may come up from behind and strike him. Misfortune.' Which in the text came down to this: 'At certain times extraordinary caution is absolutely necessary.' Which was not exactly earth-shattering advice, given the present circumstances.*

The couple have disappeared over the hill. There is no one else in sight. Byrne uses a dead branch to push back the overgrowth, then steps down into the ditch. There is little smell in the hollow now, the flesh from her corpse having completely decomposed. Her eyeless sockets stare up at him, not accus-ingly, he imagines, but with the same resigned expression with which she had succumbed to death. Not much blood in the old bitch anyway, he recalls, he'd had to rip half her throat out before he could even get a mouthful. And then it was old blood.

The bones are dry. Good. Like the wood he uses for his wood-ash glazes, the bones need to be dry. The wood he uses for the glazes usually lies in the storeroom for a year, year and a half before he burns it and begins the painstaking process of sieving and decanting the ash. That long. The bones, though, need much less time and, for rush jobs, can always be dried gently in the kiln first.

And Kimono can definitely be classed a rush job.

Gideon Byrne straddles the ditch and begins sorting through the bones. The skull is an obvious choice – plenty of ash there. As in the femur and humerus bones. How about the hip bone for a change, or the tibia? Byrne looks up at the sky considering this. Decisions come hard on such a glorious afternoon. Crickets chirping, birds singing, the sound of the River Calder like a distant chorus of excited mutterers ... All induce in him a sense of contradiction, of belonging simultaneously to two irreconcilable worlds, his and theirs. Sometimes he feels this so intensely, this sense of being torn apart, that it's almost physical. On the one side, the relentless obligations of his mission; on the other, a yearning for peace of mind, acceptance, an end to it all. Days like today, he feels his head is going to explode under all the pressure that such emptiness exerts.

We are mere vessels from which others may drink the essence of life.

And Byrne is a vessel yearning to be filled. But on afternoons like this he is filled only with an aching loneliness, a desperate need to be understood, admired, and respected. Tears will come as they always do. Tears followed swiftly by anger.

At Ardrossan he waits in line as the ferry docks, and cars and passengers disembark. He is good at waiting. He can spend hours in the cockpit of his car, watching, thinking, waiting. He feels secure behind the wheel, comfortable, can just let his mind drift on the tides of his fantasies, see where they end up.

There are three cars ahead of him, about twenty behind. On the passenger seat next to him lies the bag of bones he's selected for the glaze. He'd settled for the skull, left humerus and right femur – when the body is eventually discovered he wants everyone to know it's one of his. He hopes it will be soon.

The cars ahead pull away. He starts the Subaru and follows them down the ramp and into the bowels of the ferry. Fourth on, fourth off. He locks the car, leaving the bag of bones in plain view on the passenger seat, crosses the car-deck, and climbs the companionway up to the quarter-deck. The bar is empty, still closed, so he makes his way for'ard to the café. Although many of the tables are already taken, the servery is shuttered. Byrne curses to himself, heading for the top deck. All he wants is a fucking drink, something to lubricate his parched throat, take the edge off his mood. He can feel it hanging over him like some towering great thunderhead about to rip the sky apart. The air around him charged. What he needs is a damn good earthing.

It is quiet on the top deck, kids mostly, running out of control and making too much noise, their squeaks and squeals piercing his concentration like a flight of vicious barbs. Kids should be seen and not heard, that's what his mother always said any time he tried opening his mouth. His father, who had a dry wit when he could be bothered using it, always replied, 'Parents should be obscene, not absurd.' And that's exactly what they were, Gideon's parents: she was obscene and he was absurd. Some legacy.

The ferry backed away from the pier, manoeuvred out through the narrow harbour gates. When the winter winds came down from the north-west or up from the south-east and chopped up the already racing Clyde, the ferry couldn't enter the harbour here, would have to divert up the coast to Gourock. You had an appointment you couldn't miss on the mainland, you could count on the ferry being diverted. But this evening the sea is calm, a speckled silvery-grey beneath the cooling sun, Arran directly ahead, clear cut against the western horizon.

Reminds you of Spain, doesn't it, but there it was the early morning sun slanting in over the bay at Cadaqués, the beachfront cafés already open, cremat *for the fishermen,* café con leche *for the early-bird tourists come to look at Dali's house further down the coast. Long summer days spent prowling the beaches, scouring the cafés, down the coast to Rosas, sometimes even further, Bagur, Tamariu, Llafranch, Calella, once as far as Palamos. You were a lot younger then, your beliefs unformulated, like so much smoke eluding your grasp. But you had the urges, and it was a great place to practise your trade.*

A few more people on the sun-deck now, some sprawled on the benches, others leaning on the rail. A gangly teenager in baggy clothes and a back-to-front baseball cap walks by, skateboard under arm and a shouldered ghetto-blaster blaring in his ear. Gideon Byrne glares at him, and is ignored. He almost reaches out to grab the little shit but stops himself in time, remembering the warning in last night's reading of the *I Ching*. '*At certain times extraordinary caution is absolutely necessary.*' Which rules out the use of excess violence in a public situation. So a fuming Gideon Byrne glances at his watch, then heads down to the bar on the lower deck. Has to wait a couple of minutes while the barman serves a couple of dithering tourists, then orders a pint of heavy, no, better make it two. By the time the barman's finished pouring the second, Byrne's already drained the first. The barman makes some inane comment. Byrne ignores him, starts on the second. The barman is waiting for payment.

'Another,' Byrne tells him, wiping his lips, pushing the empty glass forward. The barman obliges. Byrne pays, then takes his drink over to a corner table splashed by sunlight. The seat is warm, the ashtray clean. Some radio programme playing ceilidh tunes behind the bar. A guy over at the bandit, pushing coins in the slot and punching buttons the way all the professional losers like to do. So far Byrne has seen no one he recognises, which suits his turbulent mood fine. Small talk is for small minds.

And you're thinking big, Giddy, aren't you. You've got big plans in mind. Show these fuckers a thing or two. They think the Ripper was bad, Hindley and Brady, Nilsen, the Hangman. Think they've seen it all, nothing new under the sun. Wrong. Very wrong. You've only just begun. Police floundering around, chasing their tails, saying an arrest is imminent, what have you got to be scared of? Nine strangles and not even a knock at the door. Unless you count McMorran.

Gideon Byrne takes his empty glass up to the bar, orders another pint, returns to his seat. A middle-aged couple two tables along are joined by two more couples. Beginning to encroach upon his space. One of the women has a laugh that makes him want to stretch across the table and slap her face to the floor. They are from Manchester. Probably live down in Whiting Bay, the village Arranites now call Little Lancashire. For obvious reasons.

Should you count McMorran? Difficult to tell. McMorran's a strange one, not like any of the other cops you've met. Something lurking deep in the guy – you saw it in his eyes that night – that you can't quite put your finger on. Something unpredictable, you feel, dangerously unstable. Like he could lose control at any given moment. Signs of it in the newspaper article you read a week or so back, before he came out to the pottery. How he'd been suspended from duty for killing a guy while trying to arrest him. How many cops manage to do that? Only the lucky few. The question is, how much of a danger is he to you? He knows you only as a potter, and then hardly at all. And all that talk on the TV was just that, talk. Nothing more than sticks and stones, hoping to provoke some kind of reaction. But you're not like that, are you. You are the cause and he is the effect. He can do nothing.

Gideon Byrne looks away from the porthole through which he

is blindly staring, and takes in the bar. He almost jumps from his seat.

McMorran!

The bastard's standing at the bar, ordering whisky. Doesn't even look over this way, just pockets his change, picks a folder off the bar and saunters out on to the deck.

Byrne can feel his heart hammering, can almost *hear* the bloody thing. He catches the woman with the hideous laugh staring at him, but she turns quickly away. He drowns his shock in beer, draining the almost full glass in four heavy gulps. His thoughts are screaming.

The fuck is McMorran doing here? On *this* ferry? There are plenty of other ferries during the day, why specifically this one? Had he noticed Byrne in the corner? Of course he had, the guy was a cop. Cop walks in a bar, he clocks every face in the room and files it away. That's the kind of thing they do. By habit. So if McMorran had spotted him, why didn't he come over to pass the time of day? Why just pick up his stuff and leave? The answer of course is he didn't want to be seen. Because he's on a job.

Coincidence? No. Byrne does not believe in coincidence. Not this kind of coincidence. He feels the tears welling up inside him again, the unfairness of it all. Some inferior little shit like McMorran following him around. It can't be happening. The police can't be on to him, not yet, no way. But there he is, keeping out of sight, probably watching the bar, waiting for Byrne to leave. How long has McMorran been trailing him? All day? Up to Mistylaw Muir and back? It doesn't bear thinking about.

But you're forgetting something, aren't you? The Book of Changes. Go to all that bother throwing the bones last night and now you want to ignore its advice. Is that the act of a superior man?

Byrne struggles for coherence of thought. Couple of the people from the nearby table are looking at him now, concern shadowing their eyes. He removes his glasses and they dissolve into vague blurs. He rubs his brimming eyes, massages his temples. Can feel the tenseness creeping back, the one that always presages the headaches. Then it comes to him, like lightning lighting up the night. Of course!

'If one is not extremely careful, Somebody may come up from behind and strike him. Misfortune.'

It has been ordained.

Suppressing his tears now, Byrne goes up to the bar, orders a bottle of Newcastle Brown. No, he tells the barman, he doesn't want it opened, he doesn't want a glass, just the way it is. Strong and heavy. Tears making way for anger now. He drops the bottle into his jacket pocket and strides from the bar.

No McMorran.

Byrne climbs to the top deck. No McMorran. He walks round the guardrail, checking out the deck below. No McMorran. He checks the café, the shop, the queue at the purser's cabin. No McMorran. He heads aft, the anger rising within him with every stride. The injustice of it, the sheer—

McMorran. There he is near the stern, behind the flight of steps leading down from the upper deck. You wouldn't notice him unless you were looking. And from there he can watch the stairs down to the car-deck. Crafty bastard. Well, Byrne thinks, two can play at that game. He finds a spot where he can watch unobserved, and wait.

And he waits.

He doesn't hear your approach. You are using extraordinary caution. You have a charming, toothy kind of smile ready in case he turns around. The deck is clear, none of the crew working at the stern now, all is perfect. It has been ordained, foreseen. Somebody may come up from behind and strike him. *Indeed. The bottle is in your hand. The weight is right. McMorran has his back to you, is leaning against the rail, projecting his thoughts out across the water that will soon be his grave. You raise the bottle and bring it down hard.*

Misfortune, indeed.

30

Turbines.

I hit the water sideways on, the force of the fall like a punch to the solar plexus, expelling what little air was left in my lungs. I sank, choking and disorientated, into a churning whirlpool of darkness, light and noise. The noise was intense, like nothing I'd ever experienced before, the vibrations jolting every cell in my body, my blood thrumming as though I were in a microwave oven, cooking from the inside out.

Turbines.

Stunned and breathless, I had only one thought in mind, *Get away from the screws!* But I was tumbling through a maelstrom with no sense of place or direction, no idea of up or down, didn't know whether I was struggling towards the props or away from them. In one of those flashes of imagination that seem to accompany mortal danger, I recalled the kitchen in which I'd worked as an apprentice chef in my early teens, and the whirling blades of the mincing machine into which I'd forced the leftover scraps of meat. In my mind's eye I could now see myself being sucked into the whirling blades of the screws and emerging as so much bloodied mince. That image, though, was enough to flood my system with adrenaline and kickstart my organism into the fight for survival.

I could now feel the tow of the screws tugging at my legs. I kicked out, crawling against the tow towards the light I hoped was the surface. The harder I kicked out, the less headway I seemed to be making. By now my lungs were aflame; I'd hit the water with barely a swallow of air and now that was gone, but I'd managed to control the spasmic choking, had contained that, but my lungs still needed oxygen, my brain needed oxygen, and I had to use my brain fast if I wanted to survive. But fast was not fast enough. The couple of seconds I'd been in the water seemed to have lasted for ever and it would only be another couple of seconds before I hit the screws. I could already feel my body tensing for the blow and another image flashed to mind, that of a young woman who'd taken her first parachute jump over an airfield and as she descended the wind had caught the 'chute and blown her off course and she came down through the rotors of a helicopter about to take off. It was a story I'd read in a newspaper a few years back and the absolute horror of it had caught my morbid imagination for days, I'd see myself in her position, floating slowly down towards the rotors and knowing there was nothing I could do, that in a few seconds' time I'd be sliced thinner than salami. So my body was tensed, awaiting that final explosion of blood and pain, even as I hauled my body through the churning water, another second gone, another, and then . . .

contact

. . . the shock making me draw in breath but there was no air down here, only water, and I began choking again, fighting so hard to stay alive that I didn't even wonder why I wasn't dead, why I hadn't been torn to shreds by the screws, aware only that I must have air and that the air was a long way away, in another world far up there beyond the noise, beyond the turmoil of this desperate struggle for existence where consciousness was now beginning to fade, mind and body sliding into a comforting warm numbness, a kind of resigned apathy, a feeling of oneness with the water, of returning I don't know where, but returning nevertheless, the sensation not unpleasant, all I had to do was give in to it, let it take me, open my mouth and breathe in and it would all be over . . .

I opened my mouth and breathed in.

Choked on air. A cool fresh air that seared down my throat and scorched my aching lungs. I opened my eyes. I could barely see through the blinding light, the salted sting of water and tears. I retched and heaved, my body reacting beyond my control. I was swallowing water but I didn't care because it soothed my burning throat and I was also gulping down air and that was the important thing, it didn't matter if it didn't stay down, there was a skyful of the glorious stuff to breathe and it tasted so good, it tasted better than anything I'd ever tasted before, and I wanted more of it and more of it, and so long as I brought the choking under control and didn't drink too much more, I'd be able to taste as much as I liked. But it was close, my friend, as Mungo Spinks would say, it was close.

Still bobbing in the ferry's wake, still coughing and spluttering, I turned and watched the ferry sail away. With half a mile already between us, I waited and waited for the pitch of its turbines to change, for it to slow and then begin the long turn through one hundred and eighty degrees that would bring it back upon its wake and eventually to me. But it didn't slow, it didn't alter course, its blunt stern only continued to diminish on my low horizon. I could see the little blobs of crew and passengers and I thought surely someone must have seen me go overboard, have already raised the alarm. But with each passing minute my hopes subsided until it became clear my plight had gone unobserved and I was out here now in the middle of the Clyde with only a few hours of daylight left and I was tired and weak, battered and bruised, and I knew I didn't have the strength to fight against the tide, and that it would take me like so much flotsam round the south of the island and, if I was still alive or afloat by then, around the Mull of Kintyre and out into the Irish Sea. And the thought came to mind – not one I'm proud of, since it wasn't the kind of thought I would normally entertain; but the circumstances, you must admit, were not exactly normal – a fearful little voice inside me saying perhaps, my friend, you should have just let yourself go, relinquished your grip on life back there a few minutes ago when you had the chance, saved yourself the headlong plunge from the heights of hope to the depths of despair. But the struggle for life is not always a conscious decision, and the organism's basic instinct for survival had brought me out from under the screws and back into the world of the living, and the fearful little voice in my mind was no more than the pitiful baying of a hound at the moon. I was Frank McMorran, goddammit, and, obstinate to the end, I would bloody well survive.

Look on the bright side, I told myself. It wasn't raining or snowing or blowing a force ten gale; I was in a fairly busy shipping lane and the sea was calm, it wasn't freezing, and as long as I kept my body moving, I wasn't going to succumb to hypothermia. I'd been in far more dangerous situations in the past and had survived them all; this would be no different. So, treading water, I did a quick body check, running my fingers cautiously through the inventory of my injuries.

There was a large lump on the back of my head, still swelling and painful to the touch. In the centre of it, what felt like a one-, possibly two-inch gash, still seeping blood. It would need at least half a dozen stitches, I reckoned. The resultant headache from the blow lurked just behind my eyes, piercing me intermittently with its rapiers of pain. Not much worse, I thought, than my usual Sunday-morning hangover. I moved on, fingers now exploring my left shoulder, which had taken the full force of my fall to the water and then, a few moments later, my collision with what I now realised had been the ferry's rudder. It wasn't broken or dislocated, just stiff and numb and, I imagined, heavily bruised. It wasn't my only bruise. There would be another one in the centre of my back where the powerful punch had hit me seconds before I went over the rail, and one more around my left knee, also a result of my collision with the rudder. Apart from all that, I reasoned, I was in the fullness of fitness and health.

By now I'd stopped coughing and retching, and was

breathing almost as normally as one can in the circumstances. I considered my boots. They were my favourites, a pair of Spanish-style cowboy boots that I'd bought in Malaga five or six years ago. They were good on land but heavy in the water. I've never before contemplated sacrificing comfort for style and I certainly wasn't going to start now, however stylish a corpse I might make. So one by one, I pulled them off and, reluctantly, let them drop towards the sea floor. Now I was dressed only in T-shirt, socks and jeans; unless my assailant was a thief as well as an attempted murderer, my flying jacket would still be lying where I'd left it, along with the folder of reports, on the deck against the bulkhead. The jeans were heavy, yes, but the layer of water trapped between them and my skin would act as insulation and, as the night cooled, I would need all the insulation I could get. And if I tired before the night was out, at least I'd have the makings of a life buoy: tie the legs together and trap some air inside.

By now the ferry was sinking into the horizon, and I could tell by its course that I had already drifted between half a mile and a mile to the south. The ferry would not be picking me up on its return to Ardrossan.

I'd gone overboard about midway across the Clyde. It was a spring tide – I knew that because the Fangman's full moon had been on Wednesday – and would run, I estimated, at about four knots. Say four miles an hour. I had maybe another three, three and a half hours of daylight left, by which time I would be somewhere off the south-east coast of the island. I wondered how close the current would take me. Perhaps if I conserved energy now, I thought, then I might stand a chance of making it to the shore. Maybe, perhaps, if and might. The terminology of hope.

I flipped up my legs and floated on my back.

I'd been putting it off, not wanting to think about it because it was all still so vivid in my mind, how close I'd come to dying. It is not a pleasant thought knowing someone not only wants you dead but is also willing to make it happen. And I didn't have many doubts as to who that person was. I could go round and round the track of reasoning but I always came back to where I started. I saw only three possibilities. One: someone I'd put away in the past had been released from jail and had been, either purposely or coincidentally, on board the ferry; had seen an opportunity for revenge and had taken it. Possible, yes, but unlikely. Two: there was a killer on the loose and I was nothing but a random victim. Highly unlikely. And three: the only person I could think of who might realistically want me dead, who would have seen me on television yesterday and now have a motive to kill me, a man who had already personalised our relationship by sending me an anonymous note, the Fangman. Like I said, not much room for doubt. And, if I was right in my assumption, I was left with another two choices. Question: what was the Fangman doing on the ferry? Choice one, he had picked me up somewhere on the mainland and had followed me on to the ferry. Choice two: he was on the ferry anyway, had noticed me and then taken his opportunity.

I reran the events of the weekend through my mind to try and see where he might possibly have picked up my trail. After clearing with DI Fullerton and Commander Kettle yesterday afternoon, I had left the locus with Mungo Spinks and taken him to a small country hotel bar for a much-needed drink. He'd still been shaky when we reached his car, so I volunteered to take the wheel. It was a brand-new BMW, jet black, and moved sweetly beneath my fingertips. The psychic business can't be all that bad, I remember thinking; either that or Spinks had foreseen himself a winner at Haydock.

The bar, being Sunday, was packed. Inside, it was all smoke, noise and sweat, so we'd taken our drinks out to the beer garden, found ourselves a table and sat. In the next hour and a half I had learnt a little about the man himself, a lot about the kind of work he did, enough about the *I Ching* to understand its origins, philosophy, and how to use it, but nothing at all about the experience that had so deeply shocked him up at the locus. I probed gently but, with all the skill of a blind surgeon, failed to open him up. When John Fullerton joined us later, having completed his duties at the locus, Spinks had excused himself and left. Fullerton felt uncomfortable sitting in a bar and, because of his car, unable to drink, so we too left not long after, returning to the operation's incident room at Kilmarnock. There I hung about for several hours while Fullerton brought himself up to date with the investigation's progress – a lot of stuff already coming in from the small army of DCs doing house-to-house; but all this information first had to be written up, fired into HOLMES, and then collated. Not a small matter of hours – and made a minor dent in the bodywork of administrational paperwork that is the ball and chain of every detective inspector in the land. It was already dark when we left the station and headed back to Fullerton's house. We stopped for a Chinese carry-out on the way and, back at his house, we ate and drank and didn't once talk about the case, preferring instead to relive our shared experiences at the Tulliallan training college. It was before midnight when Fullerton retired, and only a matter of minutes later that I fell thankfully into a deep and contented sleep. It had been a long day.

I resumed treading water. My head was still a heavily throbbing ache atop my shoulders, but the stabbing pains had receded and the salt no longer stung the open wound. My throat though was about as dry as a dead dingo's crotch and my knee was stiffening up; I would have to keep it moving. The ferry by now had long disappeared over the horizon and I was alone. The Clyde could have been the Atlantic, the way I felt right then, the sense of loneliness settling on my mind with all the delicacy of a professional wrestler.

Could the Fangman have been watching the police station at Kilmarnock? I wondered. It was possible. We had returned there, John Fullerton and I, the next afternoon – *this* afternoon, I corrected myself; already I felt as though I'd been in the water for hours, though it was probably not even one. If the Fangman had been watching the station, then he'd been waiting for me – what else could he gain by watching officers enter and exit the station? Certainly no indication of how the hunt for him was progressing. Perhaps, then, he got a kick out of being so close to his pursuers. Either that, I thought, or his intention to kill me was already fixed in his mind by then. In which case I must have really struck a nerve yesterday on TV.

If he hadn't picked me up at Kilmarnock then it must have been while waiting at Ardrossan for the ferry, or on the ferry itself. Which possibilities raised their own particular questions. Like why was he on the pier? Had he just disembarked when he spotted me? Or was he, like me, waiting to embark? Did he perhaps live on the island? And if he did, then maybe the whole thing was an accident, maybe he hadn't followed me from Kilmarnock at all, had just been on his way home – from where? – and had seen me there on the deserted lower deck and had grasped what must have seemed a golden opportunity to both rid himself of me and really hit the headlines. A masterful stroke, if successful – and, I was reluctant to admit, it could still prove successful.

I changed position again, began a slow, lazy breaststroke towards the island, riding the gentle swell, eyes squinched against the blinding sun. Holy Island was directly due west. The ferry would have docked at Brodick by now and I wondered what Monica would do when I failed to disembark. Would she hang around until she was sure everybody had got off or would she think that maybe she'd missed me and just head off home? Like me, Monica was not renowned for her patience. I asked myself what I would do if the roles were reversed. She knew I was on the ferry and she knew I was on foot, so she'd probably drive Mike 30 on to the pier and wait there. When I failed to appear ... what? How long before she boarded the ferry and started questioning the crew? Would she insist on instigating a search? And if she did, would the search find my jacket where I had left it? And if it did, how long before an alarm was raised and the coastguard called out? Too long, I thought. To search the ferry thoroughly would take hours. Even if they didn't wait that long before raising the alarm, it would still take precious time to scramble one of the Sea Kings from HMS *Gannet* and launch a lifeboat from Lamlash. Too much time, I thought. Looking on the bright side – and I was, clinging to it like it was the prover-bial straw – I only had a couple of hours of daylight left and depending on the speed of the tide and a whole lot of other factors a search party might have to take into consideration, I was – again – a proverbial needle in a haystack. A piece of flotsam on the Clyde. Once darkness fell, the search would be postponed until first light. By then, I felt, still looking on the bright side, I would be fodder for the fish. I did not want to think about nightfall and what might happen out here unwitnessed by anyone except the man in the moon. Would there even be a moon tonight? The chances were good: the sky was clear, only a few wispy threads of cumulus high over Holy Island and the western horizon. But I didn't want to think about that. I had to forcibly turn my thoughts away. Concentrate on the Fangman, I told myself, occupy your mind with pleasant thoughts, like what you're going to do to the bastard when you catch up with him. I reverted to floating on my back. I was beginning to feel the cold.

But I didn't want to think about that either.

The Fangman had a car, generally thought to be a light-coloured estate or hatchback. Had he taken it on to the ferry? If he lived on the island, the chances were good. And if so, the chances were even better that his car would be one of perhaps a hundred recorded on the ferry's manifest. It was a comforting thought. So was Billy Murdoch, skipper of the Lamlash lifeboat team and a man with whom I'd shared several drunken dawns since arriving on the island. He was a large barrel-chested man in his early forties, with a full white beard and a wicked sense of humour embellished by sparkling blue eyes. If not physically, we still had a lot in common, not least the fact that both of us were extremely stubborn, and thus unwilling to give up on something until it became absolutely impossible to continue. I hoped with all my heart that he was on duty tonight. If called out.

When called out.

A couple of seagulls wheeled overhead, curious, I suppose, about the weird-looking human-type thing below. Glad they weren't vultures, I yelled at them to fuck off home, that I wasn't dead yet. It made me feel a little better. I was pleased, though, when they didn't take my advice: they were a sign of life and made me feel a little less alone. Perhaps, in the same way that vultures can direct trackers to a corpse, the gulls might lead a search party to my position. Another slender straw, but I clutched it anyway.

I wondered where Kyoko was right now, and how she might react if she knew what I was going through. But thinking about Kyoko was a painful reminder of a future that could probably be measured in hours. Much safer to stick to the past, I decided, where all the issues had been resolved, and all the pain and suffering was either long forgotten or at least bearable.

Cathy. I'd met her in Ballaig about a year ago, a tiny village north of Callander. I'd been on the trail of The Edinburgh Hangman, Dominic Bain, and had stayed in her guest-house while I furthered my enquiries. I'd known nothing of Bain then, neither the fact that I was staying in the same room as he had as a child, nor that he and Cathy had been childhood friends. Cathy had never left the village for the city, had elected to stay even after her parents died, eventually marrying a man almost thirty years her senior. Widowed by Bain in his last few hours of freedom, she had come down to stay with me in my High Street flat. It had been good for a while, at times brilliant, but she had missed Ballaig and found she couldn't adapt to life in the city. I hadn't been much help. I was at the time fighting a

372

rearguard action on my ambushed career. Principle witness in the Fatal Accident Inquiry into the death of Ruben Maxwell, I'd been heavily censured by the sheriff – even though the verdict was 'death by misadventure' – who not only made a determination that I had been 'overzealous' in my attempts to place Maxwell in custody, but also submitted his findings to my deputy chief constable. With both press and public wanting blood, mine was a natural offering. I was brought swiftly in front of a disciplinary hearing chaired by the DCC, and subsequently busted down through the ranks. So it was against this rather fraught and tenuous backdrop that both Cathy and I had tried to come to terms with our own particular losses, and with each other. And as if that had not been enough to cope with, I'd also started drinking again. Cathy was back in Ballaig by Christmas.

There was hurt for both of us, but we also had other hurts to contend with, and perhaps it was easier this way to lick our wounds and heal and rebuild in our own space and time.

Ah, but the light of life looks so much brighter when studied from the shadows of death. Which was probably why I was now slipping into melancholia.

Out of habit I glanced at my watch; it still showed six thirty-three, had probably stopped a few minutes after I hit the water. How long ago? An hour and a half, maybe two, judging by the sun now sinking slowly below the hills of Arran. I realised I was shivering again and the realisation made me shiver even more. I rolled over on to my front so I could at least exercise my muscles. My body cried out for action. I wanted to move, to strike out for the shore, to do *something*, but there was this little nagging voice inside me telling me no, don't waste your energy, you need it to keep you warm, just lie back and float and you'll still be alive come morning. But I didn't want to think about morning because that would mean thinking about the long dark hours of night ahead of me, drifting blind and alone, with no source of reference to cling to, and suspended above God knows how many feet of water by only the tenuous thread of my ability and will to survive. Shivering, I reminded myself, is the body's way of keeping itself warm. I rolled on to my back again, stared at the empty sky.

Lockerbie. Ask any cop who was called out on that fateful Christmas when Pan Am Flight 103 was blown from the skies over Lockerbie if they still suffer from the dreams, the nightmares, and most will tell you they still do, and probably always will. Most coppers I know don't even want to talk about it. If they're anything like me, then something died in them that night – perhaps some faint spark of hope for humanity – and was then buried deep in the ensuing days as we scoured the surrounding countryside for bodies and bits of bodies. My memories of those days out in the fields, on the moorland, up on the hills, are now little more than snapshots, brief and vivid scenes that pass before my mind's eye a hell of a lot slower than I would wish.

I remember going up on to the moorland and as I crested the rise, the cold wind hitting me, the church up ahead, the snow crunching underfoot, I could see maybe sixty, seventy uniform cops just standing around – every single one of them standing beside a body. That's when it really came home to me the enormity of what we were dealing with up there.

It's not that I haven't seen bodies before – I have, quite a few, and none more recent than that of Arthur Thomas. And I can live with that, I have to. It was something that went hand in hand with my role in the SCS. And there were days, sure, when I'd be down in the mortuary and would maybe see a couple laid out on the tables, half a dozen more in the fridges. But they never seemed to register as being the bodies of people who were once alive. Everything there very clinical, comfortingly real.

Out on the moor, though, it was very different. Seeing all those cops out there standing over the black bags the Army had used to cover the bodies, knowing there were bodies underneath – the whole scene seemed bizarre, incredibly surreal.

I yelled in sudden panic and almost shot from the water as something solid brushed against my legs, something dark and alive that conjured up grotesque images of sharp white teeth and dorsal fins. Whatever it was, it squirmed back into the depths with a flick of its tailfin, certainly no monster, and certainly nothing to scream home about. It took minutes to regulate my breathing again, more than five before I could relax enough to float on my back again. The cold was beginning to eat through my flesh now, my extremities already numbing in the cool breeze. I didn't want to think about it, didn't want to think at all. But it wasn't a matter of *cogito, ergo sum* – I think, therefore I am – it was more like *sum, ergo cogito*.

So I thought.

Like I'd come down off the hill for canteen, and there was this Salvation Army soup kitchen set up by the road, these women working there – the nearest they get to a violent situation is maybe standing outside a pub selling *War Cry* – and there's all these army ambulances and trucks driving up and down the road with all the PCs and bodies in the back, and these women knew what was happening and yet they were standing there serving up the tomato soup like it was quite normal for them to be parked there and have groups of PCs come up and get mugs of soup. It kind of brought a sense of normality to the whole unusual situation, the fact that you were getting a bar of chocolate, a cup of soup, an apple. Like they were parts of normal everyday life that I could identify with instantly. I couldn't identify with body bags, but the bar of chocolate seemed to bring me back to some kind of reality where I could realise my feet were cold, that there was still a world spinning around beneath me.

* * *

Sea, sea, sea and sea. My escort of gulls had gone, deserting me for a warm nest somewhere – somewhere on land I might never feel beneath my feet again. Darkness crowding the horizon now. The cold working its way through my body like a creeping anaesthetic. How long before the cold numbed me completely and I could no longer move my muscles? Should I count my future in minutes or hours? I didn't want to think about it.

Second, maybe third day we were up there, the 27th, I had to relieve a young PC up by the farm, stand over his body and wait for the dedicated teams to arrive and do what had to be done – the CID to label the bodies, the doctors to certify death, the photographers to take pictures *in situ* – before the body could be loaded on to one of the trucks and taken down off the hill.

And before long I was standing there thinking about this guy – there but for the grace of God, and so on – trying hard not to, but it wasn't easy, he was lying there in front of me, naked but for his tie – the way he landed – both his hips on the same side, both his shoulders, his face practically unmarked, and there was nothing else to do but think. There was just me and him, and fifty yards away another cop standing by his body, five yards beyond him, another cop and another body. And so on. So it was almost impossible not to think about this guy, who was he, was he married, a father, was that his luggage over there, the one with all the Christmas-wrapped gifts?

There were stories, too, to fuel the imagination, stories that spread faster than wildfire, coming from so many sources at the same time it was difficult to tell if they were true or not. About the guy they found with his fingers crossed. About the couple the Chinook found, still in their seats, holding hands. About—

I heard it long before I saw it. A distant rhythmic throbbing that seeped up through the lower levels of my brain into consciousness like some long-forgotten song rising to the surface. So faint at first that I thought I must be imagining it, the sound fading in and out as I rose and fell in the swell, some sadistic trick of the approaching night, I felt, to raise my hopes and then dash them, death never coming easy.

At first I searched the sky, looking for the blink of lights, the blink of anything. But there was nothing there, nothing in sight, even though the sound was getting louder all the time, a thrumming drone, undulating like a huge swarm of flies battling against the breeze. With senseless fingers, I fought to remove my T-shirt, almost drowning myself at the same time, sinking below the surface, limbs responding sluggishly to my panicking commands as I hung there for what seemed ages in the cold and soundless, airless dark.

But eventually I surfaced again and drank the breath of the night, swallowing greedily, the air burning my throat like a dram of raw whisky, intoxicating me. I waved my T-shirt over my head, forced a series of broken, cracking yells from my lungs. The sound was much louder now, not the sound of rotors chopping at the air, but that of powerful engines surging through the sea, coming out of the bloodstained west. A shout. Another.

And then there it was, ploughing through the waves towards me.

31

They'd kept me in overnight for observation. It was a small two-bed ward with a broad window overlooking Lamlash Bay, and I remember insisting on taking the bed furthest from the window. Even here the sea was far too close for comfort. The other bed was thankfully unoccupied; I was not in the mood for conversation. Despite the sedatives, I'd slept fitfully, waking often in the grip of terror, disorientated, choking on air, the taste of salt in my mouth: in that limbo world between unconsciousness and consciousness, I was still there, out on the Clyde, fighting for my life. This morning, however, with the advent of daylight, I was feeling a little more as though I belonged on land and back in the land of the living.

They'd all been here last night, a welcoming committee I'd found very much welcome. Adam Yuill and Jim Tennant, Monica and Bob Gillies. All crowding my bedside, concerned, visibly relieved, and taking the piss out of me rotten. It had touched me, that, and I had felt for the first time that I was really part of a family, their family. Return of the Prodigal, that kind of thing.

Sergeant Yuill arrived first, mid morning, just after the doctor's rounds. The doctor, a young man I had met briefly only twice in the course of my duty, assured me I would live but that he'd like to keep me in a couple more days for further observation. I didn't bother arguing with him.

I was sitting by the window in dressing gown and pyjamas,

looking out over the sunlit bay and Holy Island, when Yuill
came in. His mood was unusually expansive.

'Glad to see you up and about,' he said, removing his cap and
sitting down on the edge of the bed. 'We've got a busy day ahead
of us and'll need all the help we can get.'

'You what?'

His broad expressionless face cracked into a smile. 'Only
kidding, Frank. You take your time.'

'Hospitals depress me,' I said.

'They're for the sick.'

'Exactly. I need to get out.'

'Doctor says a couple more days—'

'Today. Soon as I can. Now.'

Yuill nodded. 'Can't say I blame you.' He gave it a moment's
thought. 'Monica said she'd drop by later. I'll ask her to bring
you some fresh clothes, then she can drive you home. How's
that?'

'Fine,' I sighed wearily. I was bone-tired, aching all over, and
could feel the tendrils of last night's sedatives still clinging to my
brain. I felt uneasy, jumpy, like a fish out of water. 'Fine,' I
repeated.

'How're you feeling?' Yuill asked.

My expression said it all.

'Aye, well,' he said. 'At least you got what you wanted.'

'You mean half-drowned?'

'In on the murder.'

'Yeah, well, you know me. How I love tripping over bodies
and wading through blood. Who's been talking?'

'Sergeant Dowie. Apparently he was in touch with Commander Kettle this morning.' Yuill allowed himself the luxury of an
enigmatic smile. 'And reading between the lines, I'd say he got
an earful and is now a well-chastened dog. I imagine you'll be
seeing him later on.'

'That's all I bloody need.'

'You'll be surprised, I think. Kettle apparently told him that if he ever wanted to be a good detective, let alone a great one, then he would be advised to stick close to you. His words. Watch, listen and learn being the order of the day. Said, I understand, in a tone that brooked no argument.'

'Who told you that?'

Yuill tapped the side of his nose with his forefinger. 'I have my sources,' he said. Probably someone in the Division's control room, I thought.

'Stick, then.'

I was finding it hard to believe, all this bonhomie from Kettle. It was out of character. It disturbed me. Either the man was cracking up under the pressure of the investigation or he was playing me as a pawn again in one of his ambitious political games. Or, I reasoned, maybe he was just as desperate as I had been last night, clutching at straws, however insubstantial.

Yuill rose from the bed, joined me by the window. I knew it was coming any second now, could see it in his eyes, his mind working out how to say it without sending me through the roof. I recalled the gratitude I had felt at my reception last night and decided, what the hell, I'd go against my grain and make it easy for him.

'I didn't fall overboard last night,' I said. 'I was pushed.'

He stared at me blankly for a few moments, that special cop-to-cop kind of look, then slowly nodded his head. 'Yes,' he said, 'I know.'

'Who told you?'

'Give me credit, Frank, I'm a cop, I've dealt with lies all my life. And if there's one thing I've learnt, it's that cops make the worst liars in the world. Of course I bloody knew.'

'I just didn't want to talk about it then,' I explained lamely. 'Needed to think it through.'

'And now you've thought it through?'

'I reckon it was the Fangman.'

Yuill gave me another blank stare, then sighed and shook his head. 'I think you'd better explain,' he said.

I did. I took him through my reasoning, step by sketchy step. He listened patiently without interrupting, his moist black eyes never shifting from mine. When I finished he turned away and, hands in pockets and eyes on floor, paced slowly from window to wall and then back again. Ten paces.

'So,' he said, looking up from the floor, 'what do you want to do? Obviously you have a reason for not telling me about this last night' – his brief smile was not as convincing as its predecessors – 'perhaps for the same reason you never told me about the letter from the Fangman?'

'Is that the way to talk to an invalid?' I said, showing him he didn't have the monopoly on bullshit smiles.

He said, 'The way I see it, if it was the Fangman who tossed you over the side, then you don't want to let him know you're still alive. Is that it?'

'Part of it,' I told him. 'And certainly for the next couple of days. What I want to do is get hold of yesterday's manifest list from CalMac, see who was on board.'

'You won't get many of the foot passengers on the list. Only the ones who booked in advance.'

'Whatever,' I told him. 'I don't think it'll matter. If it was the Fangman, then he'd've been in his car. I'm sure of it. These guys almost live in their cars when they're out trawling.' I looked out the window at a groundsman tinkering with the engine of his lawn mower as I tried to pick my next words with care. 'Anyway, I know it's a long shot but ... hell, I've just got a feeling about this, I think this might've been his second big mistake, pushing me overboard. Up till now he's been really careful about everything he's done, planned every move and left us with barely a clue since he began this murderous campaign.'

'You think he did it on impulse.'

'On the evidence, wouldn't you?' The groundsman had got the mower going now, was letting it idle awhile. 'I mean, it's not the kind of situation you *can* plan carefully. Too many variables.

Too many potential witnesses. No. I think he just saw the opportunity and took it.'

'You said "second big mistake" – what was the first?'

'Killing Arthur Thomas. The second was trying to kill me. Both, I think, were impulsive, opportunist attacks and, unless he's got the luck of the devil, he'll have left a trace somewhere, something we can pick up on.'

'Let's hope you're right,' Yuill said, glancing at his watch. 'I saw your piece on TV. Nice style, if a little unorthodox. Did Kettle know what you were going to say?'

I shook my head. 'He didn't seem to care. I think he just likes to see me dig my own grave.'

'And if something good comes out of it, he takes all the credit.'

I laughed. 'You obviously know the man well.'

'Not him,' Yuill said, 'but many like him. Just watch your back, Frank, that's all.' The big man's expression turned reminiscent, as though he were now looking back on his own career and his own personal Nemesis. I let the silence stretch for a few moments while I tried to rally my sluggish, unruly thoughts into some kind of coherent form. Gave up eventually, and asked Yuill if he had any suggestions.

'About what?'

'The manifest. How I should handle it.'

'You're asking my advice?' The Sergeant seemed genuinely surprised. 'Well, first I'd wait until you've seen that detective sergeant chappie. Dowie. Maybe you'll find a use for him.'

'You mean keep him off your backs.'

'You scratch mine . . .' Yuill said.

'And you'll . . . ?'

'See if I can make some time to go through all the people on the manifest list. Or were you planning to do it all yourself?'

'No,' I told him. 'You're just way ahead of me this afternoon.'

'Morning,' Yuill corrected.

'See what I mean?' A phone started ringing somewhere along the corridor. Someone, probably the sister, answered it on the seventh ring. 'Anyway, you're right. I would appreciate some help checking out the manifest. How's your case-load at the moment?'

Yuill shrugged. 'Bearable. I've managed to get Bob and Jim back from Dowie, and they're now manning the station, handling all the day-to-day stuff while Monica and I concentrate on the Wallace rape. Division are getting impatient for a result.'

'Any progress?'

'Monica's tackling it from the Wallace end, I'm still working on Ryder. Progress? No, I wouldn't like to call it that.'

'You could always ask Ryder what he was doing last Wednesday night,' I suggested. 'The night of the full moon.'

'He was there? Up on Machrie Moor?'

'Unless he's got a twin.' I told Yuill about the ceremony I'd witnessed, the part Ryder had played in the sacrifice.

'A chicken?' Yuill said, incredulous. 'He slaughtered a chicken?'

'And then they all took turns to drink its blood.'

'Jesus, whatever next?' The Sergeant was still shaking his head. 'You think these cultists are responsible for the slaughter of those sheep of yours?'

'The first sheep I found down above Kildonan, no. That had been bludgeoned to death first and then stabbed. The second, I'm not too sure. Its throat had been cut, which is certainly more the style of a sacrifice, but it still doesn't explain how it ended up in the Distillery's water-tank.'

'What about the man in the mask, the Big High Chief or Priest or whatever they like to call themselves? Any idea who he might have been?'

'I don't know,' I said. 'There was something about him that

made me feel I'd seen or met him before. The way he walked or stood, I'm still not sure. Anyway, he didn't remove the mask the whole time he was there,' I added. 'Not even when the orgy began.'

'He participated in that?'

'I wouldn't call it "participated". He had a couple of his acolytes give him a blow-job, but that was about it.'

'Any other faces you recognised?'

'Apart from Ryder, there were three other people I felt I'd maybe seen before, but the rest were complete strangers.' I rubbed the back of my head gingerly, trying to relieve the itching of the seven stitches I'd received last night. Succeeded only in making it worse. 'You know what I think? I think maybe there's just a small core-group of them here on the island who organise the so-called "events", and the rest just come across from the mainland for the party. Like it's some special kind of Club 18–30 holiday for cultists, complete with a live sacrifice thrown in.'

Yuill's smile was distracted. 'What about the guy at the pottery? Byrne, isn't it? What's he got to say about all this?'

'His attitude seems to be live and let live,' I said. 'He reckons it's all pretty harmless, says people have been performing fertility rites out there on the Moor for hundreds if not thousands of years.'

'He has no cause for complaint then?'

'None that I'm aware of.'

'Pity,' Yuill said, but didn't elaborate further. 'Still. I'll maybe take your advice on that one, shake Ryder's tree a bit and see what falls to earth.' He glanced at his watch again, smiled. 'Anyway, some of us can't afford to lie in bed all day when there's work to be done. I better go and relieve Monica, she'll be wanting the car. Anything I can get you in the meantime?'

'Just out of here, that's all.'

'Consider it done.'

* * *

385

I considered it done almost four hours later when Monica came and sprung me from the hospital under the disapproving gaze of both doctor and ward sister.

'Sorry about the delay,' she said, holding the car door as I eased myself carefully into the passenger seat. 'I was just on my way out here when we got a shout from Bob, a TA up near Merkland Point. Guy came round the corner wrong side of the road, hit a tour bus and went over on to the rocks.'

'Fatal?'

'Fortunately only one,' she replied with a sigh. She closed my door, then went round the bonnet and climbed in. 'Driver of the car. Still in his teens, the bloody idiot. Him and three pals over from Saltcoats in his father's car. Could've been a lot worse.'

'I wondered what all the action was,' I told her. I'd heard the ambulances arrive about an hour ago, a lot of shouting and hurrying footsteps. Had been too damn tired even to consider satisfying my curiosity.

'The three passengers in the car walked away with hardly a bruise. We brought them in anyway, they were still pretty shocked, as were several passengers on the bus.' Monica hammered the steering wheel with the palm of her hand. 'Christ, Frank, when will they ever bloody learn?'

'Usually,' I told her, 'when it's far too late.'

She didn't answer, instead slammed the car angrily into gear, the wheels spinning on gravel as we accelerated up the road. I'd seen her like this before, had seen many cops react in a similar manner, disguising true emotions behind a thin mask of anger. Am perhaps guilty of it myself. It's a natural reaction, a defence mechanism against the horrors we often have to witness, and is always magnified when we come up against life wasted young. To divert the train of her thoughts, I asked her if Sergeant Yuill had brought her up to date.

'Why didn't you say so last night?' she said, her tone hurt. We turned right at the junction, began the long climb up the hill past the golf course.

'I didn't trust Yuill not to take it further.'

'And now you do?'

I thought about it for only a moment. 'Yes,' I said, 'I do. We seem to have arrived at some kind of understanding.'

'About bloody time. How long've you been here? Six months? Seven, eight? Christ, people meet and get married in less time than that.'

'Yeah, but I'm supposed to work with Yuill, not shag him.'

'Maybe that's why it took so long – you hurt his feelings.'

My laughter was infectious enough to bring a smile to her face.

I said, 'How you getting on with the Wallace case? Any progress?' Keep her thinking about something else, I thought, she'd have plenty of time tonight for the nightmares that always come.

'So-so,' she replied, shifting up a gear. 'In other words, so far, so little. A big fat bugger-all from the Social Work Department, nothing from the Wallaces themselves, and all of Julia's teachers I spoke with say she's a good pupil, though is quite shy and tends to keep herself to herself. Not many friends. They also all feel that she started coming out of herself a bit more when she was going out with Ryder last year. Apparently after they split up, Julia's marks suffered for a couple of months but then picked up again. In the last few weeks – understandably, I think – her marks have begun to dive. But nothing from the teachers on Julia's parents.'

'Her classmates?'

'Most said the same as the teachers – that she keeps herself to herself. Like I said, no close friends. Regarded by some as a bit of a tomboy. No girl friends as far as I could tell, they seem to think her shyness is snootiness. Boys? Apart from Ryder, none, though they do let her hang around with them sometimes. In all, a strange girl, lonely I don't doubt, but otherwise nothing in her life out of the ordinary.' Monica glanced in the rearview mirror. 'Jee-sus!' she said. 'Take a look at this guy!'

As she spoke, a flame-red Ferrari flashed by, overtaking on the long bend all five cars in front of us, cutting in only seconds before a tractor lumbered round the corner. On a parallel plane of existence, perhaps, you might have heard the *click click* of two pairs of eyes instantly clocking and recording the Ferrari's registration as it shot on by. Monica offered me a glance with eyebrows raised. I shook my head.

'Not now, Mo, please,' I said. 'All I want is home and a warm bed. You can call the reg in from the cottage, get Bob or Jim to handle it.'

'Guy was doing at least a ton.' We dropped down into Brodick, turned right at the foot of the hill and parked outside the Tourist Information Office. 'Won't be a sec,' Monica said, and jumped from the car. I didn't need to ask where she was going. She returned a minute later, shaking her head. 'Well, he wasn't rushing to catch the ferry, that's for sure.'

We completed the rest of the journey along Brodick's main street without incident, arriving at the Ormidale Hotel a few minutes later. There were a few cars parked outside, but Kyoko's, I noticed, was not among them.

'Place was a wee bit musty,' Monica explained as we walked around the back of the hotel to the cottage, 'so I opened a few of the windows. Otherwise, I was impressed.'

'Impressed?'

'How tidy it is. Like everything in its place. You know, the dishes washed and dried, the empty whisky bottles in the bin, that kind of thing.'

'Ha ha.'

I pushed inside – I don't lock the door because I have nothing worth stealing – with a sense of welcome relief. A long, arduous journey finally completed. I felt as though I'd been away for weeks, rather than days. I slumped down at the kitchen table. While Monica phoned the station in Lamlash and reported the speeding Ferrari, I sifted through my mail. Two were bills, phone and electricity; one was from a bank manager concerned about my overdraft; one was junk and went straight in the bin; the last was a postcard of Edinburgh Castle. On the back she had written *Wish you were here* but hadn't signed her name. Likewise, Kyoko, I thought, likewise. I levered myself off the chair and filled the kettle.

Monica came off the phone and sat at the table. She was dressed in her scruffy don't-give-a-shit look this afternoon, baggy sweatshirt over baggy jeans, worn canvas shoes. She leant back in the chair, stretched out her long legs. 'Make it black, make it sweet, make it strong,' she said. 'And for God's sake make it quick. I'm just about dead on my feet here.'

I dropped three heaped spoonfuls of continental roast in the cafetière, added the boiling water, left it to steep. 'You back on tonight?'

'Aye,' she sighed. 'Will this summer never bloody end?'

'Think of all the overtime and the money you're saving.'

'But will I live to spend it, that's the question.' Her ice-blue eyes, I noticed, had lost their usual lustre and moved almost listlessly in their sockets. Suddenly, she put a hand to her mouth. 'Oh, I almost forgot,' she said, and dived through to the bedroom. Returned a second later with my leather flying jacket.

'Ya beauty!' I cried, meaning both her and the jacket.

'Found it on the ferry, stuffed in one of the luggage lockers. Soon as I saw it, I knew something was wrong. You wouldn't've left it behind voluntarily.'

'Nothing else?' I asked. 'You didn't find anything else?'

'Like what?'

I shook my head. 'Nothing. I just wondered.'

She gave me the look that let me know she knew I was lying but wasn't going to push it any further. I was glad. I could already see the shit I was going to land in the moment the folder of reports was found and handed in to either police or press. My only reprieve – albeit a temporary one – was if the Fangman had picked them up. And if that was the case, I was already guilty of jeopardising the whole investigation – one more reason for not

389

broadcasting the failed attempt on my life. I was beginning to see my future in terms of abject obscurity. It was time to change the subject.

I depressed the plunger on the cafetière and said, 'What about Julia's father? Have you interviewed him yet?' The mere smell of the coffee was enough to set my heart pumping.

'I've tried,' Monica sighed. 'But he's not being very cooperative. Seems to be treating the whole thing as some kind of childish prank his daughter has dreamed up, a cry for attention. I don't think he cares for her much, says she's just like her mother, that this was just the kind of stupid thing his wife would do. A definite misogynist. When I reminded him of the injuries Julia had sustained, he just sort of waved it away as though it was nothing, and I a prejudiced participant in what is obviously a female conspiracy to undermine male superiority. I tell you, Frank, I felt like reaching across and slapping his face to the floor. He does that to you.'

'You think he's capable of doing something like that to his own daughter?'

'I've certainly considered it – nothing I'd like better than to slam his arse away for a stretch. But, bottom line, I just can't see it. He doesn't seem to care, and doesn't mind if you know it.'

I poured the coffee into cups, added sugar and stirred. 'What about the possible bruises on his wife's arms?'

'I think he's definitely capable of that,' Monica said, 'slapping his wife around. I have no problem imagining that at all.'

'And is she scared enough of him not to report him?'

'Absolutely, I'd say. Which is why I'm going to run him through CRO, see if he's got any previous record of violence.' Monica grabbed her coffee and, holding the cup with both hands, blew on it awhile.

'Works for the forestry, doesn't he?'

'Aye.'

'And tells his son, Bobby, not to talk to the police. That we're *nasty people*.'

'Oh he does, does he?' Monica seemed to consider this new piece of information. 'And there's another interesting fact, one I keep coming back to. The only person whom we know for a fact was in the area when Julia was raped was her father.'

'Like you say, interesting,' I said, 'but ultimately inconclusive.' I tasted my coffee: it was perfect, just the right temperature. I drank it down in four hefty gulps. 'Until, of course,' I added, 'the other people in the area come forward and you eliminate them from the enquiry.'

'Tell me about it,' Monica said dejectedly. 'All those posters we've put out and not a single response. I can't believe they were all tourists.'

'Head up, Mo,' I told her. 'Something'll break soon. Yuill's going to have another shot at Ryder tomorrow, who knows what he might turn up.'

'Aye, maybe you're right.' She drained her cup and pushed herself to her feet. 'I better go,' she said. 'Get some shuteye in before the next shift. Anything you need?'

'Just the same,' I said. 'Sleep and more sleep.'

'See you later, then.' She leant down and kissed my cheek. I stared at her. She laughed and, turning at the door, said: 'Don't get any funny ideas, Frank McMorran, I'm just glad to see you safe.'

I was too tired even for ideas.

The sound of someone hammering at the door dragged me choking from a tumultuous sea of mountainous waves back to the painful shores of reality. My body ached all over, my head throbbed under a ceaseless barrage, and my knee buckled and almost gave way as I stumbled towards the door. I was also getting a strong sense of *déjà vu*.

I opened the door on Detective Sergeant Dowie. He stood there awkwardly, unsure at first what to do with his hands, or which expression to wear. Settled eventually for professional formality.

'Constable,' he said. 'Sergeant Yuill said I'd find you here.'

'And here I am.' I wasn't going to make it easy for him, no way. Penance had to be paid. 'So what do you want?'

'May I come in?' He was wearing the same suit he'd worn on Saturday morning but had changed his shoes and, I noticed, there were fresh bags under his eyes. Mine, however, were heavier.

'I'm tired, Dowie.'

'This won't take a moment.'

'What won't?'

Dowie shuffled his feet. 'I'd like to . . .' He trailed off, looked at the ground, then cleared his throat and tried again. 'I'd like to apologise for my behaviour the other day.'

I said nothing, merely regarded him expectantly.

'I got carried away,' he explained.

'I was the one who got carried away,' I told him harshly. 'In fucking handcuffs.'

Dowie shrugged, spreading his arms in a what-more-can-I-say gesture. 'Like I said, I apologise.'

'And like *I* said, I'm tired.'

The detective's tone lost its former contriteness. 'Look, McMorran, it's clear we don't like each other, but there's not much we can do about that. On the other hand we do have a job to do. Right?'

Yah, I thought, we do.

'So I don't see why we can't put our animosity aside for the time being and work together. Concentrate on the more important issue, solving the murder of Arthur Thomas.' Now it was Dowie's turn to look at me expectantly.

Kettle had been right. The guy's accent did get right up my nose. Perhaps, though, the ever-present hint of condescension I detected in his tone was merely a product of my own paranoia. I decided not to let it get to me. Too much.

I sighed and stepped aside. 'Ten minutes,' I said. 'Then you're on your bike.'

We sat at the kitchen table. He glanced at the two empty cups I hadn't cleared away, but said nothing. I didn't offer.

He cleared his throat and leaned forward. 'Commander Kettle has instructed that we work together, and I would be lying if I said I didn't object in the strongest of terms. The Commander, though, was adamant. And here I am.'

'Get to the point.'

Dowie flinched, but recovered his composure fast enough to flick me the briefest of diluted smiles. 'The point is that I'm professional, McMorran, and I take my job seriously. Kettle says I can learn from you – okay, I want to learn.'

'And exactly what do you want to learn?'

Dowie slouched back in his chair, slipped his hands into his pockets. 'For a start,' he said, offering me another insincere smile, 'how come you got that bash on the head? And how come you were fished out of the Clyde by lifeboat last night?'

'Didn't Sergeant Yuill tell you?'

'He said you would take care of that.'

'Nice of him.' I stared out the window at the tiny square of overgrown lawn cut only by the few weak rays of evening sun that had managed to penetrate the screen of cypress and cedar surrounding the hotel. I had two choices: I could show Dowie the door and go it alone, or I could do as I'd been told and cooperate with him. Going alone was out of the question: in my present condition I wasn't going anywhere. I would have to follow orders. Now, I supposed, was as good a time as any to start.

For the third time that day, I recounted the events of last night and the reasoning that led me to believe it was the Fangman who'd attempted to take my life. I'd expected Dowie to ridicule my shaky line of reasoning, but no, he listened intently, every now and then nodding his head. When I finished, he sat there awhile, absently playing with the teaspoon in the sugar bowl, his expression pensive, intense. I waited. His question, when it came, took me by surprise.

'You think the Fangman killed the two sheep?'

I nodded.

'And Arthur Thomas?'

I nodded again.

'And that he lives on the island?'

'Almost certainly.'

Dowie lapsed into another minute's silence. I hoped it wasn't for my theory. Apparently not.

'It's a long shot,' he murmured as though to himself. 'But worth a try.'

'Enlighten me.'

'The ferry's manifest. If it *was* the Fangman who pushed you overboard, then he might be on the manifest.'

'My thoughts entirely.'

'I could check with Caledonian MacBrayne.' He snatched back his cuff and glanced at his watch. 'The office will have closed by now. First thing in the morning then.'

'My thoughts entirely.'

'Then we get all the manifests for the dates on which the murders were committed.'

Perhaps Kettle was right about Dowie, I thought, maybe he did have potential. He was certainly no slouch on the uptake.

'And then?' I asked.

'Run it all through HOLMES, and see if we come up with a name.'

'Mm,' I said doubtfully.

'No?'

'Let's just keep this to ourselves,' I suggested mildly. 'For the time being, anyway. In case we're wrong.'

The Detective Sergeant frowned. 'You think we might be?'

'No, not for a second. Covering arse is all. I have a good feeling about this. I think the Fangman's made his last big mistake.'

Dowie nodded thoughtfully and rose to his feet. 'I hope you're right,' he said. There was no threat in his tone, only ambition. 'In the meantime, we'll just keep this between ourselves, right?'

'Now you're learning.'

I awoke in a darkened room, my scalp bristling. Something out of place in the room – a sound perhaps – had seeped into my unconscious mind and brought me back from sleep. I closed my eyes again and lay there waiting for the sound to repeat itself. A minute later it did. A small scuffing sound. Behind me.

There was someone else in the bedroom.

Sitting or standing perfectly still. I could now hear his shallow, regular breathing. Coming from on or near the chair by the wardrobe. I regulated my own breathing and, gradually opening my eyes again, let them become accustomed to the dark. I was facing the window. The curtains were drawn. I couldn't remember closing them. After Dowie had left I'd returned to bed, not with the intention of sleeping, merely to rest my bones. How long ago, I wondered, two, three hours? I could hear sounds from the hotel bar: someone sorting bottles, sudden laughter, the murmur of conversation. It wasn't that late then. Back of ten maybe. If the person meant me harm, I thought, why wait? How long had he been standing there? Had his arrival woken me? My breathing may have been relaxed but my body was tense, adrenaline pumping through muscles screaming for fight or flight. If the Fangman lived on the island – not a very big if as I lay there, hackles raised, waiting for the blow to come – he might know where I lived, might have heard that I had survived and had now come to finish the job. He had watched Arthur Thomas for hours, maybe days, from the trees above Ravensbank. Had he also crept into the man's house while he was asleep, stood over his bed, relishing his power over life and death?

Another sound. This time it was the low growling rumble of his stomach that almost startled me into action. I couldn't lie here like this much longer; patience has never been one of my

395

virtues and waiting around to die is just not part of my nature. Anyway, I reasoned, I had the advantage of surprise. His advantages were something I didn't even want to think about. Hesitation kills. So grasping the covers in my fists, I made a few of the snuffling sounds I've been told I make when I sleep, and slowly turned over and then hurled myself from the bed.

As motions go, it wasn't my most fluid. But I had the element of surprise and momentum, my body shielded by the covers as I threw myself at the vague form in the chair. There was a sudden reaction, a small scream, the chair toppled to the floor and then I had him entangled in the covers. I was pulling back my arm to rain in punches when the man screamed again.

'Francis!'

Not a man, but a woman.

'Francis!'

Not just any woman, but Kyoko.

I helped her up off the floor, sat her on the bed, turned on the light. She was shaking violently, her eyes wide, hair dishevelled. I wasn't that calm myself and, shaking though I was, it was from sheer relief. I sat down next to her, wrapped an arm round her shoulders.

'You scared me to death!' she said, still breathing hard.

'Bad dream,' I told her. 'I thought you were . . . someone else.' She had both arms round me, holding me tight, the scent of her hair in my nostrils. I could have stayed there like that all night. 'What were you doing anyway, sitting there in the darkness? Why didn't you wake me up?'

'You were supposed to phone me, remember? I thought you'd forgotten or were still working, so I called the police station and your partner, the one with the long legs, she told me you were here.'

'So you broke into my house and crept up on me while I was sleeping . . .'

Kyoko punched me playfully in the chest. 'I did not! I was worried. The policewoman said you'd had an accident, that you were recuperating. She said perhaps I should check and see if you were all right, if you needed anything. She didn't tell me you'd gone insane.'

She was looking up at me, her lips only inches from mine. I kissed her. She didn't respond but she didn't pull away. 'Totally insane,' I said. 'Demented with passion.' I kissed her again. This time she responded, but only briefly, then she pulled away.

'No, seriously,' she said, standing up to smooth herself down. She was wearing her Eagles starter jacket over a white silk blouse, denim skirt over green tartan tights.

'I am serious,' I replied, 'about wanting you.'

She lowered her lashes and looked away. 'You must have been hit on the head.'

'I was.'

'Let me see.' She took my head in her hands, found the shaved patch and track of stitches. 'My God!' she exclaimed, touching the bump tentatively with a finger. 'Does it hurt?'

'Terribly,' I told her.

'Good. That will teach you not to go around frightening people all the time.' She sat down on the bed again. 'What happened?'

'Someone hit me on the head with a bottle and pushed me off the ferry.'

'You poor man . . .'

'I know. Kiss me again.'

'Who was it?' Concern was etched in the lines of her face. 'Did you get him?'

I shook my head. 'Some kind of nut probably. He'll be long gone by now.' No point in telling her about my suspicions, and scaring her as much as I'd already scared myself. I was happy to change the subject. 'Never mind me, what about you? How was your weekend?'

'Obviously not as eventful as yours.' Kyoko shrugged, chewing her lower lip with one of her gorgeous eyeteeth. 'Boring mostly. The men, all they wanted to do was talk business.

Which was all right, I suppose. My uncle's cousin, Junko, took me shopping along Princes Street, and then we went round the city on one of those tour buses. That was fun. It's a beautiful city.'

'The parts they show you.'

'Then this morning we all visited the Castle. The view was fantastic. We could see all the way over to . . .'

'Fife?'

'Yes, Fife. Then we had lunch in a restaurant on the High Street, and after that we said goodbye. And here I am.'

'I'd noticed. Perhaps you ought to sit a little closer so you can catch me if I faint.'

Kyoko edged away, laughing. 'Perhaps I should go to my own bed,' she said. 'It's been a long day and tomorrow I must accompany my uncle again to the Distillery. I'm sure you will survive.'

'Or you could stay . . .'

Kyoko acted as though she hadn't heard. 'Will I see you tomorrow?'

'The moment you open your eyes.'

'I'm sorry, Francis,' she said, getting up and kissing me softly on the brow. 'But you'd be no good to me, the state you're in right now. Believe me.'

I did, but I didn't want to.

'Please,' I called after her. 'Stay the night.'

'Goodnight, Francis. Sleep well.'

I heard the front door gently close.

32

'Shock goes hither and thither. Danger. However, nothing at all is lost.
Yet there are things to be done.'

Things to be done.

Yes. Many things. It's *busy busy busy* as a blue-arsed fly. All the threads in the tapestry of your life that have to be drawn together and woven into the overall pattern. Not much time now, events picking up speed and overtaking you. Hard to keep a thought in your head without thinking of that cop, McMorran. You took a chance on the ferry the other night, didn't give yourself the time to think it through. Now what? The cop is still alive and you've got this feeling inside that maybe he caught a glimpse of you as he tumbled over the rail, or maybe spotted you in the bar beforehand and has already put two and two together. Whatever. The bastard's still alive and the whole fucking force might be standing on your doorstep in a matter of minutes. So it's *busy busy busy* as a blue-arsed fly. You wonder if this was how your mother felt the day she killed your father and left him sitting in his armchair in front of the telly, throat gaping and blood spurting, while she continued with all her chores? Maybe. Maybe it ran in the family.

So many things to do.

The Kimono woman, for instance. Wanted a pot with one of your special glazes but did she have any kind of idea the processes you have to go through? No, she did not. People like her don't have a clue what sacrifices have to be made on the road to perfection. They see a pot they like and think only about its colour, shape and form, and what a conversation piece it will make. Do they care about the delicate elemental balances of earth, fire, air and water intrinsic to its making? Do they hell. Do they understand the empiric nature of your craft, the years of trial and error coupled with the broad scientific knowledge necessary to calculate and predict the results of a certain glaze? Not a chance. They think making pots is just a hobby for the bored middle classes, a simple matter of tossing a lump of prepared clay on to a wheel and throwing it. Anyone can do it.

Sure, like anyone can murder. Yet how many people have the courage to take that irreversible step?

Your mother for one.

Maybe it did run in the family. There she was scurrying about the house cleaning this, dusting that, hoovering all the places she'd never hoovered before, and all the while your father's sitting in his blood-drenched chair, dead as dead can be, vacant eyes staring at the flickering screen. She must have been totally gone by then, no knowing what was going on in her mind. Way past midnight and she'd switched on every electrical appliance in the house, radio, TV, hi-fi, all turned to maximum volume, washing machine going, food-mixer whirring in an empty bowl, kettle whistling, all the rings on the cooker burning red, lights ablaze... What had been going through her mind? Why the sudden obsession with so much minutiae when all around her her world was hastily falling apart? Why the sudden mania for housework she'd never done before when any second now the police would be knocking on the door? It didn't make sense. Then or now. Where was her sense of purpose, of a mission to be accomplished?

But that's where you're different, see. You're *busy busy busy*, sure, but you've got purpose. Things to be done. Things that won't wait.

Like the mask.

It gets cold in the chamber when the kiln's not firing. No matter that the sun's shining up in the other world, it never penetrates down here. What use anyway, outer, physical warmth? The warmth that matters is the one inside, that fireside of memories, furnace of dreams, kiln of desires. That is the warmth that will sustain you day and night through all of the seasons. A fire you can always build on, and one that never dies.

Kimono, another pot in your kiln.

Why had you agreed to make her one of your specials? As if you didn't already have enough to do. Another impulse. Like in the last few weeks it seems to be becoming a habit, jumping at situations before you've even thought them through. As though you've forgotten all the teachings in the *I Ching*, all that stuff about *exceptional enterprises needing the utmost caution observed in their beginnings and in the laying of their foundations*. Your mind in two minds, pulling you one way and then the other. Like you're caught in the middle, being stretched to your limits ... and beyond.

Still, at least the calcination of the strangle's bones is now complete. Washed and dried, the ash is now ready to be added to the other ingredients of the glaze.

For your less unique glazes in which you use bone-ash – your semi-matt whites and browns – you just buy the stuff in. Mostly it's the calcinated bones of horses, sheep, donkeys or cows. Obviously, though, for your special glaze – which, if anyone asks, and for obvious reasons, you call *Simone's Bone-Ash No. 1* – you have to process all the bones yourself. Which is a laborious and often time-consuming task, first removing the fat with benzine, then the gelatine with steam, under pressure in your pressure cooker. Then you have to calcinate the bones slowly in the kiln to remove any other organic matter, after which you hand-pick the bone, grind it wet in an open pan before washing out any residue soluble alkalis. Then it must be dried.

Do you think Kimono appreciates all the work involved in

making just one ingredient for the Simone glaze recipe? Do you hell. Perhaps, you think, you ought to tell her. That would be fun. Bring her down here when her pot is ready and show her what happens to all your strangles' brittle bones. Maybe take her through the Sutherland strangle, step by gory step. Tell about the old woman turning her back on you and how you couldn't hold yourself back any longer, just had to chew up her neck or explode. Then show her your holy shrine and your collection of skulls and see if she orders any more of your pots. Fun, yes, definitely.

Your mother, you recall, had made no attempt to get away, the kitchen knife she'd used to cut your father's throat as he sat watching *Grandstand* that Saturday afternoon still lay on the floor where she'd dropped it. You noticed how she made a point of hoovering around it later on, after he'd been sitting there six or seven hours. Once in a while she'd come into the room and stand there arms akimbo in the middle of the floor, looking around as though checking there was nothing she had overlooked. Once, earlier in the evening, she had stood over her husband, looking down at his corpse for a full five minutes before she took another step forward and slapped his head across his shoulders. 'There,' she had said, before turning and leaving the room. As though making a point.

You, though, she had overlooked completely. It was as though you weren't even there. Perhaps you were already dead in her eyes, you don't know. You'd been sitting on the floor by the fire, looking at the telly but not seeing the telly, when she came in with the knife and walked up behind your father. You had watched her with a kind of detached curiosity as she had grabbed your father's hair and yanked back his head, drawing the carving knife across his taut throat in one long, fluid motion that had opened up the floodgates of blood, sent it spurting across his chest and legs, carpet, chair and you. You remember the sounds he had made, the rasping hiss of his final breath, followed by the gurgling of blood in his lungs. It was somehow hypnotic, like the gentle murmur of Machrie Water, down by the Goat's Leap Pool.

Of course he had thrashed about a bit. Had grabbed his throat with both his hands trying to stem the flow of blood but it had spurted out like geysers between his fingers. You were in the way of one. You remember the blood running warm down your face. How you had raised your head and let it run down into your mouth. How strange it had tasted, yet how silky the texture. How you had glanced towards your mother and seen her standing there with an expression on her face you can only describe now as triumphant rapture.

As though for the first time in your life you had done something right.

You'd felt nothing for the loss of your father, though. He had betrayed you long ago, left you in the hands of this woman, escaping his responsibilities by running away to sea. A coward supreme. You hardly knew the man, yet you could see in his eyes, with the kind of clarity only children can see, that he *knew*, he just knew what was going on behind his back, about the men in his wife's life, about the abuse you were forced to suffer . . . How could he not know? Perhaps he too had been forced to participate, had been so humiliated that retaliation was out of the question. Caught in her web of obsession the same way you had been caught. Maybe. But he was a man, while you were just a boy. And he left you behind, abandoned you, and finally paid the price.

Someone must always pay.

Hastie, Hastie, Hastie. What to do, what to do? Giving you the big round eyes these last few days, touching you now when she talks, getting in close enough you can smell her middle-age scent and all those fucking dogs. Like a bitch in heat. The other night you imagined her – after wondering what she sees in all those dogs – sort of lying there naked, maybe rubbing her tits and

403

pubes with whatever it is dogs like to lick. Then lying there, legs spread, cooing the way she does, *Come on, Jess, come and get your din-dins* ... Later – getting into the fantasy here – she gets down on all fours, wiggles her fat arse at them, says, *Come to Mummy, Brutus, give Mummy a bone* ... Like all the lovers she'd ever need, up there on the hill, she can take her fucking pick. Why else keep all those dogs?

Anyway. Still. The mask is coming on. Almost there now – just the gauze for the eyes to do, and the zipper for the mouth. Do a little work on it tonight after the news, another session tomorrow night, and then, who knows, maybe give Hastie a preview, a dress rehearsal before the big opening night, the special performance for the visiting dignitary, the Jap bitch. Kimono.

Scheduled for not soon enough.

33

'Look at the postmark,' Detective Sergeant Dowie said, flipping over the envelope with the tip of his pen. Repeat of last night, we were back at my kitchen table, though this afternoon Dowie was in shirtsleeves, the back door was open and we each had a bottle of beer close at hand.

'I know,' I muttered. 'It's local.' Everyone else out doing something productive, me housebound and feeling oh so sorry for myself.

Still, not everyone was out enjoying the sunshine. In the Brodick office Dowie had inherited from DI Fullerton, two of his DCs were anchored to their phones, wading their way through the CalMac ferry's Sunday manifest, while another of his officers was down at the estate agent's office, waiting for a faxed copy of all the other manifests to come through.

'Which would suggest you're right about him living on the island.'

I shrugged but didn't reply. It all seemed too simple. After taking so much care in the planning and execution of his murders on the mainland, why would the Fangman now be making such obvious mistakes and drawing attention to the Isle of Arran? It was a disturbing thought. Suppose everything since the murder of Arthur Thomas had been designed by the Fangman to divert the focus of the manhunt away from the mainland to Arran? Suppose the slaughter of the sheep, dumping it in the Distillery's water-tank, the murder of Arthur

Thomas, the subsequent communications with me – suppose they were nothing but individual parts of a huge red herring intended only to waste the inquiry's time?

Nothing seemed simple this afternoon.

It would be another glorious day, the weatherman had said on the early-morning news, the temperatures perhaps exceeding yesterday's optimistic predictions. Breweries all over the country were recording a massive increase in sales. We hadn't had a summer like it in almost twenty years, he'd said, and I'd spent the rest of the morning trying to remember exactly what I'd been doing and where twenty years ago.

Dowie tossed his pen on the table and said, 'Population of the island is what, three, four thousand? How many men between the ages of sixteen and sixty? No more than a thousand, anyway. What we do is set up a clinic and take blood samples, compare the results with the Fangman's DNA. We'd have the bastard in a matter of—'

'Months,' I said. 'By which time he'll have definitely killed again.'

Perhaps Kettle and Fullerton were right, I thought, in playing down the significance of the Arran angle. Or they knew something I didn't know. In which case I was again being played like a dispensable pawn in a game whose overall strategy was beyond my ken. Would that explain Kettle's uncharacteristic bonhomie, the unnatural ease with which he had let me become part of the island inquiry? Was I being used by Kettle to lull the Fangman into a false sense of security while Operation Dentist closed in from another direction? The more I thought about it, the more probable it seemed. It was certainly more Kettle's style.

Dowie, unperturbed by my curt response, asked if I knew what the letters DNA stood for. I told him sure, deoxyribonucleic acid. He shook his head.

'Wrong,' he said. 'The National Association of Dyslexics.'

I gave him a smile for trying.

The envelope had arrived at the Lamlash station first post this morning. It had been addressed with the same typewritten print as used in the previous communication. The card inside also appeared to be the same as the one I'd found embedded in faeces up at Ravensbank. The wording, though, was not the same.

IF ONE IS NOT EXTREMELY CAREFUL,
SOMEBODY MAY COME UP FROM BEHIND AND
STRIKE HIM. MISFORTUNE.

Misfortune indeed, I thought. I felt worse today than I had done most of yesterday. I had slept fitfully and awoken early, had dragged myself from clinging sheets to make a breakfast that I immediately brought up again. I had returned to bed and just fallen asleep when the phone rang, Sergeant Yuill in another buoyant mood saying I'd got another letter from the Fangman. It was back to reality.

'Posted yesterday,' Dowie said. 'Which also suggests he lives on the island.'

'How d'you work that out?'

'How else could he find out so quickly that you were still alive?'

'Maybe he didn't know,' I said. 'Just sent it anyway, knowing it would be opened by someone at the station.'

'You really believe that?'

Again I didn't answer. I didn't know what to believe this afternoon. I felt disorientated, out of touch, as though I were having an out-of-body experience. I wished it was the real thing. Perhaps another beer would help, I thought, and was about to get up when there was a knock at the front door.

'Round the back,' Dowie called, and a moment later one of his officers appeared hesitantly at the door, manila folder in hand. 'You get it all?' the DS asked.

'All in here,' the DC replied, tapping the folder with a fingertip. 'All the dates you specified.'

'Good man.' Dowie took the folder, glanced inside, then

tossed it on the table between us. 'Okay, Davies, better go back to the station and give Bryce and Thompson a hand with the manifest. Take the number of the phone here and let me know the moment you've finished.'

Davies was halfway through the door when I called him back.

'Any luck?' I asked.

He shook his head. 'No, sir. Not much call for that kind of thing over here, the woman said. I'm not quite sure what she meant by that but she said she could order a copy for you, if you give her all the details.'

I thanked him and he left.

'Little shit called you "sir",' Dowie remarked. 'Never calls me that.'

'He obviously recognises a superior intellect when he sees one.'

'Intellect, hell.'

While Dowie subsided into a broody silence, I went and got another beer from the fridge. Later, I decided, once the DS had gone, I would take a beer and go sit at one of the tables on the hotel lawn. Soak in some sun and wait for Kyoko to return.

Dowie emerged from his sulk with a question. 'So what *is* this *I Ching* book the Fangman's sending you quotes from?'

I tried to recall what the psychic Mungo Spinks had told me about the *I Ching*, sitting in the beer garden after we'd come down from the locus. He'd also referred to it as the Book of Changes.

'It's an ancient form of Chinese oracle – even older than Confucius – and, I understand, is still used by many people to this day. Maybe oracle is the wrong word . . . I think it's more like a book of wisdom you can consult for advice.'

'You mean like some kind of cosmic agony aunt?'

The way Spinks had described it was more like a wise old friend one turns to at times when advice from a superior source is needed.

'Aye,' I smiled. 'Something like that.'

'So how does it work?'

'You throw coins,' I said, struggling to recall the layman's terms the psychic had used. 'Three coins, six times. In the old days they used yarrow stalks but apparently these days coins will do. What you do is ask the book a clear and concise question as you throw the coins and, I hope I got this right, depending on how the coins land – heads or tails – and the various permutations thereof – two heads and a tail, for example, or three tails – you end up with two trigrams, each trigram being made up of three lines, one line for every time you throw the coins. These two trigrams then make up one of sixty-four different hexagrams. You then look up that particular hexagram in the book and Bob, as they say, is your uncle, you have your answer.'

Dowie was looking at me askance, his lip curled. 'And what, all you need to consult it is a degree in nuclear physics?'

'A certain amount of wisdom helps, I believe.'

'So now we've got a wise murderer on our hands. Great.'

I said, 'As I understand it, the fundamental concept of the book is the idea of change and the transitory nature of life in the physical world.'

'You're not serious, are you? Where the hell do you get all this stuff?'

'I listen.'

'Listen to this then,' Dowie said, leaning forward eagerly. 'The Fangman's sitting in his house bored out of his skull, doesn't know what the hell to do next. So he takes out the book, asks it what he ought to do next, and throws the coins. The book says go stab a sheep, next thing you know, you're digging a dead sheep out of a water-tank. Or the book says go hit someone on the head, and next thing you know, someone comes up and hits you on the head. The only misfortune is that you survived.' Dowie stretched his thin lips into the resemblance of a grin and added, 'From his point of view, of course.'

'There were two sheep,' I reminded him. 'How d'you explain that?'

Dowie thought for a moment before shaking his head. 'Maybe he got the same advice twice,' he said with little conviction.

'Or,' I said, the idea forming as I spoke, 'he got it wrong first time, so had to do it again.'

Dowie scowled. 'I don't get it.'

'Look. The first sheep I found down by Kildonan had been bashed over the head and then stabbed. I've been wondering about that. Why kill the sheep with a blow to the head and then stab it fifteen, twenty times? Answer – so *no blood flows*. Like it says in the quote he sent me.'

'What about the other sheep? The one found in the Distillery's water-tank?'

'That's it, you see. Although it was discovered after the first one, it was in a greater state of decomposition. Not only that, but its throat had been cut and its fleece still showed evidence of matted blood.'

'So he killed that one first and when he saw all the blood . . .' Dowie broke off, frowning.

I took it on from there, the idea gelling as I chose my words with care. 'If he really believes in the *I Ching*, you know, if it's become such an integral part of his life, his philosophy, that to admit its fallibility would constitute a disintegration of all that is holding him together, then maybe what he's done here is manipulate the means to justify the end.'

'You mean like forcing facts to fit a theory, rather than conceiving a theory to fit the facts?'

'Exactly. A case of conscious self-delusion.'

'It makes sense,' Dowie acceded. 'But how does that help us?'

'I don't know,' I said. 'Not yet. First we need to get hold of a copy of the book. But where?'

'The library?' Dowie suggested.

I shook my head, then wished I hadn't as a dagger of pain cut through my wound. 'It's a mobile. Comes round a couple times a week. Too small.'

'The psychic then?'

'No, but . . .'

I fetched the phone over to the table, hunted through the island's thin directory, found the number I wanted and dialled. Listened to the tone ring and ring. Maybe she was serving a customer, I thought, or working in one of the other pottery buildings. Or the potter was in the middle of making a pot, couldn't leave the wheel. I let it ring another three minutes then replaced the receiver. 'I'll try again later.'

The phone rang almost immediately. Dowie snatched it up, barked, 'Yes?' Listened for a few moments, then said, 'Great. I'll be right down.' He glanced at me. I shook my head and tapped the table. The DS nodded, said, 'Second thoughts, bring it up here. Soon as you can.' He replaced the receiver with exaggerated care. 'They've narrowed it down to twenty-seven,' he told me.

'And of those, how many are hatchbacks?'

'Nine.'

'And estates?'

'Seven.'

We were still in with a chance. I said, 'How do you want to handle it?'

'I'll do it myself.' He made a rueful face. 'Tonight.'

'What about your team? DCs Bryce, Davies and Thompson? You tell them the score?'

'Only what they needed to know to complete their phone enquiries. That we were looking for the man who pushed you overboard, and that it was all in the strictest of confidence, not to be discussed with anyone outside the ops room.'

'Good.' I tapped the bulky folder Davies had collected from the estate agent. 'It can wait until tomorrow, you know.'

Dowie looked at me as though I'd just asked for his hand in marriage. 'No way. I'll do it myself. Tonight. Shouldn't take more than a few hours.'

I didn't want to disillusion him by telling him it would probably take at least twice that – unless, of course, he was lucky, and hit the jackpot with the first car he cross-referenced.

'That's settled then,' he said, climbing to his feet. His beer, I noticed, was still untouched. 'I'll call you if I get anything.'

'Do that,' I said.

Part of me hoped he wouldn't.

She answered on the tenth ring, out of breath.

'Sorry. I was cleaning out the kennels. How can I help you, Officer?'

I said, 'Remember that book you were telling me about, the *I Ching*? I was wondering if you had a copy.'

'Mm. Somewhere, I'm sure. Might take a while to look it out.'

'I'd be very grateful.'

'Run out of ideas, have you?' Her tone was gently teasing. 'Looking for that vital spark of inspiration?'

I laughed politely. 'Something like that.'

'I'll see what I can do. When do you need it?'

'I could pick it up tomorrow . . .'

'I'll be working out at the pottery for most of the day. If you don't mind coming out there . . .'

'No problem,' I assured her. 'I'll see you then.'

Back of eight. We were sitting at one of the Arran-shaped tables in the bar, feeling relaxed, digesting our dinner with Armagnac and coffee. The bar was quiet, a few regulars at the counter, a couple at the table by the window, a collie dozing by the unlit fire.

Kyoko's mood was effervescent, her eyes alive with humour and the glint of something else I couldn't yet put my finger on.

Compared to her, I felt about as lively as a maggot-ridden corpse.

'No,' she said in answer to my question. 'He's with Farquharson. Going over figures again. Fine-tuning, he called it. Then they're going for a meal at some posh hotel, after that, who knows?' There it was in her eyes again, the glint. 'He told me not to wait up.'

I stretched out my legs, relaxed some more. The day's nausea had passed, my headache had gone, and enough energy had returned to my limbs to get me from the cottage to the bar without the aid of stretcher-bearers.

'Masao-*san* was wondering if you'd managed to clear up the matter of the sheep.'

'He was, was he?' I glanced up as Alec Brodie, tweed coat and all, pushed into the bar, ordered up a pint, caught my eye, nodded, and looked away again. Still too sober to be sociable, I thought, and returned my attention to Kyoko. 'Is it important to him?' I asked.

'It's an imponderable,' she said with a knowing smile. 'He hates imponderables. Everything must go in its rightful place. When it doesn't, he can't sleep.'

I knew the feeling. 'Tell him it won't be long,' I said, if only to give the old man encouragement. As far as I was concerned, I'd already reached a dead-end at the Distillery. Try as I might, I just couldn't resolve the question of how – and especially why – the Fangman had deposited the sheep in the water-tank. Unless, of course, Farquharson was the Fangman. Or Archie McDonald or John French. In which case, why draw attention to himself? It didn't make sense.

'You mean you have a suspect?'

The only way it did make sense was to assume the two sheep had been stabbed to death by two different people. Which was far too great a coincidence even to consider. So how did the Fangman connect with the Glen Chalmadale Distillery?

'I'm what we call "pursuing a promising line of enquiry".'

413

Kyoko laughed. 'In other words chasing your tail, going nowhere.' She flicked a strand of hair away from her eye, then reached across and rested her hand on mine. 'Don't take it so seriously, Francis, I'm only joking.'

She could joke as much as she liked, I thought, so long as she didn't remove her hand.

'You're closer to the truth than you realise,' I said, and took a sip of Armagnac. Molten silk. As it slid down my throat I wondered if I should explain the connection between the sheep and the Fangman. Kyoko had obviously not seen my three minutes of fame on the TV – otherwise she would have mentioned it by now – so maybe it would be better not to muddy clear waters and perhaps jeopardise her uncle's delicate negotiations. There would be time enough if my hunch was right and Dowie came up with a result.

'Penny for your thoughts?'

'I was thinking how I seem to have run out of suspects.'

'Mm.' Kyoko retrieved her hand to roll a cigarette. 'You want to know what I think?' she said after lighting up. 'I think Maggie did it.'

'Maggie? The secretary? What makes you say that?'

She gave a little shrug. 'Just a feeling. Call it woman's intuition, if you like.'

'Intuition is impotent in court,' I said. 'It won't stand up.'

She giggled wickedly behind her hand. 'I hope *you* don't have that problem.'

'Not in court,' I told her, bathing in her laughter, feeling it wash away my doubts and fears, soften the temper of my mood.

'Thank God for that,' she said, the glint back in her eyes for a second. Then gone, as she added, 'But seriously . . .'

'Why Maggie? What possible motive could she have for doing a thing like that?'

Kyoko raised a delicate eyebrow. 'Fury of a woman scorned?'

'Scorned? By whom?'

'Farquharson?'

'You're kidding.'

'Have you ever noticed the way she looks at him?' Kyoko asked, propelling a stream of smoke towards the ceiling. 'No? Well, I have. She's totally in love with the man. Yet he ignores her. And when he's not ignoring her, he treats her like dirt. Then she hates him and hates herself. You can see it on her face: she loves him, she loves him not. she hates him, she hates him not. She doesn't know which way to turn.'

'So she goes out, kills a sheep and drops it in the water-tank. Happens all the time.'

'I knew you wouldn't believe me.'

'It's not that I don't believe you ...'

'No?' Kyoko stubbed out her cigarette in the ashtray. Stubbed then ground it. 'What then?'

'I just find it a strange reaction for a jilted lover.'

'Oh, you have a lot of experience of jilted lovers, do you?'

It was my turn to place my hand on hers. 'Please, Kyoko, let's not spoil such a pleasant evening.'

'Then give me a chance.'

I raised her hand to my lips, kissed her fingers. 'Take as many as you like.'

A shadow loomed, a voice intervened. 'Is that no' sweet?' Alec Brodie chortled. 'Like a pair o' teenage lovers.'

Kyoko snatched back her hand while I gave Brodie the evil eye. He stood there, still in his heavy tweed coat, clutching his pint glass close to his chest. He lifted his long chin and peered at Kyoko down his hawk-beak nose.

'Y'all right, hen?' he asked. 'Man's no' annoyin' you, is he?'

'*He* isn't, no.'

'Tha's guid. 'Cos if he was ...'

I said, 'Alec, do me a favour—'

'An' what wid that be, son?' Brodie said, turning his rheumy gaze on to me. 'Drag you oot the Clyde again?'

I gave him a conspiratorial come-with-me type flick of the head, then took his elbow and led him back to the bar, ordered him up a pint. He licked his lips as Freddie slid it across the bar to him.

'Seen you on the box the other night,' Brodie said, as I paid for the drink. 'Flash bastard.' There was no malice in his tone, only alcohol.

I said, 'That's what I wanted to ask you, Alec. Not to mention it to the lady. I don't want to scare her off with all that talk about the Fangman. She's the nervous type, doesn't like the sight of blood, know what I mean?' Hand on his shoulder, head in close, we could've been plotting Caesar's assassination in the forum.

Alec Brodie took a moment to let it sink in, then winked and tapped the side of his nose. 'You can rely on me, son. Not a word shall pass these lips, nary a one. You have my word.'

'Thanks, Alec.' I returned to the table where Kyoko sat smiling, twirling the stem of her glass between her fingers.

'Man's talk, I suppose?' she said as I joined her.

'Mm. He says I'm on to a sure thing.'

'Does he now?' A playful light dancing in her eyes, a touch of the Mona Lisa in her smile.

'Play my cards right, he said, and I might end up lucky.'

'Oh he did, did he?'

I continued to ride on the crest of her smile. 'He said what I have to do is be gently solicitous—'

'He used the word *solicitous*?'

'Before he became a poacher,' I said earnestly, 'he was a solicitor. Likes to use big words no one else understands. Tends to "intimate" a lot when he's had a pint too many.'

'And you?' she asked, lowering her lashes coquettishly. 'What do you like when you've had a pint too many.'

'Me? I prefer to *get* intimate. Get a little solicitation going, see where it leads.'

She was chewing her lower lip again, pointy wee eyetooth plucking at the flesh: that and the sultry look in her eyes kindling fires beneath my blood.

'And where do you think it might lead?'

'Somewhere a little more private perhaps.'

'You have somewhere in mind?' Kyoko getting right into it now, the enigmatic smile promising mysteries as old as sin itself.

'Now you come to mention it . . .'

'Could it be a little white cottage not all that far from where we're sitting?'

'We could get a couple of bottles of wine and sit and talk the night away. In candlelight. Just you and me and my family of mice.'

'Talk?' she said. 'Just talk?'

'I'm an old-fashioned man,' I told her with a modest smile. 'I don't like to rush things.'

Kyoko laughed from her belly up. 'You're a lying hound, Francis McMorran, I can see it in your eyes.'

I wondered if she could hear my blood as well, simmering as it was on the heat of desire. It was all I could do to stop myself from leaning across the table and smothering her lips with mine. And as I could no longer trust myself to speak without her hearing the tremor in my voice, I said nothing, merely watched as she collected together her tobacco, papers and lighter, tucked them away in the top pocket of her denim jacket, and rose from her seat.

'Go on then,' she said.

My voice cracked. 'Go on what?'

'Go and get the wine.'

We made it three steps along the hall. No talk, no candles, no wine, I just closed the front door and turned around and she came into my arms, one hand behind my head, pulling my face down to hers, the other going for flesh. That was it. All control gone. Passion at its most instinctive. Basic, primal need. Her jacket hit the floor seconds before mine. Breast to breast, thigh to thigh. Her fingers at my buttons, mine tugging at hers. Rasp of zippers, rasp of breath. Hands diving, finding, grasping. Lips slipping on a duel of tongues. Synchronised cannibalism.

She broke away, gasping. '*Bedroom*.' Her voice hoarse with hunger. We peeled clothes along the hall. T-shirts by the kitchen, jeans by the bathroom. Panties and Ys at the foot of the bed. We slid together, the smack of flesh on flesh. Chewed and sucked, rubbed and probed. Moans breaking from feasting lips. '*God, Kyoko . . .*' She, pulling me now, down, her legs parting, '*Now, Francis, please . . .*' parting wide, inviting me down, me, '*God . . .*' smothering her, crushing her small frame to mine, finding the warmth, the heat, pressing her, into her, slowly, sinking in, deeper now, her eyes closing for a moment, ankles locked at the small of my back, hips thrusting, pushing at me, devouring me, hands on my buttocks, driving me down, faster, harder, '*Fuck me, fuck me, fuck me*,' nails clawing, heavy-lidded eyes smoky with passion, neck arched, mouth seeking mine, finding it, filling it with her rasping breath, her darting tongue, her grinding passion taking me there, lifting me to a height of ecstasy I'd never experienced, the cry starting low in her belly, rising in pitch and intensity as the shudders began, her whole body suddenly convulsing, twitching, her orgasm explosive, triggering mine, bathing me in warmth as she gripped me, milked me, drained me, slowly bringing me back down to earth, to the cottage, the bedroom, the bed, her.

God, Kyoko, what are you *doing* to me?

The curtains were drawn now, the candles lit, the bottle of wine almost empty. We lay beneath the single sheet, her head resting in the crook of my arm, fingernail tracing circles on my chest. She'd already found the knife scar on my left shoulderblade, the bottle scar on my right forearm, and the little ball of fluff in my belly button. Her explorations apparently leaving her exhausted.

'Promise me you will,' she said, her voice husky with satiation.

'Will what?' I must have drifted off for a moment into that dreamy kind of post-coital transcendence.

418

She raised herself to an elbow, smacked me not so gently on the chest. 'You haven't listened to a word I said, have you?'

'You want me to go see Maggie, put her under the lights,' I said. 'Pull out her fingernails, torture some kind of a confession from her. Isn't that right?'

Kyoko giggled and slapped me again. 'Just talk to her, Francis, that's all. Do you promise?'

'I promise. First thing tomorrow.'

'Second thing tomorrow,' Kyoko corrected, grinning wickedly as her hand slid beneath the sheet, down over my belly to grasp me. I hardened in seconds.

We took our time. A tactile and lingual exploration of each other's bodies that was more a sensual reawakening than the ravenous passion that had engulfed us earlier, sapping us dry. It had been a long time – for both of us. All those lonely nights craving intimacy, to touch and be touched, to love and be loved, to hold and be held, they all came to the fore now, concentrated in the tip of a finger, tip of a tongue, a stroke here, caress there, soft moans of pleasure, giving and taking, gentle words of direction, *yes, mmm, there*, time existing only in the subtle rhythms of response, telescoped to the now as we moved sensuously among the soft shadows of the flickering candlelight.

Later, minutes or hours, she sat astride me, riding me slow, cuntipulating me, her dark conical nipples rubbing against mine, hair tickling my face, watching me through her heavy-lidded eyes, every now and then her teeth plucking at her lower lip, sending me, *Kyoko, what are you*-doing *to me? Why was it never like this before?* easing herself down, filling herself, gyrating as the first few moans escaped her parted lips, her skin goosepimpling beneath my fingers as I squeezed her buttocks, responding now, unable to stop myself, rising to meet her, the juices flowing, her back arched, soaking me with her come as the spasms began and she—

That was when the telephone rang.

—came again, crying out, panting, breath soughing from her lungs as she implanted herself again and again, each plunge forcing a groan, a shudder, another racking orgasm—

And went on ringing as I slipped back from the brink, cursing, already softening inside her. I reached over and grabbed the phone.

'You bastard.'

No, Francis, please...

'DS Dowie. Hope I'm not disturbing you?' A triumphant smugness in his tone.

''Course you bloody are. Get to the point.'

'I think we've got him.' Not just triumph but also excitement. 'We have a name.'

Kyoko groaned, quivering atop me, breath slowing, winding down now, sinking forward to lie on my chest as I said:

'Whose name?'

Dowie said awkwardly, 'I can, er, ring back later if you like.'

'Whose bloody name?'

'The Fangman. I've just finished checking through all the manifests. One name appears both on Sunday's manifest and all but two of the ones relating to the murders. It has to be him.'

'Has to be who?' I was losing patience fast.

'Man by the name of Byrne. Know him?'

'The po—' I broke off just in time. But Kyoko's eyes were closed, her breathing slow and warm on my chest.

'Potter,' Dowie said. 'Yes, him. Gideon Byrne. Drives a grey Subaru estate. Lives out on—'

'I know where he lives,' I snapped, then lowered my voice. 'I was out there with him the night of the last full moon. The night before Helen Falconer was killed.'

'You were? Hold on a sec.' I could hear the rustle of paper down the line. Then, 'Yep, he was on the mainland that day. Caught the last ferry home.'

'Who were the victims when he wasn't on the manifest?'

420

'Alice Drummond and Jean Sutherland.'

'Drummond, eh?' The nurse from Cumnock. 'You remember where her body was found?'

'South of the border, wasn't it? Cockermouth or something.'

'Exactly,' I said. 'The kind of long drive that could make you miss a ferry, if you weren't too careful. You know what we need to do?'

Dowie sighed. 'I can hear it coming.'

'Check out the manifest for the day *after* Drummond was killed. Same for the Sutherland woman – though until her body is found, we can't be absolutely sure she's even one of the Fangman's victims. Check anyway. And also check the day Arthur Thomas was killed. We don't want to find out the Fangman was on the mainland that particular day.'

'Shouldn't we put some kind of watch on the guy, the potter?'

'And risk letting him know we're on to him?' I said. 'No, Sergeant, we've got a long way to go yet. There's a world of difference between knowing he did it and proving he did it. First we check the manifests again. If he's still in the picture then, we'll go through all the forensic reports, see if we can find something to place him at one or more of the scenes. Then, maybe then, we'll have enough to put the whole case in front of Kettle.'

Dowie was quiet for a moment. I could feel the doubt hanging there in the silence between us, could imagine the frown on his bland face, the wispy blond brows furrowed, meeting in a V on the bridge of his nose. The nose which, I reflected, just a few days ago I was ready to punch clear through his brain.

That is why the human race has survived so long, I thought, because of the ease with which we adapt to changing situations. Survival of the fittest.

Something to do with the size of our brains.

On my chest, Kyoko was still, breathing heavily, already asleep. Her skin glistened with the sheen of sweat, felt like raw silk beneath the run of my fingers. From this exciting new perspective, the world looked good, a place in which I could adapt and survive.

I said, 'You've done a good job, Dowie, and if we pull this off, you're the one who's going to share the limelight with Kettle. Not me. I'm running in a different race here, and the finishing tape is still a long way off. You do the business now, do it like I say, and you'll never look back. Believe me.'

'I'll do as you say,' he said softly, after a moment. 'Don't you worry.'

'I won't.'

'Goodnight, sir.' The phone went dead in my ear.

Sir? I wondered. Well, why the hell not?

Kyoko stirred in my arms. Now, where was I?

34

Potter.

Gideon Byrne. The potter. Lived by himself out on Machrie Moor. *Nice man, very quiet, keeps himself to himself, wouldn't harm a fly . . .*

How many times have I heard that before? Far too many to be surprised any more. Cops my age know anybody is capable of anything. Without exception. So no surprise when Dowie had mentioned his name. Just dead interest.

What did he do with their bones?

The first streaks of dawn seeped in through the open window, bathing the room in a buttery glow that took me back through space and time to childhood summers spent on this very island. A small Victorian B&B back off the main street at Whiting Bay, all delicate porcelain, lace curtains and antimacassars. A list of rules for the younger guests tacked on the wall in the hall: NO shoes to be worn in the house; NO sweets to be eaten in bed; NO football to be played in the lounge. Days spent with my Great-Aunt Joan down on the beach or climbing up through the forest to clamber over ruined Iron Age forts and play in the rock pools at the top of Glenashdale Falls.

A solitary man, I remember thinking about Gideon Byrne the night of the the last full moon when he had left the room to get more beer. A man who has no past, or no time for the past. A simple man with simple needs. Who devours newspapers, documentaries and current affairs programmes, and looks at the world through a TV screen. An armchair philosopher, content to watch it pass him by.

Sounds coming in through the window now, the hotel coming awake. Clatter of pots and pans from the kitchen, someone whistling out of tune, early birds singing for their breakfast.

A tidy, meticulous man, Byrne, though shy and ill at ease in the presence of others. At once charming, yet abrupt and sometimes rude. Touchy on the subject of pottery. A lot of . . . was it bitterness I'd detected? Or just anger? Anyway, he was certainly very defensive about his art or craft or profession or whatever the hell he preferred to call it.

A van came up the hotel drive, past the cottage to the deliveries' entrance. A Bedford. One of its rear doors squeaked as it opened. The baker's van. Driver's name was Ross or something. Played in the hotel darts team. I heard the murmur of voices, a round of laughter, then the van door squeaked shut and a moment later the van reversed down the drive.

Gideon Byrne. Yes. Who also drove a grey Subaru estate, and was a large man who wore glasses. Who was on the mainland when most of the murders occurred, and on the ferry the day I was pushed overboard. Who knew, or was at least acquainted with, Arthur Thomas. The 'coincidences' were stacking up nicely.

Kyoko made a wistful sighing noise, rolled over on to her side.

I studied her with something akin to wonderment. That she could lie there with all her defences shut down yet feeling secure enough to entrust me with her vulnerability. Something I'd read in a book once, about sleep being possibly the most important single function of an animal's life. The kind of thought guaranteed to bring out the protectiveness in me.

I closed her gently in my arms, snuggled in tight. Breathed in the scent of her body, the fragrance of her hair. She stirred, pushing back at me as she slowly came awake, her buttocks squirming against my groin. Nature took its predictable course and we made a slow, languorous love, barely moving, the snug fit of our bodies enough to take us where we wanted to go, and further.

All days should begin like this.

Detective Sergeant Dowie was already in the office making coffee when I arrived. He looked like he'd slept only a few minutes more than I had. There was, however, a sprightliness about him that I could not even think of matching. I didn't try.

'Good night?' he enquired jauntily.

'Black and two sugars,' I said, dropping my helmet on the desk, throwing myself down in the chair behind it. 'Could've been better, people didn't keep phoning me up.'

Dowie laughed. 'Only a cop would interrupt his coitus to answer the phone. Admit it, you're a slave to your conditioning.'

'Maybe you're right.' The way I felt this morning, I could agree with almost anyone, even Dowie. I'd caught myself yesterday afternoon – and was doing it even now – glancing at the DS and wondering if Kettle was right – had I really been like that eight, nine years ago? And then seeing new facets of Dowie's character every time I looked that told me, yes, I probably had been very much like that. Which was why, against all my former instincts, I was beginning to not dislike the guy. It wasn't his fault his accent got right up my nose.

The kettle boiled. Dowie poured water into both cups, added sugar to one, stirred it and brought it over. 'Estate agent opens in half an hour,' he said, returning for his own coffee. 'Fax'll be through shortly after. I was thinking then maybe run Byrne through the CRO, see what comes up. What d'you think?'

'You're the OC, you tell me.'

'Can't see any harm in it.' Dowie sat on the edge of the desk, warmed now by a watery beam of sunlight.

'Me neither.' I sipped at my coffee, caught the scent of Kyoko still on my fingers. I decided never to wash them again. 'Long as you keep it routine,' I added.

'And you? What're you going to do while I do all the work?'

'Thought I'd go and buy some pottery.'

'You're going out to Machrie Moor?'

I shook my head. 'One of the other ones. I need to find out more. Like what kind of traces we ought to look out for once you get all the forensic reports sent over.'

Dowie nodded, made a note in his book. 'I'll arrange that as soon as Bryce or Davies come in. If there's no one coming over on the ferry this morning, I'll send one of them across to pick up the reports. Anything else?'

'VideoFits from the *Crimewatch* programme earlier this year. See if you can get hold of a hard copy. Also any of the witness statements which might point to Byrne. We want as tight a case as possible if we want to put it up in front of Kettle.'

Dowie made another scribbled note, glanced up. 'How about I try to get hold of the psychologist's profile? We may find something useful there.'

'Sure, why not? Just keep it routine though.'

Dowie, I had now discovered, was a notesman. Had to see things written down to imprint them on his memory. He consulted his wee black book, tapped his pencil on his teeth. 'Did you get hold of that woman last night? The one with the book?'

Yeah, I told him, I'd arranged to pick it up this afternoon. He must have sensed the concern in my voice, raised an eyebrow in question.

'She works out at Byrne's pottery,' I explained.

'Ah, I see. And you think she might be in danger there?'

'Working alongside a deranged serial killer? There's a slight possibility.'

426

'The Yorkshire Ripper never touched his workmates,' Dowie said defensively, 'nor Dennis Nilsen his.'

'Their workmates were neither whores nor down-and-out homeless gays.'

Dowie cocked his head as the station door opened and footsteps approached along the hall. DC Bryce popped his head round the door.

'Mornin' boss.' To me, a polite nod.

'Give us a minute, Joe, will you? Thanks.' When the door closed behind Bryce, Dowie turned back to me. 'So ... what? You want to warn her, suggest she hand in her notice?'

'In the circumstances...' I said.

Dowie nodded. 'Better on the safe side, yah.'

'It's got to seem natural, though. We don't want to spook Byrne. He's going to be in the hyper-phase now, all senses tuned to screaming pitch, paranoia on red alert. Anything out of the ordinary happens and he's going to turbo-thrust into outer orbit.'

'Give her a ring then. Arrange to pick up the book when she gets home this evening. That'll give you time to think of something.' Dowie consulted his watch. 'Meantime, we'll RV back here, say midday.'

I said midday. Dowie nodded and left the room. I pulled across the phone and dialled the number for the Glen Chalmadale Distillery.

Maggie answered on the third ring.

I filled up the tank at the pumps in the centre of Brodick, bought a newspaper at the store next door, then climbed back on my bike and headed for Lamlash. Although the sun was getting warmer as it climbed the morning sky, there was a chilly breeze coming in off the Clyde, tiers of cloud already gathering over the mainland. I took my time, content to let the cool fresh air clear away the cobwebs in my mind. My head was still a gently throbbing ache attached to my neck, but I think that was due more to a lack of sleep than a residue of my injury. The kind of lack of sleep I could definitely handle more of.

Mike 30 was already parked outside the Lamlash office when I arrived. I jacked my bike on its stand and went inside, met again by the smell of coffee in the making.

'Black and two sugars,' I called by way of a greeting. Like that film, I was probably going to relive this day over and over again for the rest of my life. Still, I thought, it could've been worse.

They were in the small kitchen through the back, Yuill making the coffee, Monica leaning against the sideboard, chewing on a piece of buttered toast.

'Well, well,' Yuill said. 'If it isn't the Return of the Walking Dead.'

'And after three pints, he rose again,' Monica added, around a mouthful of toast.

'Man's off sick and turns up earlier for work than he does when he's healthy.'

I beamed at them.

Monica stepped back. 'See that?' she said incredulously. 'He smiled. And it's not even opening time. We better call a doctor, fast.'

Yuill said, 'Just give me a dozen of whatever he's on.' He pushed a mug along the sideboard towards me. 'On second thoughts, make it two dozen.'

'He's got that look in his eye, Sarge,' Monica said. 'If he had a tail, it'd be wagging his arse all over the shop.'

'At your age, Frank – I'm ashamed.' Yuill led the way back through to the office.

I followed, smiling as I shook my head. 'Jealous is what you are, both of you.' We sank into chairs simultaneously. I pulled across the Duty Log, read the brief entries. Monica was down for a follow-up on a B&E in Whiting Bay, a couple of Copy Complaints – one in Sliddery, one in Blackwaterfoot – and an interview at home with a Mr Jack Wallace. Yuill had booked himself an hour in the interview room for the afternoon.

'Ryder?' I asked him.

Yuill nodded. 'Thought I'd have one last shot. He's agreed to come in voluntarily, said he doesn't need representation.'

'Then he's either innocent or a complete fool.'

'Let's hope the latter. Anyway, this is the last chance. If I can't break him down, we're going to lose him. It might not matter, though. Mo seems to be making better progress her end.'

'Yeah?' I said, turning to her.

'I ran Wallace through CRO,' she said. 'He's about as clean as the Clyde. Moved over here with his family three years ago when he got the job with the Forestry Commission. Prior to that he was living in Dundee, the last two years unemployed. During that time he was done for two Assaults, one indecent, and one with the intent to ravish. Got hefty fines for both, and was bound over for psychiatric evaluation. Also, seventeen domestic call-outs, and one restraining order. Since he moved over here, though, absolutely nothing. Not even a parking ticket.'

'His own daughter, though . . .'

'Stepdaughter. The perfect kind of victim for a sick fuck like him.'

'You going alone?'

'Mm.' Monica nodded thoughtfully. 'Like I told you before, the guy's a misogynist. He's not going to take it too seriously, being interviewed by a mere *wo*man. At least that's what I hope. Maybe he'll give something away. And I want to see how he reacts when I confront him with his previous.'

'Just be careful, Mo,' Yuill said quietly. 'Any sign of trouble and you drop it, okay?'

'Is that an order?'

'Bloody right it is. You've been hanging round McMorran far too long. You may have caught some of his bad habits.' Yuill offered me the benefit of his smile. 'How's your ambitious young detective sergeant?' he asked. 'Keeping you busy?'

'We're still checking up on the manifests,' I said, playing it down. 'May have a lead though. Man named Byrne, Gideon Byrne. Know him?'

'Of him, aye. Potter, isn't he, has a place out on Machrie Moor? Quiet sort of guy, keeps himself to himself?'

'That's the one. He was on the ferry last Sunday and, as far as we can tell, on the mainland most of the days the murders were committed. We're still waiting to confirm though.'

Yuill frowned. 'Wasn't it his house you watched that pagan ritual from last week?'

'The same.'

The Sergeant shot me a sidelong glance. 'Informed Fullerton yet?'

'I will,' I said. 'Soon.'

'Make sure you do.' Sergeant Yuill drained his coffee, rose and got his cap from the peg behind the door. Adjusted it in front of the mirror, then fetched a personal radio from the recharger on the front desk. 'Ready, Mo?' he asked.

She was. A minute later I was alone in the office.

I popped a couple of painkillers, washed them down with lukewarm coffee, then pulled out my newspaper and spread it on the desk. Skimmed through it page by page, mood sagging under the depressing weight of its headlines. Turned to the sports pages. Had to look hard, but at least there I detected a few faint traces of hope between the lines. I studied the crossword for a few minutes, then gave up, folded the paper and tossed it into the bin. Was just turning away when a small headline at the foot of the front page caught my eye. I retrieved it from the bin. In the Latest News column, it read FANGMAN SUSPECT IN CUSTODY.

Five minutes later, I got through to John Fullerton.

The pottery was half a mile up a steep pitted track that cut north of Kilmory through pastureland dotted with grazing sheep and cattle. I slalomed round the potholes in low gear, thinking maybe I should have opted for the trial bike I'd seen in the showroom when I bought the Triumph. Still. The pottery was open when I got there, and the woman inside both pleasant and helpful when I told her what I wanted.

'House used to be a steading,' Jenny Howitt explained as I took in my surroundings. 'And this was the hay barn. We only completed it last year.' It was an old stone building, recently renovated, one half dedicated to the display of pots, the other half where all the hard work was done.

She was working now as we talked, wetting her fingers every now and then as she pulled handles for the worktop full of mugs in front of her. She was in her late forties, with intelligent brown eyes and long brown hair, and wore a pair of baggy blue overalls. Sunlight slanted in through a window at the back of the room, capturing her amidst the dance of a billion motes of clay dust. Her accent was from somewhere south of Watford. I asked how long she'd been living on the island.

'We came out here in sixty-eight, I think it was. A lot of people did. Part of the whole hippy thing, I suppose, get back to nature and all that. We saw an advert in a paper, thought, why not.'

'An advert?'

'Mm.' She smeared the handle into position on the mug and then continued. 'Because of the declining population at the time – young people leaving the island to seek work on the mainland where the prospects were greater – the Council here adopted a policy of trying to attract younger people to come and set up small businesses on the island. Especially in the crafts and, you know, like cottage-industries. So, like I said, we thought, why not give it a try?'

'Were you the only potter to come over?'

'There were already several established at the time. I don't think Gideon Byrne was one of those. I think he arrived shortly after we did. Set up his business up on Machrie Moor.'

431

'I've met him,' I said. 'Nice man. Seems to be doing quite well for himself.'

Jenny Howitt frowned, brushing a lock of hair from her eyes with her wrist. 'Summer season, maybe,' she said. 'But rumour has it – and there's a lot of rumour obviously on an island this size – that he's overextended himself. Trying to fulfil too many orders on the mainland and falling behind.'

'Does he exhibit his stuff at all?' I asked. 'I noticed he had some very unusual pots on display.'

'He's talented, I'll give him that.' A grudged admission, I noticed. 'But no, I don't think he exhibits. He's very kind of, well, secretive about his glazes, won't share his recipes. Doesn't attend any of the conferences or meetings, or even associate with any of us. I think he feels we're all beneath him or something.'

'Mm.'

Not only pots on display, I noticed. There were also rainbow-coloured wall-hangings and tapestries, candles in various shapes, colours and sizes, varnished wooden ornaments, even a milking stool. In the centre of the floor a black woven carpet with the kind of design I felt would be more at home in a Hopi *kiva*.

I said, 'Isn't it possible for a potter to study a glaze and work out its ingredients? Like the way a chef might do with a sauce he hasn't tasted before.'

Howitt laughed. 'Possible, yes, but only to a certain degree. Like I could tell you Gideon uses bone-ash in a lot of his glazes. No big deal, that. You can tell by its translucence, the calcium forming tiny opalescent bubbles as it oxidises. What you can't tell, though, are the percentages of each ingredient he uses, or the thickness of application, or the temperatures to which he fires the pots, and at what temperatures he reduces and for how long. Whether he fires in his woodfire kiln or one of his electric kilns. You see, all these things are individual to each potter, a matter of lifelong experimentation.'

'He has three kilns and you only have one?'

'There.' Jenny Howitt placed the mug on a shelf lined with other completed mugs, then washed her hands in the basin, dried them on her overalls. 'I only need one kiln,' she said. 'I prefer a gas one' – I'd already noticed the two tall red bottles against the wall by the kiln – 'he prefers electric. Is into gadgets, I think, uses a computer to control the firing. The woodfire kiln I'm sure he only uses once in a while, mostly pre-season. It's a lot of work for just one person.'

I picked up a bowl, admired its contours, studied its base the way I'd seen Kyoko do that afternoon out at Byrne's. No initials, I noticed. It was a sea-green glaze, speckled with white like flying spume. I took it over to the counter.

Jenny Howitt rummaged around in a drawer, came out with a book which she pushed across the counter. 'Try that one. It should tell you everything you want to know. Maybe even inspire you.'

The Potter's Book by Bernard Leach.

'Name seems familiar,' I said, flicking through its pages. It was an old copy, well used.

'He used to be regarded as *the* guru of Western pottery,' Jenny Howitt said. 'Studied in Japan under Ogata Kenzan, one of the old masters. Brought East and West together. If you can't find what you're looking for in there, I've got other books you can borrow.'

'Thanks.' I handed her the bowl. 'I'll take this. I have a friend who'll love it. Japanese. Her grandfather was a potter.'

Jenny Howitt grinned. 'I hope she's not *too* critical,' she said. As she handed me my change, she added, 'I still don't understand why you need to know all about the materials we use.'

'Ah,' I said, giving her the most enigmatic of smiles. 'The mysteries of rural policing.'

The Ross – the road which climbs west out of Lamlash through Monamore Glen and then descends, following the Sliddery

Water south-west through the picturesque Glen Scorridale – was built, as were many other by-roads and bridges on the island at the time – early nineteenth century – by tenants of the land who had to donate up to ten days' labour free of charge each year. We have a similar system in operation today, only now politicians like to call it a 'Public Sector Wage Freeze' or 'Inflation-Linked Performance Bonuses'. Or words to that effect.

I pulled up at the Free Church at the Bennicarrigan junction at the foot of The Ross, and wondered if I should return to the station at Lamlash for a couple of filled rolls, or head on up the west-coast road to Blackwaterfoot and have a three-courser at the hotel, appease my suddenly renewed appetite.

No contest. Appetite won.

I parked the bike by the hotel wall against which I'd had my little tête-à-tête with Ryder a couple of weeks ago, made my way inside.

On my former inspector's salary I might have been tempted to go for the fresh Scottish salmon and all the trimmings, but I was having to forgo such necessary little luxuries now in order to keep up the payments on my High Street flat. So, instead, but not at all reluctantly, I ordered soup of the day, sausage, beans and chips, and a banana split, then took my bottle of LA across to one of the window tables overlooking the beach. I briefly took in the bathers, the sunbathers, the kids building in the sand and exploring the rock pools, the sun blinding off the silvery Sound, the Mull of Kintyre twenty miles distant, the speedboat curving in to the shore, then pulled out the book on pottery and began to read.

An hour later I was back where I'd started the day in the Brodick office, this time with Dowie behind the desk and me perched on the edge. The Detective Sergeant was having trouble with his self-control.

'I don't fucking believe it,' he said, tossing the file he'd been reading into a drawer, slamming it shut. 'I mean, we've just about got this Byrne guy sewn up and now he tells us he's already got a sodding suspect in custody. Like thanks for keeping us informed, DI bloody Fullerton.'

'You speak to him yourself?' I asked.

'Too bloody busy for the likes of me,' Dowie sneered. 'All I got was an arseload from some automated desk-jockey reading me the fucking press statement. Like, yah, that's really going to help my investigation.' He shook his head and sighed. 'How about you?'

'He gave me the gist, no more.'

'The gist, eh? That was nice of him. How thoughtful. Did you tell him about *our* suspect?'

'I told him we have what seems to be a very promising line of enquiry. He likes that kind of jargon.'

'I can believe it. So what did he say?'

'He said to follow it through and keep him informed.'

'Sure. Like he did us.' Dowie popped his Parker, wrote down a word on the pad in front of him, underlined it heavily. 'You tell him about Byrne? The ferry manifests and what-have-you?'

'Briefly. He didn't sound too convinced, though. Maybe he's got other things on his mind.'

'You mean like a tumour?'

'Like getting it right. He's probably got half the nation's press on his case, not to mention Kettle breathing down his neck, demanding a result. I know what it's like, I've been there. All the limelight in a case like this, you pull a suspect in, you leave no stone unturned. You don't want him walking out with two fingers in the air due to lack of evidence. You should know that by now.'

''Course I bloody know it,' Dowie snapped. 'Only thing pisses me off is I have to read about it in the bloody paper – *after* one of my own DCs tells me about it.'

I sympathised. Really. But I'd been left out of things for so long now I was almost getting used to it. 'He said he wants a report on his desk, Friday at the latest.'

'A full one? The attempt on your life, the note the Fangman sent you, the lot?'

'Everything.'

'He didn't think all that was one coincidence too many?'

'He said it was "interesting". But nowhere near conclusive.'

Dowie shook his head in disbelief. 'Christ, he must have some suspect over there. I mean, what, did they find him wanking over the Sutherland woman's body or something? Has he confessed?'

'The contrary. He's denied everything.'

'So why all the excitement?'

'Because they found him hanging round superstore car parks. Not just one, but several. Followed him for two days, watching him let down car tyres and then wait for the women to appear, offer them a ride home. Tried it four times the first day, eleven the second. Only one woman fell for it, and that's when they picked the guy up, just as he was helping her into her house with the shopping.'

'Jesus!' Dowie said, angrily scoring out the word he'd written on the pad. It now looked like this: ~~BASTARD~~. 'Sounds pretty convincing, I must admit. Unless he's just another copycat?'

'*Another* copycat?' Did he still secretly feel the murder of Arthur Thomas was the work of a copycat? Mm, I thought, interesting.

'*A* copycat, then.'

'Seems doubtful.' I explained about the couple who'd seen a man acting suspiciously up on Mistylaw Muir last Sunday, how they'd then discovered Jean Sutherland's body and reported it to the police. 'Bones missing, lying in a ditch, no doubt at all she was the Fangman's fourth victim. Anyway, Fullerton brought in the couple and asked them if the man they'd seen acting suspiciously on Mistylaw Muir was in the line-up. No hesitation, Fullerton said. Identified him immediately. Separately.'

'So who is he, the suspect?'

'Apart from the fact that he's mid thirties, fits the description, has a history of deviation, lives in Kilwinning and is unemployed, Fullerton wasn't saying.'

'Fuck,' Dowie said. 'And I thought we had something here.'

'I still think we do.' I picked up the latest manifest, the one for the day Helen Falconer died. 'Have you checked this yet?

Dowie nodded apathetically. 'He's there.'

'And the forensic reports?'

'Coming. Soon as Davies arrives off the ferry.'

I dropped the potter's book on the desk. 'Check out the chapters on clays and glazes,' I said. 'You should find all the materials you need to look out for there.'

'What about you?' Dowie whined. 'I'm the one supposed to sit around on my arse all day giving orders, yet here I am doing all the sodding work while you tour the island's pubs at your leisure.'

'I'm a sick man, Sergeant, I need my rest.' I picked up my helmet, shrugged into my jacket. 'And in case you've forgotten, I'm still attached to the island force. I have vital duties still outstanding. A question of national security. Like the matter of a sheep found in the Distillery's water-tank to clear up. Life goes on.'

'Tell me about it,' DS Dowie sighed.

If Maggie was guilty of dumping the sheep in the water-tank as Kyoko believed, then by now, I hoped, she would be a quivering mass of nerves. I had phoned her earlier for that express reason. In the intervening hours she'd have run the impending interview through her mind, sorting out her answers, getting everything in order, composing herself for the task ahead. At the same time, though, she'd be worrying: worrying there was something she had perhaps overlooked; worrying that maybe someone had seen her, or that I had some new piece of damning evidence; worrying that I might see through her fragile façade.

If she was guilty.

And if she wasn't, I would know in the first few minutes.

I parked in shade and followed a straggle of tourists up the hill. Another tour, led by a tartan-skirted guide, was just leaving the Malt Barn Reception Centre, making its way down towards the shop. I crossed the log bridge and got there first. Maggie was serving behind the counter. She saw me, did a quick double-take, smiled nervously.

'If you'd like to wait in the office,' she said, 'I'll be with you shortly. Jan should be back any minute.'

'Mind if I use your phone?' I asked. 'Quick call, local.'

'Be my guest.'

I sat behind her desk and dialled the Machrie Moor pottery. Ros Hastie answered. I told her I wouldn't be able to make it out there this afternoon, could I pick the book up later this evening when she got home? No problem, she said, she'd be home sometime after six. I said great, I'd see her then, and rang off. I sat there for a few minutes looking through the window at the tourists toing and froing, then crossed to the door to Flora Farquharson's office and knocked lightly. When there was no reply, I poked my head round the door. Empty. Cover on the computer, red light on the answerphone flashing, and no Chanel No. 5 lingering in the air. Flora Farquharson had not been in today. I closed the door and returned to the window. A minute later, Maggie bustled into the office, all dramatic sighs and exasperation.

'Typical! Busiest day of the week and half the staff decide to come down with some kind of bug. We've got four tours booked for this afternoon and only the one guide, so guess who's the Muggins who'll have to do that as well as watch the shop, answer the phone, fill out the orders and God knows what else? Me.' She sighed again, sank into the chair behind the desk. 'So, anyway, how can I help you? I must say it all sounded very mysterious when you phoned this morning. Is something afoot?'

I didn't answer immediately, instead stretched out a silence to study her openly, thoughtfully. I put her age somewhere in the late twenties. She wore a grey pleated wool skirt, pastel-pink blouse, grey cardigan. Reminded me a little of Dawn French, I thought. Maggie, though, lacked the lines of humour, her doughy, round face shy of make-up, her long mousy hair scrawled back from her forehead and clasped at the back. She squirmed uncomfortably beneath my gaze.

'Something is afoot, isn't it?' she said.

I pocketed my hands and studied the floor for a moment before looking up.

'Maggie Boyd,' I said. 'Is that your full name?'

She nodded hesitantly. 'Yes, why?'

'I think you know why I'm here,' I told her softly.

Her eyes slipped away from mine. 'No. I'm afraid I don't.' She began doodling on the back of an envelope. 'Has something happened?'

'I think you know why I'm here,' I repeated.

And one look in her eyes told me she knew. Told me all I wanted to know. She knew it and I knew it.

'I think you better leave,' she said, her voice cracking.

'I can't do that. Not yet. Not until you've told me what I want to know. I've got all afternoon.'

Maggie glanced anxiously about the room as though seeking a place to hide or escape.

'Or I could ask you to accompany me back to the station and we can do this by the book. Make it official, call in your employers, that kind of thing. Choice is yours.'

Stubbornly, like a spoilt child. 'I haven't *done* anything.'

'Tell me about the sheep, Maggie. How it happened, why.'

She lowered her head on to her hands, shook it and rubbed her eyes. 'I can't!'

'Tell me about Farquharson then, about Findlay. You're in love with him, aren't you?'

Shake of head. I was getting nowhere. I slammed my fist on the desk. That brought her head up.

439

'You love the man,' I said, letting my impatience loose. 'You worship the ground he walks on, you love his bones, you'd do anything for the man. He knows it, yet he treats you like shit. He walks all over you, Maggie. He hires in guides from the mainland, shags them right under your nose. He shouts you out in front of them, them with their tight young bodies in tartan skirts and flimsy white blouses, so much younger and prettier than you'll ever be, responding to his flirty advances, flutter of lashes there, flash of thigh here, I bet you see it all, the greedy little thoughts running through their naive little minds, thinking they're in now, they've hit the big time here, marry the boss, live in the lap of luxury the rest of their lives. Girly dreams, Maggie, the kind of dreams you discarded years ago . . . or did you?'

Tears welling up in her suddenly big, sad round eyes. Sympathy tugged, but I pushed it away and continued.

'You're sitting down here in the office, you watch him take her up the lane to the Malt Barn Centre. You're sweating away in a stuffy little office doing all the work that keeps the Distillery ticking over day to day, all the work he should be doing, the boring stuff, orders, numbers, sales figures, and you're looking out that window, you're looking up that lane and you don't need X-ray eyes to know what's going on in the building up there because you've seen it before, maybe once, maybe a dozen times, guy doesn't lock the door 'cause he likes it, doesn't he, when someone walks in, likes it even more when that someone is you, because something happened once, didn't it, something between you that makes him act the way he does, like each time he does it now he's getting a little piece of revenge, he's rubbing it in your face, that's the way it is, isn't it, Maggie? Tell me I'm right. Because I know it, I can see it on your face, it's written there bold and clear, it says, *I, Maggie Boyd, put the sheep in the tank because I wanted to pay that bastard back for all the hurt he's putting me through.* Tell me I'm wrong.'

She was crying openly now, the tears coursing down her cheeks. I went and looked out the window, giving her time to compose herself. I'm such a considerate guy that way. After a couple of minutes her sobbing subsided and she blew her nose. I turned away from the window as she began to speak, her tone tinged with sadness.

'I'd come in here like I do every night – you know, to check the bar, see if it needs stocking up, make sure there's no one still here, lock the place up – only this time there he was, over in the corner there with . . . I can't remember her name, but one of the new girls. They were . . . doing it. Didn't even stop when I came in, just said, "Hi Maggie" and carried on like I wasn't even there.'

'You couldn't have been too shocked by this time,' I said. 'You knew what was going on.'

'He *lied* to me!' she cried. 'Don't you see? The little shit lied to me!'

'I don't see—'

'He told me he always took precautions. *Always*. Said he didn't want to die of AIDS, he had so much to do, a whole future ahead of him. He said between *us* it was different, it was so good, it'd be almost like a sin using condoms.'

'He wasn't using a condom, then?'

Maggie shook her head. 'That was enough for me. I ran out of there and jumped in the car and just drove. Didn't care where, so long as it was the hell away from him.'

'And then?'

'I had to think. Just sit somewhere and think the whole thing through. I was on the road home but I didn't want to go home, so I pulled over and parked. Then I went down to the shore. The moon was out. I sat on a rock for a while, I don't know how long.'

'And that's when you saw the sheep and decided to kill it?'

She looked at me in total astonishment. An Oscar's-worth. 'Me? Kill it?' Her laugh taking me by surprise. 'Don t be silly! I

441

couldn't kill anything. I have spiders in the bath older than I am.'

'So . . . what, then? You dumped it in the water-tank and the Wee Folk came in the middle of the night and did it for you?'

She shot me a look of pure disdain. 'You're an arse, you know that? A right fucking *prick*.'

'I have my moments.'

'I didn't kill that sheep. That's how I found it. Maybe the man who dumped it did, how should I know?'

'What man?'

'The man in the car. Pulled up when I was down on the shore, opened the back of his car, dumped the sheep over the wall, then drove away. That man.'

'Describe him.'

'It was dark, dammit.'

'The moon was out, you said.'

'He was, I dunno, large. Wore glasses. And overalls, I think.'

'You ever seen him before?'

'Couldn't say.'

'What about his car?'

'Silver, I think. An estate.'

'So what did you do then?'

'I went over to see what he'd dumped. Anyone would.' She blew her nose again, tucked the tissue up the sleeve of her cardigan. A habit that always makes me cringe.

'And then?'

'I saw the sheep lying there all covered in blood. It was like semi-wrapped in a black tarpaulin. I could see it had been stabbed, its throat cut. It was horrible, but I remember thinking how much I wished the sheep were Findlay, because that's what I felt like doing to him, just stab him and stab him and stab him. I wanted him to see that, to know how far he was driving me.'

'What did you do next?'

'I don't know, I think I must've been crazy. All I could see was that little bastard and the girl. I wanted to hurt him. I remembered that he had these important negotiations coming up with the Japanese. It meant a lot to him, he wanted it to go really well. I suppose that's when I first thought about using the sheep. You know, like some kind of voodoo curse or something. A warning. I was just going to leave it where he always parks his car. Then I thought of the water-tank. Put it in there and ruin a run, that would hit him where he hurts most, in the pocket. I felt if he found the sheep in his tank, he'd somehow know it was me, that he'd maybe realise things had gone too far, that he'd better change his ways. So that's what I did. I knew Archie checked the tank most mornings, so I knew it wouldn't be too long before it was discovered.'

I said, 'You understand that you have committed an offence, that charges may be brought against you?'

Maggie sniffed and said nothing for a moment, staring out the window. Then, in a small voice, 'So what happens now?'

'I want you to show me where you found the sheep,' I said.

35

'Perserverance brings the woman into danger. The moon is nearly full.
If the superior man persists, Misfortune comes.'

Dear oh dear.

Gideon Byrne doesn't know what to think now. Tidying up for the day, getting ready to close up shop and what does he find lying by the cash register? A book. More specifically, the *I Ching*. Not his one either. So it must be Hastie's. Which is one hell of a big coincidence, he feels.

Trouble is, he's not in the mood for coincidences, not now when things seem to be getting a little out of hand, beyond his control. Hard enough trying to keep the whole show rolling, like ahead of the game, when the momentum inside him, that little ball of fire that drives him, seems to be dying away, diminishing his power. Maybe this was how his mother felt those last few days when she was contemplating slitting his father's throat, her mind unravelling, falling apart. Pick at a loose thread here, a loose thread there, and watch as the whole tapestry of your life unravels. A kind of deconstruction taking place. Interesting in a weird sort of way.

Like he could see it happening inside his head but it was like watching it happen to someone else. An out-of-mind experience. Feeling more and more these days a sense of detachment, of goodbyes already said, everything accomplished bar the screaming. As it were.

But then Ros Hastie goes and spoils it all. Gideon thinking this last week or so, shit, she's not exactly unattractive for a middle-age bitch. Okay, not a candle to Simone, but hell, it's been a long time. A long, long time. And she seems to be wanting it, giving him the signals in something only a little less subtle than semaphore. Flashing her green eyes at him, giving him long looks from under her lashes, looks not even he, inexperienced as he is, can mistake. Every now and then he'd glance up, catch her watching his crotch, something in her eyes he wasn't sure what the hell it was. So he'd stopped wearing underpants now, letting the beast move about freely inside his overalls, enjoying the sensation, aware of himself all the time now, aware also of her gaze, those sneaky wee peeks of hers, caught by the hypnotic swaying of his cobra.

And he'd noticed how she was always touching him now whenever she got in close. A hand on his arm as she made some point or other, her hip brushing against his as she discusses some tiny inconsequential detail, like where to display a certain pot so it catches the right light to show off the colours of its glaze. That kind of thing. A tactile bitch who needs to feel the things around her to remind her she's still alive, in the physical world.

And Gideon beginning in the last few days to engineer these little scenarios, getting turned on by them, standing there next to her with the old cheesy nudger half-engorged, she trying hard not to look down, see it pushing at his buttons, getting all fluttery the way she does, hands fingering the pendant at her neck, breath a little faster, going all pink with the blood rushing to her head, Gideon knowing all he has to do is touch her and she'll have a multiple whipped cream on the spot. But holding back, always holding back, because the mission was still running, things to do, things to do.

But a lot can change in just a few days. Things can just disappear from your mind, never to be found again. Like large chunks of memory. Vanishing into that black hole that wasn't there before. And it seemed to be growing bigger. Swallowing up little bits of his past, a bite here, a chomp there, some kind of Pacman eating him up from the inside. Like yesterday – or was it the day before? – he'd spent the whole day trying to remember the events of last Sunday, did he really push that cop off the ferry or was it just another jagged shard of the fragmented dreams that now littered his nighttime hours? He had only resolved the question when he found the dossier of police reports down in the chamber. But that's just one example. There are others.

Like the fine print of his mission. It all seemed a little blurred, Gideon no longer sure of the orders, which direction to take. More and more, growing like a seed inside him, the wish for peace, for an end to this manic confusion, a relief from this heavy burden of responsibility. To stop, that was it, just stop. Wind down. Lay himself down in some lush meadow beneath the Moon, look up at the stars and not feel this thing driving him, propelling him this way and that, surging through his brain like an army of occupation, never letting go. Peace and quiet, the simple life. Let the whole thing blow over, the dust settle. Then maybe work something out with Hastie, come to some kind of arrangement where she didn't need to be around the whole time, like give him space to breathe, to think. Have what they call a loving relationship. Kiss and cuddle, that kind of thing, hold hands in the dark. Let her get in a little closer and show him a few things he's not too sure about, the stuff women seem to know naturally without having to be taught it. Teach him how to make love without having to bite her throat out.

And so what if she was a little rusty in that department. He'd probably get down there and have to sweep away the cobwebs, do a little dusting around her socket, maybe polish her knockers while he was at it. But so what? He wasn't exactly Mr Shag-A-Night Byrne, was he? He'd probably have a whole bunch of his own cobwebs if he didn't spend so much time in front of the mirror doing the five-finger shuffle.

But all that was then. Before this afternoon. Now things have changed. Like life can never be simple, the way you want it. Someone's always got their own ideas about how they want to fuck it up for you, stick their poky little noses in and stir the shit. Hastie now in bed with the cop, the one you wish you'd never set eyes on. The two of them working together, hand in hand, to bring Gideon down, shatter his simple dreams. McMorran phoning her this afternoon, all whisper whisper whisper behind his back. Her giving McMorran the *I Ching*, and arranging to meet him later for a little suck-fuck therapy most likely. The two of them plotting their back-stabbing schemes and laughing at him, thinking how fucking clever they are, getting one over on Gideon. Well, not for long. Gideon has his own plans. Mission isn't over yet, not by a long chalk. Still plenty of things to take care of. What was that old saying? *Mony a pickle maks a muckle.* Take care of the pennies and let the pounds take care of themselves. In other words, take care of the cop and the woman, let the rest take care of itself.

Go lock the doors, Gideon, there's a good psychopath.

You look at her. Sprawled there on the floor, face concealed by her tumble of hair, cotton dress riding high over her pale twisted legs, one arm stretched towards the door, as if reaching out for the life beyond, the world to which she would never return. Shame, you could've been so good together, made such a handsome couple. People would've pointed you out, said things like you were made for each other, a match made in heaven, that kind of thing. Now the bitch would have to burn.

You unlock the door, check it's clear outside. Could still be a few tourists around, the kind who don't understand the meaning of CLOSED, come wandering down into the yard like they own the bloody place, have no respect for another man's property. But there's no one there. You pick her up, that familiar tingle flushing your skin as your hands touch her bare flesh. You carry her out across the yard, through your front door, up the stairs and into the bedroom, where

448

you drop her on the bed. Then stand there awhile rubbing your chin, thinking things through, a little thought never hurting anyone.

The cop. Is bound to miss her. Will go round to her place sometime this evening and find her house all locked up, no lights in any of the windows. What would he do then? Come round here, start poking around, ask tricky-dicky questions trying to catch you out? Or what? Think maybe she'd forgotten about the rendezvous, or something else had come up, and go on home? It was possible, what any sensible man would do. But the cop wasn't sensible. He was a cop for a start. Which meant his suspicious little mind would be working overtime, jumping to wild conclusions, one of which might just be right. So, yeah, he might well come out here looking for her.

Dusky light trickling through the window. Out there by the standing stones, a young couple who look like hippies, long hair, hats, shades, the guy playing a guitar, both of them singing, probably tripped out on the mushrooms that grow all over the Moor here, strumming along the great hypnotic groove into oneness. No cop, though, crawling through the long grass, binoculars trained on your window. Maybe he wouldn't come at all, like couldn't get hold of a warrant this time of night. Maybe he didn't even suspect you, was just following up those I Ching letters you'd sent him, Hastie an innocent party all along. But you can't convince yourself of that, no matter how hard you try. You fucked up, Gideon, story of your life. You acted too hastily and he saw you as he fell over the side. The only reason they haven't come for you yet, they're playing it cool, checking you out on their computers, collecting evidence, building up a case tight enough to secure a warrant. So if not today, tomorrow.

Time now of the essence.

You cross to the wardrobe and fetch four of your ties. Ties you've never worn. All except the black one. You've had a lot of use for that one in the last year, funerals happening all over the place. Strangles dropping like flies everywhere you look. You cross the great water and study the grief on all their faces, like a shopping arcade, all the relatives standing round, easy pickings if you're in the mood, the Moon sucking at your bones.

You turn her over, tear at her floral-patterned dress, buttons popping and zinging all over the place. Fuck. All those buttons down the back, she must be some kind of contortionist to get dressed in the morning. Maybe that's why she always arrived late and flustered, wasn't the dogs at all, was from all the contorting she had to do just to get her dress on. Wasn't easy being a woman by the look of it. Spend all that time getting all dressed up and then some guy comes along, just rips it off her back. A hard life.

And getting harder. You drag the dress off her body, stand there amazed. No bra. No knickers. No nothing. Like, shit, she must've caught on, was playing you at your own game. All those times she was standing next to you, rubbing up against you like some cat on heat, you never thought once to imagine she might be letting the breeze rustle through her pubes and cool her bubbling cauldron. Never once. Juices probably sliding down her thighs as she stood there with a hand on your arm trying to sneak a peek at your crotch, see if anything's stirring down there. And you never knew.

Using the ties, you secure her in position, tying each hand and foot to one of the legs of the bed. You test them, pulling each one tight – bitch is one of them contortionists, you mustn't forget that. As you do so, she makes a small strangled kind of sound at the back of her throat, just below the red weal where the bruise is now beginning to show. Making those coming-round kind of noises. You draw the curtains on the burnished stones, the dancing hippies, the dying day.

'I think you've got a problem.'

'Me?' Hastie says, seemingly unconcerned that she was tied to a bed, naked, spreadeagled, guy in a mask standing naked in the doorway, spotlit, happens every day. 'Me got a problem? I don't think so, Gideon. Forgive me for being so blunt but I think maybe you're the one with the problem, you're the one should be waiting in line to see the man in the white coat.'

'I agree, Ros. I really do. I admit I have a problem keeping people alive around me. But I also think it's a little late now to go changing my ways. I've kind of grown used to the lifestyle. It suits me, suits my temperament, probably says so in my horoscope, am I right?'

Ros Hastie doesn't answer right away, she raises her head from the pillow, studies him as he stands there motionless in the doorway, naked but for the patchwork leather mask that looks more like something Ned Kelly might've worn than the sort you'd wear to a masked ball.

'I had you wrong, Gideon. I didn't think you were the kind of man into all this kinky stuff with masks and bondage. I had you down as a sensitive man, a man with a little respect for the opposite sex. Definitely not the type who comes up behind you and half-strangles you to death, then ties you to the bed while he stands over you fingering himself, drooling behind a mask.'

Gideon looks down. Yeah, she's absolutely right, he's getting all distended down there, the beast swelling out under manipulations he wasn't even conscious of. Lucky she reminded him.

Sees she needs a little reminding herself. 'I don't think you appreciate, Ros, the gravity of your situation.' Gideon enjoying himself with this verbal sparring, the fancy big words rolling off his tongue like to a manor born, adding a touch of class to the proceedings. 'I mean we're not discussing here the petty ramifications of sexual diversity. The issue on the agenda at this point in time is of a much more serious nature and one I feel you should take on board with a certain degree of alacrity if I were you.'

'For God's sake, Gideon, what on earth are you talking about? Have you totally lost your senses?'

'In a manner of speaking, I suppose I have. There are those who are even tempted to call me crazy, a moon-howler of the highest order, bats in the belfry guaranteed.' Gideon smiles into his mask. Nice touch that. Getting into the flow of it now. 'Your friend, for example, the nice policeman, the one you're on such intimate terms with. He believes I'm a paranoid schizophrenic

451

with delusions of grandeur, that I don't know how to relate to people unless they're dead.'

'I think you've gone far enough now, Gideon.' Using the mother voice now, trying to make him feel small. 'Untie me, please, and give me back my clothes. I'll be on my way and we won't mention this unfortunate incident again.'

Still hasn't got the message yet. Like what's he got to do to make her understand that it's all over, end of game, she won't be picking up any trophies or ever going home again? Impress it upon her, obviously, in a way she can't fail to understand.

Gideon enters the room, leaving the door open, the hall light capturing her now in a yellow coffin on the bed. He approaches, still in hand, to stand over her. The black gauze eyeholes of the mask diffuse the light, put the world a touch out of focus. Seeing her the way a fly might, made up of millions of tiny dots. He sits on the edge of the bed, admires the view.

'You shave that yourself?' Gideon asks. 'Like sit in front of a mirror, rub the shaving cream in, cut and shape it all on your own? I mean, I'm not criticising, I like it. The heart shape's a novel touch, goes so well with your red hair. You could patent the idea, like start up a business, call yourself a pube technician or something. What d'you think?'

She's looking at him now like he's insane, giving him the same kind of look Simone gave him, trying hard not to believe anything's seriously off kilter, still deluding herself she's going to climb off that bed without having to endure a little pain.

'You're insane, Gideon. I warn you, the longer this goes on, the worse it's going to be for you.'

'Simone. Did I ever tell you about Simone?'

'No, you didn't.' Patronising him now. 'Perhaps you forgot, with all the stress you're obviously suffering from.'

Swelling up nicely in his hand now, he notices. She can't tear her eyes from it, doubtless never seen one this size before.

'Takes a while for it to fill all that tissue with blood,' Gideon tells her. 'If I rush it, go too fast, I'll probably starve my brain of oxygen, faint on the spot. Happened once before, you know, with Simone. Put it straight in her mouth and that was me, gone, lucky I was already lying down at the time.'

'You're sick, Gideon. You need help.'

'You're right. I need help holding this damn thing up. Simone said it was the biggest one she'd ever seen, and you can take my word for it, she'd seen a few.'

'It's not the size that counts,' Ros Hastie sneers, 'it's what you do with it.'

'Which figures,' Gideon replies. 'Simone used to say that the woman who says size doesn't count is either a virgin or married to a poodle. You a virgin, Ros-a-lind, or talking about one of your pet poodles?'

She has nothing to say. Run right out of words. Which means maybe she's getting the picture now, coming to terms with the fact that dinner is going to be her.

'You ever do it with a dog, Ros-a-lind? One of them big Alsatians you look after?' Giving him the silent treatment now, the baleful glares. Any second now, he can feel it, he's going to burst out crying. 'Or maybe you prefer pack sex, put on a show for all the jumpy little bitches, show 'em how it's really done? That what you're into?'

No reply. She's beginning to get on his tits now. What did he ever see in her? he wonders. All those wild fantasies, love and marriage, couple of kids fighting in the yard, what the hell had he been thinking of? Must be going mad, loosing a few slates off the old church roof.

'Okay, no problem. You don't feel you can contribute to the conversation, fair enough, you probably have a lot on your mind right now. I can appreciate that.' Gideon reaches into his bedside-table drawer, scrabbles around, comes out with a tube of lipstick. Scarlet Extra Gloss, for those extra-special occasions. 'What I can't appreciate is the way you went behind my back, informed on me to that nice policeman. You betrayed my trust. So it's not exactly my fault, Rosie, that you lie here in what

453

some might call a rather unenviable predicament. Not my fault at all.'

Gideon begins to apply the lipstick. She squirms, jerks her head away, leaving a glossy red track across her cheek. Gideon has to slap her, pinch her nipple hard, to get her attention. He gets it all right, and more.

'Pucker,' he says, and she puckers. He licks his finger and wipes away the smears. That looks much better, gives her rather lacklustre lips a semblance of life. Tears well in her eyes, ready to overflow. Good. Gideon likes the tears bit, it always makes him harder, like hot to hump.

'Now, you see, I don't have any choice. I need to know what you two've been plotting behind my back. It's what we call the need-to-know basis. I need to know, and if you don't assist me in my enquiries right away then I shall be forced to resort to tactics one of us is going to find rather distasteful, not to mention painful. Do I make myself clear, Rosie?'

'You're mad!'

'Of course, you're entitled to your opinion. I'm a fair man. Freedom of speech is the cornerstone of our great British democracy – where there is discord, let there be harmony, that kind of thing. So feel free to speak to me, pour your little heart out. Gideon is all ears.'

Rosalind Hastie starts babbling, the words tumbling over themselves in the scramble to come out. 'He wanted to borrow a book, that was all. The *I Ching*. He never said why, just that he'd pick it up later. That's all I know, honest!'

Dear oh dear. Not getting through at all. Gideon sighs, then straddles her, kneeling, buttocks on her heart-shaped mound, beast swinging like a metronome, hypnotising her. Ten and a half inches long, last time Simone measured it, circumference of seven. Even named a fucking shop after you, What Every Woman Wants.

'Let me tell you a little bedtime story, put you in the picture,' he says, still keeping calm, his tone polite and conversational,

another cup of tea, vicar? kind of thing. 'Are you lying comfortably? Good, then I'll begin. Once upon a time there was
a bitch called Simone. She looked a bit like you, Rosie, slim,
long red hair, green eyes, you know, freckles across her nose,
nice pair of legs. Only she had tits you could get a hold of, had a
bit of life in them, didn't just lie there like someone let out all the
air. Anyway. She was a social-work-type person, which meant
all she could ever think about was sex. She like took me in hand,
as it were. I was twelve, she was twenty-six. I was a big boy even
then. She showed me the way, she did, took my virginity,
became my special tutor. But there was this other side to her,
Ros, a mean side. Like my mother, she had to put people down
to enhance her own self-esteem. She had to debase them, exert
her power, hurt them. It turned her on. Which was where the
whole thing kind of fell apart. Me, see, all these power games
you bitches like to play, give me the world's biggest hard-off.
You think you can just fuck around with our heads and that's
the end of it, we're going to forget all about it, carry on with our
lives the way they were before you came storming into them
with your eager little plans and greedy little cunts—'

'Get to the point,' Hastie interrupts with a sneer.

Obviously he has to slap her a couple of times. Like she's
asking for it. Isn't that just typical? Like it's some basic ingrown
need bitches have to be humiliated. Punishment for all the guilt
they feel because they want what they can't have. What book
was that in? Or was it the cop, the nice policeman, the time he'd
come up and told Gideon all about the Fangman? He'd
mentioned guilt and punishment, that much is certain, so
maybe it's just the same thing but wrapped in different clothes.
Anyway. Get to the point, she says.

'The point is this. The very tip of the point is I don't forget. I
don't forgive and I never forget.' Which is a lie, but since Hastie
doesn't know about the black hole swallowing up large chunks
of his memory, it doesn't matter. 'I met her again, lot of water
under the bridge but she was basically still the same, couldn't

wait to bewitch me again. So, why not, I went along for the ride. Invited her out here for a weekend, come and see the pottery, what a success I was making for myself, the fruits of all her labours back in the Aphelion Centre. She's married by now, a couple of brats under her wing, so she tells the husband she's going to some social-work conference down south, then heads over here. You maybe saw it on the news at the time, how she went missing, just vanished off the face of the earth? Well, now you know. She ended up down in the chamber.'

Hastie's looking at him peculiar, something between a frown and disgust on her face. Then Gideon realises she's never been down in the chamber, doesn't even know it's there beneath the pottery.

'The chamber's a special place, Ros, a very special place. You'll see it later. It's where I keep all my souvenirs – and, of course, the kiln where I calcinated Simone. Am I getting to the point fast enough now?'

'You killed all those poor women . . .' A genuine sadness in her voice, thinking about all the strangles rather than herself. 'And poor old Arthur Thomas.'

'At last,' Gideon exclaims. 'I thought for a while I was going to have to draw you pictures.'

'Frank McMorran will find you, Gideon. He'll come here looking for me.'

'He may. But he won't find you. No one will ever find you. It'll be just like Simone all over again.'

'You burnt her in your kiln?'

'Now you're getting there. See what a little imagination does?' Gideon can feel it gathering down there at the base of his balls. Waiting for the big spurt. A globule of cum oozing out already on to the glistening crimson knob. 'The difference this time round is due to the advance of technology. When Simone burned, I didn't have the benefit of a computerised timer. So you can consider yourself an experiment, Ros, a pioneer in state-of-the-art pottery. You should feel honoured.'

Yup, she's using that fertile imagination of hers now. Something looks a lot like pantie-filling fear peering out her eyes. The business, in fact.

Lift-off.

Spurt, spurt, spurt.

Book Four

The Clinging Fire

36

'I told you so.'

'You certainly have,' I said. 'At least five times. You must be going for the record in the world's longest gloat.'

Only a few days ago we did most of our talking across a table or sitting at a bar. Now it seemed we had no use for bars or tables, did all our talking in bed – that is, when we could find the breath. Funny that.

'But it's true!' Kyoko said, propped on an elbow, hair all mussed. 'You only went out there to humour me. You didn't believe me for a second. I saw the look on your face when I called it intuition.'

'Okay, so maybe I was a little sceptical.'

She punched my arm, working on a new bruise now. 'Is that why you almost wet yourself laughing?'

'I might have giggled. But that was the wine laughing, not me. You know how much respect I have for—'

'Yourself. Exactly,' Kyoko said, prodding me. 'That's the point I'm trying to make. In this country, if you're a crazy old man, they call you eccentric, and if you're a crazy old woman they call you a crazy old bat. Same thing – you have a hunch, you take it so seriously you'd risk your future on it, but when I tell you about my intuition, you look at me like I'm in league with the fairies. So damn right I'm going to tell you I told you so.'

'Okay, okay,' I said, 'I submit.'

'That's more like it.' She was astride me in a flash, pinning my wrists to the pillow. 'Submissive is how I like my men.' She smothered my mouth with hers, tongue probing deep. To this kind of torture I was more than willing to submit.

Some time later. She lay on her back blowing smoke rings at the ceiling, me propped by pillows, chewing on peanut-buttered toast.

Kyoko said, 'So I can now tell my uncle there'll be no more sheep in water-tanks?'

'Tell him the Ovine Avenger has once more made the island a safe place for ordinary sheep to carry on their daily lives in peace. There shall be no more bleating in the glens, upon that you have my word.'

'And Maggie? What'll happen to her?'

'Depends on Farquharson,' I said. 'But I think he'll see the wisdom of letting sleeping sheep lie.'

'You have to tell him?'

'Mm,' I said through a mouthful of toast. ''Fraid so. I've arranged to see him tomorrow afternoon. Should be fun.'

After a few moments' silence, in which Kyoko stubbed out her cigarette and rolled over on her side, she said, 'You know, I still can't imagine Maggie doing a thing like that. Cutting that poor sheep's throat.'

'She didn't. That's how she found it down on the Imacher shore. Somebody else killed it, then dumped it over the sea wall.'

'Thank God for that,' Kyoko sighed. 'Do you know who the sheep belonged to yet?'

'Farmer down near Machrie Moor. Said it went missing three weeks ago.' The second farmer I'd phoned after returning to the station. Blamed it on the cultists, his manner suggesting he blamed them for everything including the weather.

'Which reminds me,' Kyoko said, 'I still have to pick up that pot. He said he'd phone me when it was ready but maybe he's forgotten.'

'Shit,' I exclaimed, glancing at the clock, then jumping from bed. 'I was supposed to pick up that book this evening.' I crossed to the telephone, dialled Hastie's home number. It rang and rang. After four minutes, still no reply. I dialled the pottery. No reply there either. 'Shit,' I said again, a sudden knot of foreboding tightening in my stomach as I stood wondering what to do.

Kyoko held up the cover. 'Come back to bed, Francis, there's nothing you can do about it now. The book'll wait, you know, it won't run away.'

She was right. There was nothing I could do about it now. Maybe Hastie had just gone to bed early, unplugged her phone. I slipped back beneath the cover but could still not quell the sense of unease I felt. What if Byrne had . . . No, I told myself, stop. If I started on the what ifs I'd be awake all night, wasting my time. I pulled Kyoko to me and she snuggled in close, her warm breath on my chest.

'I want you to promise me something,' I said.

'That sounds ominous.'

'When you go to pick up that pot, you don't go alone. You let me come with you, okay?'

She leant her head back to look up at me. 'Do I detect a spark of jealousy, Francis?' she teased. 'Don't you trust me alone with that charming man?'

'Seriously, Kyoko. I mean it. There are things going on here of which you're unaware. I don't want you getting involved.'

'I can look after myself.'

'Look,' I said, 'I'll buy you another pot. We can go up to the pottery I visited this morning, woman there has plenty of pots you'll like just as much.'

'How do you know what I'll like?'

No answer to that, so I said, 'I bought you one this morning but stupidly left it back at the station.'

'I've never seen a glaze like the one out at Machrie Moor. That's why I asked him to make me one. Now you're implying . . . Well, I don't know what you're implying. Has the charming potter done something wrong?'

'I'm trying not to imply anything. I'm asking you a favour, that's all.' I left it at that, feeling if I pushed any further, it'd have the adverse effect. Anyway, I thought, if all went well Byrne would be under arrest long before he finished her pot. And, chances were, he had a lot more to worry about right now than completing a one-off commission. So I told Kyoko what Jenny Howitt had said about Byrne using a lot of bone-ash in his glazes, asked if her grandfather had also done so.

'Of course,' she said, not entirely mollified. 'Though not as much as wood-ash. He preferred to use the traditional stoneware glazes of his village using ground local stone. *Kaki*, a rust-red glaze; and *tenmoku*, a rich black one, using wood-ash.'

'I mean, I've heard of bone-ash before,' I said, 'but just never imagined it was real bones, ground down. What are they, animal bones?'

'Cattle, usually. You know, cows, horses, sheep.'

'And you what, buy it ready-made?'

'Sure. The percentage you use in a glaze is pretty low, from maybe one to fifteen per cent. A couple of kilo-bags is going to last you a while.'

'Could you use human bones?' I asked with an air of levity I did not feel. 'Like would human bone-ash have a different effect than animal bone-ash?'

'God, you're morbid!' Kyoko laughed, shaking her head.

'It's what you like about me.'

'Among other things,' she said, hand wandering beneath the cover. 'But to answer your question, I don't think so. I imagine all bones, human and animal, are made from the same stuff, and therefore the effect would be the same.' I squirmed sensuously beneath her gentle manipulations. 'But it reminds me, though, of a story my grandfather once told me. I can't remember too much of the detail, but it's set back in China's Sung Dynasty, and is centred around a master potter whose talents are only mediocre compared to the heavy-handedness with which he treats his young apprentice, an orphan. One little mistake and the apprentice is severely punished by the master. Anyway, it's the habit of the master to leave all the work to his apprentice while he goes off doing whatever it is master potters and policemen do when they're not being conscientious – womanising, drinking, gambling, you tell me.' A little nudge, a soft squeeze, a peck of a kiss before she continued. 'So before the master goes off on one of his excursions, he tells the apprentice to finish off what is a very important job, a special commission for the Emperor. But while the master is away, a tragedy occurs, and the apprentice accidentally breaks one of the Emperor's pots. When the master returns a few days later in time for the Emperor's arrival, he finds the kiln has been fired but the apprentice has disappeared. When he unpacks the kiln, though, he finds inside one amazingly glazed pot. He can't understand what's going on. He can't find the Emperor's pot. He can't find his apprentice, all he's got is a single pot, the beauty of which he has never seen anywhere before. By this time, though, it's too late to start another pot for the Emperor, so when the Emperor eventually arrives, the master potter offers him instead the pot with the amazing glaze, hoping it will be a more than acceptable substitute. He is right. The Emperor is immediately taken by the pot, so much so that he orders that the potter make him another one, identical, so that brother and sister pot could sit one on each side of his throne. He tells the potter he will return in six months to collect the sister pot, and then departs amidst a swirl of entourage.'

'You tell a good story,' I said, lying there with my eyes closed, carried by the sound of her voice, drawn into the story, picturing the wooden shack with its earthen floor, the simple wheel, the pots stacked against the walls, the master bastard standing there scratching his balding head as he watches the Emperor's back disappear through the doorway, wondering what the fuck he is going to do now; he knows what happens to those foolish enough to disappoint the Emperor, they end up on the chopping block, the wrong end of an axe.

'Go on.'

'The master potter then spends the next few months searching all across the land for his young apprentice. He thinks if he can find him, he can learn the secret of the glaze, live happily ever after on riches untold. He searches everywhere, in every city, town and village, but to no avail. Eventually he has to concede defeat and decides to return to his pottery and try to reproduce the glaze himself. He seeks advice from all the other potters in the area but no deal, he's been such an odious creep for so long, none of them want anything to do with him. Panicking, he sends word to the Emperor that, due to unforeseen circumstances, there'll be a minor delay in delivery of the sister pot. The Emperor, being an emperor, returns word that in two months' time he will send a prince to collect the pot, and that the prince will return to the Palace with either the pot or the potter's head, wasn't too fussy which.

'The potter, in despair, tries everything in the next two months, from scouring neighbouring provinces for materials to poring over his former apprentice's notes and books. Again, all to no avail. So a couple of days before the Emperor's prince is due to arrive, the master potter fires his final kiln. Rather than lose his head to the Emperor's axe, he decides instead to hurl his weary bones into the mouth of the kiln. When the prince arrives two days later, he finds the pottery empty, no sign of the master potter, no sign of the pot he is to collect. Then he notices the kiln and, seeing that it's cooling, orders it to be unbricked. And – guess what? Lo and behold, there inside, he finds the sister pot with its amazing glaze, absolutely identical to its brother. And that's it, end of story.'

I stirred after a moment, drifting up through dreamy layers of consciousness, emerging into the now feeling cleansed, my mind at ease, knowing with an absolute certainty why the Fangman took bones from the bodies of his victims.

'Anyway,' Kyoko said, 'I told you so.'

'Any particular reason?' Gideon Byrne asked, his syrupy tone enough to make me gag. 'Perhaps I can help?'

'No, just routine, I'm afraid. It's about the bike that ran down one of her dogs. If she comes in, could you tell her we have a suspect and would like her to come in and identify the bike. To phone me as soon as possible.'

'Won't be till Monday,' Byrne replied. 'She asked for a few days off, wanted to go over to the mainland, attend some kind of astrological conference over there. I told her it left me in rather a difficult position, this weekend being one of the busiest of the year, but she insisted, so what could I do?'

What you do to most of your victims, I wanted to say. Instead I asked him if Ros Hastie had mentioned where the conference was being held.

'Not a word, I'm afraid.'

'Well, thanks for your help, Mr Byrne. Have a good weekend.' A weekend he'd remember for the rest of his life, I hoped. I hung up, and looked across at Dowie.

'Well?' he said.

'Says she's taken a few days off for some astrological conference on the mainland.'

'You believe him?'

I didn't answer. I'm a cop, I don't believe *any*body. I was also in a foul mood, no particular reason, just one of those days. I'd woken late and alone, with vague recollections of Kyoko slipping from bed in the early hours, dressing, planting a lingering kiss on my lips before closing the door quietly behind her. I'd lain there for a few precious minutes assembling my thoughts, then jumped from bed and thrown on my clothes, a glance out the window at the overcast sky enough to send me digging out my waterproofs. Two minutes later I'd been mobile.

'So what do you want to do?' Dowie asked. 'If we go out there looking for her, chances are we'll spook the bastard.'

'Don't tempt me.'

'Says the man who advised patience and caution.' Dowie's mood was a reflection of my own, he just needed more practice. He stood by the window of his office, fists deep in pockets, glaring out at an afternoon that was both close and grey, clouds brighter to the east, darker to the west. 'Looks like rain,' Dowie commented, as though to himself. 'Front coming in, the weather girl said, expect heavy showers and gale-force winds.'

'Summer arrives at last.'

Dowie shook his head, off on another plane. 'I can't believe he's clean. It just doesn't ring true. I mean, you don't just become a serial killer overnight, these kind of people are in and out of YOIs most of their teens. But he's got no prison record, nothing.'

'A late developer perhaps,' I said. 'Or he's changed his name.'

Dowie's mind was in interview mode, jumping around all over the place. 'There must be some kind of stargazing society listed somewhere. We could try and find out where the conference is, check the Hastie woman really is there.'

'Why not?' I said, dropping my feet on the desk and leaning back in my chair. 'Put one of your boys on it.'

'If they ever return from lunch,' Dowie growled. He was dressed in jeans, sweatshirt and trainers, and looked almost human from a distance. Maybe the mood came with the suit, I thought. On the desk by my feet, the camera he was going to take out on to Machrie Moor the moment his two DCs returned, and a case containing three rolls of film and a telephoto lens.

I said, 'What's the latest on Fullerton's suspect?'

Dowie snorted derisively. 'You think they'd tell me?' He turned from the window and began pacing the floor, six steps turn, six steps turn. 'Seems like no one over there is prepared to say he is the Fangman, or he isn't. Everyone playing it very close to the chest. Only snippet I got, and this was from Davies when he was over yesterday, was that the suspect is now claiming he was only hanging around the supermarket car parks so he could meet his hero. He says he wanted to offer the Fangman his services and, if the Fangman was into it, work together. You believe that?'

'Sounds like the kind of thing a nut would say. A copycat. But not the Fangman.'

'My thoughts, too,' Dowie said. 'What I understand about serial killers is that usually they readily confess to their crimes. It's like a huge weight off their shoulders to be able at last to tell someone all about it. They don't try to deny it, come up with some second-rate lie. They want the glory, the headlines, it's the moment they've been waiting for.'

'And working towards.'

'Exactly,' Dowie said, kicking out at a chair and missing. 'So sod them all on the mainland – Fullerton, Kettle, the lot. I'm going out on the Moor this afternoon and I'll take pictures of the real bloody Fangman. And I'll make sure it's all in the report, too, all neatly documented how forthcoming they've been, how accommodating.'

'You do that.'

On Dowie's authority, DC Davies had spent all afternoon yesterday trying to gain half an hour's access to HOLMES in order to print up a hard copy of all the collated forensic reports. In vain. Far too busy, he was told by the duty officer; all the terminals were now concentrating on the data coming in concerning their prime suspect. No time to fart around on some wild-goose chase like the Arthur Thomas enquiry, that was yesterday's news. Come back after the weekend.

Hence Detective Sergeant Dowie's displeasure.

The first drops of rain spattered against the window, at first tentatively, then with growing confidence. Dowie kicked out at the chair again, connected, sent it crashing into the filing cabinet.

'First spot of rain in weeks,' he said, 'and I have to spend the afternoon out on the Moor. Just great. That's going to look really natural, a tourist standing out there in the pouring rain for three hours taking photos of the standing stones.'

'It'll clear,' I told him. 'Don't worry.' Well, in a couple of days perhaps, I thought with an inward smile.

'Byrne's going to look out his window and see cop.'

'All the more reason for not going into the pottery. Two decent photos are all we need, one of him, one of his car. Once you have them . . .'

'Okay, McMorran, I've got the message.' Dowie picked up the chair, set it down by the desk and sighed down on to it. 'That witness of yours, the one who saw him dumping the sheep?'

'Maggie Boyd,' I said. 'She's coming in tomorrow afternoon. I'll get her statement then.'

'And you want Farquharson along as well?'

I nodded. 'If you ask him, he'll come. If I ask him . . .'

Dowie made a brief note in his book. 'I'll see what I can do.' The outside door opened and he jumped to his feet. 'At bloody last.' He strode angrily from the room to confront his tardy DCs.

I glanced at the clock as his voice rose outside in the hall. I had twenty minutes till my appointment. Time to go. I donned my waterproofs and headed out into the rain.

I waited an hour and a half in the waiting room, read the previous week's *Arran Banner*, skimmed through long-out-of-date coffee-table magazines, then counted the tiles on the ceiling, the tiles on the floor, and was just about to give up and reach for a *Reader's Digest*, when the receptionist called my name.

Dr David Hunter rose from behind his desk to shake my hand. He had a handsome boyish face, lightly tanned and topped by sandy hair parted at the side. A pair of pince-nez hung from a cord around his neck. Last time I'd seen him, he'd been kneeling on the floor up at Ravensbank Cottage, examining the body of Arthur Thomas in his role as police surgeon.

'How's the head?' he asked, motioning me to sit.

'It's felt worse.'

'I don't doubt it.' He glanced at the file in front of him, then came round behind me, examined the stitches. 'Couple more days, then they can come out. Any headaches to complain of?'

'Not today.'

He lifted my eyelids, peered at my bloodshot eyes. 'Double vision? Trouble focusing, anything like that?'

'No more than usual.'

His laugh was professionally polite. 'Lightheadedness? Nausea?'

I shook my head.

'Loss of appetite?'

'The opposite,' I told him. 'Can't stop eating.'

'Must be love,' he smiled. He returned to his seat, flipped over a page in the file. 'How about your knee? Any problems there?'

'Apart from stiffness in the morning, none.'

'Ribs?'

'Still bruised, but it doesn't hurt any more when I breathe.'

'Good.' He made an illegible note. 'I'll make an appointment for you to come in on Monday, have those stitches taken out. Anything else I've overlooked? No? Good.' He rose again and accompanied me to the door. 'How's the sleuthing coming on? I heard you were on TV last week. Any further forward?'

I shrugged and shook his proffered hand. 'You know how it is.'

'I keep wondering about all that broken crockery,' Dr Hunter said. 'You know, around Thomas's body. I remember thinking how awfully strange it seemed at the time. As though arranged, placed there for a purpose. Have you managed to find out why?'

'We've a pretty good idea.'

He nodded thoughtfully, as though I'd suddenly made everything clear. 'Good,' he said. 'Good. I wish you the best of luck.'

It was still drizzling down when I came out of the hospital, and Holy Island across the bay was already shrouded in a heavier veil

471

of rain. I thought what the hell, it's only two minutes' ride from the hospital in Lamlash to the police station. I'd risk it without waterproofs. Two minutes later I was soaked to the skin.

Jim Tennant was busy on the phone when I arrived dripping all over the floor. He smiled, raised his eyes towards the ceiling, continued talking into the phone. 'Yes, sir, I understand that... I know... We *are* doing the best we can... If that would reassure you, sir... Yes... Yes... I'll do that...'

I peeled off my jacket, went through the back to look for a towel. Voices came from the interview room. I looked up, saw the red light on over the door. Interview in progress. The voice talking was Sergeant Yuill's. The other voice would be Julian Ryder's. I returned to the office, towelling my hair. Jim was off the phone.

'How long's he been in there?' I asked.

Tennant glanced at his watch. 'Almost forty minutes. Shouldn't be long now.'

'Having any success?'

'Monica was through a few minutes ago,' he said. 'It's looking good, she said.'

'Ryder's talking?'

'Hasn't stopped since he arrived. Yuill got hold of Ryder's girlfriend, Carol, the one he was using as an alibi. Had her waiting in here when Ryder arrived. Didn't let them talk, just ushered one out and the other in. Worked a treat.'

'Some people get all the fun.'

Tennant smiled and tossed across the form he was working on. 'Take your turn, Frank, it's about time Yuill had this urgent report that just came in.'

I glanced at the form. It was an application for a firearms certificate. I took it through the back, knocked on the door, entered.

Monica said, 'PC Frank McMorran has just entered the room, I'll pause the tape here. The time is sixteen-oh-seven.'

Ryder had both elbows on the table, hands cradling his

lowered head. Beneath his long blond fringe I could see the gloss of tears staining his cheeks. He turned his head to watch sullenly as Yuill rose and came over to the door. I handed him the sheet and he pretended to read it without a word, every now and then glancing back at Ryder as though he couldn't quite believe that the report he was reading concerned the young man he was interviewing. I stood there giving Ryder the look we usually reserve for beasties. He looked away. I asked Yuill how long and he shrugged, told me five, maybe ten minutes. I gave Monica a wink and she suppressed a smile. As I turned to leave, she unpaused the tape and said, 'Interview resumed at sixteen-ten. Present are . . .'

Back in the office, Jim asked how it went.

'He'll've thought everything he's ever done wrong was down on that piece of paper,' I said. 'At least that's what his expression said.'

'How long do you think?'

'Five, ten minutes.'

It was closer to twenty. Yuill came out first, immediately washed his hands in the sink, like a brain surgeon after a difficult operation. It was a habit I'd seen him perform several times before. Not exactly the Pontius Pilate Syndrome, but close. Ryder and Monica emerged a minute later. Monica complete with a signed statement.

'So what happens now?' Ryder demanded, manner surly.

'You bugger off out of here,' Yuill growled, 'and hope you don't ever come back.'

'What about a lift home? There's no bus for ages.'

'What about a boot up your arse, laddie?'

'But it's pissing down!'

Monica propelled him towards the door. 'Should've thought about that before you started lying,' she snarled. 'Now get the hell out!'

The moment he'd gone, she let out a yell of triumph and punched the air. 'Gotcha, ya bastard!'

Yuill, Tennant and I took it in turn to shake her hand, hug her, and kiss her cheek respectively.

'Nice one, Mo,' Yuill said. 'Calls for a little celebration, I think.' He pulled a half-bottle of single malt whisky from the bottom drawer of his desk, four plastic cups.

'You going to let me in on this,' I asked, 'or do I have to beg?'

'Beg,' Monica said, laughing.

Yuill poured a dram into each cup, handed them round. 'To Mo,' he toasted. We drank.

'And a ten stretch for Wallace,' Tennant added.

'Ten?' Monica said. 'Let's hope it's twenty.'

'So it was Wallace after all? The stepfather?'

Monica said, 'No doubt about it. Bastard almost admitted it to me when I interviewed him. Not in so many words, but in his attitude. Arrogant is not the word. He sat there smiling his way through the whole interview as though it was all a big joke. When I suggested he might be in serious trouble, he actually laughed and asked if I'd ever heard of something called proof. Like he's so sure of himself, of his hold over his family and Ryder, he just doesn't care.'

'And Ryder?' I asked. 'What's he saying?'

Yuill gulped down his whisky, spoke over his shoulder as he washed his plastic cup in the sink. 'Those cultists you witnessed out at the standing stones last week?' he said. 'Call themselves Church of the Fertile Seed, or some such nonsense. According to Ryder, Wallace is the guy in the mask you told me about, the Big Cheese, Penis Nose. You know, Prince of Potency and Son of Spermatazoa, the Lord of Lust.' Yuill chuckled as he returned his cup to the drawer, and sat down. 'Apparently he got Ryder involved in the cult when he started going out with Julia, then made Ryder one of his special acolytes, giving him just enough power to keep him nice and obedient. Ryder says Wallace was always trying to persuade him to bring Julia along, have her initiated into the sect. For reasons, I add, which are now obvious. Ryder, however, refused. Julia was his girlfriend after all, he didn't want to share *her* with anyone else, especially not her father. So Ryder found himself in a quandary. He wanted to hang on to the benefits he reaped from the sect, but by now Wallace was putting on the pressure, saying if he didn't introduce Julia soon, then he would excommunicate him – or whatever it is they do in these cults.'

'Vasectomise?' Tennant suggested.

'Whatever.' Yuill chuckled again, then continued. 'Wallace said he would also ban Ryder from ever seeing his daughter again. So Ryder took what he saw as the easy way out and dumped Julia, began seeing his present girlfriend, Carol. He then told Wallace that if he was disrobed he would tell the world about Wallace's intentions with regard to his own daughter. This little spot of blackmail seems to have checked Wallace's intentions, at least for the six months or so leading up to the rape.'

'Why the hell didn't Ryder tell us all this earlier?'

Monica said, 'Have you met Wallace? I tell you, he's not a nice piece of work. You can see the violence in his eyes, barely restrained. He's scary, Frank, has an aura of menace about him which he uses blatantly. He enjoys the effect it creates, you can see him just lapping it up, getting off on the whole big power trip.'

'So he threatened Ryder?'

Yuill nodded. 'Wallace said he'd take Ryder with him if he ever got sent down. Put him there when the rape took place.'

'What about Carol, Ryder's supposed alibi?' I asked. 'Has she made up her mind yet?'

Monica said, 'Ryder *was* with her, she now says. She was scared to admit it before because she'd told her father she was spending the night at a girlfriend's. Apparently her father doesn't approve of her relationship with Ryder, especially as Ryder works for him part-time at his store.'

'O what a tangled web we weave...'

'...when first we practise to deceive,' Monica added.

'Exactly. If it hadn't been for those two playing their silly little games, we might've had this cleared up weeks ago.'

'What do you think actually happened?'

'I think Wallace probably got drunk one night, began brooding, then came home and went into his daughter's room and raped her. Maybe his wife tried to intervene and that's when he beat her up.'

'You think it was his idea to put the blame on Ryder?'

'Almost certainly. God knows what goes on in that house, but I think his family are terrified of him. I don't see any of them standing up against him, not while he's still free.'

'What happens now?' I asked. 'You going to bring him in?'

'First thing tomorrow morning.' She winked, indicating Yuill with a flick of her head. 'Our good sergeant here has a thing about dawn raids, obviously has nothing better to do in the mornings.'

'Of course not, he's married.' I asked if they wanted an extra body along.

Sergeant Yuill shrugged, glanced at his watch, then climbed to his feet. 'Sure, why not? The more the merrier. We'll meet here oh-five-hundred hours. And wear your uniform.' He crossed to the public counter, checked out a PR, then donned his cap. 'Meanwhile, some of us have work to do.'

As the sky darkened and heavy rain now slanted in against the window, Sergeant Yuill climbed into Mike 30 and pulled out, heading south. I reached for the phone and for the third time in as many hours called Ros Hastie.

Still no answer.

37

Cramp.

The pain was excruciating, inescapable. Like nothing she had ever experienced before. Each spasm tearing through the muscles in her legs as though she was being slowly ripped apart, tissue by tissue, tendon by tortuous tendon. She could think of nothing else, her whole mind and body screaming for relief she now knew would never come. If she'd had a knife she'd've gladly sawn off both her legs if only to stop the pain. To die through loss of blood would be a blessing compared to what she knew was going to come. To sink into unconsciousness...

But Byrne, true to her astrological predictions, was as conscientious as ever in the sating of his desires. He had removed the brick from the airhole at the top of the kiln, allowing the flow of oxygen to feed her imagination – now running wild in fearful flight, unable to flee the clutches of impending death – as it would soon feed the flames that would consume her. It also meant she could hear him as he moved around the chamber talking to himself and, every now and then, to her.

'I don't know what I'm going to do without you, Ros, I really don't. I mean, in four weeks you've managed to turn the business round, make it almost profitable. I was just checking the books and we're up almost a thousand on last year's sales already, and we've still got another couple of months to go. How d'you do it, Ros, read it in the stars or what?'

It's hard to carry on a conversation when you're screaming,

not so easy to focus the mind. The air inside the kiln was heavy with clay dust. It already coated her lungs and throat, mouth and nostrils, every breath a choking rasp, like swallowing a sheet of sandpaper. If she could just forget the pain for a few minutes – well, if not forget it, at least ignore it – then perhaps she could manoeuvre her body round a bit, inch by agonising inch, angle her head up, get her face near the bunghole. Breathe some real air, oxygen for the brain, maybe get an idea, a flash of inspiration that will deliver her from this torture.

'You ever look back on your life, Ros, and wonder what might have been had you chosen another path somewhere back there?' She could hear him over by the open fireplace, rustling paper, humming to himself. 'How many different lives we could have led, how many different people we could have been? I've been thinking about it a lot lately. It's really fascinating when you get into it.'

Of course she had thought about it. It's what growing old was all about. Regrets. Wishing she knew then what she knew now. Wishing she could somehow go back to that time and place, make a different decision, embark on some exciting new adventure that didn't lead to a cramped and stifling kiln in a dark stone chamber. Wishing now she'd told him yes all those years ago, dear Timothy, the only man who ever bent his knee to her, asked for her hand in marriage. But she'd been young then, full of life's potential, and the idea of settling down with a professor in economics ten years her senior had seemed like throwing in the towel, a form of cowardice, of retirement from the human race, why not just lay down and die. But even that conventional form of suicide now seemed infinitely more preferential than the choice she had made, the path she had set out upon which had led her down that long and winding road to here, Dead End Street, the place where she would die.

Forcing from her mind the terrifying images of what would happen once the programmed computer initiated the kiln's firing process, and biting back the cries of rage, the tears of frustration, the screams of her protesting body, she squirmed a few more precious inches, her bare skin scraping raw on the brick walls and floor of the kiln. Byrne continued his monologue, his tone oddly reminiscent.

'It's like we are moulded by the world around us, yet every minute of every day we have the choice to break that mould, to form another one free from all our former restrictions. Do we, though? Change, I mean. No, the majority of us don't. They stagnate, then wonder why their lives stink. The inferior man lets himself become set in his ways, imagining there is security in intransigence. Surrounds himself in material comforts he thinks will cushion him from the harsh reality that is life at its most exciting. Senseless Ones, Ros, living in prisons of their own making. So scared of dying, they lock themselves away in their tiny castles, pull up the drawbridges, flood the moats, go down to their stuffy little dungeons and turn on the television, there to pass the livelong day with no expectations but that once in a while their cowardly justification may be proven right. You know the kind I mean, Ros?'

She was almost there. Had managed to angle her body sideways, her legs now drawn under her, not so much the foetal position, more one of supplication, the muscles no longer cramping so heavily because she'd gone numb down there, could no longer feel her calves. Already she could taste the fresher air flowing in through the bunghole. The oxygen doing the trick, knowing what she had to do now, perhaps her last and only chance.

'*In the light of the setting sun,*' Byrne was now saying, '*Men either beat the pot and sing, Or loudly bewail the approach of old age. Misfortune.* You recognise that, Ros? You should do. It's in the book you were going to give to that nice policeman. I think it's kind of fitting, don't you, considering all we've just been discussing. The reading makes it clearer, though, less of all that Confucian imagery crap. I'll read it to you, it may give you courage in your dwindling hours of need. It says, *Here the end of the day has come. The light of the setting sun calls to mind the fact that life is transitory and conditional. Caught in this eternal bondage, men are usually robbed of their inner freedom as well. The sense of the transitoriness of life impels them to uninhibited revelry in order to enjoy life while it lasts, or else they yield to melancholy and spoil the precious time by lamenting the approach of old age. Both attitudes are wrong. To the superior man it makes no difference whether death comes early or late. He cultivates himself, awaits his allotted time, and in this way secures his fate.* Well, what d'you think, Ros? Have you cultivated yourself enough to secure your fate?'

She'd been still now for almost five minutes, moving not a fraction, controlling her breathing, keeping it slow and quiet, choking off the cries of spasmodic pain by jamming her bicep into her mouth, biting down hard enough to draw blood. It appeared to be working.

'Ros? You still there? You've gone awfully quiet. I hope you're not sulking, that would really shatter my good impression of you. Ros?'

She heard his footsteps cross to the kiln and stop. He was listening. She held her breath. For what seemed like an eternity. Had to force her thoughts away from the intense pressure building in her chest. To self-recrimination. Like why had she been so blind? Poring over his chart for the last two weeks, she should have recognised the signs, known him for what he was. Scorpio. The Scorpion. Symbol of death, mutilation and regeneration. Influences the kidneys and genitals. The stone, the fiery red carbuncle, representing bloodshed. Scorpio. Him with his Capricorn ascendant and Saturn conjunct. Hardly surprising then that he was an extremely, powerfully, saturnine man. He wasn't physically dark, but yes, she had witnessed the sombre moods, the long brooding silences. And he *was* very heavily built, had strong hands, and was determined if not totally stubborn. Also true to form, he was absolutely deadly serious and earnest in his life's work and, so it would now

480

appear, in his perversions. She should have recognised the signs as soon as she saw them and kept well away.

'Ros? Talk to me, Ros. I know you're in there.'

But no, she always knew better, always liked to see the good in people, would concentrate on that, pretend the dark side of their characters didn't exist. But there was more to it than that. She had to admit it, the dark side also intrigued her. The fear of the unknown like some kind of aphrodisiac worming through her veins, stimulating those secret places in her mind she seldom dared explore, even in fantasy.

'I can hear you breathing, Ros. I can hear your gorgeous little heart a-fluttering in your chest, so stop playing games and be a good girl, tell me you're still alive.'

And then, of course, there was the Mercury square Uranus in his chart. Which suggested he was opinionated, eccentric, very ingenious, intellectual, arrogant, and liked to deceive authorities. Also that he was discontented and had self-exalting beliefs. Like the size of his Thomas, for example.

Up there in his bedroom, him behind his mask – like he couldn't face her, let her see him as he really was – and playing with himself, calling it 'beast' and bragging how big it was the last time the woman Simone measured it. Ten and a half inches? She would have laughed if her situation hadn't been so precarious at the time. Laughed her head off. Talk about self-delusion. Byrne could count himself lucky if he had four inches to get a hold of. Him talking about poodle-dicks and wondering if she did it with her Alsatians, and she thinking at the time how she'd probably get more satisfaction from one of them than from four of the likes of Byrne. When he'd eventually stopped playing his power games and had climbed on top of her – well, exactly, that proved it, he'd deflated faster than a burst balloon. Had then exploded in a tantrum of violence, punching and kicking her, blaming it all on her, calling her bitch this, bitch that, all the whores under the sun. Then he'd dragged her out of the house by her hair, across the yard, down here into this

481

gruesome chamber with its bare stone walls and open fire and display of human skulls on a shrine in the corner. Two, maybe three hours ago now.

'Ros?' He was standing in front of the kiln door, doubt clearly evident in his voice.

Any second now and he'd open the door. At least she hoped he would. And in that split second she would summon all the strength at her command and launch herself through the door and out into the chamber. Try to grab a piece of him and hurt him so bad he'd . . . Well, whatever. That was her plan, pathetic as it was. Better not to think about her useless numb legs and stuff like that. Think positive. Stop worrying about Bundle and Puffin and Loppy and Lindy, and who's going to look after them and feed them when you're gone . . . Think positive – and act.

'Okay, Ros. I'm going to open the door. But I'm warning you . . .'

And there it was, the soft click as the door disengaged. The moment was now. She hurled herself forward, a yell exploding from her aching lungs as her shoulder hit the door and sent it flying into Byrne. A jumble of snapshot images as she tumbled from the kiln on to the stone floor, Byrne staggering back, clutching his face, the kiln door swinging, the flicker of the open fire, candles glowing around the shrine of skulls, Byrne cursing now, raging, one hand still holding his cheek, the other bunched into a wildly swinging fist as she scrambled about on the floor trying to find her legs which were there somewhere below her waist, she could see them, could see the bruises from his earlier assault, the grazes where she'd scraped away the skin trying to manoeuvre in the kiln, but they would not function, they would not obey the screamed commands from her mind to get up off the floor, to stand, to run, to get her the hell out of this nightmare, they just lay there like dead joints of meat on a butcher's slab, useless, totally useless.

And then he was upon her, the blows and kicks raining in, her world a sudden whirlwind in which she was tossed like so much chaff from wall to floor to wall and back again, all the while his voice rising, the fury blazing from his eyes, not human now, not animal, worse than anything she had ever witnessed, just evil, pure evil looking out at her, devouring her, eating her alive.

'So inconsiderate. Isn't that typical. Just like a bitch. All you can think of is yourself. Me, me, me, selfish to the bloody core. No consideration at all, how I might feel. Eh?' *Kick*. 'Eh?' *Kick*. 'Never mind that I've got an early rise in the morning, things to do across on the mainland far more fucking important than the small matter of your ineffectual little life. Never mind I've now got to worry about a fucking cop sniffing round my heels because you thought it would be a good idea to help him put me away someplace where they can silence me with drugs and put me under a microscope and find out what makes a superior man superior. Never mind all that. I can handle it. I've secured my fate, Ros-a-lind, I don't care if death comes walking through that door right this minute, I'm cultivated. I'm that kind of guy, I cultivate and I crop. I've got them all waiting for me across the great water, they're mine, you understand, my people, they belong to me, I own them the same way I own you, every little bit of you is mine to do what I bloody well will with, you're just a doll, bitch, a rag doll I'm going to play with and then just toss away.' He grabbed her by the hair and dragged her back across the floor to the kiln.

That was when she really began to scream.

38

Drizzle seeped from the grim leaden sky, the early morning already veiled in shades of grey that set the sombre mood for the day. A day for mourning another summer come and gone, strangled in its infancy.

The milkman left four pints of milk and two cartons of cream on the door step, collected the half-dozen empties and made his way back down the concrete path to his float. For the second time in as many days I was up with the birds and, for the third time in as many minutes, Sergeant Adam Yuill glanced at his watch.

'Five minutes,' he said. 'Then we go in.'

We were parked fifty yards away and on the opposite side of the street from the Wallace house, engine running and fans on.

'Monica and I'll take the front,' Yuill said. 'You, Frank, take the back. Soon as the door's answered, come in.'

'And if the door's locked?'

'Kick it down.'

'Alternatively,' Monica said, turning in her seat, 'there's a key under the plant pot to the right of the door. I saw Mrs Wallace use it the other day.'

'Where,' I said, 'is the fun in that?'

Monica shook her head ruefully. 'Who'd be a man?'

The milk float whined down the street, the driver casting us a long, curious look as he passed. He couldn't have seen much through the rain-speckled windows, just three dark shapes fidgeting nervously as the seconds ticked by. A minute later and the street was once again cushioned in silence.

'Two minutes.'

Between the nearest two houses and through the hanging gauze of mist, I could just make out the slate-grey waters of Drumadoon Bay. Distant Kintyre was but a vague blur, so vague it could well have been just a product of my imagination.

'I'll cuff him up,' Yuill said to Monica, 'and you can read him the statement, okay?'

'You've already gone over it twice.'

'Just making sure.' He glanced at his watch again. 'Okay, that's it, let's make hay.'

'Make hay?' Monica smiled, then put the car in gear and fired us across the road to the end of the Wallaces' drive, braked with a squeal of rubber that almost put Yuill through the windscreen.

'Jesus Christ!' he exclaimed. 'We're not the bloody Flying Squad, Mo!'

'Slip of the foot,' she said with a twitch of a grin. 'Sorry.'

We climbed out, donned our caps, and closed the car doors silently. Were just about to make our way up the short drive when the front door opened and Wallace appeared in his dressing gown and pyjamas. He bent down and picked up the four bottles of milk, straightened, then suddenly noticed us standing there watching him. For a moment he just stood on the step, his eyes popping, jaw hanging, caught like a rabbit on a runway, not knowing which way to run.

But run he did.

The bottles smashed on the doorstep, the front door slammed. Monica was already in motion. Yuill close behind. I didn't need telling. I leapt a low trellised fence, sprinted down the concrete path along the side of the house, hurtled round the corner. As I arrived at the back door, I heard the front one crash open, the sound of more breaking glass. Somewhere in the house a woman screamed.

I tried the door. It was locked. I stepped back and kicked it just above the lock with all my force. It burst open and almost caught me on the rebound as I dived inside. I ran through the kitchen and found myself in the hall. There were screams and shouts coming now from upstairs, footsteps heavy overhead. And then the threat we dread the most, isolated, it seemed, from all the other commotion, a quiet pool of deadly reason amidst all the chaos.

'I've got a gun!' Wallace yelled. 'I'll kill her, I will!'

Then Monica's voice. 'Hold it, Sarge, he's got a gun!'

I was at the foot of the stairs, looking up at Yuill. He motioned me to stay where I was.

A door slammed. 'Come in here and I'll blow her fucking head off!'

Yuill: 'Where is he?'

'In the bedroom,' Monica said. 'He's got his wife in there.'

'And the gun?'

'Looks like a shotgun. Shit!'

'Where are the kids?'

'The room over there.'

'Get them. Hurry!'

A moment later, Yuill was carrying them down the stairs. Bobby and Julia, still half-asleep, not knowing what the hell was going on. I took Bobby from Yuill, carried him into the living room, deposited him on the sofa. Yuill was telling Julia to be a brave girl and look after Bobby, everything would be all right in a minute, just to stay in here and not open the door.

'Jesus!' he exclaimed outside the door. 'This is all we fucking need.' He yelled up the stairs. 'Mo? You all right?'

'Sir!'

'Keep away from the door, let me know the moment he moves.' He turned back to me. 'Frank. Any suggestions?'

'How about a nice cup of tea?' I said. 'As long as he's stuck up there, Wallace is going nowhere.'

'You mean we sit and wait? Wait for bloody what? It's not like we can just call up an Armed Response Unit, have them here in a matter of minutes. It could take them hours. By that time it might be too late for Mrs Wallace.'

'Okay. So we talk him out. First, we want him out of that bedroom and down the stairs.'

'How the hell do we manage that?'

I was just about to reply when Monica yelled that the door was opening.

'No! Please! Get back!' The voice was Mrs Wallace's, trembling in desperation. 'He's coming out. If you try to stop him, he'll kill me. Please don't try anything, just do as he says. I don't want to die.'

'Okay, Irene, don't worry.' Monica sounded calm, her voice full of authority. 'You're not going to die. Everything's going to be fine. Look. See? I'm moving away. I'm going down the stairs now, no one's going to stop him, just relax, just relax.'

Wallace's voice now. 'One wrong move and she gets it, copper! You understand that?' Desperation at screaming pitch.

'I understand.'

'Now toss your radio on the landing. There, where I can see it.'

Monica glanced down at us, the question in her eyes. Yuill nodded. She dropped her PR on the landing.

'Now back away. Downstairs. Move!'

She joined us at the foot of the stairs. Whispered to Yuill, 'Where's yours?' Meaning his radio. He jerked his head ruefully towards the car. 'Great,' she said. 'Now what?'

Wallace appeared on the landing, arm round his wife's neck, twin barrels at her throat. Her eyes were red, her cheeks stained with tears, her nightie torn from neck to breast.

'Where're the kids?' he demanded.

'Living room,' I said.

He squinted at me menacingly as he deliberated. I kept my eyes on his, but my concentration firmly on his right arm and shoulder. If he was going to bring the shotgun to bear, I would see the first movement there. He reached a decision.

'Okay,' he said. 'All of you into the living room. Slowly. Keep your hands where I can see them.'

We backed into the living room, a shuffled retreat as he descended the stairs, keeping us all in sight. Bobby and Julia were still huddled together on the sofa, the small boy snivelling in his sister's arms. We stood in the middle of the room and waited while Wallace edged himself and his wife through the door. It was a large, airy room, with deep, wide windows letting in all the poor light the morning had to offer. Modern furniture, beige carpet, video and large TV in one corner, hi-fi in another, family snapshots on the mantelpiece over a coal-effect fire, coffee table in the centre of the three-piece suite.

Wallace said, 'Bobby, Julia, go sit on that armchair.' When they didn't move, he bellowed, 'Do as I bloody say!' They almost jumped from the settee.

'Right. You three. Over on the couch.'

We sat, each of us aware, I think, that we'd totally lost the initiative. The settee was deep and soft, discouraging any thoughts of sudden action. He had us exactly where he wanted. Or so he thought.

I said, 'Now what, Jack?'

'Shut up and let me think!'

'Not much to think about, Jack, is there really? I mean, what are your choices? The moment you picked up that gun, you narrowed them down to live or die, simple as that.'

He shook his wife as though rubbing her in our faces and hissed through gritted teeth, 'Haven't you forgotten something, copper?'

'I'm talking about you, Jack, not your wife. Irene doesn't have much choice right at this moment. But you do, Jack.'

'I want your car.'

'Jack, where the hell's your head, man, Planet Jupiter? This is Arran, remember, tiny wee island in the Clyde? It's not Hollywood, it's not New York, it's not even Glasgow. You've got to understand that no one's going to lay on a jumbo jet, let alone a ferry, to take you away from here. No way. You're stuck here, Jack, this is as far as you go. Any decisions you're going to make, you're going to have to make them right here. And soon.'

'Aye?' Wallace sneered. 'Why soon? I've got all fucking day.'

'Because soon is when the Armed Response Units arrive.' I glanced at Yuill. 'How long d'you reckon?'

The Sergeant shrugged. 'Fifteen, maybe twenty minutes.' He did not look a happy man. Probably thinking about the PR he'd left in Mike 30, how it would look in the report he'd have to write.

'There you go, Jack,' I said. 'Fifteen minutes make-your-mind-up time.'

'Shut the fuck up, you!'

I held up my hands in a placatory gesture. 'Hey, I understand, Jack, it's okay. You need to mull it over. That's good thinking. It's not an easy decision, live or die. Deserves careful consideration. These guys from the ARU are not always the crack shots they're made out to be. Those clean kills you see on TV, the sniper takes the guy out with a clean head shot ... pure fantasy, Jack. These guys spend all day sitting in a car waiting to respond, by the time they get to a scene they're nervy, jumpy as hell. I've seen them – fuck, even *I've* got steadier hands with the world's worst hangover than most of them.'

Wallace stared at me open mouthed. I could almost see his mind lurching to keep up. I was disappointed. I'd expected, I don't know, someone bigger, meaner, the real thing. A couple of crazed eyes and drooling lips. But Wallace? Nothing but a runt. Medium build, stocky, with short red hair, thinning on top. Darting narrow eyes set astride a sharp broken nose, mouth a Ralph Steadman gash above a chin like an executioner's block. I'd met his kind before and already I despised him.

Monica said, 'That guy in Paisley, was it, last year? Holding the hostages in the bank? Thought he had it all worked out, came out the bank to climb in a van, first shot took off one of his ears, second took his arm off, the one with the gun, just below

490

the shoulder, third caught him in the knee. He just kind of stood there with this stupid look on his face, not understanding what the hell was going on.'

'That's right,' I said. 'And the fourth one took off the top of his head. Which was not a pretty sight.'

Yuill had this look on his face, one of total disbelief. He followed our conversation as though watching a game of tennis, about to say something but always a step behind.

'Not that they go for the head shot any more,' Monica said, leaning forward on the sofa, ignoring Wallace as though he wasn't even there, all of us here on a social visit, chatting over a cup of tea, nights are fair drawin' in, wouldn't you say? 'They've got a new training video I managed to get a peek at last time I was across. Seems some criminal psychologist somewhere has come up with the theory that if you shoot a guy's bollocks off, he's going to go down quicker than any head or heart shot. Something to do with the instinct for survival.'

'I've heard about it,' I told her, 'but never saw the video.'

Monica screwed up her face in disgust. 'Wasn't very nice, Frank, the guy took a long time dying. He was in some pain, too. Marksman must've taken out half his intestine as well, those nickel-plated bullets they use. I hear they kind of flatten out on impact, dum-dum style, tear a hole big enough to drive a tractor through. Ugh.'

'Just shut it,' Wallace roared, 'the pair of you!'

'Jack,' I said, 'you don't seem to understand. We're none of us going anywhere. We're all in this together, whether we like it or not.' Create bonds, the manual says, personalise the situation. 'You might as well get used to the idea, Jack. You've about ten minutes left before the troops arrive. If you've still got that gun in your hand by then, you'll die, no doubt about it. But if you put it away before they arrive, just drop it on the floor there, we'll pretend it never happened.' I turned to Yuill. 'Isn't that right, Sarge?'

Yuill nodded sagely and said, 'Let's not make it any worse

491

than it is, Jack. You put down the weapon and we'll forget it was even here. We'll just place you under arrest and walk out of here, no one will be any the wiser. What do you say, Jack?'

'I say you're full of shit, copper!'

But there was now a subtle lack of conviction in his voice, a tiny worm of doubt. That's what selling is all about, sowing the seeds of doubt. We were trying to sell Wallace something he didn't appear to want – life, and the next ten years or so in prison – and, like any good salesperson, we would lie through our smarmy teeth to make that sale.

'He's telling you the truth, Jack,' Monica said. 'Put the gun down and we'll talk this through sensibly, see if we can work something out. Maybe even put a good word in for you, tell the procurator how helpful you were. You see what I mean, Jack? You help us, we help you.'

'You know what these mainland cops are like, Jack, they're not going to give a shit about you.' Yuill, getting into the swing of it now. 'But we do. We live here, we're all in the same boat. We know what it's like, how the pressures can get to you. You need us, Jack, more than you've ever needed anyone else.'

Wallace's eyes darted from Monica to Yuill to me and back again. 'How do I know I can trust you?'

The first crack in the dam wall.

'I was in a similar situation in Inverness once,' Monica said, her tone cooly reminiscent. 'Just like this, only the man'd already killed his wife, she was lying there in a pool of blood when I arrived, first on the scene. He stood about as far away from me as you are now, Jack, had the barrel of the shotgun pressed under his chin, screamed he was going to blow his head off. You know what I said to him, Jack?'

'What?' Said with grudging interest.

'I said, "Go on, Uncle John, do me the favour."'

She'd never talked about it before. Now I understood why.

Yuill asked softly, 'What happened, Mo?' Like Wallace wasn't there, all attention, even his, focused on Monica.

492

'He pulled the trigger,' she said in almost a whisper. 'Took his whole face off. Bits of teeth and bone stuck in the ceiling, his nose . . .'

'Jesus.'

Silence in the room for several long seconds.

'He survived, though. Is still alive now, if you call being a vegetable "alive". Missed most of his brain. He can still hear, though. The doctors say he understands what's going on.' Monica sighed, rubbed an eye with a fingertip. 'So I used to go up there to the hospital, talk to him. Tell him how much I hated him. I told him my aunt had survived, and would tell him all these stories about what she was doing, how much she was enjoying life now that he was out of the way, how she'd remarried, this French businessman, and now jetted all over the world, life one big holiday. I'd tell him all this and watch his eyes, hoping to catch the slightest glimmer of response there. Once in a while I imagined I did. It was enough. Sometimes I'd tell him I'd put him out of his misery, come in one night and switch off his life support. Then next time I'd tell him I'd changed my mind. I did that maybe ten, fifteen times. I really loved my aunt, you know. Hated him for what he'd done.'

This time the silence lasted even longer. Somewhere in the house, a clock chimed the hour. Outside, the drizzle had turned to a light rain that now tapped sporadically at the window. It was Irene Wallace who broke the silence.

'Jack? Please?' she said. 'Hasn't this gone far enough?'

A sob burst from his trembling lips.

'Daddy!' Bobby struggled to free himself from his sisters grip. 'Daddy!'

The sob became a groan and all the life seemed to drain out of him and he sank to his knees, the shotgun slipping from his hand to the floor, his face falling into his hands as his shoulders heaved.

Even before the weapon landed we were out of the settee, halfway across the room. No more finesse, no more false pity or sympathy, no more fucking around. We piled into him, hit him hard, knocking him backwards to the floor, restraining him with all the force that tends to build up inside you when you share a room with a shotgun you know can blow your head off at any given second. He didn't stand a chance. A minute later, he was face down on the carpet, hands cuffed behind his back, Yuill leaning on his neck, Monica reading him his rights.

'I am detaining you under Section Two of the Criminal Justice (Scotland) Act 1980 because I suspect you of having committed an offence punishable by imprisonment . . .'

I broke open the shotgun, dropped the two cartridges into my pocket.

Ten minutes later, Irene Wallace and her two children were settled with neighbours, Wallace was in the back of Mike 30 with Sergeant Yuill, and Monica and I had just finished collecting all Wallace's clothing for evidence. As I secured the bin-bag, Monica said, 'That was a bit risky, wasn't it, winding Wallace up like that?'

'Marginal,' I told her. 'One thing I've learnt about men like Wallace, they hate pain, even the thought of pain. It's why what they do turns them on so much.'

As we descended the stairs, I asked her was it true about the ARU marksmen now aiming low.

She gave me her most beatific grin. 'Just wishful thinking, Frank,' she said. 'Don't worry.'

By the time we'd done all the paperwork, taken the necessary statements, bagged the evidence and organised a detail from the mainland to come and collect Wallace for transferral to Division HQ at Kilmarnock, most of the morning had disappeared. A testy phone call from Detective Sergeant Dowie in Brodick reminded me that I had arranged a meeting with Findlay Farquharson and Maggie Boyd, and that I was already fifteen minutes late and he couldn't hold them much longer. I told him ten more minutes, and was there in twelve.

Dowie had brought a couple of plastic chairs through from the locker room next door, had parked them the other side of his desk. Maggie Boyd sat nearest the window, staring out at the murk, while Farquharson fidgeted on his chair by the door. There was just enough space for me to squeeze through and sit on an edge of the desk uncluttered by Dowie's impressive display of paperwork.

Both Dowie and Farquharson glanced at their watches but elected to say nothing. I felt a bit like Hercule Poirot arriving late for one of his classic denouements. I cleared my throat and twirled my waxed mustachios.

'You may be wondering why I asked you to come along this morning . . .' I began, focusing on Farquharson.

'Detective Sergeant Dowie has already explained,' Farquharson said loftily, directing a smile of complicity at the young DS.

So much for that, then. Poirot would have to wait.

I glanced at Maggie. There was something different about her, I couldn't put my finger on it just yet, but whatever it was had fired a spark in her, brought the fire of life to her eyes. She met my glance, offered me the briefest of smiles.

Triumph? I wondered. Could it be triumph?

I turned to Dowie. 'We have a statement?'

He picked up a buff-coloured file, opened it, passed me a statement form. I read it briefly, nodded, handed it back.

'Photos?'

Dowie gave me them one by one. Four in all, two of the car, two of Byrne. 'Ms Boyd has identified them positively as being both the car she saw that night and the man she saw tossing the sheep over the wall.'

'That's right,' Maggie said in a rush. 'It was definitely him. It was the glasses, you see. Even from a distance I could tell the lenses were thick. And the car, I remember that sticker on the rearside window.' She glanced at Farquharson, as though for approval.

'And you, Mr Farquharson?' I asked. 'Have you reached a decision yet?'

'Decision?' he frowned. 'About what?'

'Whether you wish to press charges or not?' There was also a change in Farquharson, I noticed. Not just the nervousness he portrayed with his constant fidgeting, nor anything to do with the sleek haircut and shorn ponytail. Something deeper, core-deep.

Farquharson looked at Maggie. Maggie looked at Farquharson. In that look, a story a million years old. I looked away.

The cork-board along the wall behind them had been covered with a dustsheet, presumably to keep from the public eye any scrutiny of Dowie's murder investigation. I smiled inwardly. If nothing else, Dowie was certainly paranoid enough to make a good detective.

'Yes,' Farquharson said eventually. 'You'll be glad to hear that I have made a decision.' Pompously, as though bestowing a great favour upon us.

Dowie and I caught each other's eye. A copper's look. I liked that, he was working on the same wavelength.

'Tell us,' Dowie said. 'Please. In your own time.'

Farquharson reached across and took Maggie's hand in his. Puffed himself up dramatically and said, 'Well, put it this way – I could hardly bring charges against the woman I love and intend to marry, now could I?' He held up her hand so we could both admire the lump of stone set in gold.

I looked around for a sick-bag.

It was Farquharson's turn to clear his throat. He made a meal of it. Obviously a speech coming up.

'I don't mind admitting that I have been acting like a bloody fool recently,' he said, patting Maggie's hand. 'If I have offended either of you, please accept my sincerest apologies.' Where was that sick-bag, quick, I thought. 'I have been so caught up in these negotiations that I have seriously neglected other aspects of both the business and my personal life. For bringing me to my senses, I have Maggie and, indirectly, both of you to thank for that. You are looking at a new man here, gentlemen, and, dare I say it, a much happier one. I thank you.'

I didn't know whether to bow or applaud, so I did neither. Maggie and Farquharson rose in unison, shook hands all round. I pulled Farquharson aside.

'There's still the small matter of your former employee,' I reminded him. 'John French.'

He took my shoulder and brought it down so he could speak sincerely into my ear. 'As I mentioned, I'm a reformed man, McMorran. After Maggie and I sorted out our differences and realised that we lov—' He broke off to look away embarrassedly for a moment, then recovered his composure. 'Well, anyway, Maggie insisted I speak to his prospective employer at the Field Studies Centre. I did that yesterday. Told him in no uncertain terms that he'd be a fool not to employ someone of John French's ability and integrity. I think you'll find that your friend has got his job.' Looking at me now as though I was supposed to drop to my knees, slobber on his ring.

I said, 'Okay, wee man, you're free to go.' As an officer of the law one must retain one's authority.

He gave me a withering glare, said, 'Come along, Mags,' then stalked from the room.

Maggie rose on tiptoe, pecked my cheek. 'Thanks,' she breathed. Then, in a swirl of skirt, she almost flounced from the office.

Hell, I thought, I must be doing something wrong.

The front door closed. Dowie and I looked at each other for several long seconds. Then burst out laughing.

We took the Land Rover south down the east-coast road, through Lamlash and Whiting Bay, the road climbing now through heavy slanting rain, the grey sea merging with the grey sky to our left, the mainland out there somewhere, or at least it had been yesterday. Dowie was behind the wheel.

He'd changed out of his suit, now wore jeans tucked into hiking boots insulated by thick white woollen socks, a heavy-knit jumper, a waterproof jacket and a flat cap several sizes too large – all but the jeans courtesy of the Mountain Rescue Team's locker room. I, too, had changed out of my uniform, and now wore much the same as Dowie, but no hat. We anticipated a long, cold, wet afternoon, if not evening.

'I tried,' Dowie said, 'but he was still unavailable. At another case conference, apparently. That makes two now in a week.'

'They must be really taking their suspect seriously.'

'What else has Fullerton got to go on? Nothing, far as I can see. The CCs will want to make as much of this as they can, show the public how diligent they are.'

'You written out your report yet?'

'What do you think I was doing all last night?' Dowie slowed as the road turned sharply to the right, diving into a steep wooded gully, dog-legged left, then climbed out again into the gloomy daylight. 'Certainly not what you were doing anyway,' he said with a strained wee laugh. 'Have you been seeing her long?'

'A while,' I shrugged.

'Nice-looking woman. You're a lucky man.' He'd met Kyoko briefly last night, having tracked me down to the hotel bar. No prizes for his powers of detection there.

'You married, Dowie?'

A single shake of the head. 'Neow.' Said with an air of finality that closed the conversation down for the next mile and a half. Okay by me. I spent the time daydreaming about Kyoko and the evening and night ahead of us. Maybe tonight we'd actually find time to sleep.

'Next right,' I said.

Below us, the village of Kildonan lay smothered in mist, the lighthouse on Pladda winking lethargically out to sea, the rocky coastline a cemetery of wrecks that had failed to heed its warning. Further west the black cliffs of Bennan Head rose sheer from the foaming Sound, while above us sloped the field and the stone where I'd discovered the first of the two stabbed sheep ... hell, was it only four weeks ago?

Dowie slowed and turned up the track, the Land Rover making easy work of the potholed surface, the churned mud. No recent tracks, I noticed, at least none made since the rain had begun. Hastie's cottage emerged from the mist like a ghostly galleon adrift on the Sargasso Sea. Dark windows, no outward sign of life. Only the rising chorus of barking dogs.

Dowie parked on a square of gravel by the near side of the cottage, tooted the horn twice before cutting the engine and climbing out. We tried the front door first. It was locked. Peered through the living-room window. Dark nothing. Walked round the back to a crescendo of barks and howls.

'Bloody hell,' Dowie exclaimed, taking in the kennels, the dogs lining and leaping at the wire-mesh fence. 'What's she doing, running a retirement home for pandered pooches?'

'Something like that,' I replied. 'Picks up strays, the story goes.'

'What a racket. It'd drive me crazy.'

'Likewise.' I circled the perimeter of the compound, keeping well back from the fence, my progress followed by an agitated pack led by a snarling Alsatian. My stomach churned, as it had on my last visit.

'She should try feeding them,' Dowie observed. 'That would shut them up for a while.'

I, too, had noticed the empty bowls.

'I don't like it,' I said. 'She wouldn't go away for a whole weekend without leaving them enough food. She cares for these dogs. If she couldn't feed them herself, she'd arrange for someone else to come and do it.'

Dowie looked towards the cottage. 'We could force one of the windows ...'

Perhaps he felt the same sudden sense of urgency as me. 'Let's do it,' I said.

It took a matter of seconds. I pushed the window up, brushed the glass from the sill, then clambered inside and picked my way through the gloom of the living room to the front door where I let Dowie in. Switched on a few lights.

Dowie glanced around, screwed up his nose. 'I'll try upstairs,' he said, breathing through his mouth. He didn't wait for a reply, took the pine stairs two at a time.

Nothing, it seemed, had changed since the last time I'd been here. Still the cloying smell of dogs, the fusty air, the barely controlled chaos of the book-littered living room. I went over to the desk, rummaged through the papers there, eventually found her desk diary. Flicked through the pages until I came to today's date. No mention of any conference there, just a note that said *Mary – 4.30*. I turned to Saturday. *Sandra and Felix arriving p.m.* and below it: *Prepare guest room – more wine!!* Sunday's page was blank. I heard Dowie cross the room above, the sound of drawers and doors opening and closing. I skimmed through the rest of the diary, found what I was looking for on the page for 18 May. Dowie thundered down the stairs.

'Any luck?' he asked.

I showed him the diary. 'Friends or relations arriving tomorrow by the look of things,' I said. 'But check out the eighteenth of May.'

Dowie did so, then whistled through his teeth. 'So Byrne was lying. The conference has already been and gone.'

'Unless she lied to Byrne . . .'

'You don't believe that for a second,' Dowie said.

He was right. The sense of urgency was quickly becoming a heavy knot of concern inside me. Dowie replaced the diary on the desk, absently sifted through the mess of charts and papers.

'Nor do I,' he continued. 'Overnight bag is still in her wardrobe upstairs, nightie still under her pillow, toothbrush and make-up bag still in the bathroom. I don't think she's gone any-fucking-where.' He suddenly peered hard at the chart he'd picked up. 'Hullo – what's this?'

'One of her horoscope charts,' I said. 'She's an astrologist of sorts.'

Dowie held it out for me to see. 'Recognise the name?'

I didn't even need to look. 'Gideon Byrne,' I said. 'I remember she mentioned she was doing his chart.'

'Christ, listen to this,' Dowie said excitedly. 'This is what she says about him. "*Jupiter square Pluto. Rarely agrees with accepted codes of conduct, a law unto himself, arrogant, adventurous, cynical, destructive, sarcastic, violent and explosive.*"'

'Sounds like our man.'

'It gets better. Listen. "*Mars conjuct Pluto. Restless, intense, irritable, overreacts, has a strong sex drive, may be attracted to surgery, will probably die violently.*"' Dowie lowered the chart and met my eye. 'I mean, the guy slices up his victims for their bones and Hastie's got it down here, "*may be attracted to surgery*". It's unreal, man.'

'Which reminds me,' I said. 'An idea I had about the bones, why he takes them.'

'Yah?' Dowie regarded me expectantly.

'I'll tell you in the car.'

His eyes came alight. 'Are we going to see Byrne?'

'I think it's long overdue, don't you?'

We locked the front door, turned off all the lights and left the cottage the same way we had entered. Were met again by the howls and growls, yips and yelps, snarls and barks of the hungry dogs. I made a quick mental note to phone a joiner and the RSPCA as soon as we had a chance, then followed Dowie round the building to the Land Rover.

As we manoeuvred down the track into the rain, Dowie said, 'Well, between you and me, I hope she got the last bit right about Byrne.'

'Which bit was that?'

'How he'll probably die a violent death.'

39

*'The source of nourishment.
Awareness of danger brings good fortune.
It furthers one to cross the great water.'*

Thing about these fucking places is the smell, the stench of shit and piss barely disguised by disinfectant. But worse than that, the smell of burnt-out brainwaves. A riot of mental energy pinging off the walls, all that confined psychic electricity in the air short-circuiting, blowing multiple fuses in the minds of all the moon-howlers here. A distinct taste of scorched brains in the atmosphere.

'If you'll just wait here, Gideon,' the nurse says, 'I'll go and find your mother. Won't be a tick.'

Sometimes it's difficult to tell who's the guard in here – or nurse, as they prefer to call them – and who's the cashew cluster. Nurse Simmons, for example. Big butch bitch with short fair hair, looks like her face caught fire and someone beat it out with a spade. Tits way out to fucking there, dwarfing her name badge so Gideon has to squint at it, find out she's a Betty as well as a nurse. First time he visited here, August last year, same day he picked up the Hegarty woman, the social worker, in Kilmarnock, took her up on to Whitelee Hill and chewed her throat out, that was when he first met Nurse Betty Simmons, mistook her for one of the 'patients'. Something familiar, he felt, back there in her eyes, the same kind of hungry look his mother used to have before she gave him a whipping. That and the sloppy way she dresses, baggy jeans and an oversize woollen lumber-jack shirt, all part of the new regime here, one big happy family.

Reflected, too, in the visiting room where he now waits for his mother to show. Looks more like someone's living room, what with the bay windows looking out on the vegetable garden, the tasteless flock wallpaper, the settee and armchairs gathered around a long low coffee table, the pictures on the wall, all the patients' own work. One of his mother's there, too, a riot of blacks and reds supposed to signify something going on in her mind. Look at it long enough and yeah, he can see it, a headache coming on. And there just inside the door, the desk where the nurse usually sits and pretends she isn't listening, flicking her way through some home-furnishings catalogue or chewing the end of a pencil trying to think of a three-letter word meaning obese.

Only not in the last three visits, Gideon has noticed. Nurse Betty Simmons apparently having arrived at the conclusion that it's a waste of time watching over Gideon and his mother because nothing's ever going to happen, him such a nice boy, such a devoted son, keeping his mother up to date, prattling on about this and that, she sitting hunched over on the edge of the settee, never saying a word or meeting his eyes, locked away in her own little world, not here at all. No need for supervision, this pair. Like what could happen? A nice, gentle giant like Gideon, the kind of son who'll visit his deranged mother regularly every month, what harm could he do? And his mother? Frail little old woman half his size, what, was she going to overpower him and escape? Hell no. So why not just leave them alone, give them an hour's privacy, head along to the canteen for some tea and biscuits, pick up on some of the day's juicy gossip.

So when Nurse Betty Simmons eventually leads his mother into the room, sits her down on the settee and finally finishes fussing over her, that's exactly what she does. Leaves them alone.

'Just ring the bell when you're ready, Gideon,' she says as she's leaving. 'Someone'll come and show you out. Bye now. Be good.'

Which is a four-letter word meaning not naughty.

Gideon stands, hands in pockets, over by the bay windows, watching the tranqued-up zombies in the veggie garden, digging, pruning, hoeing, one guy down there on his knees cutting the lawn with a pair of nail-clippers. Fucking mental. Like Gideon is not unaware that in the rest of society's eyes his own actions are regarded as those of a madman. The papers are full of it. But there are degrees, even in madness. Some end up like the sad fucks out there, don't even know what planet they're on, whole life focused down on to a single potato patch, life's ambition to keep that bastard lawn trimmed. Others go down in a ball of flame that lights up the sky brighter than the sun. Gideon is definitely one of the latter, ahead of his time, a superior man. Someone must show the way.

He turns from the window as the first drops of rain speckle the reinforced glass, looks at his mother perched on the settee, rocking back and forth to some loony tune only she can hear. Last time he was here, he'd suggested to Nurse Betty Simmons they call the visiting room the Nutcracker Suite, and she'd brayed like a horse and told him, really, he shouldn't say such things, someone might hear. But now it was like they shared some little secret, the bond there, both on the same side, partners in criminal laughter. She trusts Gideon now, which means she won't be coming back till the hour is up, maybe not even then.

Gideon sits down in the armchair opposite his mother. Hard to imagine he ever squeezed out from inside this tiny husk of a woman. Maybe that's what drove her crazy, when he came out he took with him everything she'd ever had, left her with nothing but a fragile shell of skin and bone. Hard also to imagine this was the woman who'd treated him worse than a dog, used him like some kind of marital aid, then shoved him away in the back of a drawer till the next time. This dehydrated sack of bones who one fine day picked up a knife and slit her husband's throat.

It's a question Gideon has asked himself time and time again: does it run in the family, this? Is it some kind of self-destructing gene they share, get to a certain point in life and the mind starts unravelling? Behind the question, of course, the nagging worry that he, too, could end up a cabbage tending cabbages.

Gideon leans forward, knocks on his mother's skull.

'Hullo,' he calls. 'Anyone in there?'

No response. None. Not even in her eyes. They just kind of look through him like he isn't there. Maybe she thinks all this silent treatment gets to him, ignore him and he'll go away. Except she's been ignoring him for six years now, ever since her last ECT treatment. A long time in anyone's book.

He runs his hand up under her skirt, along the inside of her withered thigh. No response. Just like last time. Though he hadn't been rushed then, wasn't watching the clock like today. Had gone the whole hog then, bent her over the back of the settee, taken her from behind, plumbed her back passage well and good. Had had plenty of time to mop and tidy up, get everything all spick and span by the time Nurse Betty Simmons returned and asked how they were getting on. 'Just fine and dandy,' he'd told her.

But today, well, he's going to take her in a different way. Take her all the way. Make her his for all eternity.

'You hear that, Mum?' he says, peering into her lifeless eyes. 'Mine for all eternity.'

40

Rain.

Detective Sergeant Dowie had brought along Hastie's astrological chart for Byrne, was now leafing through the pages as I drove, headlights on, through the tunnel of rain.

'Here's another one,' he said. '"*Neptune sextile Pluto. Hates conventional society, has mystical qualities, is creative and artistic. Has intuitive knowledge of dark forces.*"'

'Great. Now we've got Darth Vader to contend with as well.' I touched the brakes and slowed as a sudden deluge hammered down from the ever-darkening sky, starring the windscreen, cutting visibility down to less than thirty yards. Dowie had to shout against the rising din.

'It gets better. Listen to this: "*Pluto in Virgo. Will stop at nothing to promote obsessions on to others. Has a morbid preoccupation with death.*"'

'Tell me who hasn't,' I said, 'at one time or another.'

Dowie either didn't hear my comment or chose to ignore it. He was using the map-light now, bending over the papers on his lap, squinting at Hastie's spidery scrawl.

'Wow, look at this. Today's date on it, something called a "transit".'

'What the hell's a transit?' Having to concentrate now, the road dropping steeply into the tiny village of Lagg against the dazzle of approaching headlights. A post office, a cluster of cottages, a small stone bridge over the swollen Torrylinn Water, and then climbing out past the Lagg Inn, out from beneath the canopy of trees, back into the driving rain.

'Says here a transit indicates the energy flows from planets into the personality subconscious at the given times – whatever the fuck that means. Anyway, d'you want to hear what it says?'

Call me sceptical, cynical or just plain sober, I just can't bring myself to believe that an individual's future can be forecast through the movement of planets hundreds of thousands of light years away. Maybe I've just been a cop too long. Either that or it's because I'm a Capricorn.

'Enlighten me,' I said.

'It says, and I quote, "*Violent and disruptive energy controls, a ruthless burst of ego energy that does not take lightly to limitation. You will seek power over others by assault. You will gain great satisfaction from use of physical power. Mars brings repressed childhood feelings violently to the surface.*" That's it.'

'Strong stuff.'

'Lethal, by the sound of it.' Dowie snapped off the light, tossed the papers into the glove compartment. 'Makes you wonder why she continued working for him after finding all this in his chart.'

'Maybe she did a runner after all,' I said. 'Used the conference as an excuse, just took the hell off.'

'You'd think she'd've mentioned it to you first,' Dowie said. 'I mean when you spoke to her on the phone the other day.'

'She was at the pottery. Maybe Byrne was hanging around.'

Dowie was silent for a minute, staring out the side window at the lush green fields, the cud-chewing cows impervious to the rain, the white-capped sea, and the dark smudge of the Kintyre hills beneath the ever-lowering skies. A tractor and trailer turned the corner up ahead, lumbered past us, followed by half a dozen cars.

'That stuff about repressed childhood feelings coming

violently to the surface,' Dowie said. 'Isn't that common with killers like the Fangman? Like the murders are supposed to be a kind of re-enactment of some horrific experience in the killer's childhood . . .'

'. . . in which he reverses the roles and can thus right the wrongs he perceives have been perpetrated on him. Aye,' I sighed, 'it's a popular theory.'

'You don't think that's what the Fangman's doing, then?'

'Between you and me, Sergeant, I don't really care why he does what he does. That's someone else's job. Ours is to stop him before he kills again. Simple as that.'

'So how are we going to approach him, then?' Dowie asked huffily. 'Go in with all our guns blazing or what?'

Christ, the man was almost as sensitive as I was. I said, no, leave the guns till later, this time round we'd just wander in, take a look around, play it by ear.

'Do we tell him we're looking for the Hastie woman?'

'Can't do any harm,' I said. 'She's been reported missing, we need to check everywhere she's been in the last twenty-four hours. That should keep him quiet.'

'Shouldn't we be worried about spooking him?'

'Worried?' I glanced at him askance. 'Hell no. We should be wildly excited by the prospect.'

'I was thinking of my career,' he said lamely. 'That's all.'

'Start worrying about your career and you'll never have time to do your job,' I said, slowing now behind a black-and-silver camper with two mountain bikes secured to its rear above an Italian number plate, Roma.

'Platitude Man strikes again.'

'You what?'

'Nothing.' Dowie leant against his door, peered ahead. 'You're clear,' he said.

Tyres hissing as I overtook, the road dipping towards the shore, then straightening out as Beinn Bharrain loomed out of the gloom ahead. We took a left at The String, passed through

Blackwaterfoot in silence, headed north on the Torbeg road, on towards Machrie, the moor opening out on our right. As I slowed for the turning up to the pottery, I was thinking of Kyoko, seeing her again as I'd seen her last, head on the pillow, looking up at me through tousled hair and half-closed eyes heavy with milky satiation, eyetooth caught in her full lower lip, hand tugging at mine, not wanting to let me go.

Only this morning.

I shifted into four-wheel drive and we lurched up the rutted track, churning mud, cows to the left of us, sheep to the right, onwards we drove, on to the moor that is Machrie. Although the rain had eased off a little and the eastern sky ahead was now just a dirty dishwater grey, there were, coming in behind us over the Kilbrannan Sound, towering black thunderheads that would soon bring an early night to this late afternoon.

At the Moss Farm road stone circle, Dowie broached the rain to first open the gate and then close it behind the Land Rover.

'We just drive right in?' he asked, reclaiming his seat, slamming the door.

'You'd rather walk?'

'Beam down is what I'd rather.'

We covered the next few hundred yards in silence, the track running along the crest of a rise, the encircling hills seeming to crowd in, close out the world beyond. A flash of lightning lit up the sky, followed, ten seconds later, by a distant roll of thunder. As I pulled over on to the verge of the track at the top of the pottery's drive, I was thinking about omens and whether a storm could be considered a good one. Perhaps only if you live in the Sahara, I decided.

We climbed out, met by the bonnet, neither of us, it seemed, in any particular hurry to walk down to the pottery. From where I stood I could see no sign of life among the cluster of buildings, no lights in any windows, no car in the yard, no psychopathic potters climbing the drive to meet us.

No tourists, either.

A hundred or so yards to the east the mist wafted in silken threads through the standing stones, bringing a distinct eeriness to the scene that conjured up images far more primal than those I had witnessed at the last full moon.

'Makes you wonder, eh?'

'What does?'

'Those stones,' I said. 'See them standing there amidst all this rain, it's hard to imagine they were formed when Arran was somewhere around where the Sahara is today.' Dowie stared at me as though I had worms dropping out my nostrils. 'Hence the red sandstone,' I added.

'You wonder about things like that when you're just about to confront the world's most demented psychopath?'

'Why not?' I said. 'It helps clear the mind. Anyway, I've told you a million times, don't exaggerate. Byrne's not a demented psychopath, he's just a poor mixed-up kid.'

'Fuck, now you're turning social worker on me. That's all I need.' Dowie swept the three buildings with his gaze, slowly shook his head. Said, 'Maybe we should've called for back-up.'

'I could always hold your hand . . .'

'You? Trivia Man? Bugger off.' Dowie pulled up his collar, hunched down his neck. 'Okay. No time like the present. Let's do it.'

'You're the boss.'

There was a varnished wooden sign on the end wall of the pottery with all the weekday opening times. There was also a small wooden slide you could push one way and it read OPEN, push the other way and it read CLOSED. It now read CLOSED. We tried the cottage first, hammered on the door for a minute or two, then crossed the yard to the pottery and tried there with the same amount of success. The Subaru gone, the whole place deserted.

'What now?' Dowie said, pressing his face against the pottery window, peering into the darkness. 'Wait until he returns?'

Lightning once again forked across the sky, the ensuing cracks of thunder only a few seconds behind, getting closer.

The door caved in with my first kick, one of the panes of glass shattering as it crashed against the inside wall. Dowie stared, his mouth working hard but no words coming out.

'Two doors in one day,' I said, 'both with a single kick. I'm looking at a personal record here.'

'Christ, McMorran, you can't do that!'

'Do what? We came out here to look for Ros Hastie, found the door smashed open, obviously we have to search the building, make sure the perpetrator's not still here.'

'I'm getting a distinct sense of *déjà vu* here, McMorran, and it's not a pleasant feeling.'

'You want to stand out here in the rain, discuss your feelings, or shall we do what we're paid to do, uphold the law and maybe put a little order back in the cosmic scheme of things?'

'I should've stayed at home,' Dowie said. 'Called in sick.'

I found the light switch, flicked it on. Said, 'You check his workroom, I'll check in here.'

He stood there shaking his head. 'I don't want any part of this, McMorran, one B&E a day is enough for me. Doctor's orders. I'm staying right here. You want it checked, check it yourself.'

I did. The door was not locked. It was a workroom not much different from Jenny Howitt's, the wheel sitting against the wall facing the door, I presumed, so Byrne could watch the shop while throwing his pots. Around the whitewashed walls, shelves of unglazed pots – mugs and bowls, teapots and vases, candle-holders and jugs – awaiting the kiln which stood in the far corner, electric blue, door ajar, already half-packed. Fixed to the wall beside it, and connected to the back of the kiln, a white plastic box with lights and buttons and an LCD display, obviously the computer Howitt had mentioned. On the floor, half a dozen red plastic buckets full of different coloured liquids, what had to be glazes. But no Ros Hastie.

512

I returned to the shop. Dowie was on the doorstep, peering in. I ignored him and crossed to the counter, thinking maybe I'd been a little premature, maybe Dowie wasn't quite ready to make a good detective: he wouldn't let his curiosity get the better of him.

The money-drawer under the counter was locked. There was a box of plastic bags on the floor, next to it a pile of newspapers used for wrapping pots. On the counter, a ledger, open, listing all the recent sales. A sticky-tape dispenser, a packet of white sticky-backed price labels, a pair of scissors, ten or so pens and pencils in a mug. A pile of books – *Glazes for the Studio Potter*; *The Potter's Book*; *The Ceramic Review Book of Glaze Recipes*; *Kilns, Design, Construction, and Operation* – and magazines, mostly copies of the *Ceramic Review*. I was turning away when it caught my eye, a splash of colour down on the floor, almost hidden by the newspapers. I stooped and picked it up.

'What is it?' Dowie asked from the door. I tossed the bag across to him. He opened it, rummaged inside. 'Is it hers?'

One of these hand-woven bags, almost a tapestry in shades of red and purple, tassels hanging off its sides. 'Last time I saw her,' I said, 'it was slung round her shoulder.'

Dowie held up the book. 'And this is the one she was going to lend you? The *I Ching*?'

I left him to draw his own conclusions, pushed past him out into the rain, crossed the yard.

'Hey, what are you doing?'

The front door of Byrne's cottage was made of a sterner wood, it took three attempts before the lock splintered the frame and the door burst in. Turning on lights as I went, I searched the ground-floor rooms – kitchen-cum-dining-room, bathroom, living-room, study – propelled by a growing sense of urgency, Dowie yapping at my heels.

'You can't do this. I mean, Christ, we could lose our jobs. What if Kettle finds out? What if this constitutes an illegal search and fucks up the whole case? Hey, McMorran, listen to me. You've got to think about these things. You can't just kick your way through any closed door that just happens to be in your way. There are rules, you know, rules. Due process of law. Ever heard of that? No, probably not.' Following me up the stairs now, yap, yap, yap. 'Christ! I can see it now. *Fangman freed on technicality*. I mean, he could walk in now, sue our arses to the wall. Illegal entry. No grounds for suspicion—'

'No grounds for suspicion?' I snapped, turning on him. 'A woman goes away for a weekend conference and leaves her handbag behind? Her purse, her house keys, her make-up, her chequebook? I find that hard to believe, Dowie, how about you?'

'She may have just forgotten it.'

I couldn't keep the sneer off my lips. 'You really think so?'

There were only two rooms up the short flight of pine stairs, left, a spare room, and right, Byrne's bedroom. The spare room held a single bed, a chest of drawers, a wardrobe, and a dressing table in the dormer window overlooking the yard. No pictures on the wall, no personal touches, no atmosphere – a very spare room. I shouldered past Dowie, entered Byrne's bedroom.

First thing I noticed were the ties, one tied to each leg of the double bed. The bed was unmade. On the bedside table a couple of books with interesting titles – an *Encyclopaedia of Murder*; and *Zodiac*, 'the shocking true story of America's most bizarre mass murderer'.

Dowie like a ball-and-chain shackled to my ankle. 'Bedtime stories for your average serial killer,' he said over my shoulder. 'What did you expect?'

'Beatrix Potter?'

'Eh?'

'You want to contribute, go check the wardrobe, the drawers there.'

Dowie seemed about to argue, maybe saw the look on my face and shrugged instead, set about his search.

I looked under the bed, nothing, lifted the mattress, nothing, under the pillows, nothing. In the bedside drawer, more books on murder, a half-bottle of whisky, some pills – Quinalbarbitone and Amylobarbitone – known on the street as 'chewies', a few Spanish coins and several hundred-peseta notes, a small pocket-knife, and a plastic mug. I closed the drawer just as Dowie turned from the wardrobe and said:

'Ever see this before?' He held up a cotton floral-patterned dress that was ripped from neck to groin.

'Last time I saw her,' I said.

'It was crumpled in a ball at the bottom of the wardrobe there.'

'Nothing else? No bra or panties, tights, what have you?'

'Just this.' Dowie examined the dress, inside and out, presumably for stains, semen or blood, then tossed it on the bed. 'It doesn't look good, does it? I mean, for Hastie.'

I didn't need telling.

'What with the ties and that,' he said, 'it looks like he ripped her dress off, tied her to the bed, had his way with her.'

I pulled back the bedclothes, inspected the sheets. 'No stains,' I observed. 'Not even old ones.' I pressed each of the pillows to my nose in turn. I'd done the same thing yesterday with my own pillows, Kyoko gone a couple of hours, but her scent still there, lingering, a minefield of pheromone bombs.

'Anything?'

'Faint trace of woman on this one.' I examined it closely, found what I expected, several long red hairs.

'Hers?' Dowie was at my shoulder again.

'Well, they're not his.' I held them up. Dowie searched his pockets, came out with an evidence bag. He sealed the hairs in the bag, dropped it back in his pocket.

'What now?'

'We search the place,' I said, 'top to bottom.'

'We just did.'

'So we do it again.' I was already on the stairs, Dowie close behind.

'We do it again,' he mimicked. 'Like we haven't already torn the place apart without a warrant, without reasonable grounds for suspicion. We do it again. Check behind all the cushions this time, see if he left the body there and we just happened to overlook it.'

'Shut up, Dowie.'

'Now I've got a PC telling me to shut up. Me, a sergeant, supposed to be in charge here.' He grabbed my shoulder, spun me around, prodded my chest with his forefinger. 'Okay, McMorran, you know all the answers, tell me what we're looking for. If it's not her body – which is probably already decomposing in some ditch somewhere, if he hasn't changed his MO – then what the fuck are we looking for?'

We were in the living room, by the fireplace. All those cheap souvenirs on the mantelpiece, the Spanish dolls. I took a swipe and sent them flying. Registered the apprehension in Dowie's eyes, planted my hand in the centre of his chest and pushed him away. He staggered back, caught the back of his legs against an armchair, sat heavily, staring up at me in what was close to disbelief. That I had dared touch him!

It didn't take me long to transform the living-room into a scene of destruction. About as long as it took for my anger to burn itself out, the anger a natural reaction, easier to exorcise than the growing clot of guilt lying heavy on my mind. Dowie just sat there watching, waited until I'd finished, the storm blown out, before he climbed from the chair, went and picked up the video recorder.

'You forgot something,' he said. Then hurled it through the TV screen.

I said, breathing heavy, 'Guys like Byrne, like the Fangman, they usually have a special place, a secret place where only they ever go. It's where they retreat to, to gloat, to fantasise, to revel in their past gory deeds. The Edinburgh Hangman had a place like that, a barn at the end of his garden, where he kept all his trophies, his fetishes, the newspaper reports of his atrocities, his snakes. He told us he spent hours, sometimes days, down there, reliving his fantasies, thinking up new ones. It's where he brought the kids back, he'd show them his snakes, then throttle them unconscious, take them next door to a bigger barn that had thick high rafters, wait until they regained consciousness before he put their heads in the noose, kicked away the chair.' I paused for a second, looking out the window and through the curtain of rain, across the yard to the pottery, door open, lights on. 'You know what I'm saying, Dowie? Byrne's got a place like that, a secret place, a room somewhere, maybe a cellar, maybe out in that storeroom, behind all those logs. I don't know. But it's here, I feel it, and until we find it we've got nothing for Kettle, absolutely nothing. So let's do it, man, let's tear this place apart.'

Dowie shrugged. 'In for a penny . . .' he said.

41

*'The influence shows itself in the jaws,
cheeks and tongue.'*

Chew, chew, chew.

You need something to chew on, it helps those acid attacks,
the adverts say, aids concentration.

Gideon Byrne knew it, he'd just fucking known it. Arriving at
the ferry terminal in Ardrossan an hour or so ago, and there it
was, as expected, a sign saying that due to the severe weather
conditions the ferry would be leaving from Gourock. Which had
meant another hour's drive north, and ahead of him now a two-
hour crossing guaranteed to have him puking in the toilet for at
least half of it. Doesn't seem to matter how much whisky he
drinks, he always ends up on the big white telephone if the sea's
anything steeper than a ripple. Just *looking* at the sea over the
Gourock harbour wall, as he's doing now, is enough to make his
stomach churn, try to turn itself inside out. The sea crashing in,
drenching him in spray, still another few hours of daylight left
but already it's like night, thunder growling in the broiling sky,
the rain lashing down.

He removes his glasses, wipes them for the hundredth time,
thinking he should get one of these pairs he's seen Elton John
wearing once in some magazine, a pair of pink ones with little
like windscreen wipers on them, battery-operated. Except you
have to be a stage artist, a fucking millionaire, before you can
wear a pair of specs like those and not have people laugh at you

as you walk down the street. Okay that you can wear deely-boppers or pink fluffy ear-muffs, or put rings in your nose or shave initials into your hair, that's all right, that's fashion for you. But the moment you want to wear something practical, like a pair of glasses with windscreen wipers, people look at you like you just shot the president.

Gideon Byrne turns away from the sea wall, wanders back towards the car, twenty-third in the queue. The ferry's in, cars already disembarking. Won't be long now, the train'll arrive from Ardrossan, all the backpackers with their mountain bikes and healthy fresh-air faces. Lining the ferry's rails, noses to the wind, getting all turned on by the tumultuous seas, the sense of adventure. Like they're Scott of the fucking Antarctic.

Chew, chew, chew.

Checking back along the line of cars, looking at all the passengers, the happy families, the bored couples, the golfers, the salesmen returning from a week on the road, the weekend just beginning for them, something that'll last a fuck of a lot longer just beginning for Gideon Byrne. But no one looking at him, paying him the blindest bit of notice. Which suits him fine. It means they haven't found her body yet, or if they have, they're busy looking for him somewhere else. If he can make it on to the ferry, the last of the day, then he'll have a head start.

Chew, chew, chew. Getting a bit tasteless now, losing its texture. Still, it helps concentration, and that's what he needs right now, to concentrate, stay alert, remain one step ahead. Not worry about the island cops, who're basically just small fry, glorified traffic wardens with batons.

Except *him* of course, the one whose name he keeps forgetting, the one who went on TV and told the whole bloody world that Gideon could never do it with a woman, was – what was the word he used? – impotent. Well, impotency just happens to be a subject Gideon wants to discuss with the cop's woman, the slant-eye bitch who thinks she can look down her nose at Gideon and not pay some kind of price.

Chew, chew, chew.

Once on board, check around, make sure there's no polis sniffing his tracks, then give her a ring. Directory Enquiries, get the number of her hotel, make an appointment for her to come out and have a look at the pot she commissioned. She doesn't want to come out tonight, tell her fuck it, there're plenty of other people prepared to pay a good price for his pots, what does he care. Then maybe go over to the hotel anyway, knock on her door.

The cars down the front are moving now, a guy in a uniform and waterproofs, one of the ferry's loading crew, coming back along the line, checking boarding tickets, reservations. A straggle of backpackers fighting through the slanting rain towards the gangway, the connecting train just in. Gideon wonders if he should do it for a laugh, when the guy asks to see his ticket, should he spit out his mother's tongue and make a joke out of it, say something like, 'Always did have a loose tongue in my head,' and see how the guy reacts, whether he pukes down the side of the car or what.

But Gideon decides no, better not draw attention to himself, no point in having the guy call up the cops and tell them he's just seen a guy chewing someone else's tongue, and that that someone else happens to be detached from said tongue, nowhere to be seen. It would only lead to trouble. So Gideon spits it out into his hand, tucks it away in the ashtray. Maybe leaving it a while will improve the taste.

Still, maybe the Kimono bitch will appreciate it later, your tongue-in-cheek sense of humour.

42

Dowie said, 'It wasn't just the smell. It was that.' He was pointing at the computer, the white box on the wall, the one connected to the electric kiln in Byrne's workshop.

I looked at it, not seeing what he meant, the wood for all the trees.

He saw my puzzled frown, said: 'See that wire there, leads round to the back of the kiln? I thought, fair enough, you punch in all the digits here and it controls the firing sequence. You can pick that much up from the instructions label there, you don't actually need to have a degree in computer science.'

'Which you probably have anyway,' I said, some of the anger still there, seething.

'And you're right, I do. But I didn't need to use that knowledge to wonder about that other wire there.' He pointed at the wire which left the computer and travelled down the wall to disappear behind the skirting board. 'All I needed to ask myself was where it led.'

'Downstairs,' I said, getting there at last.

'Exactly.' Dowie looked pleased with himself. He had a right to; I'd seen the computer and the wires leading off, hadn't even thought to question where one of them might lead. I glanced round the workshop but saw no evidence of a trapdoor or any other kind of access to a cellar.

Dowie smiled, enjoying his leading role. 'Over here,' he said, and led me across to the potter's wheel. Unlike Jenny Howitt's small power-driven wheel, Byrne's was a much larger affair, with a heavy kick-wheel below the wheel-head disc, and a bench, all attached to a metal plate on the floor. Dowie took hold of one side, motioned that I take hold of the other. He pushed, I pulled. And there it was, a trapdoor.

I said, 'Good work, Sergeant.' Through gritted teeth.

Dowie grasped the ring-pull, hauled it open.

I got a shout once, back when I was PC first time round, not on the plod very long, go check out old Mrs Duff up at Dumbiedykes, neighbours report a strange smell coming from her flat, haven't seen her about for several days. I wasn't stupid. I knew what I'd find when I got there, knew my tutor con was setting me up, all part of the training. I didn't mind, though, I thought I could handle it, all I'd have to do was breathe through my mouth, call it in, wait for the services to arrive. No big deal.

'Bloody hell!' Dowie staggered back, hand clamped over his mouth and nose.

Mrs Duff was in there, of course, well deceased. And yes, she had been dead a few days. And yes, the stench was overpowering, stuck to my skin and clothes for days, I couldn't scrub enough. But it wasn't the stink of decomposition, it was the stench of flesh burnt beyond recognition. Old Mrs Duff had been sitting in her armchair, had leant forward to maybe turn on another bar of her electric fire, had fallen forward face first on to the fire and had died like that, the electric bars burning through her face until the meter ran out.

The smell in her flat that day, the same as that now wafting up from the cellar.

I called in the Code Four Four using Byrne's telephone in the pottery. I could have used my PR but didn't feel in the mood to alert all the scanner freaks on the mainland, all the hungry journos prowling the Operation HQ at Kilmarnock. Bob Gillies took the shout, told me Yuill had gone off duty a couple of hours ago, just him and Jim Tennant in the office. I gave him the barest of details, told him to get hold of DI Fullerton or

Commander Kettle on a secure line, have them call me back at the pottery. I gave him the number, told him to alert Yuill and then stay by the phone, keep a radio handy in case of emergencies.

'You have a name on the Code Four Four?' he asked before I rang off.

I told him we'd probably have to wait for the post mortem, and maybe even a forensic examination of the teeth, before we got a positive ID. 'But between you and me, Bob, it's Rosalind Hastie.'

'The woman with all the dogs?' he said. 'Lives down Kildonan way?'

'The same. It's not very pretty, the bastard burned her in one of his kilns. Not much left but ash and bone.'

'Any idea where he is?'

'Not yet. I'm just hoping he turns up before—'

'Take it easy, Frank, let's not go flying off the handle here.'

'I'll be in touch,' I said, and hung up.

I stood in the doorway for a while, gulping down the rain-freshed air, then returned to the cellar where Dowie was on his knees, wading his way through a pile of scrapbooks. He'd found a cloth somewhere, now had it tied at the back of his neck and covering the lower half of his face, bandit style. Not much protection from the stench, but something. He said:

'He's catalogued the whole lot here. A scrapbook for every murder, press cuttings from all the papers. There's a pile of papers over there in the corner covering the Falconer murder, looks like he hasn't had the time yet to cut them out, too busy burning fresh victims.'

You came down the wooden stairs and found yourself in a cellar that extended the whole length of the building, maybe forty, fifty feet by half that wide. A wide open-hearth fireplace in the centre of the wall facing you, a workshop area at the far end – work bench against the wall, shelves, racks of tools – the kiln, what looked like an old model, rust-red, opposite the fireplace, and, tucked away in the corner beneath the stairs, an old armchair and the most sinister aspect of the stone-walled cellar, a kind of home-built shrine adorned with black velvet cloth, several human skulls, candles, and an assortment of trophies taken from the Fangman's victims. Enough evidence there to satisfy even Kettle.

Dowie said, 'Christ, here's one that goes back must be thirty years.' He was off his knees now, had carried the pile of scrapbooks over to the light on the work bench, was slowly turning pages. 'Jesus! No wonder he went off the rails. Look at this. There's a story here about how his mother sent him to school dressed as a girl ... refused to acknowledge he was a boy ... the school sent him home ... social work department took him into care for a while ...'

I joined him by the bench, opened one of the drawers as he turned another page.

'Holy hell! *Housewife slits husband's throat as he watches TV,*' Dowie read. 'His mother, that is. Mrs Byrne.' Dowie flipped a page. 'Unfit to stand trial, blah blah blah, sentenced to Her Majesty's Pleasure ... Carstairs. Could still be there, for all we know.' He glanced at the folder I was holding in my hand. 'What's that?'

'Found it in the drawer,' I said. 'It's the collated forensic reports I got off Fullerton. Byrne must have taken them when he pushed me over the side of the ferry.'

Dowie squinted at me. 'Can't recall you mentioning any files, McMorran ...' He took the folder, briefly scanned the files inside. 'Don't look much like files to me,' he said after a moment. Then, removing the papers from the folder, he folded them twice before slipping them in my inside pocket. 'In fact, I don't know what you're talking about, McMorran. You must be seeing things. Hallucinating, with all that pressure you're under.'

'I think you must be right, sir.'

'Heed a sergeant's advice, take a good long holiday.'

That was when the phone rang. I took the stairs three at a time, answered on the fourth ring. It was Commander Harlan Kettle. He didn't give me a chance.

'Straight up, McMorran, is it him?' I'd never heard him so excited before.

'Without a shadow, sir. Body in the cellar downstairs, skulls, trophies from the victims, newspaper cuttings, the lot.'

A moment's silence as he took it all in, his breath snorting down the line like that of a wounded bull.

'So,' he said eventually. 'You've done it again.' Censure in his voice as always, but also relief. 'What you doing, shagging Lady Luck?'

'We're just good friends, sir.'

'Aye, sure.' Another brief silence, through which I could hear someone tapping at a keyboard, the high-pitch buzz of a printer. After a moment, 'You know where he is?'

'No, sir. Place seems abandoned.'

'Give me the details then. Name, description, whatever else you've got.'

'Name's Gideon Byrne. Six-three or four, fifteen, sixteen stone, glasses, sandy hair, drives a silver-grey Subaru estate. He's probably—'

'Wait a minute, did you say Byrne?'

'Yes, sir. Gideon Byrne.'

'Hold on a minute.'

I could now hear the sound of voices in the background, the ops room exploding to life. It was still raining outside, though no longer a deluge, the eye of the storm having passed, thunder still a distant grumble in the east. Kettle came back on.

'McMorran? Aye. Good man. Gideon Byrne, you say? Well, listen to this. A few hours ago, DI Fullerton was called out to a place called Elderburn House, Code Four Four. It's an institution, some kind of halfway house for long-term patients from Carstairs who are no longer deemed a threat to society. Apparently they spend a few years there before reintroduction

527

into the community. Anyway, a patient there was found murdered this afternoon. An old woman, name of Byrne.'

I said, 'He killed his own mother?'

'Strangled her, left her stuffed under a desk, and just walked out. They didn't discover her body till two hours later when she failed to appear for tea. What's more, he didn't just strangle her, he bit out her tongue as well. Either swallowed it or took it with him.'

'You've put a call out for him?'

'No, I sent him a fucking invitation, McMorran, what d'you bloody well think?' This was more like the Kettle I love to hate. 'All points,' he continued. 'I just—' He broke off as someone spoke to him, then came back on. 'Confirmation just in, he boarded the last ferry. Sailed from Gourock an hour and a half ago, should be docking your end any time now.'

'You want us to wait for him here?'

'No, McMorran. I want no more fuck-ups like with Maxwell. I want you out of there now. Immediately. Stand back and secure the area. Let Byrne come in, but don't let him know you're there. Observation only, you got that?'

'Sir.'

'Can you give me coordinates?'

'Bob Gillies at the Lamlash office,' I said. 'He'll have an OS map there.'

'Okay, noted. How about terrain? Can we land a chopper nearby?'

'Should be no problem if you stick to the higher ground,' I told him. 'It's been done before.' A Navy Sea King, a few years back, according to the Gospel of Yuill. A forced landing, the chopper caught in fog.

'Okay. You hear us coming in, use your torch, let us know where you are. No radios, understood?'

I said. 'What if he tries to leave?'

Kettle seemed to hesitate. But only for a second. 'Nobble the bastard,' he said. 'Nobble him good.'

'You remember the Borthwick case?'

'You mean as in Simone?'

'Aye,' I said. We'd circled the stones and brought the Land Rover up behind a clump of trees midway between Machrie Water and the Moss Farm Pottery. While obscured from the cluster of buildings, we still had a good view of the pottery, the yard, and the short steep drive down which Byrne would surely come. We sat now in darkness, waiting, a persistent rain bouncing off the roof.

'Only vaguely,' Dowie replied, wiping the lenses then peering through the binoculars. 'Didn't get much coverage, the way I remember it.'

'Probably because those in the know reckoned she'd been going over the side for a while, then decided to make it permanent. Set up a fictitious conference in London to give her a head start.'

Before leaving the pottery, we had made two phone calls. Dowie the first, calling up his two DCs, Bryce and Davies, telling them to meet the ferry and watch out for the Subaru, to follow it discreetly and at a distance. If it turned up the lane on to the Moor, they were to wait at the turning and link up with Yuill and whoever else appeared from the Lamlash station. The second call was mine, putting Yuill squarely in the picture. We then closed the trapdoor to the cellar, returned the potter's wheel to its original place, and turned off all the lights. There was nothing we could do about the damaged pottery door.

'Is that what they thought?' Dowie asked

'It's what the canteen cowboys thought at the time.' A couple of years ago I'd been assigned alongside one of the cops who'd been on the case, had been forced to listen to the whole story during one long and seemingly endless night on a futile surveillance operation. The cop, I remember, had a monorail mind that led from one part of the female anatomy to another, no rest stops along the way. A heavily-built Scouser who scratched his balls and farted a lot. He'd told me about the Borthwicks – their open marriage, the partner-swapping, the photographic and video evidence found at their home – in avidly lurid detail. Such sexual liberation had not only obviously turned him on, but had also fired his imagination. He had many theories about what had happened to Simone Borthwick – including one which involved her being kidnapped by a sex-slave ring masquerading as a travelling circus – and I had had to listen to them all. The only scenario he had not envisaged was that she might have been abducted and murdered by a psychopathic potter with a bent for baking his victims alive.

Dowie must have read my thoughts. He lowered the binoculars and said, 'It's not your fault, McMorran. There was nothing you could do.'

I said, 'I could have gone to see her when I said I would. If I had, she'd still be alive today.'

'She was probably already dead by then.'

'The kiln was still warm, Dowie.'

'So? Who says she was alive when he put her in there? Maybe he was just disposing of her body.'

'Yeah? Did you happen to notice the scratch marks on the inside of the kiln door?'

Dowie shook his head. 'Look. If you want to torture yourself, go ahead. But not here, not now.'

'Why the hell not?' I said.

He had the binoculars to his eyes again.

'Because I think that's Byrne just arriving.'

Sure enough. A few seconds later, a pair of headlights arced across the sky, dipped down into the yard of the Moss Farm Pottery.

The Fangman had landed.

43

'Waiting in the mud
Brings about the arrival of the enemy.'

Better wash and clean up, change into something a little more comfortable. Scrape a blade across his stubble, at least make the effort. Mission might be running towards the endgame, but a superior man always finds the time to make himself presentable. Especially when a lady's calling.

Eyes.

Gideon Byrne stands at his bedroom window, the room in darkness, looking out across the moor. They're out there somewhere, he can sense them. Maybe looking at him right this moment. Biding their time.

Gideon comes away from the window, enters the bathroom. Runs hot water into the basin, studying his face in the mirror as the steam rises. Doesn't look that much different from this morning. More haunted, perhaps, his expression, but what the fuck, it's not every day you kill your mother, not every day you come home to find your house trashed. Still. A shave will do the trick. Last thing he wants is that Kimono bitch whining about his stubble when he eventually gets to grips with her.

Out there somewhere, getting soaked by the rain.

He doesn't resent them. It's like they're all part of the game. When the curtain finally comes down, they'll respect him. They will, no doubt about it. Thing about the police, they don't take

531

these kind of things personally. It's just a job to them, they try not to get involved. They meet a superior intellect, hell, they respect it. They like a challenge. Give them a good old-fashioned murder hunt and they'll respect him for it. Bring him tea in his cell, whatever he wants. Maybe even come in and shake him by the hand, say, 'You led us a good chase there, Gideon, really gave us a run for our money.' That kind of thing. Experts flying in from all over the world – maybe even that Clarice Starling bitch from the FBI Behavioural Science Unit at wherever it is, Quantico – to study him, try and find out what makes him tick. People writing books about him, front page in all the papers, the courthouse under siege, all those bitches wetting their knickers, wanting to marry him, make him change his ways. See? That's how a superior man does it, all worked out to the last detail, no room for error. The bitch walks in, Gideon says let's go over to the pottery, see if your pot's ready. She follows him across the yard, rushing to get out of the rain, doesn't want it to spoil her hair, fuck no, dangerous stuff, acid rain, when it mixes with all that gunk they put in their hair nowadays, likely to explode or go up in flames.

Gideon lathers his face, finds a blade that's only been used twice. Notices a couple of hairs sprouting from his nose that weren't there the last time he shaved. He wonders when that was, but can't remember. No problem. There'll be plenty time for remembering when all this is over. Time to relax at last, bathe in the glory, the recognition he so deserves.

Okay. So she's standing there. Gideon hauls the wheel off the trapdoor, tells her in a confidential way – maybe even drops his voice a little for the dramatic effect, whispers it in her ear, getting a good look at her neck at the same time, like sizing her up for the big bite – that this is where he keeps all his special pots, that only his special customers get to see down here. Yeah. Do it like that. Just go down the steps, leave her standing there, how long before her curiosity gets the better of her and she comes tentatively down the steps? A minute, two? No way.

More like seconds. Then, soon as she's down, yank the string, pull the trapdoor shut, and shoot the bolt. Turn on her and tell her maybe she ought to just step out of her clothes if she knows what's good for her. Then see what happens.

Gideon has to take off his glasses, wipe them. Getting all steamed up already and the bitch not even here yet. But coming, definitely coming. Gideon recalling how excited she'd sounded on the phone, then hesitating a moment, saying something about some guy called Francis, then saying what the hell, it wouldn't hurt. Gideon smiling when she said it. Then telling her he was sorry but she wouldn't be able to stay long as he had a date to keep this evening, hearing her voice relax as she said that was okay, she couldn't stay long either, not sounding like a Jap at all, her accent educated, English almost, but with that air of snootiness still in her voice, like she was doing him a favour, not the other way round. Still, that's what life's all about, things coming full circle. The idea of change. Bad becomes better, better becomes worse.

Maybe shaving wasn't such a great idea. Two cuts already and he's only done half his face. Still. Better persevere. Perseverance furthers, as it says in the *I Ching*. You just bet it does. Throwing the bones last night, he'd come up with all kinds of weird readings, had to keep throwing them until he came up with one he liked the look of. That's what's called 'perseverance'. Superior men succeed because they persevere, inferior men give it all up at the first hurdle, spend the rest of their lives bewailing the approach of old age. See? That's the difference. That's what the world will recognise when the time comes. They'll understand.

Gideon peers at the mirror. Crazy. There's like a million little beads of sweat on its surface. Distorting his face so much he almost has to check he's wearing his glasses. Not an ugly face, no. Catch it at the right angle and he looks almost boyish. The woman this afternoon, she – well, it's escaped him now, exactly what he was thinking of, but no matter, plenty more thoughts in that brainy old head of his, enough there to keep him thinking the rest of his life.

Wondering now where the fly spray is. Couple of weeks ago, he'd had a whole fucking nest of bluebottles in the house somewhere, he'd get up, open the bedroom door and it'd be like walking through one of those bead curtains, only they weren't all threaded through bits of string. Still. Sounds like they're back now, a whole swarm of them, heading this way. Except . . .

Except bluebottles don't have headlights. Nor do they pull up in the yard, climb out of their shiny blue and black shells, and slam the door. None that he's met, anyway.

The doorbell rings.

Doesn't she just look the business? She does. All dressed up for you, too. Black leather jacket over a simple red dress, nice pair of legs in those black and red tartan tights, pity about the Docs though. All this under one of those collapsible umbrellas, red. Worried dark eyes staring at you, probably wondering what the fuck you're doing standing there in your boxer shorts, shaving cream all over your face. As if it isn't obvious.

'I'm sorry,' she says. 'I didn't mean—'

'Follow me.'

You start across the yard.

'But what about your shoes?' she says, scampering after you.

You stop, look down at your bare feet. Yup, sure enough, she's right. You've gone and left your shoes somewhere. Bit of a gaffe, that, not quite the done thing for a superior man. Was that before or after you came off the ferry? You can't recall. Still. It doesn't matter. That's what you tell her, it doesn't matter. She shrugs, looks at you funny, the line of her neck stretching taut. The rain coming down, caught in the porch light, another bead curtain, this time of a billion drops of crystal sliding down invisible wires, splosh, they land in the mud, splat, they splash off her umbrella, splunk, they bounce off the bonnet of her car, same Jap thing, you notice, all black and shiny and new, probably got a jacuzzi in the back seat, and little electronic voices talking to you, telling you to buckle yourself in, get a haircut, go buy a suit that doesn't make you look like you just dropped out of your chairman's arse. Nice looking car, though.

Except...

Trouble is, bitches, you just can't trust them. Doesn't matter how deep you bury them they always come back to haunt you. Got to get that last fucking word in, no matter how hard you try to silence them. This one a case in question. You tell her to come alone and she says sure, fine, no problem, then turns up with some guy sitting like a garden gnome in the passenger seat. Like she doesn't trust you.

'Who the fuck's that?'

'Sorry?' She's looking at you kind of funny, chewing that pouty little lip of hers, trying to decide whether to keep that frown on her face or what.

'Man in the car,' you sigh. 'Mr bloody Moto.' It's been a long day.

'You mean my uncle? He's—'

'Going to sit there all night, is he?'

'Well ... no, I mean ...'

You stand there, arms akimbo, as she rounds the car, speaks some gibberish to the man, almost drags him from his seat. Stands there holding the umbrella over the old fart as she makes the introductions, the little man like a cock pecking dirt, bowing his head three times, saying how honoured he is.

And you saying, 'Yeah, yeah, the honour's all mine,' while sizing up the suit – the guy's physique, you notice, not exactly straining its seams. Good. No sign of tattoos either, and the guy still has all the joints of his fingers intact. Better good. Last thing you need right now is the Yakusa on your back as you prepare to send the Kimono bitch into the land of the setting sun.

She says something you don't quite catch.

'You what?'

She's looking at you really strangely now. 'I mean, you're getting soaked standing there.'

Getting soaked. You just bet they say exactly that in Japan. Getting soaked. Still. She's got a point. The two of them following,

535

*you splish splash through the mud to the pottery door, go in and turn
the light on.*

She's still not happy.

'What happened to your door?' she says.

'Visitors,' you tell her. 'The uninvited kind.'

'Did you call the police?'

Like, oh yeah, he might've forgot.

'They said they'd be along any minute.'

*That seems to cheer her up, bring a little light into her eyes.
Probably thinking of – she'd used his name on the phone – that's
right, Francis. Getting all hot down there, just thinking about him.
You can hear the material of her tights rubbing as she walks across
the pottery to the display cabinet. Nice arse, but a little on the small
size. Snazzy leather jacket cut short like that, what you want is
something down there with some life in it, get your eyes moving good
and proper, like hypnotised. Your tongue hanging out. Which
reminds you . . .*

*The old man fidgeting with the brolly now, over by the door.
Shaking off the water, leaning it up against the door-jamb, all very
neat and tidy, actions precise. Probably has a slide-rule in his pocket
to calculate how much cuff to show. Glancing at you now, the look in
his eyes wondering what kind of land is this where your host greets
you in his underwear, shaving cream all over his face. The Land of
No Return, you feel like telling him.*

*Because now the immediate future seems a lot more complicated
than it was a few minutes ago. Police closing in and a bitch to burn,
and now this Uncle Something-san to contend with. Who could be a
black belt in some martial art, come at you with one of those praying
mantis type attacks, all shuffle-shuffle, wiggly fingers in your face.
So you cross to the wheel, shunt it off the trapdoor. She's watching
you now, you can sense it. Admiring your physique, no doubt, the
way your muscles clench in your boxers, all that beef, as you raise the
trapdoor.*

*'What are you doing?' she asks, like it's any of her fucking
business.*

You stare at her.

Something about your special pots, isn't it, what you're supposed to say next. Or is this when you get your mother's tongue out and make some witty remark you can't remember? Things getting all confused – the old man's fault – your mind a jumble of inconsequentialities: what to do, what to say, who to kill first? Worrying now about the etiquette of murder!

You shake your head – sad world – and disappear down into the chamber. Notice immediately that the mice have been playing while the cat's been away. Drawers open, your private files and scrapbooks littering the workbench, some of them scattered across the stone floor, the door of the kiln wide open, Hastie's burnt remains in full view, her scorched skull lying on its side, glistening in some places, charred in others, her sooted teeth bared in a screaming grimace . . .

. . . that reminds you of Simone, the way she looked when you took her into the big strangle, your first bite at that most forbidden of fruit, her lips pulling all the way back to expose her teeth as you drove your thumbs deep into the flesh of her throat, her naked body thrashing against yours as you drove into her again and again, your weight pinning her there, the beast rampant, you, watching all the while, studious, wanting answers, noticing the numerous fillings in her teeth but mostly intent on her eyes, trying to see it there, the moment of triumph, see what she was seeing as her focus changed and she passed into the great forgetness, capture it for ever, that feeling of transcendence, of godlike potency, of total exultation over death . . .

. . . but no time to ponder, not now, you have to keep your mind focused on the job in hand, the bitch upstairs and the old man, her uncle, getting jumpy already, take too long and they might turn their fluffy tails and make a run for it. As you rummage through your toolbox, you can already hear them plotting whispered plots upstairs. Haste now the name of the game.

The hammer is there, down in the second level drawer of the toolbox, the same ball-peen you used on the sheep to make damn sure the blood didn't flow. This time though, it doesn't matter whether the old Grasshopper's blood flows or not, just as long as he goes down and stays down.

They stop whispering as you climb the stairs, hammer in hand.

44

Lying there in the mud, looking up at the starless sky, the rain thudding down, drenching me, cooling me. It all seemed perfectly normal, lying in a bog in the middle of a thunderstorm – happens all the time. You get used to it. You have to. It's all part of the job.

It's quite easy really. You just kind of lie there for a while and wonder what the fuck you're doing, rain trickling into your mouth, bouncing off your face. Sometimes it takes seconds, sometimes minutes, sometimes hours before you arrive at any sane conclusion. That's the fun part.

The not so fun part is when you come to that conclusion. When it suddenly dawns on you that lying on your back in a bog is not the best place to be when several hundred yards away there's a psychopathic fuck about to roast your favourite woman, turn her into bone-ash. That's when dazed wonderment takes a dive out the window, leaves you scrabbling in the mire.

I scrabbled. Like a fish floundering on the shore. In the equation of the moment, the common denominator was pain: movement equalled pain, immobility equalled pain. So I scrabbled. To my knees, to my feet. Stood there on the edge of the world, fighting gravity, the wind and the rain.

'Dow – ie?' My voice cracked, the word snapping in two as a gust of wind snatched it away into the darkness of the night. The Land Rover lay on its side, front end buried in mud, rear wheel still spinning. Dowie had dragged himself from the wreck, was now sitting on a boulder, head in hands, blood running down the side of his face, his neck, his shirt. The gash over his temple looked deep.

'You fucking idiot,' he groaned.

I glanced back along the tracks, saw for the first time the submerged boulder that had sent us spinning. In the distance through the curtain of rain, the cluster of buildings where Byrne now entertained Kyoko and her uncle. The sense of anger that had fired me into action – and caused our present predicament – still burned strongly within me. As did the overwhelming sense of foreboding. The image of Kyoko and Masao Hayashi following a half-naked Gideon Byrne across the potter's yard was still tugging urgently at my mind, demanding immediate response.

I staggered over to where Dowie sat, brushed away his hand and examined the wound. It wasn't as deep as I had previously thought but would still need at least half a dozen stitches. I told him where to find the First Aid box in the Land Rover, then left him sitting there shouting for me to come back, we were under orders and a lot of other stuff I didn't hear because of the sound of my own voice yelling at Kyoko to get away from there, just run, Kyoko, run. The words, though, were whipped from my mouth and bludgeoned into silent submission by the squalling wind and rain.

Two hundred yards that seemed like a hundred miles. One of those nightmarish scenarios where you're running, trying to escape some terror behind you and the ground beneath you is like quicksand sucking at your feet and you daren't look over your shoulder, confront your innermost fears, you just pump your legs faster . . .

. . . but it's like you're running on the spot, getting nowhere and not very fast, the beast's rasping breath hot down your neck, your legs like pistons, desperately pumping, and then somewhere around there you slip and stumble and fall to the ground and, as you turn to confront the face of your torment, that's when you wake up and realise that everything's all right, it was only a nightmare, the demons are gone . . .

. . . except I couldn't wake up, not this time, because I wasn't asleep, and still the marshy ground sucked at my feet and I hardly seemed to be making any progress at all, falling, picking myself up, ploughing on, trying to ignore the searing pain in my knee, the grinding of cartilage in my hip which I'd caught on something hard when I'd been flung from the cab of the Land Rover. And now the cloying, restrictive weight of my clothes, covered in mud, drenched right through, slowing me down so that every stumbling step I took became an agonising frame by frame journey through an endless succession of microcosmic landscapes, time slowed down almost to a halt as I battled against the gusting wind, the slanting rain, knowing then how Neil Armstrong felt, Buzz Aldrin, the first time they stepped out on to the surface of the moon, one small step for them, yes, but no giant leaps for me, no way, I was stuck back here on Earth with fuck knows how many pounds psi of gravity pressing down on my back as lightning suddenly forked across the western sky, lighting up the night for a few frozen seconds before the thunder rolled, cracked and then boomed, a mile off, maybe two, but heading this way. I'd glimpsed the broiling stormclouds in the lightning flash, seen too the pottery in vivid silhouette up ahead, still a long way off, hundred yards, maybe more, difficult to tell now, the darkness closing in and having to concentrate on the marshy ground again, place my feet with care on the small grassy knolls, try and keep the rhythm flowing, the breathing in time, focus on the immediate and ignore what lay ahead, push from my mind the crowding images of what might be happening right that second in the pottery, just press on, one step at a time.

Easier said.

None of this past-flashing-before-my-eyes kind of shit, not me, save that for the drowning fraternity. What I could see was my future passing before my eyes. And I can tell you this, it wasn't much of a future, and certainly not a pleasant one, not without Kyoko there, pretty damn grim if you really want to know, empty, the prospects of a happy life for either of us diminishing with every passing second, Kyoko possibly even this moment struggling in the hands of Gideon Byrne, perhaps already lying limp on his pottery floor, me trying to work it out now, how long it might take from the moment the thumbs first dig into the neck, closing off the carotid, pressing down on the voice-box, the thyroid, cutting off the flow of blood and oxygen, how long before the brain finally shuts down? Not long, no, not long at all. You're talking how many seconds it takes Linford Christie to sprint a hundred yards, a hundred yards on a track and at the peak of his fitness, that's what you're talking, not a hundred yards through wind and rain across treacherous marshland in almost total darkness on two broken legs and only half a lung . . .

. . . but no, I was getting ahead of myself, letting the fear take over. I'd forgotten about her uncle, Masao-*san*, he was there too, maybe his presence would be enough to steer Byrne off his murderous course, if not indefinitely then at least temporarily, long enough perhaps for me to get there, me with my useless knee, my wracking lungs, my delicate social skills – *I say, Gideon, old chap, what say we postpone this rather indecorous attempt on Kyoko's life, and retire to the drawing-room for a well-earned pot of tea?*

Some bloody cavalry.

'*Found it,*' *Gideon Byrne says, holding up the hammer, displaying it as though the World Cup. Kimono, he notices, is still over by the display cabinet, while Mr Moto is now hovering close at hand by the workshop door. Both of them also wearing puzzled frowns, as they look first at the hammer, then at each other. The bitch is the first to speak.*

'*I don't know . . .*' *she says, her expression turning really strange, reminding Gideon of the last one, the one up on the picnic table when*

542

he had to get his toolbox out, the only way he could shut her up.
'Maybe we should come back another time . . .'

Like she wants Gideon to make up her mind for her.

He's happy to oblige.

The old man first. Gideon makes as though to walk past him then suddenly swings on his heels, the hammer coming up and round too fast for the old man's blocking arm, catching him square on the temple, the crack of his bone coinciding with the bitch's first scream. His eyes turn up even before he slumps to the floor – more squashed cockroach than praying mantis.

The bitch screams again, dashes for the door.

Gideon Byrne catches her as she's almost there, manages to clamp off most of the third scream as he drags her back into the pottery, heels dragging on the floor – squirming the way those mice used to do back in the copse when he inserted the first couple of needles – into the workshop, her teeth sinking into Gideon's hand as he reaches the trapdoor, but losing their grip as he throws her down the steps.

Tumble, tumble, tumble.

She lies there, dazed, looking up at Gideon through blurry eyes as he descends the stairs, turns to yank the string and then reaches up to bolt the trapdoor.

There.

She's up on one elbow now, shaking her head confusedly, her red skirt all hitched up round her waist, her pins spread, stockings and panties there for all to gape at, stupid bovine kind of look on her face.

They just never learn.

Still . . .

'Maybe you ought to just step out of your clothes,' Gideon says, giving her a smile to end all smiles. 'That is, if you know what's good for you.'

Now all he has to do is see what happens.

Fifty yards. Driven now only by fear and anger. Fear for what he might do to Kyoko, anger because this was personal now, doubly personal. Approaching the solitary standing stone, the ground here offering grip, the clumps of long grass firm islands in the bog, the silhouette of the woodfire kiln coming up on me now, the tall, crooked flue rising from its domed roof, the storeroom beyond, thirty yards, twenty, stumbling, breath a hoarse wheeze burning my throat as I heard the first of the screams, definitely Kyoko's, pierce the sodden blanket of rain, slicing me to the quick as I staggered off the moor and into the yard on leaden legs and mud-clogged boots, slipping again as I heard another scream, this one choked off midway through. I lay there in the yard, exhausted, scarcely able to breathe, washed by the pelting rain, bathed in the light from the pottery window, trying to summon what last vestige of strength I might have somewhere in reserve . . .

. . . and finding it, perhaps not strength but pure innate stubbornness, this bastard was not going to win, he wasn't going to take Kyoko from me or this life, he was going to pay, yes, for everything he'd done to all those poor women, he was going to pay for Arthur Thomas, he was going to pay, if I had my way, and pay and pay and pay . . .

I struggled to my feet and stumbled and skidded the last twenty yards as once again lightning lit up the sky. I crashed through the pottery door to the sound of cracking thunder, the eye of the storm directly overhead. The shop was empty. I glanced around. Saw an umbrella dripping inside the door. Saw Kyoko's bag on the floor over by the display cabinet. Saw through the workshop door that the potter's wheel had been pushed back, the trapdoor to the cellar lying exposed but closed. Saw the foot just inside the workshop door, unmoving.

Masao Hayashi lay there in a twisted heap, blood pooling below his left cheek. A ball-pen hammer lay on the floor nearby. He looked very old and small, and very much unconscious. I loosened his tie and felt for a pulse. As I did so, a soft groan sighed through his lips. I felt the relief begin to flood through me but it was shortlived, interrupted by a scream, Kyoko's, coming from the cellar. The sound of something else, too, but I wasn't sure what, didn't have time to think because I was already at the trapdoor, hauling on the ring-pull with all my might, but it wouldn't give, the trapdoor was bolted, it just wouldn't fucking give!

My eyes darted around the workshop, the eyes of a cornered rat desperately seeking salvation. Tools, godammit, I needed tools! Something to jemmy the trapdoor. But all the tools were down in the cellar, no bloody use to me there. A crowbar, that's what I needed. But potters don't use crowbars, they use their hands, they like to wrap them around the supple necks of their victims, imagine them as pots on a wheel as they squeeze and squeeze and squeeze . . .

Panic took hold of me, forcing me out of the workshop and into the rain. Adrenaline stampeding through my veins, I sprinted – like a semi-crushed cockroach – across the yard to the storeroom. Cursed when I saw the padlock on the door, turned and headed for the cottage. There had to be something I could use there, had to be! Rounding the two parked cars, I suddenly stopped, skidded in the mud, fell on my arse.

Of course – the cars!

I picked myself up and yanked open the rear door of the Subaru, scrabbled around, found the spare tyre under the floorboard but no tools, nothing I could use on the trapdoor. I tried the Nissan. Found the boot locked, shit, but the keys, thank God, were still in the ignition. I tugged them free then dropped them in the mud as I rounded the boot. Had to stop and wipe them clean before fumbling the right one into the lock. Lifted the floorboard and hauled out the spare and there it was in the hollow below, just what I needed.

I grabbed the tyre-lever and ran.

Gideon Byrne knew it, he just fucking knew it. It was so typical. Like you come from somewhere in Asia and you have to be related to

Bruce fucking Lee. Here, they send you to school and teach you how to hate yourself, over there they teach you the spiritual oneness of mind and body and how to kick the living hellfuck out of someone twice your size.

Gideon rubs his side as though to erase the sudden pain there, looks at her through watering, though definitely more cautious, eyes. He mustn't underestimate her, he realises now, that would be foolish. He remembers reading something in the I Ching about underestimation being the folly of inferior men. Too true. Experimentally, he touches the spot again where her kick had landed, winces in pain.

'Kidney,' she says, a look of satisfaction on her face.

'Yeah?' Gideon is genuinely surprised. He'd always thought his kidneys were round the other side, somewhere down below his heart. Well, well, well.

She's standing off now, controlling the centre of the floor, her body angled side-on, poised, not quite the praying mantis stance, but close. No fear in her eyes, nothing Gideon can read there, no handle on the situation. So he watches her feet instead, recalling the speed with which they had moved. Skinny wee bisom like her, it's a wonder she can even lift those Docs off the floor, let alone swirl and kick in the one fluid motion that had taken him completely by surprise. Still, next time he'll be prepared.

'So where's the liver, then?' he asks, standing there at the foot of the stairs, arms akimbo, inviting her in close. 'You want to—'

Again she moves, her speed across the intervening yards incredible as she feints to the right, Gideon responding, unable to help himself. He tries to correct his balance and throw in a block, but is far too slow, her knuckled fist jabbing in below his forearm, catching him under the ribs, the instant pain excruciating as she dances – fucking dances – away. Gideon can't believe it! He sinks to one knee, tries to draw breath. It's like he's on fire down there, as though someone just ran him through with a red hot poker.

Blinking away the tears and suppressing a moan, he regains his feet. Stands there clasping the pain, crouched over, exaggerating his condition. She's back in the centre of the floor now, same old stance, *same old look of satisfaction on her face. Already underestimating him. Good. Third time lucky. All he has to do is draw her in, then pounce. Use his bulk, his weight.*

'So . . . that's . . . where . . . it . . . is . . .' *he gasps, laying it on thick, the pain. As long as he remains by the stairs, there's nowhere for her to go.*

She smiles benignly but says nothing.

'I always . . . thought . . . it was . . . like down . . . there.' *Gideon pulls down the elastic of his boxers, touches a spot just above his pubes, opposite his appendix scar, noticing at the same time the beast down there, swinging free. All the fun and excitement and he'd clean forgot. He pulls the boxers right down, kicks them away.* 'Well . . .' *he says,* 'what . . . d'you . . . think?'

The Kimono bitch doesn't even blink. Sure, she has a wee peek, maybe that's why the dreamy smile on her face, her tiny mind imagining all the fun she could have. But then it's suddenly back to business as sounds come from upstairs, right overhead now, someone hammering at the trapdoor, trying to haul it open.

The old man regained consciousness, Gideon wonders, or the cops? Or maybe just an angry customer who wants her money back, teapot spout doesn't pour right, stained the lace tablecloth that's been in her family since Bonnie Prince Charlie used it once to blow his nose. You never fucking know. But the Kimono bitch looking all hopeful now, like she thinks it's all over, her cop friend come on a white charger to rescue her, carry her off into the sunset.

Not a good idea.

Gideon feels the anger rise in him as the sounds from above diminish, feels it burn through his veins – the fucking injustice of it all – then explode in his brain as he charges across the floor at her, fists flailing, taking her by surprise, leaving her no time or space in which to defend herself, his momentum like that of a runaway truck, smashing her to the ground, pinning her there, dazed but thrashing, wriggling this way and that, squirming, yes, the way the mice used to do, as his fingers claw inexorably up her body, seeking her neck, arched now, trying to escape his grip, as his thumbs close in on that beautiful stretch of taut unblemished skin, this the moment he's been waiting for, dreaming of, lowering his face to lick her clean, savour that salty sheen of fear, just a sample at first, a nibble, test the texture between his teeth, breathe in the subtle scent . . .

. . . the fight going out of her as his thumbs gradually increase the pressure, Gideon raising his head now to watch her eyes lose focus, trying to see it there, the moment, the crossing of the great water, see it in her eyes, the bitch not so snooty now as her life force drains into his, becoming his, no stopping it now, this is the way, the way of the superior man . . .

Thunder ripped the night apart, an explosive barrage of sound that seemed to stun the world in its tracks, shake it to the core. The old man, Masao-*san*, was conscious now, groaning wheezily and trying to sit up as I re-entered the workshop and hurried across to the trapdoor. I could hear no sound from down below; the silence, though, was loud enough, screaming up at me to *get a fucking move on* . . .

'Flancis . . .' the old man moaned.

But I ignored him, he was still alive, and Kyoko was down there with Byrne and I didn't want to think what might be happening, *what might already have happened*, because to do that was to give in, relinquish what little strength I had left, and if she was still alive then I would need all that strength. I would need every cell in my body to combat the manic might of Gideon Byrne, every nucleus of every cell . . .

I jammed the tyre-lever into the crack by the trapdoor bolt, hammered it down with the heel of my boot. Wood groaned . . . but that was all. I hit it again. Wood splintered, but still it did not give. I repositioned the lever, worming it in. Then jumped on it, both feet, all my weight. The bolt snapped, the trapdoor sprang open and somehow I was down the steps and looking along the cellar at the two of them there, Kyoko with her dress half torn off, writhing on the bare stone floor beneath the naked bulk of Gideon Byrne, his back arched as his hands clenched around her neck, a low snarl coming from deep in his throat as his lips drew back, prepared to bite.

The sound that came from my throat was a million years old, a roar of primal rage that reverberated off the stone walls and seemed to stop Byrne in his tracks. As I ran towards him, Kyoko hit out, her hands chopping at his face, his throat, her knees pumping, feet kicking out. Byrne groaned under the torrent of blows and, releasing her neck, tried to turn. Kyoko hit him with the edge of her hand across the bridge of his nose and his glasses flew across the cellar, smashed against the wall.

'I can't see!' he yelled, grabbing his nose, trying to stem the sudden flow of blood. 'I can't see!'

I canoned into him with all my force, sent him sprawling across the floor. I tried to pin him down, subdue him with a necklock, but he was too big, too strong, too far gone. He punched and kicked and spat and bit like a wild rabid dog. There was no holding him down. The tyre-lever was still in my hand. It was the only way, less-than-reasonable force. I raised it above my head just as one of his wildly swinging fists caught me on the temple, knocked me backwards off his body. The tyre-lever slipped from my hand, clattered across the floor. I lay there, stunned, the world disintegrating before my eyes. Felt his weight upon me, fingers scrabbling for my throat. I tried to fend him off, but couldn't. I was spent. I had given everything I had. My thought commands struggled pathetically through the morass of my mind. No response, body no longer listening. I felt the pressure on my throat. I couldn't breathe. Circuits exploding in my brain. A galaxy of stars in my eyes. This was it. *No More Mr Nice Guy*. I had failed. The lights dimmed.

Then came on again. Slowly I became aware that I was still breathing. No more pressure on my throat or body. I felt weightless. Perhaps this was one of those out of body experiences, I thought, any second now and I'd be zooming along a dark tunnel towards the bright light at the end, find myself in a lush summer's meadow, the birds singing, the stream gurgling, the hundreds of little white fluffy lambs flouncing their jaunty wee butts in the air, beautiful redheads parading naked around me, asking would I like a little taste of heaven . . .

But no, this was no out of body experience, this was still painful reality, the sense of weightlessness due to the fact that Gideon Byrne was no longer pinning me down, crushing me to the floor, I could see him now through barely-focused eyes, see his pale naked form stumbling around in the middle of the cellar, one of his hands held out in front of him, like a blind man searching for a door, the other hand clasping his bloodied head. Another dark stain ran from his battered nose into his mouth and down his chin.

'*Bitch*,' he snarled. '*Bitch . . . bitch . . . bitch.*'

I saw Kyoko beyond him, over by the stairs. She was standing perfectly still, the tyre-lever in her hand. It too was stained with blood.

'Over here, Mr Byrne,' she said quietly, her voice calm.

Gideon Byrne staggered towards her. Fighting back the nausea, I pushed myself up to a sitting position. Could he see her? I wondered. And why didn't she move? What the hell was she playing at?

Byrne was almost upon her when she moved. Stepping neatly to the side, she raised the tyre-lever and brought it down on his extended wrist with all her force. There was a loud crack as the bone snapped, followed by a long high-pitched scream from Byrne. As he held his shattered wrist limply in his other hand, Kyoko swung the lever again and broke that wrist too. Byrne raised his head to the ceiling and howled.

'*Please!*' he screamed. '*No!*'

He turned and ran. Blindly. Smacked into the kiln. Begging now, please, no more pain. Fingers fumbling at the door. Finding it. Opening it. Sobbing all the while. Then he folded himself in, drawing in his legs, crunching bones, brittle bones, Hastie's bones. Whimpering like a well-whipped dog. *It's not*

550

right, it isn't fair, it's not supposed to end like this. Fingers now scrabbling for the door again, pulling it towards him, a scream, one more . . .

. . . and then the door clicked shut.

Kyoko was in my arms when I turned. We retrieved her jacket and climbed the steps out of the cellar, the sound of Gideon Byrne's demented screams diminishing behind us. Kyoko looked at me, a question in her eyes.

'Let him scream,' I said. 'He'll keep.'

45

'Its coming is sudden;
It flames up, dies down, is thrown away.'

Gideon Byrne thought at first it was something to do with his broken wrists. Some kind of bodily defence mechanism to keep his body warm, reduce the pain. The body was good at that, repairing damage. Cells knitting together, forming new tissue, whole bones, fresh skin. The organism's fight for survival as intrinsic as his own.

He shifted his weight, felt one of Hastie's charred bones crack beneath him. Poor old Ros. Things had been different, well, who could tell what might have happened. The two of them living to a ripe old age, maybe even a couple of sprogs to follow in their footsteps. Weirder things had been known to happen. Now she was gone, the mission at an end, she wouldn't even live on in the glazes of his pots. Sad really, when he thought about it.

Of course, the mission wasn't really over yet. Not by a long chalk. Soon, in a matter of minutes or hours, they would take him from the kiln, load him into a police van and take him off to hospital. First they would set his bones, then they would probably fly him across the great water to some secure place on the mainland. Wherever – that was irrelevant. What *was* relevant was that the media would be there in their hundreds, maybe thousands. Flying in from all over the world. To see *him*. To hear *his* story.

Finally, they would *understand*.

553

In a way, Gideon felt glad it was now all over. In the last couple of months things had been getting way out of hand, like he'd somehow lost control of his life, was slowly going crazy. Now it was like a heavy burden had been hoisted from his shoulders, the relief almost overwhelming. He felt buoyant, as though floating on air. Perhaps he would be able to sleep now that the responsibility had been wrested from him. Rest and recuperate. Say goodbye to those long dark hours of manic thought, the total exhaustion, the almost constant state of panic. Maybe even wave goodbye to the utter loneliness, the sense of absolute isolation in having no one with whom to share his burning secret. Now that the secret was out, maybe he would make some new friends, people who understood what it was like to bear so much responsibility alone for so long, who understood the sheer pressure involved in being a superior man.

The first twinge of cramp clutched at his left thigh. There was nothing he could do about it, with so little room for manoeuvre. No matter. They would come for him soon – and what's a little pain to a superior man? Pain, like rain, always passes.

It was strange finding himself in here amongst all the bones and ash. Almost a tragic irony to it, in fact, him now trapped in the same kiln where both Ros and Simone had finally burned. Their spirits, perhaps, imbued within its very walls. Simone who had sparked him off, igniting the fire within him, sending him hurtling along the track that had now, years later, come full circle, bringing him back. Simone. If he hadn't met her that day on the mainland, Gideon wondered, would things have turned out any different? Would all those other bitches still be alive today? Although doubting it, Gideon could not be too sure. *We are mere pinballs*, he told himself, *our actions and reactions but cause and effect*.

Another spasm of cramp took hold of him. This time it lasted longer, the pain not so easy to dismiss. And it was getting warm. Which was odd, to say the least. There should be plenty of cool air coming in the bunghole: he could tell by the light slanting in that the brick was definitely not in place. Perhaps it was his body heat, then, or his breath, warming up the kiln.

He could hear nothing. Had heard nothing for a while now, not since the cop had said something about letting Gideon scream, he'd keep. Then the sound of the cop and the bitch climbing the stairs, the trapdoor slamming down. Gideon feeling no animosity towards them now, the match well over, time to shake hands all round. It had been a good game while it lasted, and now it was back to the dressing-room for the post-match *post mortem*.

Gideon shifted again. It was becoming difficult now not to think about stretching his legs, breathing some fresh air into his lungs. Decidedly muggy now inside the kiln. His throat and mouth were dry, and he could feel the sweat dripping from his brow, his armpits, his chest. Which was strange. He rarely sweated. In fact, only when he fired the woodfire kiln. Maybe it was some kind of emotional fever, he thought, brought on by the relief he felt. It certainly couldn't be—

No.

It couldn't be that. No way. Just paranoia creeping in.

He leant back against the wall. Then jerked his body away with a screech as the element hissed through his skin.

They *couldn't*! Not that. It was against the fucking *law*!

It had to be a joke. They were just teaching him a lesson, that was all. Any second now they would come down into the cellar and let him out. Of course they would – this was *Britain*, after all.

But they didn't.

Not when he began kicking at the door, nor in response to his desperate screams.

Not even when his skin began to peel and burn.

Nor did they come when his hair burst into flames and he slowly began to melt.

In fact they didn't come for quite a long time.

By then, though, Gideon Byrne was well past screaming.

46

The chopper slanted in against the wind, hovering over the three standing stones, correcting its trim, steadying, before finally settling in the pool of light cast by half a dozen headlights. The cabin door slid open and the second contingent of men climbed out, fought free of the down-draught, tramped up towards the Moss Farm Pottery.

The storm had passed and the rain had eased to barely a drizzle, the air now fresh and clear, loaded with the scent of the wet moorland.

We were all there now, the whole island force, sitting or leaning against the rounded stones of the circle at the top of Byrne's drive, looking down on the chaotic scene in the yard, not saying much, happy to be on the fringe, leaving all the dirty work to the murder squad. Monica was there, and Yuill, Jim Tennant and Bob Gillies, and Kyoko, of course, in the crutch of my arm, wrapped in a blanket but shivering still, smoking, her other hand warm against the skin of my back. Her uncle, Masao Hayashi, was already being treated by medics down in the ambulance parked in the yard.

I watched as Commander Kettle, uniform and all, climbed the churned-up drive towards us.

'Bloody fine piece of work,' he said, coming to a halt amidst us. 'Bloody fine.' He held out his hand to Yuill. 'Don't think your contribution will go unmentioned, Sergeant. The success of this operation is purely down to you and your officers.' He then shook everyone's hand – bar mine – saving Kyoko's till last. 'And you, Miss, I commend your bravery. Damn fine piece of work, from what I hear.'

He turned to watch as two more ambulances crested the hill and manoeuvred cautiously along the track towards us. Then he turned again and dropped his baleful eyes on mine.

'You, McMorran,' he growled, 'come with me.'

I followed him down the drive, behind the ambulances. He spoke to the driver of the first, telling him where to park, where to take the stretcher. He then called over one of Fullerton's plainclothes officers and issued more instructions concerning the ongoing search of Gideon Byrne's cottage. I could see Fullerton himself through the pottery window, standing by the workshop door and talking animatedly into a PR.

I crossed to the ambulance where Masao Hayashi was busy receiving attention. He was sitting passively on one of the bunks as a young medic concentrated on cleansing his wound with a cotton-wool swab. I asked how it was going.

'He'll need a few stitches,' the medic said, bagging the swab and tearing off another. 'Apart from a mild concussion, he's fine.'

'McMorran!' Kettle beckoned me over to the pottery door.

I told Hayashi we would catch up with him at the hospital, then limped my way wearily across the yard. The sight of the beds in the back of the ambulance had served only to remind me how exhausted I was. Without a word, I followed Kettle down the stairs in to the cellar, where four ID Branch officers were already at work, taking photographs, dusting for prints, collating and bagging evidence. The stench in the cellar, that of badly burned pork. Commander Kettle led me across to the kiln and jerked open the door. A blast of hot, noxious air hit my face.

Gideon Byrne was still steaming. He was totally unrecognisable. Hunched into the corner, his charred, blackened skin looked as though it would crumble to the touch. His sooted teeth were bared in a snarl, and from the sockets of his eyes seeped a grey gungy ooze.

'Right, McMorran,' Kettle snorted. 'Take me through it again. From the moment you forced the trapdoor.'

I took him through it again, omitting nothing. When I got to the bit about Byrne climbing into the kiln and closing the door, Kettle rammed his fists into his trouser pockets and shook his head in disbelief.

'You really expect me to believe that?' he sneered. 'That with two broken wrists he just climbed in and shut the door all by himself?'

'It's exactly the way it happened,' I shrugged.

'Then what? Once you'd left, he let himself out and climbed the stairs, switched on the computer, then came back down and crawled back in to the kiln? Is that what you're saying?'

'Fuck you,' I said, suddenly tired of it all, tired of Kettle and his brutish ways.

'No, McMorran, it's fuck *you*,' Kettle snarled, jabbing a forefinger into my chest. 'You call us up and tell us you've got the suspect secured – *alive* – and then the next thing we know, said suspect's burnt to a fucking crisp. Questions are going to be asked, McMorran, and you better have some answers.'

I smacked his prodding forefinger away. 'You want answers, why don't you ask him?' I yelled, pointing at the scorched remains of Gideon Byrne. 'I'm sure he'll save your arse for you, if you ask him nicely.'

All activity in the cellar stopped. Kettle retreated a pace and turned away. Maybe he'd recognised the tone in my voice, the look in my eyes. Wise man. He turned on the spectating officers.

'What're you all looking at?' he demanded. 'Never seen a frank discussion before? Get back to your work. And Nicholls? You want to smoke, ask for a transfer. Got it?'

'Sir.'

Kettle took my arm, led me across to the stairs. On the shrine in the corner, all the skulls and fetishes had already been bagged, were waiting now for the evidence officers.

'Okay,' he said. 'So you closed the trapdoor. Then what?'

'Detective Sergeant Dowie arrived. We carried Mr Hayashi across to the cottage, laid him on the couch, checked he was all right. Then we called in.'

'Dowie put the call through, right?'

I nodded. 'Then we waited.'

'And no one else went down in to the cellar?'

I shook my head. 'Fullerton was the first.'

Commander Harlan Kettle lapsed into thought. I waited, and said nothing. It was his problem, he was the one in the firing-line. There was little I could do or say.

'I don't know, McMorran,' he said eventually, exasperation dripping from his sigh. 'I just don't fucking know.'

I said, 'How the hell could anyone have known he had the computer preset to switch on the kiln at a certain time?'

Kettle leant forward, his voice an angry hiss. 'You could have bloody checked, man.' I could see from his barely concealed disdain that we were now firmly back on familiar territory. No problem. I could live with that. Preferred it, in fact.

'I could've,' I said. 'But I didn't.'

'You could have bloody checked,' he repeated, though now there was more weariness in his tone than anger.

'So put it in your report,' I said. 'Do what you always do, cover your arse.'

His smile was sudden, tight, and dripped contempt.

'Count on it,' he said. Then turned and, without another word, climbed the stairs.

I found Detective Sergeant Dowie in the back of the second ambulance, the first one having already left. He too was being treated for the wound in his head. I told the medic to leave us for a moment. He seemed about to argue, but then shrugged and climbed out of the ambulance. I pulled the door shut.

'What's up?' Dowie said, regarding me askance. 'You seem troubled, McMorran...'

I said, 'Funny things, computers. I just don't understand them at all.'

'No? How's that?' With an air of confidence I hadn't seen in him before.

'That one in the pottery? I'm sure when I looked at it earlier, it was in the RESET mode. Like someone would have to punch in a whole new firing sequence before it would work again. And yet . . .'

Dowie offered me his guileless, baby blue eyes. 'Perhaps you were mistaken, McMorran.'

I stared at him for what seemed a long time, searching for something in those pale blue eyes, anything to dampen the fires of my suspicion. But he didn't flinch or smile or back down, just sat there waiting, returning my gaze, the same way I'd just done with Kettle.

So after a while I just said, 'Yes, Sergeant, I think perhaps I was.' And left it at that.

Then went looking for Kyoko.

I consulted the *I Ching* that night while Kyoko slept, kept her in mind as I threw the coins. The hexagram I came up with was *Hsien*. The judgement read:

> *'Influence. Success.*
> *Perseverance furthers.*
> *To take a maiden to wife brings good fortune.'*

The Author's Last Word

Obviously this is a work of fiction and, as you might now agree, there has probably been more crime committed within these pages than has occurred during Arran's long and sometimes bloody history. But that's crime writers for you – give us paradise and we'll fill it full of bodies.

Fortunately, though, today's reality is in total contrast – a peaceable island community policed by often less than half a dozen officers. And while I am indebted to the people of Arran for many reasons, the characters portrayed herein are but products of my sometimes over-fertile imagination. Likewise the Glen Chalmadale Distillery. While it is based physically on the Edradour Distillery near Pitlochry, its owners and staff bear no relation to those at the Edradour who so generously gave me both their time and assistance (and, almost as importantly, a bottle of their superb Single Highland Malt!). I now read, however, that there are plans afoot to build a real distillery in Lochranza – not quite life imitating art, but close enough. Another Single Highland Malt? I'll drink to that!

Finally, I would like to thank the following for their invaluable time, enthusiasm and encouragement, and often a lot more besides:

Arran: Pete McMillan, Carol Furze, Henry & Eunice McNicol, Tommy Gilmour, Stuart Blake. **Brentford:** Campbell Distillers Limited, and Debbie Fyrth. **Campbeltown:** Angus Martin,

Robbie & Gloria Lang. **Edinburgh:** Nigel Gatherer, Paul Tebble & Junko Shibe at the Meadows Pottery, Ewan Skinner, Charlie Drysdale, Iain McKinna & Kirsty Anderson, Colin Simpson, Simon Pia, Davy Pringle, Brian Gourlay, Mark Miele, Joe McEwan, Angus McPheep, Valerie Hogg, Paul Kirk, John Edwards & Andy Watters, Dave Sharpe, Eddie Curry, Tam & Drew Hendry, Mike Fraser, Big Ian; All at the Tron, especially Cy, Allan, Freddie & Brian; All at the West Pilton Neighbourhood Centre, especially Johnny & Jimmy Muir. **London:** Caroline Oakley (Editor), Arthur Sparks. **Pitlochry:** The Edradour Distillery and its staff, especially Donny McLeod and Barbara Sadler.

MC
High Street, Edinburgh, April 1994.

More Compelling Fiction from Headline:

— GALLATIN WARFIELD —
STATE v. JUSTICE

A SEARING COURTROOM DRAMA...
WHERE PRIVATE PASSIONS RUN OUT OF CONTROL

A brilliant first novel as spellbinding as *Reasonable Doubt*

'Fast and compelling. A fascinating courtroom thriller'
– David Morrell

'Legal know-how and polished narrative skills...Warfield's
authority in the courtroom and the clarity of his prose sustain
this promising debut' – *Publishers Weekly*

When a body is found murdered in deserted woodland, it
seems just another shocking incident of routine atrocity. The
obvious suspect is T.J. Justice – a psychopathic drifter with a
glaring police record. He is swiftly arrested and charged. But
when the victim is identified as a Russian diplomat's son, the
case develops a totally new dimension.

Prosecuting attorney Gardner Lawson is determined to lock
up Justice permanently. But his opponent is Kent King, a
ruthless and manipulative defence attorney who sets out to
obscure the trial with dubious clues and confusing evidence.

Gardner's assistant Jennifer Munday watches in growing
desperation as her boss and King battle above and beyond the
law. And what once seemed a clear-cut case of sexual
perversion and murder blossoms into a baffling mystery with
shadowy governmental interference and a vendetta fuelled by
dark personal secrets.

FICTION/THRILLER   0 7472 4064 7

A selection of bestsellers from Headline

HARD EVIDENCE	John T Lescroart	£5.99	☐
TWICE BURNED	Kit Craig	£5.99	☐
CAULDRON	Larry Bond	£5.99	☐
BLACK WOLF	Philip Caveney	£5.99	☐
ILL WIND	Gary Gottesfield	£5.99	☐
THE BOMB SHIP	Peter Tonkin	£5.99	☐
SKINNER'S RULES	Quintin Jardine	£4.99	☐
COLD CALL	Dianne Pugh	£4.99	☐
TELL ME NO SECRETS	Joy Fielding	£4.99	☐
GRIEVOUS SIN	Faye Kellerman	£4.99	☐
TORSO	John Peyton Cooke	£4.99	☐
THE WINTER OF THE WOLF	R A MacAvoy	£4.50	☐

All Headline books are available at your local bookshop or newsagent, or can be ordered direct from the publisher. Just tick the titles you want and fill in the form below. Prices and availability subject to change without notice.

Headline Book Publishing, Cash Sales Department, Bookpoint, 39 Milton Park, Abingdon, OXON, OX14 4TD, UK. If you have a credit card you may order by telephone – 0235 400400.

Please enclose a cheque or postal order made payable to Bookpoint Ltd to the value of the cover price and allow the following for postage and packing:
UK & BFPO: £1.00 for the first book, 50p for the second book and 30p for each additional book ordered up to a maximum charge of £3.00.
OVERSEAS & EIRE: £2.00 for the first book, £1.00 for the second book and 50p for each additional book.

Name ....

Address ....

....

....

If you would prefer to pay by credit card, please complete:
Please debit my Visa/Access/Diner's Card/American Express (delete as applicable) card no:

Signature .... Expiry Date ....